Praise for *The Eighty-Year-Old Sorority Girls*

"I love books that represent the values of female friendships and supporting one another. The way these women show up for each other is truly inspiring."
—**Pat Mitchell, Co-Founder and Curator of TEDWomen
and Author of *Becoming a Dangerous Woman:
Embracing Risk to Change the World***

"*The Eighty-Year-Old Sorority Girls* is a heartfelt book that will inspire women of all ages to stop, pause and reflect on one's life journey . . . to embrace it with open arms and reminiscence the friendships and the opportunities they have experienced. Robin Benoit has provided a beautiful collection of magical and memorable moments that will bring laughter and smiles of joy, and tears of love and compassion. Page by page and chapter by chapter, *The Eighty-Year-Old Sorority Girls* is a must read as one's life comes full circle. Don't let it pass you by . . . enjoy, and thank you to our author and storyteller Robin Benoit."
—**Deborah S. Phelps, Executive Director of
The Education Foundation of BCPS, Inc. and
Author of *A Mother for All Seasons: A Memoir***

"Robin Benoit's touching story is a celebration of the enduring bonds of sisterhood. Whether you are 18 or 80 years young, women need women in their lives, and this book is a beautiful testament to that."
—**TJ Condon, President of Kappa Alpha Theta Foundation
and Award-Winning Author of *Some Assembly Required:
A True Story of Love and Organ Transplants***

"I think fans of *Steel Magnolias* will love this book! I recommend it wholeheartedly!"
—**Carey Conley, Co-Author of *Keep Looking Up*
and Co-Founder of Infinite Nation™ Community**

"I find this a truly endearing book, and the style of writing conveys just that message. I recommend this book for all women to enjoy. We all need our tribe, our pride and to think about our special relationships and their lifetime impact personally and on future generations."
—**Robin White Fanning, President of Phi Mu Foundation**

"Robin Benoit has written a heart-warming story that celebrates the bonds of friends, family and sisterhood. This is a beautifully crafted novel complete with memorable characters, witty dialogue and a compelling narrative about lifelong friends in their golden years."
—**Kristina Seek, Author of *The Hashtag Hunt***

"This is a heart-warming book that redefines the bonds of sisterhood and the sorority experience beyond the formative years of adolescence. All women can embrace this unique story that celebrates friendship and be inspired that life-long relationships persist despite the challenges of adulthood."
—Erica D'Angelo Ochs, Fraternity Vice President at Kappa Alpha Theta and Vice President Americas at NNG LLC

"*The Eighty-Year-Old Sorority Girls* was so easy to fall into and enjoy. Robin Benoit's story features some of the best female characters I've encountered. She brings her characters to life with humor and grace. They are lovable and believable, and I was invested from the start. Sorority sister or not, this book is an incredible portrayal of sisterhood and friendship that will warm your heart."
—Kelin Kushin, Chief Business Development Officer at Vivid Vision

"For every girl who has loved her sorority sisters for a lifetime, this book is like a warm hug. Robin's heart for the enduring bond of sisterhood amid the cruel pain of Alzheimer's disease comes alive on every page. In even the most difficult times, Robin's characters show us that sisterhood reaches across generations and encourages us in ways we never imagined."
—Jill McClelland

"I absolutely loved this book! This story has it all . . . laughter, tears, joy, sorrow . . . and all of it found within a lifetime of sorority sisterhood! Whether you have a sisterhood of your own, would love to understand how deep the bond of sisterhood can go, or have no idea about any of this, but love great stories with wonderful characters, this book is for you! After you turn the last page and put away your tissues, you will find yourself thinking of these characters again and again . . . and each time you do, you will smile."
—Deb Vander Bogart

"*The Eighty-Year-Old Sorority Girls* is a poignant look at authentic friendships and Greek sisterhood through the lens of advancing Alzheimer's disease. The book follows four alumnae of the same sorority and the promises they made to each other and their sisterhood. The book also offers an educational look at the Alzheimer's disease process. It's obvious that the author, Robin Benoit, is a member of a sorority and cares deeply for Greek life. The novel accurately portrays the bonds that develop between women who are active in Greek life, especially after their time as collegians. I've had similar experiences in my own sorority and sisterhood. I found myself examining each of the characters and pondering who I most closely resembled. This book is extremely relatable, especially to initiated women in sororities as well as young women considering sorority recruitment. The process is accurately portrayed using the most current language and procedures. I enjoyed this happy portrayal of sororities and the power of female friendships."
—Alice Ashmore

The Eighty-Year-Old
Sorority Girls

The
Eighty-Year-Old
Sorority
Girls

Robin Benoit

BROWN BOOKS
PUBLISHING GROUP

The Eighty-Year-Old Sorority Girls

Brown Books Publishing Group
Dallas, TX / New York, NY
www.BrownBooks.com
(972) 381-0009

A New Era in Publishing®

Publisher's Cataloging-In-Publication Data

Names: Benoit, Robin, author.
Title: The eighty-year-old sorority girls / Robin Benoit.
Description: Dallas, TX ; New York, NY : Brown Books Publishing Group, [2022]
Identifiers: ISBN 9781612545516 (hardcover) | ISBN 9781612545523 (ebook)
Subjects: LCSH: Older women--Fiction. | College sorority members--Fiction. |
     Alzheimer's disease--Patients--Fiction. | Female friendship--Fiction.
Classification: LCC PS3602.E485 E44 2022 (print) | LCC PS3602.E485 (ebook) |
     DDC 813/.6--dc23

ISBN 978-1-61254-551-6
LCCN 2021921727

Printed in the United States
10 9 8 7 6 5 4 3 2 1

For more information or to contact the author, please go to
  www.RobinBenoit.com.

In loving memory of my mother,
whose battle with Alzheimer's inspired this story.

Acknowledgments

First and foremost, I am grateful to God for this story. As I wrote the words and developed these darling characters, I knew it was inspired by Him and the wonderful people He has put in my life.

I wish to also extend my heartfelt gratitude to two sorority sisters: Lynn McGraw and Jillian Benoit. Lynn was the first person to read a single line of this story. Her enthusiasm and encouragement to "keep writing" led me to do just that. To me, it is downright scary to let someone read my words, which are deeply personal. But I found myself easily sending Lynn a few chapters at a time, typos and all, and gained so much from her insight and suggestions. As I cried writing it, she cried reading it, and we bonded that much more over the love of our mothers.

Jillian is both my daughter and my sorority sister. Like Lynn, she was an insightful editor of my book and tremendously helpful in bringing Lottie to life. I remember getting her on the phone more than once while she was away at college to help me with young adult lingo. She said after reading the manuscript that if I didn't call Milli Brown, she would.

And boy do I love Milli Brown of Brown Books Publishing Group! This is the third book that Milli and her team have published for me, and I am so, so grateful. They always make the book publishing process so easy and special, and their unique perspective and unyielding support is second to none. Thank you to Milli, to my managing editor Kelly Lydick, and to everyone else at Brown Books.

Thank you to my family! To my husband, Brian, for listening to me read this in rough manuscript form as we drove to Colorado on vacation and insisting I publish it. Thank you to my daughter, Annelise, for her unwavering support, and to my sister, brother, sister-in-law, nieces, and nephews who all lived through our beloved Nana's Alzheimer's battle and know so much of this book is true. I am also grateful to my wonderful Bible study girlfriends. Much of this story grew out of our lessons together, and I appreciate your support so much.

And last, but not least, to my sorority sisters. You have inspired me for forty years. Thank you for every moment, each experience, the laughter and tears. Thank you for showing me that the sorority experience does not end with college or remain within the boundaries of our home state. Thank you to the real Vivian, who held my hand when I was in my thirties and she was in her nineties, singing sorority songs and telling grand stories. She really did go to China before President Richard Nixon (on a humanitarian mission). She inspired my fictional Button, and I'm sure my sisters will see themselves in the lives of Laney, Helen, and Ida. Love in Our Bond, Sisters!

Helen
(Button's sorority sister)

Nick
(Devon's brother
& Lottie's friend)

Henry
(resident at
Button's assisted
living center)

Devon
(Button's
nurse)

Vivian
"Button"
|
John
(Vivian's husband,
deceased)

Laney
(Button's
sorority Big Sis)

Ida
(Button's
sorority sister)

Robert
(Laney's husband,
deceased)

Charlie
(Ida's husband)

Marie
(Button's sorority
Little Sis)

Ava & Joe
(Ida's daughter &
son-in-law)

Bobby & Judith
(Laney's son &
daughter-in-law)

Charlotte "Lottie"
(Laney's granddaughter)

Jennifer
(Ida's granddaughter)

Jake
(Jennifer's
boyfriend)

Payton
(Jennifer's
best friend and
sorority sister)

Dear Diary,

I'm moving to Enduring Grace Assisted Living Center tomorrow, and I think it will be much like moving to college. Just like the sorority house, I will have my own room and many sweet people with whom I can chat. I will eat my meals in the dining room and have a number of fun activities to do. What is there to dislike about that? They say, "Once a sorority girl, always a sorority girl." I think it's true! No matter our age—even at eighty, we remain sorority girls at heart.

Laney, Helen, and Ida will be there for me no matter where I live. They are my family!

It's amazing, Diary, how women need women in their lives. I think that's what is so special about sororities. We can't live forever and ever, but our sisterhood can. I love that my sorority will carry on my role as friend, advocate, encourager, and mentor with generations of young women I will never meet. It's inspiring to know my tiny role over the past sixty-two years could be felt for years to come.

Things are changing as I grow older, but I'm not scared. Many people might complain about the loss of their home, car, and independence (Laney will definitely complain about this), but I won't. I have chosen this path and expect it to work out splendidly.

Much love,
Button

The Road Not Taken

By Robert Frost

Two roads diverged in a yellow wood,
And sorry I could not travel both
And be one traveler, long I stood
And looked down one as far as I could
To where it bent in the undergrowth;

Then took the other, as just as fair,
And having perhaps the better claim,
Because it was grassy and wanted wear;
Though as for that the passing there
Had worn them really about the same,

And both that morning equally lay
In leaves no step had trodden black.
Oh, I kept the first for another day!
Yet knowing how way leads on to way,
I doubted if I should ever come back.

I shall be telling this with a sigh
Somewhere ages and ages hence:
Two roads diverged in a wood, and I —
I took the one less traveled by,
And that has made all the difference.

Vivian (Button)

When Plans Call for a Little Lipstick

Her favorite color was pink.

Miss Vivian, as they called her at the Enduring Grace Assisted Living Center, was born Vivian Susanne Kincaid in Charleston, South Carolina. An absolute sweetheart, Vivian was a favorite among the residents. Her innate charm disguised her quirks and idiosyncrasies, and many people wondered what possible health problems led to Vivian's need for skilled nursing care.

Every morning she asked one of her nurses to help her find something to wear in "a lovely shade of pink or rose." It wasn't hard; almost everything in her wardrobe was her favorite color. She had a private bedroom, which, in all honesty, was a barely disguised hospital room. Her private room was one of few in the facility and, from time to time, the nursing staff allowed someone to "sleep over" for a few nights. Vivian was blessed with the financial capacity to live in a single room, and everyone agreed it was the best option for her. The center director approved a guest to stay with Vivian only in a strictly temporary overflow situation.

She was a little bit of a talker and, although everyone liked sweet Miss Vivian, temporary guests and their families had a history of reporting that she wasn't the best roommate. In addition to being a talker, she'd been labeled a night owl and an insomniac. She failed to understand that the curtain separating the two twin beds was essentially a barrier with a *Do Not Disturb* sign on it.

Vivian would have taken offense to comments slighting her hospitality as a roommate had she heard them. She would have noted that none of her sisters had ever complained about sharing a room with her, nor her husband, who, quite obviously, only had lovely things to say. She was definitely a people person who valued her role as a former welcome leader in her neighborhood. Why wouldn't that same courtesy be afforded to those moving into her room as well? Vivian fit the description of a true southern belle to a T. She took pride in sharing her parents' decision to name her after actress Vivien Leigh, who played Scarlett O'Hara in *Gone with the Wind*.

Enduring Grace was the newest assisted living center in town, designed to look like a resort at the seashore. It was rather like a resort in that one building accommodated independent living retirement apartments and the other housed the assisted living center. Outside, it was quite welcoming, painted in light blue with white trim. The stunning foyer was grand, with pale yellow walls, beautiful windows, and high ceilings. The living room filled the majority of the space with lovely furnishings in a combination of light blues, yellows, and corals. A gleaming black grand piano was positioned in the corner. The dining room, although smaller than one might see in a resort, was just as lovely and situated behind the living room. A small card room, a large game room, TV room, and huge recreation center were to the left of the main area. Offices for employees and a public restroom were to the right.

Just beyond the offices was a door that led to the residents' private rooms. An extra-wide door opened with a mere push of a button on the wall. Despite their commitment to excellent care, it was still a rather jarring experience as the giant door whooshed open and you entered the outer wing of the facility. Walking through the door was equivalent to walking into a different world. The welcoming, cozy colors and beautiful furnishings disappeared much like Dorothy leaving colorful Oz and returning to a movie-version, black-and-white Kansas. The smells of potpourri were joltingly replaced with disinfectant.

The nurses' stations were fashioned in a slight horseshoe, and each was poised in front of a hallway leading to residents' rooms. The nursing staff kept their area cheerfully decorated year-round with holiday themes. Vivian's room was down the right-hand corridor, last room on the right.

She didn't particularly like sitting alone in her room. It was tragically colorless and brought her no joy. Prohibited from hanging anything on the walls, the floral window curtains were the only decoration. The matching rug she had enjoyed for a pop of color and to warm her feet had been taken away by staff to prevent her from falling. They replaced the rug with no-skid socks for her feet.

On the windowsill sat three little frames of photographs and a small green plant that looked like a tiny cactus. Vivian was glad the plant was not demanding of care because her husband had said there was not a plant alive she couldn't kill. As harsh as that sounded coming out of her sweet husband's mouth, it was absolutely true.

Despite the fact that she often gazed out her window, her view was nothing grander than the parking lot. Of course, everyone knew she wasn't focused on the cars as she stared out the window for hours on end; she was lost in memories of long ago. Whenever her eyes did leave the outdoors and she gazed around her room, staring immediately to the left of the window, she saw a dark wood wardrobe cabinet with an ugly and loudly ticking clock hanging next to it on the wall. Her television hung from a bracket in the ceiling, always on, with the sound adjusted for either watching or ignoring it. Continuing a scan along the wall to the left, she saw a small sink and mirror followed by a door leading to the bathroom, which housed a toilet and handicapped-adapted shower.

Across the room, she had a comfortable rocking chair and a hospital tray table with wheels. She rather liked that it could be used at her chair or adjusted as a food tray if she was still in bed. Her nightstand, tucked neatly between her twin-size hospital bed and the rocking chair, had a small pile of papers on it, notes perhaps. The walls were a dreary cream color along with the trim around the door. The door and every piece of furniture in the room was a dark wood tone. It all felt foreign to her. She'd longed for home at first, but no longer mentioned it. Some days, she would admit, were fairly good ones. Like today and every Monday, when she had special visitors coming for lunch.

Vivian's nurse, Angela, draped her tiny, fragile shoulders with a delicate pink shawl as Vivian proudly shared, "I was Miss South Carolina, you know." Angela simply smiled. This was one of her other charming idiosyncrasies. Vivian did not state this with vanity. It was simply her way of sharing something about herself in hopes others would reciprocate. Many thought she was being boastful, but she was simply stating a get-to-know-you fact. *I was married, I had a dog, I went to college, and I was Miss South Carolina.* She didn't realize she shared her get-to-know-you facts at least once a day.

When Vivian moved into the assisted living center earlier that year, she had insisted on "putting on her face" every morning. She loved fixing her hair and wearing pink lipstick, usually in a shade too bright for her pale complexion. She had been trained to perfect her look by professionals—never a hair out of place. Her demanding mother had instilled in her that a lady never left home without lipstick. Unfortunately, trying to keep that unnecessary promise now often left Vivian resembling a little girl playing unsupervised in her mother's makeup. It was much better when her nurses lent a helping hand.

Nurse Angela applied a simple pink-tinted lip balm to her lips. "Look how beautiful you are, Miss Vivian!" They both glanced into the mirror. Angela saw a lovely eighty-year-old woman whose blonde hair had turned silver gray. She saw sky-blue eyes and an infectious smile that, when big enough, showed off matching dimples. Vivian saw strangers. She saw an older woman and a younger one. She studied the beautiful woman with the glowing ebony complexion, who wore her long hair pulled back in a thick ponytail. She rather thought the kind woman needed a little lipstick, but shared honestly, "You have such beautiful skin."

"Thank you!" Angela beamed at Vivian. She knew that was high praise coming from this petite pageant queen. Angela knew, although Miss Vivian didn't look in the least like an eighty-year-old woman, that her body and mind were losing their fight with age and illness. "Shall we be off to see your friends?"

Angela pushed Vivian down the hall in her wheelchair. She smiled as Vivian waved to fellow residents and nurses; she made everyone smile. They paused for a moment outside the room next door to speak with Vivian's "lovely Asian friend," whose name Vivian couldn't recall. She meant absolutely no disrespect in calling her neighbor by such a description and the sweet woman never seemed to notice that Vivian didn't call her by her name, Margaret. After speaking for a minute, Vivian reached over and gently squeezed the other woman's hand. "I'm sure your husband will be by today. Please come join me for lunch if you'd like." The woman smiled at Vivian and nodded as everyone continued in the original direction they were headed.

Angela took Vivian beyond the giant whooshing doors, pushing her into the dining room where three lovely older women sat in their usual spot at the table by the window. She adjusted the brakes on Vivian's wheelchair and left with a smile and slight wave to the ladies.

"I traveled to China even before President Richard Nixon," Vivian stated emphatically in lieu of greeting her longtime friends, whom she insisted were her sisters. They were sorority sisters she had known for more than sixty years, which made her statement true, but most thought this was just one of the many things she had confused in her mind. "My husband, John, was a congressman. I think he secretly worked for the CIA," she shared in a whisper with her sisters as they sipped coffee out of white foam cups.

"Or *you* worked for the CIA, Button." Laney, the oldest of the sisters by a few months, laughed. Button, as in "cute as a button," was a nickname from childhood. Much to Vivian's dismay, it was a name that followed her through life. She tried repeatedly, especially upon marrying Mr. John Upton, to be known as Vivian. But the name Button Upton was just too funny for her friends to let slide.

"Well, anyway, I guarantee whatever Chinese food they presume to be preparing for lunch in that kitchen—isn't," Vivian asserted.

Her friend Laney asked, "Isn't what? Edible?"

"Chinese food," Vivian answered.

With a chuckle, Laney reached over to squeeze Vivian's hand. She seemed to be doing so well today. Laney noticed how beautiful Vivian's hands still were with perfectly manicured nails, polished pink. Her hands showed only the slightest signs of aging, the skin becoming softer with a few lines rising up to the knuckles, but they were still so lovely. Vivian's fingernails had always been a source of pride for her. "They're long, strong, and can be used in a pinch like a screwdriver," she used to say.

Laney looked at her own hand next to Vivian's. It was tan, more than a little wrinkled, with a few age spots. Laney loved the outdoors and her skin always had a healthy, sun-kissed glow. She had a few more wrinkles than Vivian, but her dark hair, now short, had only hints of gray. It had never been color treated, much to the dismay of her friends. Laney had recently started using a cane to assist with walking. She'd used one many years before following knee surgery and rather liked the confidence it gave her. It also worked well as a pointing stick or to make grand gestures. She especially liked that.

"They say we elderly lose our taste buds," said Helen, who no doubt knew because Helen read everything and knew everything. She had been a walking encyclopedia since long before high school. She turned to say thank you to the staff member who brought their lunch to the table. Helen pushed her glasses up on her nose and studied the plate in front of her. Her red hair, once her pride and joy, was now gray, short, and a little too curly for her liking. She had gorgeous brown eyes that seemed to twinkle when she smiled. "We are born with as many as eight thousand taste buds, but those start diminishing around age sixty-five," Helen shared.

"I don't really think that's true," Ida, the eternal optimist, muttered. She remained the envy of her friends with her slender and dressed-to-perfection style. She wore her gray hair, once curly blonde, in a classy bun and, today, looked particularly spiffy with a bright red beret. Her ensemble was perfected with a light touch of red lipstick. Looking from Helen to Laney, she spoke a little louder. "They just say that so we won't blame the cook."

Laney, Helen, and Ida looked at each other and laughed as they said simultaneously, and a little too loudly, the name of a man they'd never forget. "Virgil!"

"How that man ever managed to get hired as a cook for a sorority house is beyond me," said Helen.

Ida paused with food on her fork. "He really was a nice man despite all the scary tattoos. I think he was in the Navy. Do you remember the chicken Kiev with the orange rice? It was basic white rice with something like orange juice mixed in it? He called it *à l'orange* with a French accent."

"The man was from Albuquerque," Laney quipped, barely looking up from her lunch.

"Well, despite the orange rice incident, he did make amazing pies," Ida said, looking at the dessert next to her plate. She reached over with her fork and took a small taste. "Actually, this is an excellent apple pie. You don't suppose?" she asked jokingly and with a dramatic flair. They all turned and looked toward the kitchen, seeing several young women in hair nets. They looked back at each other, laughing at their inside joke.

"We do have the most heavenly cakes and pies," Vivian whispered.

"Vivian, would you like a petit fours with your tea? Our cook makes the most heavenly cakes and pies." As Vivian nodded and smiled, the lovely girl with long dark hair and striking green eyes continued, "I'm so glad we have iced tea. It's August in Florida after all," she said with a giggle.

Well aware of the stifling heat in the crowded but large, beautiful sorority house living room, Vivian turned her head slightly, discreetly wiping the perspiration off her top lip before removing her newly purchased black gloves. They were the perfect match to her sleeveless dress, black patent pumps, and hat. She turned back to accept her plate and cup from the pretty sorority girl who did not look warm in the least in her sleeveless, white eyelet dress. This was Vivian's last of several sorority houses to visit that day, so she did her best to casually glance at her nametag. "Thank you, Laney."

They sat face-to-face in matching floral chairs, surrounded by other girls longing to pledge a sorority and current members sharing their favorite aspects of sisterhood. Despite everyone's efforts to keep their voices conversationally low, it was a little loud nevertheless. Laney scooted her chair slightly closer to Vivian and leaned toward her as she said, "Tell me about yourself, Vivian. What are your interests and goals in coming to Redding College?"

After talking about the areas of study open to young women at the college—teaching, nursing, or secretarial—Vivian was pleased to find she had much in common with her hostess. They were both from South Carolina, loved dogs and kids, and wanted to be nurses. She was fun to talk to and giggled at everything Vivian said.

"We've been talking so much; we almost forgot to eat," Vivian said.

"I've never forgotten to eat anything in my life," Laney replied. "Especially dessert!"

They picked up their tiny cakes and, as they took a bite, they both briefly closed their eyes and made the same yummy sound: "Mmmm." Their eyes popped open and they laughed at each other.

As they walked toward the door at the end of the party, Laney turned to Vivian and said with a contagious grin, "I have truly enjoyed meeting you today."

Vivian replied, "Thank you, Laney. Isn't it funny that we have so much in common?"

"Very funny," Laney replied with an extra big smile and giggle.

Vivian was the last girl to leave the sorority party, lagging behind the others returning to the dormitory. When she entered her room, she turned on the light and went straight to the mirror above the small dresser to remove her hat. She gasped in shock and embarrassment, closing her eyes and swaying a little as she tried to remember how many times she had wiped her upper lip throughout the day. She looked down at her black gloves with hatred, ripping them from her hands. Her roommate, Helen, came into the room, her eyes widening as she saw Vivian's face in the mirror.

"I look like Adolf Hitler," Vivian cried. She motioned at her reflection in the mirror to the black glove stain above her lip and just below her nose that resembled a tiny, black mustache. "Now I'll never be asked to join a sorority."

"Of course you will. It's me who should be worried," her roommate shared.

"Nonsense, Helen. You're the brightest girl I've ever met."

"Button, do you want your pie?"

Laney got no reply. The sisters could tell from Button's glazed-over expression that her mind was somewhere else. She was no longer with them as she stared into space. This seemed to be happening more and more. Sometimes she gave them word clues that helped the sisters identify the time and place of Button's flashback, but today they did not know where her mind had taken her.

Glancing across the table at Helen and Ida, Laney motioned with her head that it might be a good time to leave. In silence, the three friends stood, left the dining room and pushed sweet Button back to her room where she could rest for a little while. After helping her from her wheelchair to bed and tucking her in for a nap, they did not linger.

Without a word, seemingly in deep thought, the three made their way through the building and into Helen's car in the parking lot. She was the only one of them still driving, and her car was her baby—her pride and joy.

"She seems much worse," Helen said, breaking the silence, as she pulled her old but pristine four-door, blue sedan out of Enduring Grace's parking lot.

"I didn't think she seemed too bad today, especially at first," Ida countered from her spot directly behind Helen in the back seat. "She was smiling and laughing about Virgil and the orange rice. She knows who we are. Many people our age have memory issues from time to time. I think, now that she doesn't have to worry about taking care of that big old house, she is much better."

Turning off the radio, Helen refuted. "She isn't. She isn't better. She's just different! She seems to be in her own little world half the time."

Ida continued to disagree from the backseat, checking her reflection in a small compact mirror and reapplying lipstick. "At least she isn't calling us on the phone every few minutes like she is stuck in a loop. This situation is so much better."

Helen's tone softened. "Bless her heart. It was so hard with her calling us off and on to report her coffee table was missing, her car stolen, or her dog lost. She hasn't had a dog in forty years. She was definitely having her fair share of senior moments. And that whole thing about her lost bicycle. What bicycle? I have never *ever* seen Vivian Upton ride a bike!"

Helen felt a little rattled as she slowed the car to a stop. Sitting at a red light, Helen took a cleansing breath. She looked toward Laney, who hadn't said a word since leaving the nursing home. "Laney, are you okay?"

Rubbing her forehead, Laney sat uncharacteristically quiet with her eyes closed for a few seconds. "I called the Alzheimer's Helpline."

Ida leaned forward as far as her seatbelt would allow. She stared sharply at Laney. "When? Why would you do that? Nobody has ever used that word about Button! No one ever said she has Alzheimer's, just dementia or memory issues." Ida leaned back in her seat and crossed her arms.

Glancing briefly into the rearview mirror, Helen replied to her, "Dementia is the general term for loss of memory. Alzheimer's is a common cause of dementia." She looked back at Laney and asked softly, "Why did you call them? What happened?"

Laney admitted, "It's not the first time I've called them. I'm sorry that I have kept some of this from you. I didn't want to burden you with it every day. You both have enough on your plates already. It actually was the helpline advice I received months ago that led me to the realization that Button needed assisted living."

"Don't apologize, but, for the love of Pete, please don't feel like you need to shield or protect us from this," Ida softly scolded. "You have always put yourself in the role of big sister. I know you have power of attorney and have handled many of Button's personal affairs, but this added stress and worry can't be healthy, Laney. It's not healthy. You need to let us be of help." Helen shot Laney a quick look, which communicated without words her agreement with Ida.

Laney turned slightly to look out her car window. After a moment, she shared, "As you know, evenings and nighttime seemed to bring about a personality change in her. One day we all went to lunch at Junie's Tea House, remember? And after lunch, we walked through those cute shops downtown. She was fine, absolutely herself. About seven o'clock, her neighbor called concerned that Button was outside calling for a dog, which, like you said, Helen, she hasn't had in decades. Another evening she wasn't answering her phone, and I was concerned. I drove over and found her outside in her nightgown. She was looking for something or someone; she was searching, perhaps, for John or her dog. She was so confused. That was when Dr. Long changed her medication, and we added a little melatonin into her evening herbal tea. Did you know they make something called Go-to-Sleep Tea?"

Helen said, "yes," and Ida replied, "no."

Laney continued to unburden herself and explained further to her friends. "We went a few days, maybe a couple of weeks, without incident. And then, we had a really bad night. She was calling that evening over and over and over, never remembering that we'd just talked. She kept asking me where John was because it was getting dark and his supper was on the table. I just wanted her to think, to remember, to pull herself together for a second and . . . and I told her, 'Button, John passed away fourteen years ago.'

"I thought she would suddenly have a moment of clarity, but instead she started screaming. She was devastated! It was just like when she heard the news the very first time. Her heart was absolutely broken and she sobbed, inconsolably, for several minutes. I told her I would come right over and hung up the phone. When I walked into her house a few minutes later, she was washing dishes and singing in the kitchen. I mean, what a relief to not find her sobbing hysterically, but what a horrific sight to see her standing there having already forgotten our phone conversation about John."

Laney continued to rub her forehead lightly; she suddenly felt the weight of those memories. "I realized for some time that I needed advice beyond that of Dr. Long. He's a wonderful physician, but I wanted to talk with an expert or someone who had been in my shoes. I kept the helpline number on my nightstand and thought about calling several times. When I got home that night, I felt so overwhelmed, so in need of guidance about our next steps, and I decided to call them. It was three o'clock in the morning, but someone answered."

Laney revealed what she learned. "I explained the situation to a nice young man on the phone and asked him what I should do. We talked for an hour. He explained 'sundowning' to me. It happens to people who have Alzheimer's disease, causing behavior changes, confusion, pacing, and wandering. He said fading light around sundown—thus, the name—seems to be the trigger, but they don't really know why it happens. Weirdly enough, just like with Button, the symptoms start in the evening, can get worse as the night goes on, and usually get better by morning. She never remembers these sundowning events the next day, thank God."

Laney continued, "We talked about John. I told the man on the phone the whole story about that night. I asked him what to do because, obviously, I made the wrong decision in trying to jog Button's memory. He told me to lie. 'Lie your butt off,' he said. 'Do or say whatever you need to because Vivian's reality is reality. Don't correct her. Don't try to jog her memory.' So, when the phone rang a few minutes later and Button said, 'Where do you suppose John is this late in the evening,' I lied to her for the first time in my life and said, 'He's still playing golf.'"

Helen had driven another mile or so and stopped at a traffic light through the conclusion of Laney's story. She felt frozen; the sound of a car horn behind them jerked her back to the green light and her responsibility behind the wheel. She drove on in silence, pulling into a parking lot at her earliest opportunity. She put her car in park, rolled down the windows, and turned off the ignition. They continued to sit there in complete silence, feeling hurt and confused. The three women had no words. Finally, Ida declared in an upbeat tone from the backseat, "Well, the golf course it is!"

She unfastened her seatbelt and scooted close to the front seat before continuing. "To live a life of honesty, integrity, and kindness . . ." She paused for a second to let the other two join in with the rest of their sorority creed. "Is the true meaning of sisterhood."

All three women nodded. Laney said, "Honesty, integrity, and kindness—until you have to lie your butt off for your best friend."

Helen replied gently, "I think that was very kind, Laney. You spared her from grief she should not have to repeat every day."

Laney reached to take Helen's hand. Ida scooted forward even further, reaching over the seat and placing her hand on top of theirs. She looked out the window and, trying to lighten the mood, said, "Does anyone need anything from the Mega-Mart?"

Laney

When Cookies Are the Best Medicine

Laney Walsh loved to bake. She didn't, however, love to cook and would happily explain the difference to anyone who asked. She had surprised Helen and Ida in the car on Monday when she'd jumped at the chance to run into the Mega-Mart. She needed to do something to ease her mind about Button, and the grocery store was just the ticket. *When stressed, bake. When really stressed, eat!*

She'd found all the ingredients she needed to make her favorite cookies. With the recipes in her mind, she snatched up the items she was missing at home, checked out at the register, and met her friends back in the parking lot in under fifteen minutes.

She had to wait two days to have the house and kitchen all to herself. Slipping on an apron, she put the CD from her favorite musical, *Waitress*, into the player her granddaughter called old-fashioned and cranked up the volume. She knew, in theory, that she could listen to music on her cell phone, but Laney loved the actual CD. It reminded her of the glorious trip she, Button, Ida, and Helen had taken to New York City in honor of their seventy-fifth birthdays. Ida was put in charge of planning and organizing because she was both a travel guru and New York City aficionado. Ida and Charlie had been there many times thanks to her love of Broadway musicals, Central Park, and New York's finest cheesecake.

They had flown in on a Wednesday and back on Sunday and, even at seventy-five, had crammed more fun into a few days than most tourists did in a week. They saw *Waitress* at the Saturday matinee, and it had been the highlight of Laney's trip. She bought the CD and a T-shirt in her favorite color of azure blue, which reminded her of the sky on a cloudless sunny day.

After preheating the oven to 350 degrees, Laney started singing along to the soundtrack, "Sugar, butter, flour." She pulled out pre-cut parchment paper for two large cookie sheets; quickly mixed flour, baking soda, and salt in a small bowl; and set the mixture aside. As she creamed butter, brown sugar, granulated sugar, and vanilla in the mixer, she couldn't help but reminisce about her childhood in which her love of baking began.

She'd always been a good eater, according to her mother. Born Delaney Diane Dandridge on Independence Day, she had been cute and pudgy and the center of her parents' lives. It wasn't long, however, before the first of four little brothers came along, overwhelming her parents. Her mother had taken to her bed often, forcing Laney into the role of babysitter as young as eight years old. Washing, ironing, and cooking took up most of her after-school hours. Unhappy with most of her chores, Laney did have one exception—making desserts. Her grandmothers taught her everything they knew and, before long, she surprised them with creations of her own.

Add eggs and blend until creamy, Laney recalled. *Add the dry ingredients and beat well.* As she worked through the steps, her thoughts drifted to special memories of her grandfather and their Saturday trips to the local library. She treasured those weekends and quickly became her family's bookworm. Reading was her passion, both books and cookbooks.

Blend in chocolate chips along with the special ingredient, drop a spoonful of dough in rows on the parchment paper, and bake for eight to ten minutes. Laney set the timer and, as her earlier thoughts and memories drifted through her mind, she washed the dishes.

An advanced reader, she remembered being moved ahead a year in school and skipping the second grade. She smiled as she thought of her third-grade teacher, who unknowingly shortened her name to Laney thanks to a simple typo on the class roster. Laney liked it so much she never corrected her teacher. Although Delaney was her mother's maiden name, she much preferred the shortened version for her first name.

She was proud to be a Dandridge and loved her family history. She'd been raised with family stories, and her favorite was that she was a direct descendant of George Washington. When Laney was in high school, she wrote a paper in history class about her lineage to President George Washington and his wife Martha Dandridge Washington. Her teacher gave her a *D* on the paper and wrote her a personal note in red ink at the top of the page, "George and Martha Washington had no children of their own!"

She took that paper straight to her grandfather's office at the local newspaper and, together, they investigated her teacher's comment. It turned out she wasn't a descendant of George Washington at all, but she was part of the Dandridge line from Martha's brother. She requested a grade change from her teacher on the grounds of close familial association, but was denied. She made her first and only B in that history class. *Boy, that still irks me*, she thought. In all fairness, she admitted, it eventually did lead to her love of genealogy.

It may have started out as research with her grandfather, but it became her favorite pastime. She was able to find even more information during her college years at a family research library near campus. After she had traced her roots as far as she could, she took Button, Helen, and Ida to the floor of the city library where she had spent countless hours. She was far more excited than they were to discover their ancestors.

Button (aka Vivian Susanne Kincaid Upton) was of Irish descent. She had an ancestor, a many times great-grandmother of long ago, who came to the United States as an indentured servant. She had stolen food in Ireland and was transported to the United States, serving several years as a housemaid for that supposed crime. Button was proud that she had made her way to the US West, married a farmer, and raised eleven children.

Ida (officially Ida Jo Kellenbach James) was the only born-and-raised Floridian of the foursome. She was a blend of English, Irish, Dutch, and German. Laney thought her search was the most intriguing because she had also been hoodwinked by a faulty family story. She was supposedly a descendant of the famous Pocahontas, which was regretfully false. She did, however, come from a long line of women with multiple middle names, a tradition her grandmother, Adeline Cornelia Rebecca Ida Jane Branch, regretfully ended by naming Ida's mother simply Mary Jo. Laney had shown Ida her research concluding the multiple names came from a desire to name daughters after sisters. After that discovery, Laney had changed Ida's name to Ida Jo Helen Vivian Delaney! Laney still regretted that Ida and Charlie had named their daughter Ava Ann. She adored Ava, but found it inconceivable that Ida had thrown away a naming opportunity like that.

Helen's ancestry was quite the story. She was born Helen Renee Chastain in Macon, Georgia. Her ancestors were French Huguenots, who came to the United States for religious freedom and settled in South Carolina and Georgia. She came from a long line of names like Soblet, Dampierre, and Rivoire. Her direct ancestor was Paul Revere, whose father, Apollos Rivoire, anglicized his name to Paul Revere. Helen firmly believed that her feisty, gutsy nature was passed down to her from the patriot who took the famous midnight ride during the American Revolution. Laney completely agreed!

The timer began beeping in the kitchen, pulling Laney from her daydreams and alerting her to check on the cookies in the oven. The chocolate chip cookies looked delicious and smelled incredible thanks to her secret ingredient: toffee bits. She picked up the idea from a little boy on the *Kids Baking Championship Show* on television. It was crazy how well those little urchins could bake!

She popped a bite, still warm, in her mouth and knew Button would love them. She had some snickerdoodle dough in the freezer she'd made a few weeks ago. It was simple to roll dough into little balls, freeze them on a cookie sheet, and then keep the frozen dough balls in a baggie. She filled two cookie sheets with frozen snickerdoodle dough balls and put them into the already hot oven. In minutes, the cinnamon aroma in the kitchen made her think of autumn weather. Of course, autumn weather in Florida was still eighty degrees.

When the cookies were out of the oven and had cooled sufficiently, Laney took a snickerdoodle and a cup of decaf tea onto the lanai to read for a little while. She glanced quickly through the mail she'd tossed on the table next to her book. She rarely got anything exciting but was unexpectedly thrilled to find a postcard from her sorority sister, Marie Tillman Meyer, who was coming to visit that very weekend from Bethesda, Maryland. Laney laughed—the postcard was of the Washington Monument. Marie would forever defend Laney's tie to George Washington, which she agreed was, in fact, a close familial association.

Thinking about her time in college, Laney considered it nothing short of a miracle that she'd pledged a sorority. She was no debutante; she was quite a tomboy with little grace or finesse. She had not had many girlfriends growing up and found herself intrigued by the opportunity to meet fellow female students in college. She had no concept of sorority beyond her favorite librarian at home, who once mentioned she loved her sorority sisters. It was really the term *sisters* that led Laney to pledge. How amazing to finally have sisters in her life! After helping to raise four younger brothers, she'd go to her grave arguing that girls were easier than boys. How ironic that God blessed her with one child: a boy. Of course, Bobby was the exception.

When Laney was in high school, she learned of Redding College's renowned nursing program. Uncertain of her chances, she had applied and been accepted before even talking with her parents. Despite their pride in her admittance and scholarship, they had been against it. It was too expensive, too far away; they didn't know anyone there and she was only seventeen. Grandfather Dandridge had come to her rescue. He insisted on giving Laney money for living expenses and bus fare, declared she would be eighteen before moving away to school, and reminded her parents of a distant cousin who lived in Florida. He had changed her life!

She hadn't been the slightest bit nervous as she boarded the bus to college. She felt such a sense of adventure and hope. She would miss her family, of course, but would see them on holiday breaks.

She remembered feeling instantly welcome and at home on campus. Her roommate was a shy girl from Biloxi, Mississippi, who left college after one semester to marry her high school sweetheart. Instead of living alone in her dormitory room, Laney took an available bed in the sorority house in the middle of her freshman year. She lived in a room with three bunk beds, six girls sharing one room, and a bathroom down the hall. She had never been so happy! They became the sweet friends and confidants she'd always wanted. She thought of those five special sisters, two of whom were already angels in heaven. The other three had eventually moved far away and, with travel and communication in the 1950s being nothing like today, she had lost touch with them years ago.

Her freshman year, Laney welcomed her tremendously special big sister, Evelyn Mae Marks, into her life. They called her Evie. She was from Savannah and, despite looking like a beauty queen, was the most progressive girl Laney had ever met. She made their house mother crazy by coming in late, smoking cigarettes on the back steps, and dancing a little too closely to her dates at socials. She wasn't a bad girl in the least; she just skirted the edges of propriety. Laney adored her, and they'd remained close until she moved with her husband to Denver in the 1970s. They were good about exchanging holiday and birthday cards until cancer took her away a few years ago.

Evie would always hold a special place in Laney's heart. She'd not only helped her land a part-time job at the library on campus, she had introduced her to Robert Walsh, the love of Laney's life. Robert was one of the other students working in the library, and they bonded quickly over their love of books. She thought he was such a dreamboat, looking a little like Paul Newman. He was sweet, shy, and several inches taller than Laney. He was the first person she approached about changing her field of study. Although she liked the idea of being a nurse, the science courses were not her cup of tea. She found her mind wandering during those classes, longing to pull out books of her choosing. Robert said, over and over, that she was already a librarian at heart and why not pursue her first love. He was wrong about that—he was her first love! She decided to pursue both and eventually became a librarian and Mrs. Robert Walsh.

The sound of the doorbell pulled Laney's attention to the front door. She walked from the lanai, carefully navigating the living room without her cane, and opened the door to find Helen and Ida on the front porch.

She smiled and welcomed them inside. "What a nice surprise! What are you two up to this afternoon?"

Helen put her purse down on the coffee table and said, "We're on a mission."

"What kind of mission?" Laney crossed her arms and studied Helen.

"A mission to find the best snickerdoodles in town. We assumed you'd baked all day yesterday, but you made some today, didn't you? I smell cinnamon." Helen looked beyond Laney toward the kitchen. "Oh, I think I smell the amazing chocolate chip toffee ones too!"

Ida interjected, "We are not on a snickerdoodle mission. We came to see how you're doing, dear. Monday was an extraordinarily hard day. We thought you might like to talk, but if you did happen to have cookies, we could share one with you while we're talking."

"Ida, you are the worst liar. You always have been." Laney laughed.

"I never lie, dear. I may fib or stretch the truth, but I never lie," Ida corrected.

"Me, too!" Helen's outrageous statement made Laney laugh out loud.

Walking into the kitchen, Ida declared, "You've been baking and listening to *Waitress*. Do you feel better?"

"I feel so much better!" Laney put cookies for Helen and Ida on paper plates and poured them each an iced tea. She'd already had two cookies, so she simply sipped her tea. They sat at the kitchen table reliving their birthday trip to New York and wondered if being eighty-five in a few years meant they'd be too old to travel. They loved the idea of taking other adventures together, but it made them distressed to think of traveling without Button.

They changed the subject to discuss plans for Marie's upcoming visit.

"I know Button needs to stay at Enduring Grace, but why don't the rest of us have a sleepover at my house?" Helen offered. "Marie is already staying with me, and I think we should have a sorority reunion weekend."

"I'm one step ahead of you. For some reason, I've already taken a walk down memory lane today," Laney admitted.

"You thought about Evie today, didn't you?" Ida had an uncanny ability to know what Laney was thinking.

"Among other sisters too," she shared.

Ida turned slightly in her chair to look straight at Laney. "Good for you! It's important to remember them. They were a huge part of our lives and remain an integral part of special memories. So, let's have a weekend retreat. Find your photo albums, scrapbooks, and composite photos and bring everything we can find to Helen's this weekend. Does that sound like a plan?"

Laney replied with a huge smile. "Yes, ma'am, Ida Jo Helen Vivian Delaney!"

Ida grinned and Helen laughed out loud, adding gleefully, "And I'll make a Paul Revere midnight ride to the liquor store for wine!"

Ida was elated with the plans. "It will be like the old days when we took sister trips every five years during our birthday season. I mean, obviously we couldn't make plans for this year for Button's sake, but we'll make it a special weekend."

Helen admitted, "It won't be like our past trips to destinations like Key West, New Orleans, San Francisco, or Santa Fe, but we will make it the best weekend we can for Button, for all of us."

Her sisters stood and gathered their purses. As Laney walked them to the door, they poked fun at Helen when she amended her previous plan. "I will buy wine well before midnight, of course." She stepped through the door, turned back to look at Laney, and dramatically instructed, "Bring cookies!"

Marie

When a Visit Means Everything

"Marie's flight has been delayed by thirty minutes," Laney shared in frustration as she settled back into Helen's car. "I'm sorry, but I honestly don't understand why you can't talk to a human being when you call the airlines these days. The recording said my wait time was between thirty and ninety-five minutes. There wasn't a single employee at the airline counter just now either. Luckily, I noticed the delay on the arrivals board."

"We're supposed to use their website or phone app. Not that I can't do that; I just didn't think of it today," Helen replied as she pulled her car away from the front of the airport.

Laney dug around in her purse until she finally found her cell phone. "Oh, good grief. I have a text from Marie from the Atlanta airport. She says she is going to be thirty minutes late," Laney said, kicking herself for her mistake. "I am terrible about this phone. I just want my home phone, which I no longer have—phone or home."

Trying to avoid another conversation about Laney's unwanted move to her son's house and her loss of meaningful items, such as her home phone, her car, and her independence, Helen steered the conversation back to the situation at hand. "Don't worry, we can circle the airport and park in the cell phone lot to wait for her."

"They have parking just for people with cell phones?"

"How long has it been since you've been out here? They have a parking lot for everyone. It's called the cell phone lot since *everyone* is basically awaiting a text from their traveler, indicating they've arrived. It keeps us all from circling the airport dozens of times. We park and wait for the signal and then storm the terminal, hoping for a curbside spot in front of baggage claim. I thought ahead, however, and called Marie earlier in the week. She agreed to pack light for the weekend. She didn't check a bag and will head upstairs to the ticket counter entrance and we'll pick her up there. It's much less crowded!"

Helen pulled into the cell phone lot and parked her car. She dug her own phone from her handbag and shared, "Ida says Button is doing well this morning. I'm letting her know that Marie is delayed and to stall for an hour! I've pictured this reunion in my mind, and I think we should be at our dining room table when Vivian enters and sees Marie. Despite the decline in Button's cognitive abilities, I think she will know Marie."

"I hope so. I truly do."

"Marie calls every week and they talk."

"Yes, but I've sat with Button during those calls and the conversations are often just about college days. She knows Marie's voice on the phone, but I wonder what her reaction will be to seeing her little sis in person, especially when she no longer looks like young Marie. It's been more than a year, and Button has declined so much."

Helen nodded. "Did you prep Marie for Button's current situation? Her decline?"

"Oh, sure. We talk often and she is in the loop. It's just hard with her living in Bethesda and not seeing everything with her own eyes. She and Tim were very close to Button and John when both of their husbands served in Congress. Marie and Button share all of those years, those experiences, and the memories. Button talks about John, of course, although not about the time they lived in DC."

Laney and Helen were still discussing the upcoming weekend when Marie texted that she had arrived and would meet them promptly at the upstairs pick-up location.

"Poor Marie will probably be exhausted after waking up this morning for a five o'clock departure," Helen theorized as she drove toward the designated pick-up area. "I thought, after our lunch visit with Button, we could go back to my house. You, Marie, Ida, and I can visit. Marie can rest if she'd like. I assume she'll want to go back to Enduring Grace this evening to see Button again, so I put a roast dinner in the crockpot this morning to make life simple. We know evenings aren't always great for Button, but we can navigate through that if she has an . . . episode."

"Thank you for inviting Marie to stay at your house, for inviting all of us to have a girls' weekend."

"I'm thrilled to have you all and, if I'm not mistaken, there she is!"

Helen pulled up curbside in front of their sister, Marie. Much to their chagrin, Marie had not changed dramatically. Her salt-and-pepper hair was still styled much the same in a slightly shorter bob cut. She wore glasses, too, now but somehow made them a fashion statement. The cute black frames looked absolutely precious on her. She was wearing denim with a hot pink top and a flowy poncho in a rainbow of colors.

"Hello, my loves! No, please don't get out of the car," Marie said with a wave as she opened the door to the backseat and climbed in with her bright floral duffel bag. "I'm so excited to see you!"

Conversation was nonstop from the airport to Enduring Grace. The volume in the car nearly exploded! Helen smiled at Laney and Marie's bubbly, vivacious personalities. They were amazing; they could talk over each other, replying to questions and comments simultaneously without seeming to even draw breath. Their laughs were contagious. They always had been.

Helen reminisced as she drove. Marie pledged their sorority sixty-one years ago, one year after Button, Ida, and herself and two years after Laney. She and Button were opposites in looks and personality. Unlike Button's long blonde hair, Marie's shoulder-length black hair had been flipped up stylishly like a young Marlo Thomas. She preferred rolled-up jeans to Button's conservative skirts and had minimal interest in makeup. Button was flabbergasted that Marie didn't have a favorite color as she considered all of them her favorite.

Marie raved about the beaches of her hometown, Miami, whereas Button loved the South Carolina seashore. Marie was Jewish, and Vivian a Christian. They embraced their different upbringings and loved learning about and sharing each other's customs and traditions. Button thought Challah was the best bread in the world. Marie thought cutting out Christmas cookies and decorating them topped any loaf of bread. They gave each other Christmas and Hanukkah gifts because doubling up on giving made both holidays special.

Marie towered over Button's petite frame, standing even taller than Laney. She knew swear words a sheltered Button had never heard and was outspoken about her thoughts on social issues, politics, and just about every subject under the sun. They could not have been more different, nor loved each other more.

They did have a few things in common. They were both straight-A students, officers of the sorority, active on campus, and just plain likeable. Their biggest honor, they often shared, was being elected one year as the big–little sister duo "Most Likely to Take Over the World" at their sorority's annual awards banquet.

Glancing at her sisters as they continued to talk nonstop in the car, Helen knew Laney loved Marie very much. There was a brief time after she'd graduated and got married that Laney felt a little jealousy of Button and Marie's close friendship, but that corrected itself a year or two later when they graduated and married as well. With Ida tying the knot in the same year as Button and Marie, Helen remembered declaring herself exhausted of bridesmaid duties. That declaration hadn't helped a bit. In just four years, she'd been a bridesmaid eight times. When her opportunity came to marry, she eloped to Atlantic City. Eloping had not been a good decision. Actually, she corrected in confession to herself, Atlantic City was fine. It was the *husband* that was rotten. She was not used to being wrong.

Helen parked the car in the Enduring Grace parking lot and chuckled at Laney and Marie's surprise over their quick arrival. She texted Ida that they were heading inside. They made their way through the large living room to the dining room, waving to people they knew, and secured their favorite table by the window. Sweet Nurse Angela had put a hand-written *reserved* sign on the table, but their delay meant lunch was almost over and the room was empty. Helen positioned Marie in a chair facing the entryway and took a seat next to Laney on the other side of the table.

Vivian entered the room with Ida guiding her wheelchair. Helen and Laney reached for each other's hands with one last prayer.

"Howdy Do, Button Sue!" Marie stood, smiling hugely with her arms spread wide, using her old nickname for her beloved big sister, Vivian Susanne.

"Marie! My Little Sissy Sue!" Vivian said loudly just before her face crumpled in tears as she reached out to hug the very happy and thankful Marie Susanne. Button leaned forward and rested her head on Marie's shoulder as they hugged and whispered to each other. Two very different women. Same strong, lasting bond and, coincidentally, the same middle name.

It was the reunion of their dreams that Laney, Helen, and Ida had planned, hoped, plotted, and prayed for. It may have appeared it was a gift for Button or even for Marie, but the three sisters knew it was for all of them. Button was changing. Alzheimer's was an enemy they didn't know how to defeat. Time wasn't on Button's side; actually, time wasn't on any of their sides.

On that blessed weekend, time stood still. It actually seemed to rewind like a magical fountain of youth, giving these special women many moments full of joy, memories and time together that they deserved. Ironically, it was Button who slept well through both Friday and Saturday nights in her bed at the nursing home, while the crazy crew at Helen's stayed up talking until well past two in the morning. They tried to milk the weekend for every single second it would give them. They looked at pictures in old photo albums, shared favorite stories, drank a little wine, and giggled like schoolgirls. They made a toast to sisters who had passed away before them.

"I don't know how I missed the news about Fay," Marie shared. "What a fabulous lady!"

Ida picked up a photo of their sister who had lost her battle with cancer last year. "Indeed she was. I'm sorry, Marie, that we failed to call you. Laney, Button, and I were in a bridge group with her and a few other ladies. We played twice a month, rotating who would be hosting. Fay lived down the street from me, and we shared rides. One of my favorite memories of those days was her love of cherry limeades. We always stopped for one on our way home. Our bridge group has dismantled since Fay's passing, and Button's health issues."

Laney took a sip of wine. "Button was both a lucky and fabulous bridge player, and it was hard to watch her decline and struggle with the game. We wanted to keep her playing with us as long as we could. I remember one day it was her turn to host everyone at her house. We had talked a couple of times that week about the dessert she was planning to serve and a punch she wanted to make. I got to her house early that day to discover nothing prepared, no card tables set. I scrambled to throw some slice-and-bake cookies into the oven and pulled out her tea set. When Ida arrived just behind me, we set everything up as quickly as we could. It wasn't long after that when we added Marjorie to the group and paired Button with one of us as an adviser of sorts, under the guise that we needed her expertise."

"Who is Marjorie?" Marie asked.

"You'd love her. She didn't go to Redding College with us, she went to the University of Georgia. She and her husband moved here long ago, and she is part of our alumnae chapter," Laney explained.

Marie nodded. "That's marvelous. The DC Alumnae Chapter is a melting pot of sisters from all over the country, all ages. I've made some wonderful friends. It was fabulous to plug into that group when we moved from Florida years ago. Button and John hadn't moved there yet, and I didn't know a single soul. I like it. We do quite a bit of philanthropy work and enjoy some fun activities. I enjoy a happy hour group of mostly younger alums, but another sister—who went to school somewhere in Texas and is also in her seventies—loves to team up with me to crash their party. They are delightful and seem to think Beverly and I are a hoot."

Ida laughed, pointing at Marie. "I love how you just slid in the fact that you're in your seventies. Seventy-nine!"

"And don't you forget it. Holding steady in my seventies. I have ten months before I am officially elderly."

"I hate to break it to you, Sister, but retirement associations deemed you elderly at age fifty," Helen declared, and laughter erupted!

They decided, given that they were all so old, they should call it a night on their slumber party and get some rest. The next night they did more of the same.

Despite their lack of sleep, they arose early both mornings to visit Button. They tried to give her and Marie as much time together as they could, even making Halloween crafts with Button in the nursing home rec room on Sunday morning before Marie's flight.

"I'm still no better at crafts than I was sixty years ago," Marie complained, showing her not-so-scary witch to Button. "But this is pretty cute if I do say so myself."

"It's darling," Button replied. She hadn't made one of her own. Despite having the materials in front of her, she'd said, "no, thank you," when Marie and Laney asked if she wanted a hand. Nurse Devon asked her the same question a few minutes later, and she accepted his help with a smile.

While Button was distracted by Ida and Helen on her left, Marie leaned close to Laney and whispered, "I do believe someone may have a crush on a cute young man!"

Laney laughed, "Oh my, yes! He has doted on her from day one and she adores him. Actually, we all do."

"She deserves to be doted on and the center of a man's attention. Lord knows, John didn't! During their marriage, he was country and duty first, and Button second," Marie said.

"Country. Golf. Button," Laney clarified.

"Yes, in that order. God bless him, he was even on the golf course when he had his heart attack. I shouldn't speak ill of him, because he did love Button, but he also loved having a beautiful and loving wife to cook, clean, grocery shop, pay the bills, take care of all details, and be the perfect hostess and congressman's wife. He got all of that plus her brilliant mind. I know for a fact she read and edited many a bill and did background work on constituent issues his staff assumed he did."

Laney looked at Marie. "And you and Tim?"

"Not quite as much. I put my foot down early on in our marriage. I regretfully must admit though, for appearance's sake, I did much of the same. I was often so mad, so frustrated with Button during those years for allowing herself to be treated that way. I'm as bull-headed as they come, whereas Button will carry burdens in silence to avoid confrontation."

Looking around again to confirm nobody was listening, Laney whispered, "Button never talks about John in any terms other than perfection. She only recalls her favorite memories or the blissful days as a newlywed. In that regard, I love Alzheimer's."

Helen and Ida stood, finished with their projects, and gestured to Marie that they needed to leave for the airport soon. Laney looked up at her friends and joked, "Look at me using a glue gun—and nobody got hurt! Button, do you want to put these decorations on your door? I mean, even Marie's witch is display worthy."

They gathered their homemade decorations and pushed Button back to her room. They borrowed a roll of masking tape and turned her door into a festive Halloween display.

"Do you like it, Button?" Marie took her hand and motioned toward the door. "Isn't it a fun way to welcome guests?"

"This isn't my house. I don't live here."

Helen stepped forward to help Marie, worried she would feel upset about Button's statement.

But Marie simply knelt down in front of the wheelchair to look Button in the eye and took her hand gently. "Vivian Susanne! You know that home is where the heart is. My heart is here with you. Laney, Helen, and Ida's hearts are here. So where else would your home be? This is your home and you are very, very loved. And, I bet you $100 that 95 percent of the clothes in that wardrobe are pink. Am I right?"

Button reached out and touched Marie's cheek.

Just then, Devon approached Button's door and motioned toward the decorations. "What do we have here? Miss Vivian, look at your Halloween decorations! Aren't they fabulous?"

Button's mood instantly lightened. She smiled at Devon.

"Would my favorite girl enjoy a little stroll with me for lunch today?" Turning to the others, he asked, "Your usual table?"

Helen leaned toward him and murmured quietly, "We can't today. We need to get our friend, Marie, to the airport. We will come tomorrow, though."

"Won't that be fun, Miss Vivian? Your friends are coming for lunch tomorrow! Monday is always a special day. Well, let's be off on our date, shall we?" Devon said, pushing Button toward the door. Smiling at Marie, he added, "Have a safe flight. It was nice meeting you."

"Thank you, Devon. I enjoyed meeting you as well."

"Goodbye," Vivian waved. "Goodbye now. Come over again soon!"

Marie watched Vivian depart down the hallway. "That nurse is the best person in the world for Button, isn't he?"

"He is," Ida confirmed.

"I'm sorry, Marie, today was not as good for Button as Friday and Saturday. This can't be the way you wished to end your visit," Laney said softly as she put her arm around her.

"I'm fine. I'll see her again soon."

Ida

When Swear Words Are Absolutely Necessary

"Touchdown!" Ida cheered as she and her family watched their college football game on the giant TV in their living room. With her arms in the air to signal the score, she announced to her husband Charlie and son-in-law Joe seated nearby, "I yelled at the offensive coordinator in the first quarter to call the screen pass. The other team's defense is being overly aggressive and hyper-focused on sacking the quarterback. A short, quick pass to the running back just beyond the line of scrimmage and he had clear sailing to the end zone." As a joke, she declared, "It's about time that coach listened to me!"

"Grandma, you'd have made a fabulous play caller for any football team," Jennifer said from the kitchen table as she worked with her mom, Ava, to put out halftime snacks.

"Your grandma would have been a viciously brilliant football coach," Charlie said, toasting his wife with his beer raised high in respect.

"Honey, you know there isn't a vicious bone in my body," Ida protested.

"There is during football season!" Everyone chimed in simultaneously. Ida chuckled.

Known by many as the sweetest lady in town, Ida was a kind, thoughtful person. She always did her utmost to have a positive attitude and sunny disposition. She and Charlie had owned two homes in town, both painted her favorite shade of pale yellow. When giving directions, she always said her home was the happy, yellow one at the end of the cul-de-sac.

She was generous to a fault and the peacemaker in times of strife. She was a loving wife, mother, and grandmother; the very best friend and neighbor. But every weekend in the fall, similar to a Dr. Jekyll and Mr. Hyde phenomenon, sweet little Ida turned into passionate football guru and half-crazed lunatic!

It was no secret that she loved football games and was by all definitions a fanatic. She had long ago declared it her favorite season—football, not autumn. When the sun rose on the first Football Saturday of the year, Ida felt like Christmas morning had arrived. She considered it a present that lasted until the final bowl games were played in January. She watched more football games than anyone else in her circle of family and friends. Even Charlie left her many times in front of the television late at night, surrendering and going to bed. He had not, for example, cared overly much that Utah was playing Oregon way out on the west coast, but Ida knew the Utes were tough and the Ducks were fast, and she'd wanted to see which team would come out on top. That was worth staying up until one in the morning in her book!

She not only loved the game but also cherished many special memories. She prized Saturdays, adorned in her favorite team attire, even if she never left her house. She had an outfit for every holiday of the year, as well as a plethora of football garb from shirts and hats to scarves and jewelry. She threw giant watch parties with family and friends and firmly believed her football parties were the precursor of modern-day tailgating. Most of all, she treasured every opportunity to be on campus on Football Saturdays.

Many of her favorite moments had occurred over the years on that campus. Most cherished of all was the evening Charlie James asked her to marry him. It was during their senior year after a walk to a beautiful section of campus they'd designated as *their spot*. Year after year, they had retraced their steps to that special spot before football games and shared a kiss for good luck. It had become their tradition. The trees grew over the years, adding more shade, but otherwise it remained the same. New buildings had popped up all over campus, old ones torn down or renovated, but their spot had remained untouched.

They saved as much money as they could as a young married couple, and within a few years, they bought season tickets in the end zone. They'd been season ticket holders ever since. Despite numerous offers, Ida never coveted a seat upgrade to a different section of the stadium. She loved her seat. She especially relished taking her seat early before the game and listening intently for the sound of the band coming toward the stadium. It was thrilling to hear the fight song getting louder and louder, until the band marched onto the field and the stadium erupted in cheers. She loved the excitement, thrills, and traditions.

Beyond campus, she and Charlie traveled to a few away games. They felt very lucky to have attended one bowl game, so amazing it had been deemed an instant classic. Thanks to their love of travel and the joy Ida took in trip planning, they had splurged on the tour to Arizona. Not only had their team pulled out the unexpected win, they took a side trip to see the Grand Canyon. It was one of their most amazing trips ever!

Following a series of commercials, Ida turned her attention back to the game and reacted to a bad play. "Oh, poo!"

Ida looked at Joe and complained, "They made a first down on us. The ref missed a holding call on the right guard, number ninety-two." Joe nodded his agreement.

Jennifer laughed in the kitchen. "Oh, poo? Wow, Gran, that's one of the toughest swear words in your arsenal."

Ida did not swear. She had learned an unfortunate lesson as a child when her mother washed out her mouth with soap for her simple use of *darn it*. Despite hearing much worse at school, she promised herself she would not allow bad words into her vocabulary. She took this commitment seriously, even creating alternative swear words when Ava was born. Mothers definitely needed to swear from time to time without risking that their words might pop right back out of their little darling's mouth. Her curse words such as *tartar sauce, scrap,* and *Doolittle* had stood the test of time.

"Well, scrap! Doolittle line judge is blind!" Ida noticed Charlie smiling at her. "I'm just saying, honey, that the referee needs glasses. The receiver's foot was out of bounds. They'll have to overturn that call from the booth."

Charlie winked at her from his favorite chair. "I'm sure you're right, sweetheart."

Despite Ida's claim that she didn't swear, Charlie knew of one major slip-up on her part. He called it the *famous incident of 1973*. Ida often claimed college football her favorite pastime, but she was a devout NFL Miami fan as well. One Sunday afternoon while watching their beloved team on TV, Ida lost her composure.

Back then, in Ida's eyes, quarterback Bob Griese had been a superhero. He had led the team to an undefeated season in 1972 as well as a championship. Hopes were high for all Miami fans when, just two games into the new season, their eighteen-game winning streak came to an end at the hands of players from Oakland. They managed to put up just three points each quarter and yet uncannily won the game 12–7 on those four field goals. Miami scored a touchdown in the fourth quarter, but it was too little, too late.

To hear Charlie tell it, his little Ida screamed "you f-ers" as Oakland celebrated their win at the end of the game. Ida claims Charlie misunderstood her, and she really said, "you fudgers," because they had fudged up Miami's winning streak. Charlie usually won their squabbles over the event in question by claiming his hearing was just fine in 1973 and that *fudgers* wasn't a real word. Ida always claimed innocence and leaned on the fact that nobody would ever believe such a word came out of her mouth, which may have been true if not for football season!

Fortunately, their team pulled out a winning season anyway, claiming the championship for the second year in a row. Charlie and Ida spent many a Sunday afternoon cuddling on the couch and watching their favorites play. Bob Griese and Dan Marino may have been his wife's football heroes, but he knew he was her longtime, one-and-only love.

They grew up in the coastal community of Tarpon Springs, where their fathers were commercial fishermen and close friends. Their mothers were like sisters to each other, and Ida and Charlie found themselves always together. They grew up as friends, classmates, neighbors, and partners on game nights. When their families gathered to play cards or dominoes, they often were the winning team. Charlie always said that Ida could read his mind and, later on in high school, she balanced out his bad side by having so much good in her. They were high school sweethearts, marrying right after college graduation, and still in love sixty years later.

Charlie went to college to study engineering, and Ida went to college to be with Charlie. She'd sold her parents on a fervent, but pretend, desire to be a teacher, and they had supported her dreams. Once in college, however, Ida discovered a different side of herself. She blossomed into a dedicated student. She discovered a love of learning, especially history, and was inspired by the aspirations of her sorority sisters.

She never thought of pledging a sorority, but Charlie pledged a fraternity the summer before college started and suggested she might like it. He said they would have mixers and dances; Ida didn't see anything to dislike about that.

Button always said it was thanks to the Phoenicians and their alphabet that she and Ida became friends. They were placed in the same orientation group and stood alphabetically in line, Kellenbach and Kincaid, at every sorority house they visited. They were great friends by the third day and jumped for joy when they had the opportunity to pledge the same house. They loved their sorority, but for Ida, it had actually been her second choice.

Many girls had homed in on the question of which sorority on campus was the best, and Ida still remembered the director's response. She'd offered, "If you are wondering which sorority is the best, I can tell you. It's the one you love the most."

Ida had such a hard time deciding between two favorites. She liked the girls she'd met at both houses; she felt a connection to their philanthropic work. She put the other sorority first on her list because there was a girl in that house from her hometown.

She was disappointed she didn't receive a bid from them for about an hour. Once she found Button at their new sorority and met sisters like Helen and Laney, she was sure fate had lent a hand. She was certain, however, she would have been happy pledging the other sorority as well. They were equally wonderful, and she was friends with many girls who were a part of that sisterhood. Additionally, she had darling friends who pledged a variety of different sororities and just as many who did not join one at all. Pledging didn't narrow her friendship circle; it widened it.

Ida also had a strong affinity for sorority ritual. Loving history like she did, it proved to be meaningful to her. Ritual was just history, honestly, a simple shared tradition of secret meaning and purpose aimed at helping young women strive toward admirable and estimable lives. She was proud that Ava and Jennifer had followed in her footsteps. They loved their sisterhood as much as Ida, but their experiences were different from hers—as they should have been.

Sororities were constantly evolving support systems, which responded to the ongoing and ever-changing needs of women, in college and beyond. Ida was proud to pass the torch to Ava and Jennifer, whose experiences were much broader and more powerful than hers had been. It made her so happy to see women of different cultures, backgrounds, and sexual orientation finding a home within the bond of sisterhood. It thrilled her to see women today consistently going far beyond what she and her friends thought possible.

After graduating from Redding College, Ida had become a fifth-grade teacher when her pretend dream became a reality. She worked for thirty years at their neighborhood elementary school. She loved it. She paused her career for four years after Ava came into their lives when she and Charlie were twenty-five, but she started back when Ava was old enough for preschool.

Ida had gone through a very difficult pregnancy and delivery with Ava. The doctor admitted afterward that he was afraid he was going to lose them both. He suggested they'd be wise to not have additional children. Despite Ida's resolve to prove the doctor wrong, she never conceived again. Ida had worried, unnecessarily, for years about not giving Charlie a son, but he could not have cared less. He insisted over and over that he loved being surrounded by beautiful blondes!

Ida was pulled from her woolgathering when she heard Jennifer's voice.

"Grandma, are you alright?" Ida looked up to see Jennifer staring at her with concern.

"Yes, dear, I was just thinking."

"Well, I hope you're thinking up a way for our team to come from behind in the second half and win this game. And, I hope you can subconsciously float your game plan out into the cosmos for the coach. We're behind by two touchdowns." Jennifer offered Ida her hand. "Snacks are ready and the third quarter starts in about ten minutes."

Ida put her *We're #1* foam finger down on the sofa and straightened her team jersey over her black leggings as she stood. Walking to the kitchen on Jen's arm, she shared, "They need to come out and establish the running game to open up throws down field. Offensive line is going to have to firm up protection for the quarterback because he is getting flushed out of the pocket and isn't as accurate passing on the run." She explained her game plan as she grabbed a few snacks. "The defense needs to put double coverage on their wide receiver, number eighty. He's a potentially award-winning receiver and they've been leaving him wide open." Ida enjoyed her halftime break, but returned to her seat, foam finger on her hand, for the second half kickoff. *Here we go, boys.*

Unfortunately, Ida wasn't telepathic. It was a blowout win for the other team.

Long after the game was over and Ava, Joe, and Jennifer had gone home, Charlie pulled Ida's foam finger back out of the trash can, where he'd found it after countless other losses. He was pretty sure she called it "stupid, unlucky, and a 'fudging' waste of money" when nobody was within earshot.

Charlie headed back inside, placing Ida's foam finger on the coffee table. He knew she'd want it by next Saturday. And he smiled as he headed to bed. *I love my rabid, little football fan!*

Button's Halloween

When Chocolate Makes Your Day

Halloween decorations lined the hallways as Ida made her way to Vivian's room. They shared a deep love of all holidays, and Ida was excited to present Vivian with a little Halloween goodie bag. Dressed in black slacks, a black sweater adorned with festive orange jack-o-lanterns, and a matching snazzy black hat, Ida smiled when she saw her friend sitting in her room donned in a black turtleneck and fuzzy pink sweater vest covered with little black cats and candy corn. She had on matching pink lipstick.

"Trick or treat," Ida said with a big smile as she entered Button's room.

"Give me something good to eat," Button replied happily.

Ida pulled up a chair and sat next to her. She proudly showed Button the little Halloween sack filled with chocolates that she had been hiding behind her back. Button's favorite candy was chocolate, and she preferred it without any distractions like nuts or caramel.

"I wish I had a trick-or-treat bag for you, but there are no shops here," Button replied, putting her hand in the bag and pulling out a pair of pink fuzzy socks. She looked at Ida in confusion.

"Underneath the socks," Ida instructed. "I had to walk past the nurses' station, and they might frown on me stuffing you full of candy."

Button dove back into the bag once again and came up with two pieces of chocolate in her hand. Ida took the bag and sat it, along with the pink socks, on Vivian's nightstand. "Here, Button, let me help," she said as she unwrapped the first piece of candy. She put it in Button's hand and smiled as her friend put it in her mouth, closed her eyes, and made her signature "Mmmm" sound.

With her mouth full, Button motioned from the bag to Ida, but she shook her head. "They are all for you. I've had several already today, but isn't that what trick-or-treating is all about? I'll put the bag in your drawer so nobody knows. Laney and Helen are in on our little secret, and they promise to check the drawer and help keep you happily in chocolate when they visit." As she closed the drawer, Ida noticed a coloring book and colored pencils on the nightstand as well. "Oh look, a coloring book!" She turned with it in her hand and asked Button if she'd like to color.

"I suppose. I haven't colored since I was a little girl."

Ida opened the coloring book, noticing that several pages had been colored already. The completed pictures were signed and dated by Laney, Nurses Angela, Jamie, and Devon, and by Vivian herself.

Ida forced a smile for Button and sat the coloring book and colored pencils on the little table. She rolled the table closer to her friend so they could both reach the book and pencils and opened the book to a new picture for them to work on together. She picked up a pencil and started to color the parts of the page she thought might look pretty in green.

"I really don't expect many trick-or-treaters tonight," Ida shared. "I have some candy, of course, just in case. It's going to be terribly cold tonight! I always hated it when kids had to cover their costumes with a coat. Remember when my girl Ava was little and dressed up like a fairy and she couldn't wear a coat over her wings? You gave her that fuzzy blanket when we stopped at your house. Charlie and I sat in the car with the heater running and your blanket in the backseat and slowly meandered with her from house to house. She would hop out of the car, run up the neighbor's walkway and jump back in the car almost like she really was a flying fairy."

Ida glanced up at Button who was staring out the window. She reached for the pink pencil. "Here, Button, can you color all the pink parts?" Button turned back toward Ida and took the pencil.

"Button, can you color all the pink parts? The pink paint is on your side of the banner. Start on some of those candy pieces, and then paint those little cakes and the cotton candy on the other end. I'll finish painting the words, 'We're Sweet On You.' It is such a cute Bid Day theme," Ida said.

As she took in the long banner stretched in the sorority house foyer from the staircase to the living room, Vivian replied enthusiastically, "Yes, I love to paint. I'll help you! You did put down the drop cloth, didn't you?"

"Yes, ma'am," Ida joked.

"I just finished the nametags. They're in alphabetical order on a table in the dining room."

"Of course they are," Ida replied.

"What is that supposed to mean?"

Ida laughed, never looking up from painting. "Nothing. You are so organized, that's all. And thank goodness! I could never have done this without your help."

"I could never have done this by myself either," Vivian confessed.

Just then Marie bounded down the grand staircase, jumping from the third step to the tile floor. "I found the gold glitter. I knew we had some.

It was all the way in the back of the storage closet under some old, dingy dining room tablecloths."

Button explained, "House Mom Marion hid it there last year. She said she was banning glitter in the house because it is insidious. Apparently it clings to surfaces forever and ever."

Marie shrugged. "No problem. We'll just take the banner outside on the porch and splash it with a little glitz."

"Glitz is good," Ida said as Laney and Helen walked into the foyer from the direction of the dining room.

Helen disagreed. "Don't you dare get a single speck of glitter in this house! As house manager, I will have to listen to Mom Marion's tirade on the subject again. Those are the rules."

Ida couldn't help but say "yes ma'am" once again.

Laney shared, "The desserts are done; everything looks yummy. Let's get this banner glittered up and hung. We're running out of time. Our awesome new pledge class will be here in less than an hour."

"I'm ready!" Button offered. "I can't wait to see all of them. Plus, I'm starving and tonight I'm going to eat all the desserts and candies I want."

The six girls each took a section of the banner, still slightly damp, and carried it through the open double front doors, placing it carefully on the porch. Just as each of them took a huge handful of gold glitter and tossed it toward the banner, a gust of wind, later described as a hurricane force gale, blew all the glitter straight back into the house just as Mom Marion was making her way down the stairs.

Helen yelled, "Your little splash of glitz is now the golden glitter storm from hell! We're going to be cleaning up glitter until we graduate."

Mom Marion glared at them furiously, pointed toward the broom closet, and roared, "Clean up this disaster right this minute!"

The incredulous looks on those six faces was so comical even Mom Marion couldn't prevent the laughter that bubbled up inside her.

Looking at her five cohorts and their varying degrees of laughter, Ida said in the most cheerful voice she could muster, "We can clean this up in no time at all."

"And Charlie said, 'I'm sure you can fix the wings,' but unfortunately Ava had shoved those fairy wings into a tight wedge in her closet without thinking and permanently disfigured them. That costume never became a hand-me-down. It became a throw-me-out!" Picking up the picture they colored, she turned it toward Button and said, "Look at our masterpiece. I couldn't have done it without you."

Button did not look at Ida nor respond. She was staring out the window.

Ida recognized the faraway look in Button's eyes and felt like she was, once again, momentarily living in a different moment. She wished she knew what Button was thinking.

It was getting late, and Ida could see the sunset turning the sky such beautiful colors of red, purple, and pink. Her daughter, Ava, was going to make a grocery store detour after work, so she had a little extra time before her daughter would be arriving to pick her up to drive her home. Ida thought a walk outside might do her friend some good. Button adored puffy pink cloud days and, most of all, a pink-tinted sunset.

"Button, how about a little turn around the courtyard? It looks like the sky may turn a beautiful pink." She pushed Button's wheelchair toward her door, almost colliding with Devon, who had come to check on Button. "Oh, excuse me, Devon! I was just coming to ask if you'd let Button and me outside for a view of the sunset."

"Excellent idea. I will walk you out." As they walked toward the patio door, Devon smiled at Ida and said, "Happy Halloween," motioning toward her festive sweater. "Are you ready for some trick-or-treaters tonight?"

Ida smiled up at the tall, handsome young man. His dark hair, tan skin, and warm, brown eyes would have caught her eye years ago for sure, but what she adored about him now was how kind he was to Button. "I have candy, but don't really expect that many children," she replied. "Are you having a celebration here tonight?"

"Not really. I think the kitchen staff has made Halloween cookies, but they will be pretty bland." He said the last few words in whisper. "I'll make sure Miss Vivian gets a cookie since I'm sure she's had no other sweets today," he added with a wink.

Ida smiled at Devon and with her own wink replied, "Just three tiny bites of chocolate."

Devon swiped his badge and the back door clicked open. He took over pushing Button's wheelchair and positioned her along the walkway at the far end where she could see the sky and setting sun.

"Look at that beautiful sky, Miss Vivian!" Devon kneeled next to Button so she could see his face. "I love a gorgeous sunset. A red sky at night means fair weather ahead." Looking up at Ida, he said, "I hope that applies to people's lives as well."

Ida replied, "Look at you being all charming. No wonder you are the perfect match for Button. She has always been romantic about a pink sunset. I remember an argument that she and Helen had when we were younger. One night we were driving somewhere when Button insisted we pull over to admire the pink sunset. She said it was the Belt of Venus, a gift from the Roman Goddess of Love."

Devon chuckled, "I can totally picture her saying that."

Ida continued, "Well, Helen disputed Button's belief by explaining that a pink sky is simply an atmospheric phenomenon caused by sunlight shining through a denser atmosphere. Helen said it's something called scattering that happens when short-wavelengths of blue and violet are scattered by molecules in the atmosphere. It allows longer-wavelength colors of red, pink, and orange to pass through and hit the clouds."

"I can't believe you remember all that!"

"Oh, trust me, they argued about it forever. It wasn't just that one time. Button never let go of her romantic, dreamy feelings about sunsets. I think that's what hurts so much about her sundowning episodes. Sundown had always been her favorite time of day."

Devon looked at her with great empathy. "I wish I could stay longer, but I need to get back inside now. Would you like me to take Miss Vivian or would you like to stay here a little longer?"

"My daughter has probably arrived, so I'll walk with you to her room and leave her with you. Thank you for the sunset, Devon."

"Anytime. I'll make sure Miss Vivian gets outside for her pink sunsets."

When they returned to Button's room, Ida kissed her on the cheek, said goodbye, and headed for the front of the building. Button had been so quiet after coloring the picture. Ida wondered if that wasn't the best activity for her. She spotted her daughter, Ava, in her gray car in a parking spot near the door. She hoped she hadn't been waiting long after running errands.

Ava, officially Ava James Russell, now fifty-five, looked so much like Ida. Her curly blonde hair, with only a few hints of gray, was pulled back in a messy bun. She much preferred leggings and tunic tops over her mom's dressier style. She greeted her mom with a smile and little hug and asked how her Aunt Button was doing as she helped her into the passenger's seat.

"She loved her Halloween chocolates, and we colored a picture. We went outside for a little while. Did you see the sunset tonight?"

"I only caught the tail end of it, but it was definitely a Button sunset."

"Nurse Devon helped me wheel Button outside. She looked at the sky and, although she didn't say anything, I think she liked it. She looked all around, her head moving left and right with her eyes focused on the horizon."

"She was probably thanking Venus for her pink sky," Ava said with a chuckle. "Good thing Aunt Helen wasn't here to ruin it with her atmospheric anomaly lecture."

"Exactly! Thank you for bringing me today, Ava. Thank you for bringing me to see her every week. These visits are so important, so special to me."

Ava nodded and gave her mom's hand a brief squeeze. "I know, Mom. I should go in with you to see her, but it's difficult for me since she no longer seems to know who I am. The day she said, 'I know you're Ava, but where is little Ava' nearly broke my heart. I am happy to go with you, for you, if you want." Ava looked at her mom, who nodded, but didn't reply.

Trying to lighten the mood in the car, Ava said more cheerfully, "I will start coming with you from time to time. Now, let's get you home. I have ice cream in the grocery bags for Dad."

As they pulled away, Ida said a little thank you that she still had Charlie and could playfully scold him for eating too much ice cream. And for Nurse Devon, who understood the significance of chocolate candy and pink sunsets.

Helen

When Your Thanksgiving Feast
Calls for Stretchy Pants

Helen loved Thanksgiving. It was her favorite holiday, ranking higher on her list than Christmas. She found Christmas preparations rather exhausting and hadn't put up a tree in years. She was allergic to real trees. The artificial one she once decorated and displayed in the living room had lost its shape and luster. She was honest with herself and knew she had no business being on a step ladder or carrying heavy boxes back and forth from the garage. She didn't put up lights outside for the same reason; it wasn't money well spent to hire a company to string lights on her house. She did enjoy, however, hanging the Christmas cards she received on red ribbons strung on her fireplace mantel. Button always said it was the prettiest garland she had ever seen.

Her favorite part of Christmas was the gift exchange that she, Ida, Laney, and Button had shared for more than fifty years. The spending limit had been raised a little, of course. Last year, Helen chose pink tinted lip balm for Button, a scarf for Laney, and a fun hat for Ida. In return, she received a hat from Ida, a scarf from Button which Laney had picked out, and a music CD of holiday songs from Laney herself. Helen wasn't sure who the singer was, despite Ava telling her he had been the lead singer of a popular band—as if she knew the names of any boy bands. But the singer had won Helen's devotion upon listening to his rendition of "Have Yourself a Merry Little Christmas." She had his CD ready to play and a lovely wine in the refrigerator for her after-Thanksgiving blues tonight. She also had plans to watch a sappy, romantic Christmas movie. They were her guilty pleasure.

It surprised her friends, and herself honestly, that she enjoyed sentimental Christmas love stories. She concluded she liked love stories with happy endings to help her forget her own failed romance. She had her ex-husband to thank for that—and her father.

Born and raised in Macon, Georgia, Helen Renee Chastain was the middle child between two brothers. Life in the Chastain house may have appeared picture perfect, but looks were deceiving. Helen's father was an alcoholic, which probably should have been received with a modicum of revulsion from those around him, but Edward Chastain, Eddie to his friends, was loved and adored by everyone who knew him. They thought he was charming, funny, and caring; they really did not know him at all.

Helen's mother, Iris, was not Mrs. Iris Chastain. She was Mrs. Edward Chastain and there was a huge difference between the two. Iris April Clark disappeared, for all intents and purposes, the day she married Edward. Her name was not on their mortgage or bank account. She had no credit history in her name. Iris succumbed to what was expected of her and put everyone's happiness before her own. She was the epitome of a loving wife, but not a *beloved* wife. The picture of how vastly different those descriptions were had become exceedingly clear to Helen when she was about thirteen—thanks to a bottle of ketchup.

One summer evening, after helping her mother work hard in the sweltering heat of the garden and kitchen, they'd put a lovely dinner meal on the table. Her father and brothers sat down and dove into the meal without saying grace or waiting for Helen and Iris to be seated. Her mother had barely sat down, had not taken a single bite, when her father lifted and shook his empty glass of iced tea at Iris as if saying *fetch me more.* Helen watched as her mother jumped up for iced tea and refilled his glass. As her mother made it to her seat the second time, her brother said the word *salt* and Iris jumped up to bring him salt and pepper shakers. *How could they treat her like that? How could she let them treat her like that?*

Less than a minute later, Edward, without even looking up from his roast beef and potatoes, said, *ketchup*, in a one-word command. Before Iris could jump and run to the refrigerator, Helen said to her father, "Get it yourself and let mother eat."

He looked up in anger, staring at Helen, as her mother made an excuse and leapt from the table to get ketchup as fast as possible. She handed the glass bottle to her husband, murmuring what sounded like kind words. Her father, eyes still angrily on Helen, opened the lid, put ketchup on his plate, closed the lid and threw the bottle at her mother's head. By wounding her mother, he had injured Helen more than if he'd hit her instead and, of course, he knew that. She'd despised ketchup ever since.

Fear for her mother kept her quiet from that day on and, although her mother swore repeatedly he'd never done anything like that before, Helen remained skittish and uncomfortable around her father. Eventually, respect waned and love died.

Helen dated very little as a teenager, seeing most young boys as future Edward Chastains. Even her own brothers, although kind to her, coasted through life under a different set of rules. Helen was, by far, the brightest of the Chastain children, and yet her father saw no reason for a girl to go to college. Money had been set aside for her brothers, but not for her. When Helen approached her mother for help and support, she'd crumbled under the weight of her father's opinion and suggested Helen secure a job or a husband.

During high school, Helen worked after school at the drug store downtown, mostly serving drinks and treats at the soda fountain. The owner was a young widow named Alice Glenn, who had inherited the store from her family and successfully ran the operation after her husband died in a bridge construction accident. Helen adored her. Alice made Helen feel as if she could do more, be more, and expect more from life than the plan that had been drawn up for her. She saved every dime of her pay for three years and, after high school graduation, announced her plan to go to Redding College in Florida. Nobody helped her pack; nobody saw her to the bus stop.

She felt alone as she arrived at college, but much like Laney, Helen had a sense of freedom, hope, and adventure bubbling inside her. She would never forget the first day, the first time she opened the door to her dormitory room and met her roommate. Helen recalled how the beautiful girl had smiled so warmly at her and said, "Hi, I'm Vivian Kincaid, but you can call me Button. I picked this bed and left you the one by the window. The view is lovely, but if you'd like to swap, I certainly am willing. I hope you need a friend because I know absolutely no one in Florida. I brought you some welcome-to-college brownies. I do hope you like chocolate."

Button had insisted within less than an hour of knowing Helen that she must pledge a sorority and find a home away from home. She could not have proposed the idea any better. Helen longed for a new home and a loving family. Button personally escorted Helen to the office where she signed up for sorority rush. Button had coached her on having a simple, natural conversation, which felt anything but natural to Helen. As they kicked off the first day of visiting all sorority houses, she and Button were divided, alphabetically, into different groups. Before she walked away, Button hugged Helen and whispered, "Smile, dear. All day long."

Helen could not believe her luck in being offered an opportunity to pledge. She was going to have to find a part-time job, but felt she could make it work. She mentioned her desire for a job on campus to an older sister and, thanks to a tip, found herself employed promptly at the university bursar's office. It was a perfect fit of facts and figures; Helen enjoyed keeping the records and files orderly. They worked around her class schedule and she held the job until she graduated.

She found being a sorority sister was like finding a magic genie in a bottle. Wishes for a happy home, friends, love, and support—all granted. Helen discovered she never needed to be reminded to smile!

Helen dated a little in college but was not serious about anyone unlike Ida, Laney, and Button. After being a bridesmaid eight times and seeing her friends happily wed, she began to long for a special man to call her very own. As each year passed, void of an appearance by Mr. Right, Helen started feeling somewhat unchosen and unselected. Thoughts of inadequacy and unattractiveness began to nag at her and she decided to try a little harder. She finally met and dated the handsome and charming Stanley Harkins. Unfortunately, her desire to find a man of her own had blinded her to his manipulation. He purposely presented himself as an intelligent, exciting, ambitious, and devoted boyfriend and fiancé, only to reveal himself to be a senseless, apathetic, unfaithful husband.

It took several years, but Helen finally ended her sham of a marriage and focused her attention on a career at the museum that she loved. She was hired in a secretarial position and retired as the museum director.

The sound of a car horn outside brought Helen out of her unexpected thoughts. Turning her attention back to Thanksgiving, she felt so anxious for her friends to arrive. The assisted living center had agreed to let Button come today. It was hard, after sharing so many holidays together, to imagine celebrations without Button. Helen had been praying for her to have a blessed holiday season without dementia stealing her joy. She knew such a blessing would be felt by all of them. Ida and Charlie, along with their daughter, Ava and her husband, Joe, were checking her out of

Enduring Grace around noon and bringing her with them. Laney was getting a ride to Helen's courtesy of her son, Bobby, his wife, Judith, and their eighteen-year-old daughter, Charlotte. Despite being a bit self-absorbed, Bobby and Judith had raised a wonderful daughter. Lottie, as Laney called her, was a high school senior, who loved singing, dancing, and acting. Unfortunately, they were having Thanksgiving with Judith's family and wouldn't be joining them.

Helen loved having her friends, truly more like family to her, for Thanksgiving. Her home was sparkling clean, top to bottom, even if it was showing signs of age. Ida's husband, Charlie, had done some repairs and yard care for her over the years. He had stepped up when she needed him. She taught herself to fix many things around the house. She believed she was capable of doing anything she could find detailed in a book and also credited the hardware store's Saturday seminars for many of her home repair skills.

Nowadays, the teenage boy next door, a sweet friend of Lottie's, mowed her lawn, which was so much more affordable than lawn care services. She wanted to stay in her home as long as she could. It was paid for, which allowed her to get by on her small retirement account and social security. That was why she still drove her sedan. Old Blue had been paid in full within three years of buying it about eighteen years ago. At sixty-two, she had purchased it, gently used, from a lady at church. It was part of her plan to have a reliable, sturdy car paid off before she retired from her longtime position at the museum. Helen was proud of herself, proud of her accomplishments, her home.

She'd dusted the dining room table early that morning and set it for a party of seven. She would have preferred an even setting of eight at the table, but Ava and Joe's daughter, Jennifer, had been invited to share Thanksgiving with her boyfriend's family. They had dated for three years, having met in graduate school. Her boyfriend, Jacob, was a doll.

He and his family adored Jennifer. She had hopes they would have a wonderful day and that Jen would come home wearing an engagement ring. If not today, soon!

The doorbell chimed, snapping Helen's focus back to the beautiful dining room table. She quickly scanned it one more time. It looked like it belonged on the cover of *Southern Living*. Her mother's beautiful white china sat in contrast to the gold-plated chargers she bought on sale. Her grandmother's crystal and silver had been washed and polished with lots of love and elbow grease. The tablecloth was white with a plaid table runner bursting in fall colors. The centerpiece was a decorative cornucopia with two long, orange taper candles seated in gold candlesticks on each side. The napkin holders, which resembled autumn leaves, held a clean, starched white napkin. The bread plate was from her mother's china, but the dessert plates were cute orange jack-o-lanterns she'd found at the after-holiday sale at a popular home décor store. She smiled as she made her way around the corner to open the front door.

"Happy Thanksgiving!" Laney and Lottie practically shouted the greeting. In Helen's opinion, Laney's granddaughter, Lottie, was a miniature Laney. She had long, dark brown hair, green eyes, and a smile that instantly made her everyone's friend. She was a wearing a denim skirt, boots, and a deep purple sweater (Helen's absolute favorite color), which complemented Laney's dark slacks and forest green sweater. She was carrying a paper bag from the nearby grocery store.

"Happy Thanksgiving, you two. You look very pretty and festive! Please let me help you with that," Helen offered, taking the bag from Lottie. "Come in!"

Lottie grimaced. "Sorry, I can't, but thanks, Aunt Helen. Mom and Dad are waiting in the car. I wanted to lend Nannie a hand," Lottie replied, using the cute grandmother nickname she had bestowed upon

Laney as a two-year-old. "I'm sure you will have a much yummier Thanksgiving than the one waiting at my other grandparents' house. My mom's pumpkin pie is from the frozen food aisle. No disrespect to the pie company, but their pie isn't the same caliber as Aunt Ida's homemade pie. If you save me some leftovers, I'll love you forever!"

Lottie kissed Helen and Laney on the cheek and, with a final wave, slowly jogged down the square stone steps that led back to her parents, waiting in their car. Bobby and Judith smiled and waved before quickly driving away.

Laney walked into the house, immediately spying the gorgeous dining room setting. "You host the loveliest Thanksgiving, Helen. You make the day so special. And your turkey is by far the best I've ever eaten."

"Marshall Green has never steered me wrong," Helen spoke fondly of her favorite television chef. "*Eat Your Greens and Yummy Things* was sheer brilliance! I would vote for that man as president in a heartbeat. If he can rule the kitchen, he can rule the country!"

"Is that your version of *the best way to a man's heart is through his stomach*?"

Helen chuckled, "Something like that."

They unpacked Laney's bags and put food on the counter as Laney shared, "I brought the yummy yeast rolls and my cousin Rick's famous Thanksgiving mashed potatoes."

"Good, I wore my Thanksgiving pants. Those potatoes are the reason I even have stretchy pants in the first place! As much as I'd love to ask what the secret ingredient is for those mashed potatoes, I will refrain from doing so. I can only eat them once a year, and I don't want to feel guilty," Helen teased.

"Ida said they should be here about one o'clock," Laney shared, looking at the clock on the microwave. "She is bringing her famous sweet potatoes with the pecans and marshmallows, along with a pumpkin pie. Ava is bringing green bean casserole, cranberry salad, and an apple pie since Joe doesn't like pumpkin."

"I remember. I told Ava at Thanksgiving years ago that she better be sure about marrying a man who didn't like pumpkin pie. Luckily, Joe was a keeper," Helen shared, nudging Laney with her elbow as the doorbell rang.

Helen and Laney walked to the front door and opened it to find a beaming Button in Joe's arms with Ava just behind him pushing Button's wheelchair. Ida and Charlie were behind Ava, coming up the walk, arm-in-arm.

"Joe!" Helen exclaimed.

"A stone walkway is beautiful, Helen, but not the easiest with a wheelchair," Joe said in explanation. "So I just whisked up this beautiful lady like a knight in shining armor."

Joe walked into Helen's living room and set Vivian gently on the sofa.

"Isn't he strong? I feel like a queen," Button insisted, blushing more than a little.

"Well, I'd say that is the perfect way to kick off Thanksgiving. Button is officially the Thanksgiving Queen!" Laney chuckled as Button grinned and clapped her hands.

Moving into the dining room, they each shared something for which they were thankful, Ida's favorite tradition. They said grace and then filled their plates from passing bowls. Button lectured them on never separating the salt and pepper shakers, twice. "You must always pass them together whether the recipient wishes to have both salt and pepper or not."

"That's sorority class one," Ava said as she passed the mashed potatoes to Helen. "I learned more about formal dinners, time management, conflict resolution, and event management in my four years living in our sorority house than I ever have in my career as an event planner."

"Add in leadership, negotiation skills, networking, communications, and teamwork. What is in these mashed potatoes? No, please don't tell me! Please do not pass that bowl back to me no matter what I say," Helen insisted as she licked her spoon.

"And lifelong friends," Button shared softly. Every head swiveled toward Button. She was doing so well and enjoying the day immensely. Laney, Helen, and Ida shared smiles and looks with each other, having perfected their nonverbal friendship communication signals as college sorority girls. This was a great day. They felt very blessed by a perfect Thanksgiving.

"Lifelong friends and their husbands," Charlie clarified with a smile as he squeezed Button's hand on his right and his wife Ida's hand on his left.

"Yes, sir! I think I had as much fun at homecoming last month as Ava," Joe, Ava's husband, shared.

"It was such a fun day. We got to campus early enough to watch the Homecoming Parade at nine in the morning, met sorority sisters at the house for brunch, moved the brunch crowd to the beer tavern, laughed until our sides hurt, and then cheered ourselves hoarse at the football game! I loved every minute of it. I think going back to college for homecoming is like plugging into a fountain of youth. Everyone feels eighteen again and conversations flow like you just saw sisters last week instead of last year," Ava said, emphasizing her points with her butter knife.

They were surprised to realize it was already past four o'clock when they finished their pieces of pumpkin and apple pie. They had promised to have Button back at Enduring Grace by six o'clock. Feeling the day getting away from them, they all pitched in to clear the table. Helen shooed Charlie and Joe out of the kitchen, declaring they took up too much space, but whispering to them to stay in the living room with Button.

After putting leftovers in take-home bags for everyone, including an extra one for Lottie, Helen stored everything in the refrigerator while Ida and Laney dried the remaining few dishes. Vivian had fallen asleep on one end of the sofa. She was covered lovingly with a soft blanket by Charlie, who was now also napping in the big, cozy recliner. Joe sat in a chair by the fireplace watching a football game on TV.

They could not have been more content. Helen, Laney, and Ida talked softly at the kitchen table.

Ava walked into the kitchen with her camera. "I snapped a few pictures of the dining room table before we attacked it. And I took a few candid shots today including Dad snoring in the recliner just now. I wondered if I set up my tripod in the backyard if we could take a photo by the Thanksgiving tree. I can set the timer so we'll all be in the picture."

"Ava, that's a great idea. Let's do it," Helen exclaimed. "The last couple of years that tree has been without leaves at all by Thanksgiving. Today the leaves are a brilliant orange and red and it is worthy of its name, Thanksgiving tree. Unfortunately, we will need to wake Vivian, but it's almost time for you all to take her back anyway. Wake your dad and pull your husband from the game," Helen suggested, giving Ava a little push toward the living room. "I will check on Button."

From the doorway, Ava turned back toward the kitchen. "Joe can carry Button outside without her wheelchair. We will help her stand with one of us on each side of her—I know she'll be happier about that—and I would love to have a picture of this day with her standing and smiling like normal." After a slight pause she added, "I hope that didn't come out wrong. You know what I mean."

"Yes, sweetie, we know what you mean," Ida reassured her.

They gathered in the backyard, which seemed extra beautiful thanks to the lovely weather, and Ava directed them to the perfect spot in front of Helen's tree. The smiles on their faces were genuine and joyful. Ava used her remote control to take a few shots. Her favorite was the last one: the one of Button looking at the camera with her Miss South Carolina and Thanksgiving Queen Smile while everyone else had burst out laughing.

Button had just asked, "Whose house is this?"

Button and Christmas Presents

When the Right Clothes Matter

"Ida, hold the door please," Helen asked her friend as she and Laney rushed up the walkway toward Enduring Grace. It was a stormy, freezing December day. They stepped into the nursing home foyer, closing their umbrellas.

"Thanks, dear! I can't get over how cold it is this morning," Laney said. "I appreciate you both meeting me here so early, but I was worried after Nurse Jamie called at dawn about Button. I'm so glad I had my cell phone next to my bed and the volume was up high."

Ida asked Laney, "Tell me again what Jamie said. Button was disruptive in the night, unable to sleep?"

"Let's walk and talk," Laney suggested. "I don't know much. She said we should ask for Jeannie Peters in the office and she will explain, but they had to give her a sedative," Laney replied.

As they turned from the living room to walk down the hallway toward the executive offices, Jeannie stepped out of her office. Dressed in navy slacks, a blazer, and a crisp white blouse, she looked professional. Her brown eyes were serious but kind, and her ponytail swayed as she quickly approached them. "Ladies, thank you for coming. I am aware that Vivian Upton has no immediate family, and you are listed as her emergency contacts. She is resting comfortably, but I'm told last night was quite the ordeal."

"What happened?" Laney asked with concern.

"Please come in my office," Jeanie said, motioning for them to take a seat. She continued talking as she maneuvered her way to her desk chair. "From what I understand from the night shift, Miss Vivian was very confused last night, thinking she was at a holiday program. She had all the residents up singing Christmas carols and entertaining imaginary children. I confess, I think it's wonderful that the night shift was kept on their toes," Jeannie added with a grin. "However, we obviously don't want this to be a nightly occurrence."

Ida said, "Vivian has never done anything like this before."

Helen raised her hand. "This may be my fault. I was here yesterday to drop off Christmas cards from my Sunday school class. Button wasn't talking; she was staring at the TV, but not really watching it, so I decided to sing to her. She started singing along a little when I picked a few Christmas carols."

Ida said, "I think that's sweet, Helen." Laney nodded in agreement.

Jeannie took a sip of her coffee and continued, "Thank you for bringing the Christmas cards, but unfortunately this is not the first time something like this has happened. Not too long ago, she corralled several other women into being in a beauty pageant. They walked up and down the hallways as if they were wearing ball gowns, waving to an imaginary crowd! Luckily, that was after dinner and not in the middle of the night."

Turning to Jeannie, Laney said, "I'm sure it had to do with sundowning. She can get so confused at that time of day. You know that Vivian was Miss South Carolina."

"Yes, of course," Jeannie replied with a smile and slight eye roll. "Everyone knows she was Miss South Carolina!"

Laney continued, "Jeannie, what you may not know is that Vivian Upton was going to be a nurse. She was top of her class in college, extremely intelligent. She would have been a fabulous doctor, but women our age weren't given many options when we were young. Vivian's family pushed her to participate in pageants and when she was named Miss South Carolina, she saw it much less as a personal achievement and more of an opportunity to help others. She started several programs for children; her favorite was a Christmas show she organized for disadvantaged youth. She never became a nurse."

Ida said, "This was a big part of Vivian's life. Even later on, when she and her husband discovered they could not have children of their own, they did all they could to help children in need, including hosting a special holiday celebration."

Jeannie leaned back in her office chair as if the wind had been knocked out of her. "I'm sorry. She is a lovely lady. Dementia is such a difficult disease. I will ask her doctor to review her medication again. Delusions and hallucinations are common symptoms, but we hadn't seen these symptoms with Miss Vivian to the extent they emerged last night. Thank you, again, for coming this morning. We will do everything we can for her."

Feeling dismissed, Laney stood first, recognizing that Jeannie wished to move on with her day. "Can we check on her and stay in her room? We always have lunch with her on Monday."

Jeannie said, "I'm sorry, ladies, but I think she will sleep through lunch today. They gave her a sedative, and she finally fell asleep just before dawn. Perhaps you'd like to come back for dinner. We are having an early Christmas surprise."

Helen put her arm through Laney's and motioned for Ida to come with them. "Thank you, Jeannie. We will do that. Please ask the dining room to save our table by the window for us."

Later that evening, the trio was back at the nursing home awaiting Vivian's arrival in the dining room. "Maybe we should figure out a plan for one of us to come every day," Ida said, leaning close to her friends and keeping her voice down. "I'm worried, what are we going to do if Vivian's health is beyond what they can handle here?"

Laney agreed, "She is going downhill fast. We've seen her decline so much in the three weeks since Thanksgiving. I wanted to hit Jeannie Peters with my cane when she said delusions and hallucinations are common!" She sighed, regaining her composure. "It's not Jeannie's fault. I just don't want this for Button."

Ida sighed. "I don't want to accept it; none of us do. I'm scared, or maybe just sad. I looked back at my last year's calendar when I bought a new one in January. My social life has basically been going from funeral to funeral!"

"I wasn't talking about her funeral, Ida," Laney snapped. "I just think she is changing, losing more of her memory. She could live like this for a few more years."

"I hope not for her sake," Helen answered solemnly.

Laney leaned forward to hold her friends' hands. "Please. I just can't do this! I can't talk about this right now. We don't need to discuss her funeral anyway. She planned it years ago."

"Of course she did," Helen and Ida spoke at the same moment. They shared a small smile despite the pain they were all feeling.

Laney shared the details, "She wants a memorial service, but insists on a celebration of her life. Despite the fact that the church will be filled with pink flowers, she wants us to ask, in lieu of flowers, that donations be made to our sorority foundation. I have all the paperwork and instructions," she added. "They are color coded and very detailed."

"Of course they are," Helen and Ida said again in unison.

"So, we're back to needing a day-to-day plan," Ida said, distractedly. Looking down the corridor, she said, "I wonder what's taking Button so long and why she isn't here yet. Devon said Santa Claus was coming to visit all the residents this evening and he'd have her at our table in a flash."

Laney sighed. "Hopefully she hasn't made another run for the exit. She hasn't tried to leave as often since they took away her walker and made her get around mostly in a wheelchair."

Helen replied, "Good Lord, please do not remind me of that! I think that was the day I knew she was truly ill. She walked straight out of here, put her walker, folded correctly, in the back of an unlocked car and would have driven away if the keys had been in it."

Ida cringed. "You know she thought it was her car! It resembled her old white luxury sedan. I think, in her mind, she was going to the grocery store to make a special supper for John."

Helen agreed. "You know she was. What really upset me was that she fell."

Laney nodded her head sadly. "Right after that the nursing staff insisted on putting a monitor on her ankle so that the alarm would sound if she got too close to an exit door. I'll never forget the look on Jeannie Peter's face when I yelled at her, 'You seriously want to track my sister like a migrating deer?'"

Helen and Ida smiled at Laney, trying not to laugh. "And that is why we love you," Ida said.

Down the corridor in Vivian's room, Devon looked at his watch. He'd come to check on Jamie's progress in helping Miss Vivian get dressed for the Christmas party. She was sitting on her bed and acting quite out of character, pulling off shirts almost as fast as Jamie could put them on her.

Devon moved closer to her bed. "Sweet Miss Vivian, what is bothering you tonight? Your sisters are in the dining room waiting for you and, rumor has it, Santa is coming. I bet he has a present for you! You got your hair and makeup done today by those nice ladies who own the salon down the street. Don't you want to go to the Christmas party?"

Vivian's head was down, her voice was low, but he and Jamie heard her say, "I'm supposed to wear a dress. No congressman's wife should wear pedal pushers and sweaters outside the house."

"Well, let's find you a dress," Jamie replied with a light and supportive pat on her knee.

Devon put away the holiday sweaters as Jamie helped Vivian into a soft, pale pink knit dress and draped a red plaid shawl around her shoulders. Her holiday party ensemble was a little unique. She would have objected to the ankle monitor and beige no-skid socks on her feet if she'd noticed them, but much to Jamie and Devon's relief, she was finally dressed and seemed happy.

"There now, Miss Vivian, are you ready to accompany me to the party?"

Vivian surprised him with her answer. "You will marry a very lucky girl someday. Do you have a special someone?"

Jamie chuckled and raised her eyebrows at Devon. He started to make a joke and say something flippant about her being his special girl, but Vivian was looking at him quite honestly and lucidly. Devon admitted, "I don't have a girlfriend, no. I need to find time to get out and meet people, I guess."

"We'll work on that," Vivian said. "I have lots of lovely sorority sisters."

Jamie laughed loudly as she left the room. Devon chuckled under his breath and pushed Miss Vivian out the door and down the hallway. They entered the dining room where Christmas music was softly playing and a festively decorated tree sat in the corner. As he set the brakes on her wheelchair, he noticed her friends looking at her in astonishment. They hadn't said a word.

Devon offered a little explanation. "A few stylists from the beauty shop down the street donated their talents to fix up all the ladies for tonight's Christmas party," Devon said. "Doesn't she look pretty and ready to see Santa?"

Helen, Ida, and Laney stared. She didn't look like herself despite the pink dress.

Helen said, "Her hair doesn't usually look so . . ."

"Big," Laney announced.

"Old-fashioned," Ida corrected.

"Goodness, she looks much older tonight." Helen just had to be honest.

"Maybe it's her makeup too. She doesn't care for red lipstick," said Laney.

Laney stood up and went over to Vivian, taking her hand. "Merry Christmas, Button. We're so happy to see you. Santa will be here soon." Vivian stared off into space with no response.

"Santa will be here soon, darling," John said to his bride as they cuddled on the sofa enjoying Christmas music and the beautifully decorated tree. "We should be off to bed."

Vivian smiled lovingly at John and said, "Merry first Christmas, my darling! I'm so happy we got married before Christmas so we could be Mr. and Mrs. Upton for the holidays."

"My mother is still in shock that you pulled together a wedding in a few weeks," he said with a chuckle. "I could have asked you earlier, but I thought our first date may have been a little too pushy!"

Vivian hugged him a little tighter and said, "Don't be silly, I've had my wedding planned since I was sixteen! I was just waiting for God to present me with my groom. I must say, He did a fabulous job on His end."

John kissed the top of her head and stood up with her in his arms. Looking into her sapphire eyes, he said, "I am the lucky one! I declare from this moment forward, you are and will always be my favorite Christmas present."

John gently kissed her forehead. Then he kissed her so sweetly and said, with a smile and a wink, "Now, I think it's time to unwrap my present."

Vivian giggled.

Vivian giggled. "John wants to unwrap his favorite Christmas present," she said.

Ida whispered to Laney and Helen, "Surely she didn't mean that the way it sounded."

"Oh, I bet she did!" Helen couldn't help the retort.

Laney snorted when she laughed!

Mary Carolyn and Claire

When Songs Bring Back Memories

Laney, Helen, and Ida started a rotation to ensure that one of them came every day to spend time with Vivian. In addition to keeping their established Monday plans, Laney added Tuesdays and Thursdays. Helen added in Wednesdays and Ida took Fridays. They agreed Saturdays and Sundays would be divided among them, but on this particular Saturday, they would go together and arrive later than normal after attending their sorority's annual Founders' Day event. It was the first time Vivian had ever missed it.

"How is Mrs. Vivian?" One of the college girls, seated at their luncheon table, seemed concerned. "We haven't seen her at the house in two years, since I was a sophomore, and she isn't here today. She seemed to enjoy herself last year. I sat by her and we talked about her fun sorority memories. And about her being Miss South Carolina."

Ida spoke for the trio. "I'd like to say *fine*, but she isn't doing well honestly."

"I'm sorry." The pretty young woman with shoulder length auburn hair, whose nametag shared that her name was Claire, continued, "She was my mom's chapter adviser a long time ago," she said, motioning to the woman seated beside her. "This is my mom, Gina."

Gina, an older version of her daughter with shorter hair, smiled at her memories of Vivian. "I love Vivian. She was an amazing chapter adviser! Of course, I really began to understand that when I became a chapter adviser myself. She was so supportive. She stressed the importance of assisting each other, serving the community, and maintaining high academic standards. She spoke often of how sorority involvement wasn't just for college. She always shared stories about the lifelong friends she made and how they had made such a difference in her life. And, most of all, she said that bylaws have the word 'laws' in them for a reason. I stole that from her and used it a few times myself!"

Laney replied, "She loved being a chapter adviser. She did it for several years, driving more than half an hour to campus, staying late into the night sometimes. She has always been a sorority girl at heart."

The lovely young woman seated next to Claire, named Mary Carolyn, with curly blonde hair and a peaches-and-cream complexion, said, "She is the reason I pledged a sorority at all! Mr. and Mrs. Upton were the youth group leaders at my church. I remember, after Graduation Sunday for my high school class, Mrs. Upton asking me if I'd like for her to write a recommendation for me for recruitment. I'm embarrassed to tell you, I actually told her that I was a good girl and would not be pledging a sorority."

Mary Carolyn explained, "She looked so shocked! I remember she put her arm around me and told me she couldn't give away all the secrets, but her sorority creed and ritual honored God. She said for me, or for any young lady who might not believe in God, sororities imported the values we should all want in our lives. She said sororities aren't like, or aren't meant to be like, how they are portrayed on television or in movies. She told me that I might be pleasantly surprised if I gave it a chance. I'm so grateful to her. Best decision ever!"

"We will be keeping her in our thoughts and prayers," Gina said as the two young women nodded in agreement.

"Thank you," Helen answered.

"Mary Carolyn and I are singing a duet of one of our sorority songs to close today's luncheon," Claire announced. Maybe you'd like to record it on your phone and play it for her later."

"And I'd love for you to take my dessert to her," Mary Carolyn insisted. "I remember she used to love petits fours and served them at her house when we had youth group activities there."

Gina added, "Please take my program. It highlights our scholarship honorees. Thanks to her establishing a scholarship through our sorority foundation, we were able to award three deserving sisters with scholarships today!"

Blinking away tears, Laney simply nodded. She knew it would mean so much to Button. How honored and proud she would feel to know these girls remembered her and the extent to which her scholarship was helping these young sisters. Even if Button didn't remember these thoughtful, simple sorority honors beyond today, Laney felt it would be special in the moment.

A little later that afternoon, Laney, Helen, and Ida went to see Vivian and deliver all the Founders' Day mementos. It was typically much more crowded in the parking lot on Saturdays, but many families and friends must have stayed home on such a cold February day. Helen punched the code into the security pad on the front door, and with a loud beep, the door was unlocked for them. They quietly made their way to the nurses' station in Vivian's wing where the desk and walls were decorated for Valentine's Day.

Nurse Angela glanced up when she heard their footsteps. "Hello, you Three Musketeers. I just checked on Vivian, and she is awake if you'd like to visit in her room. She is having a pajama day."

"A pajama day?" Laney echoed in question.

"Yes, she wasn't feeling cooperative about getting dressed today, but we did manage to help her brush her teeth," Angela explained.

Angela turned to answer a ringing telephone and the three friends looked at each other in surprise, but without comment. They were worried about the sister they loved so much. Button was not typically uncooperative about putting on pretty clothes and a little makeup.

Laney turned first in the direction of Vivian's room, and they walked silently down the hall. Upon entering her room, they found her in bed, wearing her pajamas, her hair messy and face free of makeup. There was no pink lipstick today. She stared at her friends, but did not smile or speak.

After a slight delay to take in her appearance, Ida stepped forward first. "Hi, Button. We went to Founders' Day today and brought you a lovely white petit fours with pink flowers. Everyone said to say hello and that they miss you."

Laney walked to the other side of the bed, sitting on the edge and gently took Vivian's hand. "Look, Button, here is the program. The high-light of the day was the presentation of scholarships to three collegiate sisters. These scholarships were from the endowment you established with our foundation."

Ida and Laney looked up from the bed at Helen. She pulled up a chair next to Vivian's bed, sat down, and pulled her phone from her purse. Within a few seconds, music was playing from Helen's cell phone. It was the duet sung by Claire and Mary Carolyn at the end of the Founders' Day ceremony, a song they had known since they were eighteen-year-old pledges of their sorority.

Helen started singing along and Laney and Ida joined in quietly, "Remember your days together, today and evermore. In friendship and fraternity, you'll find an open door." They watched Vivian very carefully and noticed her lips were moving with the words of the song. Helen played the song again.

"In friendship and fraternity, you'll find an open door." Vivian looked at the circle of sisters around her linked with their arms around each other, swaying and singing a sorority song. It wasn't really her favorite as she preferred the more upbeat songs. However, this song was a tradition passed down from generation to generation and she respected that, especially on Founders' Day. She had been selected by the sorority to attend a national meeting last summer and found it so inspiring to sing this song with sorority sisters of all ages and from all across the country.

"Hey, Button, you're daydreaming again. Come on, little sis, we've got to get ready for our double date tonight," Laney said as if in a hurry. Laney grabbed Vivian's hand and tugged her toward the main staircase in the sorority house, chatting about the night's plans.

"I'm only going because I want to see Singing in the Rain. *And because Gene Kelly is totally the bee's knees," Vivian said just like a girl with a movie star crush!*

"Fine. Gene Kelly is all yours," Laney replied as they climbed the stairs.

As they ran into their bedroom, Button gasped at the mess. "Laney, did you try on everything in your closet?"

"Yep, and some from your closet. Although we may wear about the same size, the length on everything you have is a mile too short for me."

"Lucky me."

"Do you like these pedal pushers with this sweater?"

"Yes, that's cute. I thought I might wear this skirt and blouse," replied Button

"To a drive-in movie?"

"My mom doesn't buy me many casual clothes. I have one pair of rolled-up jeans," Button explained.

"Then wear those with that pink top." Laney pointed to a stack of shirts on her bed.

"Which pink top?" asked Button.

"Has anyone ever mentioned you have a problem? This one," Laney suggested, gently tossing it to Button.

As they dressed for their evening, Laney thanked Button for going to the movies. "I like Donald from my biology class, but you know my rule that first dates must be double dates. Beside the fact that you'll love seeing Singing in the Rain, you might like his friend."

"What is his friend's name again?" Vivian asked as she slipped her feet into a pair of loafers.

"Gads! I totally forget, but I'm sure you'll have a lovely time with what's-his-name."

"What's his name?" Vivian asked. Her friends did not know how to respond.

"Button, would you like to try the petit fours? It's delightful," Ida gently put the tiny cake into Vivian's hand. She took a small bite, made a small "Mmmm" of delight, and then took another tiny bite.

Ida smiled. "See, they are really yummy. What do you think?"

"The bee's knees," Vivian replied. "Like Gene Kelly."

A lightbulb went off in each of their heads simultaneously. "Singing in the Rain," the three friends replied with a smile as they followed Button's train of thought.

"It's her sophomore year, and she is at the drive-in movie theater with me on a double date. She is wearing rolled-up jeans and a pink top," Laney shared, putting together the pieces of Button's word clues. "And she really didn't like what's-his-name."

Button looked at Laney and grinned.

Sisters

When Love Feels Like a Soft Blanket

"I can't believe they have this movie," Laney said to Helen as the residents were enjoying a showing of *Singing in the Rain* in the center's recreation room.

Helen was surprised to see her and asked Laney why she was there. After she received a shrug and no reply from her, Helen answered Laney's original question. "I ordered the DVD online after Button mentioned it a few weeks ago. Angela and Jamie thought it would be a fun choice. Button has been singing along at times. And, Mr. Johnson over there thinks he is Gene Kelly. He keeps getting up to dance." Helen's tone suddenly became more serious. "But back to my original question, it is Wednesday, my day, and I'm surprised to see you. How did you get here? Did Bobby take off work?"

"Taxi."

Laney stopped with the one-word response. Helen could see that she was considering her words carefully, but Laney simply sighed and replied, "I will tell you later." Helen nodded, agreeing to postpone the conversation.

When the movie was over, the residents were escorted to their rooms for a nap or to other parts of the nursing center to read or make crafts. Helen motioned to Angela that she and Laney would take Vivian to her room.

Angela motioned for Helen to wait a moment. She walked over to them, smiled a greeting to Laney, and replied to Helen, "I'll take her.

She needs a little assistance with a visit to the bathroom. Why don't you meet me in Vivian's room in about five minutes?"

Just as Helen was about to respond that they could help Vivian, Laney jumped in quickly to reply, "Thank you, Angela. That will be fine."

"We will see you in a minute, Button," Helen said brightly before turning to Laney with her famous and intimidating stare. "OK, Laney, what is going on? You are here, on a Wednesday, and that exchange just now with Angela was weird."

Laney pulled Helen gently to a private corner. "When I was here yesterday, I inquired about Button's missing laundry basket. I thought it had been temporarily misplaced because it hasn't been here for some time now. Devon looked so embarrassed, so uncomfortable, but I pushed for an answer. I thought maybe it ended up in someone else's room by mistake. He said that Button was confused in the night about things."

"What things?"

"The location of the bathroom."

"Oh dear! Did she trip over her laundry basket and fall on the way to the toilet?"

"No, she was using her laundry basket as the toilet."

Helen gasped.

"I know. I know," Laney said, shaking her head sadly. "So they have obviously taken it away. Her dirty clothes are now in a cloth bag in the bottom of her wardrobe. And they have put her in adult diapers."

Helen had no words. She looked sadly at Laney with her hand covering her mouth.

"Ladies, I hope I'm not interrupting," Jeannie Peters said as she approached them quickly, ponytail swinging.

"Not at all," Laney said, turning toward Jeannie.

"I wanted to let you know that Miss Vivian has two visitors signing in at the front desk. They are college students. They called a few days ago and asked if they could deliver something to her on March 18. I'm not sure if you know them, but thought you might like to walk up to the front desk with me."

Laney nodded and thanked her. She and Helen followed Jeannie through the living room toward the entrance. As they got closer, they recognized the young sorority sisters they had met at the Founders' Day luncheon. Jeannie excused herself to return to her office, and Laney and Helen approached the young ladies.

"Hello, you've come to see Vivian Upton?" Helen said.

"Yes, it's so nice to see you again. You probably don't remember our names. I'm Mary Carolyn and this is my roommate, Claire. We are here to deliver a little gift to Miss Vivian from the chapter."

Helen beamed. "How thoughtful of you! I will get her from her room and meet you in the dining room," Helen added as she rushed off.

"That is Helen Chastain, who is running to get Vivian, and my name, again, is Laney Walsh. This really is so kind of you. Is this a thank you for her scholarship?"

"Well, partly," Claire explained as they walked through the living room. "We decided to launch an Adopt-an-Alum program; we pick one alumna a year and make her feel extra special."

"We picked Miss Vivian because she has done so much for our sorority over the years. We'd like her to know what a difference she has made and how much we appreciate her. You said she was losing her memory, but we hope she will enjoy this little sorority gift we made her," Mary Carolyn said, motioning toward the large gift bag she carried.

"I am sure she will love it," Laney smiled as they entered the dining room. The girls put their coats and purses down on the large table in the corner just as Helen and Vivian came into the room.

Looking at the young girls, Vivian's face broke into a huge grin, "You're here! I have missed you so much." She held out her arms for a hug. Mary Carolyn and Claire looked a bit surprised, but were quick and kind with a reciprocal embrace. Laney studied Vivian curiously.

"Button, this is Mary Carolyn and Claire, and they are here to give you a gift from the chapter for being the Alum of the Year. They are so smart to recognize how special you are," Helen said as she circled from behind Vivian's wheelchair to take the chair near her.

Claire gently put the gift bag on Vivian's lap and told her, "We tried to come up with a thank you gift for all you've done for our chapter, Miss Vivian. We hope you like this and enjoy it."

Vivian smiled up at her but made no move to take the gift from the bag. Mary Carolyn stepped to the side of Vivian's wheelchair and the girls talked in quiet words to her as they took a soft blanket from the bag and spread it across her knees.

"It's a T-shirt blanket. It's made from our sorority T-shirts," Claire said, pointing to the individual squares in the blanket. "This one was mine," she said as she knelt down on her knees in front of Vivian. "It was from a philanthropy event we did for kids. This one is an old shirt of my mom's from a Bid Day years ago. She remembers that you were there. Several sisters donated shirts for your blanket."

"This one is mine, Miss Vivian," Mary Carolyn added as she knelt next to Vivian. "I picked this national convention T-shirt because we talked about how much you loved going. And this one was from a campus Greek Week event, and it has all the Greek letters on it. Do you remember the Greek Alphabet?" She started softly singing, "Alpha, Beta, Gamma, Delta, Epsilon, Zeta, Eta." Claire joined in and they sang, "Theta, Iota, Kappa, Lambda, Mu, Nu, Xi, Omicron, Pi, Rho, Sigma, Tau, Upsilon, Phi, Chi, Psi, Omega."

Vivian looked up at them, from one girl's face to the other, and sang, "Alpha, Beta."

"That's right," Claire encouraged her. And they continued through the song again with Vivian joining them through much of it. Vivian smiled so brightly at the young girls.

"Thank you, Helen. Thank you, Laney. I love it so very much," Vivian said as she touched the blanket squares one by one. With her head down, she didn't see the brief, stricken looks on the faces of Laney and Helen. The young girls didn't correct her, nor seem distressed in the least.

"You are so welcome, Miss Vivian. I wish we could stay for a long visit, but we can't today because of afternoon classes. We will be back again soon, though," Claire said, giving Vivian a brief hug.

"Please take care of yourself. We will sing more songs next time," Mary Carolyn suggested as she gently squeezed Vivian's hand.

Regaining her composure quickly, Helen whispered, "Thank you. You have no idea what a special gift this is. What a special gift you both are to spend this time with Vivian today." The girls looked toward her and smiled at Helen's thoughtful words.

Laney finally moved from her frozen position next to the table. She seemed to be leaning on her cane for a little extra support. "I will walk you out if you'd like," she said, addressing the girls.

After they said one final goodbye to Vivian, Mary Carolyn and Claire accompanied Laney through the large living room toward the lobby. They talked about the special blanket and the song they shared with Vivian. Laney paused for a moment, and the girls turned toward her. "I'd like to explain something if you have another moment. When Vivian called you Helen and Laney, I realized she was confusing you with younger versions of us." Looking at Claire, Laney said, "When she was younger, Helen's hair was red, similar to yours. Obviously, I don't have blonde hair, Mary Carolyn, but I can see why . . ." She trailed off without completing her sentence.

"We understand. And we don't mind at all. She can call us by whatever names she wants. You are a wonderful friend, a wonderful sister, Miss Laney! The love you three have for her and each other is amazing," Claire shared.

"We will be back soon. Count on it! Claire and I are really inspired by you all. We know our futures will be full of weddings, babies, and a large variety of shared moments with each other and sisters we love. It's what sisterhood is all about, right? To have this amazing support system forever in good times and bad. I hope when we're older, we'll have each other like you all do."

"Yes, Mary Carolyn. That's exactly what sisterhood is all about. And it's changed my life. My husband, Robert, was killed in a car accident when we were only thirty-two years old. Vivian, Ida, and Helen rallied around me and my young son, and they are, without a doubt, family. Thank you, both, so much. It makes me proud to see our sorority is in such good hands."

Laney walked them to the door and gave them each a heartfelt hug. It truly was easy to see Helen and a little of herself in them.

As she turned away from the door to walk back inside, she saw Helen walking toward her. "Button is napping. She snuggled in with her new blanket and was out like a light. Don't call a taxi. I will take you home. Unless you'd like to come over for a much needed glass of wine."

Laney tilted her head to one side to ponder the idea. "I suppose I could ask Bobby to pick me up at your place on his way home from work. I just can't tell him I drank wine."

Helen linked her arm in Laney's as they headed toward her car in the parking lot. "Well, that's up to you, but a little red wine never hurt anyone. You aren't on medications that would make a glass off-limits.

As a matter of fact, part of the benefits of drinking red wine in older people is having a sharper memory. That's probably why I'm still safe to drive."

"And you don't have anyone taking your keys away and telling you that you can't," Laney laughed.

"Red wine and a divorce. My two best discoveries of 1975!"

Helen's Birthday

When You Make a Wish and Blow Out the Candle

Ida entered Vivian's room juggling her raincoat, umbrella, purse, gift bag, and a tiny birthday cake in a bakery box. She had a few small paper plates, plastic forks, plastic knife, and candles in her purse. Ava had offered to help her inside with everything, but Ida waved off her offer. She didn't want her daughter to be late for her dentist appointment this morning. Ava was such a tremendous help to her and Charlie, and Ida knew those unfortunate days of feeling like a burden to one's child were quickly approaching. To be honest, in many ways, those days had arrived.

"Good morning, Button!"

"Good morning, Lady. Did you see my husband? He just left."

Ida stood frozen in one spot. Although weighed down by all the parcels in her hands, she did not move a muscle. She looked around the room, even glancing behind her. "John was here?"

"Yes, he looked so handsome. I woke up, and he was standing by my bed. I apologized for being such a slugabed. I offered to make breakfast, but he has a tee time at the golf course this morning."

"Well, that's . . . nice," she replied, lamely. She had no earthly idea what to say. She slowly sat her belongings down on the spare bed against the far wall in Vivian's room. Motioning toward the bed, she asked, "Button, did you have a roommate sleepover recently?"

"I don't think so."

As Ida took off her raincoat, she said, "April showers bring May flowers, and this rainy month has kicked off in style. It poured most of yesterday, no April fool's joke, and it's still raining this morning. It's supposed to clear up by evening. Laney should be here shortly. We wanted to get here before Helen because it's her birthday."

Turning toward Vivian, who was still in her nightgown, Ida said, "What would you like to wear today?" With no response, Ida made her way to Vivian's wardrobe and pulled out a white T-shirt and light pink, velour jogging suit. The top had a zipper in the front and was easy to slip on and off. She walked over to Vivian's bed and pushed the button to ring for a nurse. She opened Vivian's drawers to find no-slip socks but couldn't find her bra or panties.

"Good morning, Miss Ida. How are you this rainy morning?" Nurse Jamie asked as she entered Vivian's room with a kind smile. She always wore scrubs with a fun design instead of the traditional solid colors. Today, she looked like a flower garden. Her sandy blonde hair was in a messy ponytail. Ida couldn't image how, but Jamie always seemed to have a smile on her face.

"I'm doing well, thank you, Jamie. I wondered if you had time to help me get Vivian up and dressed this morning. We have a birthday to celebrate at lunch today."

"It's my birthday!" Button beamed from ear to ear.

"It's Helen's birthday," Ida corrected her sweetly. "Your birthday is June 10."

"I'm seventy-nine today."

"You turned eighty last June."

"We're having chocolate cake," Button announced.

"We're having white cake and white icing," Ida corrected.

"And ice cream," Vivian said dreamily.

"No ice cream."

"Yes, ice cream," chimed a new voice in the conversation. Laney walked into the room with a big smile on her face, carrying a grocery bag that obviously contained a half gallon of ice cream.

Vivian clapped her hands together in glee. "I love my birthday!"

Jamie burst out laughing. "You three have made my day!" She helped Vivian from her bed and into the wheelchair. She gathered up the clothes Ida set out on the foot of bed to help Vivian dress in the bathroom.

"I couldn't find her bra and panties," Ida apologized.

"The diapers are next to the toilet and we don't bother with a bra anymore," Jamie replied as she wheeled Vivian into the bathroom and closed the door.

Ida's eyes shot straight to Laney's. She watched for surprise in her face and saw none. She raised her eyebrows, cocked her head, and crossed her arms. She even tapped her foot on the floor.

Laney confessed, "Alright, I'm sorry. I didn't tell you."

"Why is that?"

"I could say to avoid upsetting you. I could say because I forgot. Truth is, I just hate hearing the story come out of my mouth!" As she rubbed her forehead, Laney explained, "She started out having trouble at night and she thought her laundry basket was the toilet. She isn't recognizing her need to use the restroom until it's too late. Since it has become a twenty-four-hour problem, they've made a change to adult diapers. It's easier than changing her clothes and sheets several times a day. Can we leave it at that?"

"I'm sorry," Ida admitted. "That is very difficult to share. It's heartbreaking to hear. Are there any other secrets you wish to disclose at this time?"

"Not at this time, no."

"*Are* there other secrets?"

"No. Wait, yes. She no longer has shaved legs or armpits."

Ida took in a breath so loudly that Laney could hear it from across the room.

"Look, Ida, I'm sorry. That was rather harsh and not well done of me."

"No, I'm sorry. You are much more involved in the day-to-day details. I shouldn't be scolding you, Laney. I just don't want you to be burdened. A burden shared is a burden lessened, so they say."

Laney nodded. "Well, my burden is melting," she said, trying to lighten the mood again. Motioning to the bag in her hand, she said, "I better get this ice cream into a freezer."

They met at their table in the corner of the dining room. Helen's birthday cake had one purple candle and was positioned in the middle of the table with three presents set to the side. Laney made it a point to have a gift for Button to give to Helen. Books and music were the traditional choices for Helen, but this year, Laney chose two soft knit tops from a specialty store. The baby blue and soft yellow floral scarf in Button's gift box would match both shirts. Helen rarely splurged on new clothes, simply adding career pieces over the years to her wardrobe as needed. With retirement long behind her, Laney hoped she would enjoy the new, more casual pieces.

If there was a best gift contest, Laney admitted to herself Ida's choice of *Eat Your Greens and Yummy Things* book by Marshall Green would win. It was perfect for Helen, and Laney couldn't wait to read it. She loved cookbooks, even if she didn't always try out the recipes.

Helen entered the dining room, taking in her sweet friends at their table and the kind efforts they'd made to make her eighty-first birthday a special one. This was the first time they'd celebrated one of their birthdays at the nursing home. They normally picked their favorite restaurant for lunch. From April to July, their birthdays were separated by mere weeks; they referred to those months as birthday season. It started with Helen in April, Ida in May, Button in June, and Laney on the Fourth of July. She always said her birthday was best because everyone had the day off work and the day was marked with fireworks every year. It was hard to beat that!

Helen smiled. "You are the best friends in the world!"

"Happy birthday," Laney and Ida expressed sincerely.

"We're having chocolate cake and ice cream," Button shared, smiling at Helen.

Helen leaned toward Button, gently squeezing her hand. "I'm sure it will be delicious."

"Honey, I'm sure it will be delicious," John insisted as he looked at the birthday cake his young wife had made. It was sunk a bit on the top layer and leaned precariously like the Tower of Pisa. She had tried to repair a section along one side where the cake had pulled apart as she iced it. She kept that side of the cake hidden in the back.

"I'm such a bad cook!" Vivian wailed. "My mother and grandmother tried to teach me to bake, and I even took home economics classes in school. I'm so sorry, darling. I wanted your birthday to be special."

"It is special," he insisted. "You are special," he said, kissing her cheek. "Dinner was delicious, and I had an extra helping of roasted chicken and new potatoes."

"Helen helped me," she admitted. "She helped with the cake as well but had to leave while it was in the oven. I assured her I could frost the cake. Please don't tell her it ended up looking like this."

"Sweetheart, you are worrying over nothing. Slice it up and give me a big piece."

Vivian took a little breath and cut into the cake, but, much to her dismay, the very center was undercooked and looked more like batter than cake! She closed her eyes, silently cursing her luck. The cake had only cooked along the outer edges despite that fact the toothpick she inserted in the cake had come out dry. Next time, she thought, she would stab toothpicks a hundred times into the cake, especially in the center.

John gently took the knife from Vivian's hand and cut the cake in a circle, hollowing out the center. He picked up the giant round donut he'd made and put it on another plate.

"Now I have a place for my ice cream," he said with a kind smile for his bride as he motioned to the hole in the center. "We do have ice cream, right?

"We always have ice cream. And I love you immensely!"

"We always have ice cream. I love you immensely," Button said in a soft voice.

Helen mouthed the word *John* to Laney and Ida as she instantly recognized where Vivian's mind had taken her. She replied sweetly, "I love you too, Button."

"Everyone knows you can't have cake without ice cream at a birthday party."

Laney looked at Ida with a *told-you-so* expression on her face.

Helen dove into presents first and was delighted with her gifts! Laney was especially happy to see her reaction to the new tops and scarf, which she'd tied instantly around her neck with the white top she'd worn. Helen blushed at the ensuing compliments. She eagerly thumbed through her new cookbook, promising to try every single recipe.

Ida lit the birthday candle and told Helen to make a wish. She closed her eyes, thinking of a special hope, and blew out the candle. Ida sliced each of them a little piece of cake, and Laney added a small scoop of ice cream.

"It's not chocolate," Button complained loudly in a childish voice when Laney sat the plate in front of her.

"No, not today," Ida answered softly. "Today we are having white cake for Helen's birthday." She put a slight emphasis on Helen's name.

"I want chocolate!" Button grouched, unlike her true personality.

"Well, today we're having a lovely white wedding cake for Helen," Laney said, trying a different approach.

"Helen has a wedding cake," Button said contentedly. Laney helped Button put a bit of cake on her fork and she put it in her mouth. While chewing, Button looked to her left toward Helen and asked, "Where is your wedding dress?"

The next few minutes were filled with an abundance of fibs and tall tales. It started out innocently enough as Helen replied, "I didn't want an elaborate wedding dress" and ended with Button exclaiming, "And her prince carried her away and they lived happily ever after. "

Helen gave Laney and Ida her evil-eye look. "You two spun her up and now you can settle her back down." Laney and Ida agreed to her terms; they would take Button back to her room for a nap, but insisted that Helen consider it another birthday present.

She lightheartedly agreed. "Thank you, sweet sisters, for a lovely birthday. I've truly had the best time. Thank you for the gifts and the wedding cake. I feel quite spoiled!" She hugged each of them, insisting Ida take the remaining cake to share with her family. As Helen gathered her purse and gifts and turned to leave, her eyes connected with a startlingly handsome man, who appeared to be smiling at her. He was standing next to his chair at a table nearby.

Helen felt it would be rude to not offer a small smile in return, but she forced herself to not look at him further as she walked by him in the dining room. She made her way toward the living room, but paused as she heard a masculine voice behind her say, "Happy birthday!"

She turned and looked at the man from the dining room. It would be rude, she decided, to not acknowledge him and replied, "Thank you."

"Henry."

"Thank you, Henry."

He smiled. "You are very welcome . . ." He was waiting for her to supply her name.

"Helen."

He nodded, almost bowed, as if he was making her acquaintance.

She felt suddenly awkward, turned toward the front door, and practically ran for the exit.

Charlotte (Lottie)

When Granddaughters Are Truly Grand

Laney sat at her kitchen table on Saturday, just a few mornings later, sipping a cup of coffee and putting together a little Easter goodie bag for Button. In truth, it was her son Bobby and his wife Judith's table. It was Bobby and Judith's kitchen, their home. Bobby had repeatedly encouraged his mother to think of their house as her house, but Laney still felt like a guest. Her bedroom and bath on the far side of the house were lovely; she enjoyed the kindness of that privacy. She loved the extra time she got to spend with them, especially her granddaughter, Lottie, who was seventeen years old.

Laney and Lottie had bonded early in Lottie's infancy with Laney caring for her as a baby and toddler while Bobby and Judith were working. Through the years, she had picked up Lottie at elementary and middle school, staying with her in the afternoons until her parents got home. They spent many fun weeks and weekends together when Bobby and Judith had taken trips.

One year, when Lottie was four years old, she felt horribly left behind as Bobby and Judith pulled out of the driveway without her. Laney started a tradition that year, just for the two of them, by taking her to an amusement park in Orlando. They'd been back annually ever since.

Laney tried her best to support Lottie's dreams without interfering in the hopes and plans her parents had for her. Judith, especially, had pushed Lottie to follow in her footsteps at the same hometown university and similar career as a decorator. Lottie had tried to share with her parents numerous times that she wanted to be an actress. They had patted her on the head like a good little girl not old enough to know her own dreams.

Lottie had shared information privately with Laney one day last year as they'd sat side by side on the sofa with Lottie's laptop perched across their laps. "See, Nannie, I could go to Florida College of Theater and Arts in Orlando for their amazing drama program and try to get a job part-time at Big Sky Amusement Park. You know I love that place!"

"That would be wonderful for you, Lottie," she admitted whole-heartedly. She truly believed it was essential to pursue one's passion, having changed her major from nursing to become a librarian. She'd worked several years at the local library, loving every minute.

Despite the time she got to spend with her family, Laney missed her own home—the darling craftsman in which she'd raised Bobby. She and her husband, Robert, had purchased a two-story house when Bobby was a baby, envisioning the big backyard as the place all the neighborhood kids would want to play. After losing Robert, she decided it was too large, uncomfortable, and a burden filled with moment-by-moment reminders of a life without him. Many nights she found herself fixing a meal he loved or glancing up at a noise, thinking he was walking in the door.

About a year after Robert's death, she made an offer on a house, buying the craftsman just around the corner from Button and John with part of the money she received from Robert's life insurance. They almost had not taken out the policy since they were so young, but she was tremendously grateful they did; it made a huge difference in her life. She resigned from her job to focus on the life she needed to build as a single mom and, over the years, she and Bobby had found real happiness in that home. He did homework at the kitchen table; they celebrated holidays there. She marked his growth with pencil marks on the wall in his bedroom. Every year, she took his first-day-of-school photo on the front steps of their home.

She loved the front porch with the charming porch swing, the thick oak front door, beautiful entryway with the wood staircase, and the built-ins. Oh, the lovely built-in where she displayed her dishes in the dining room. She missed that.

She'd set down rules against stinky shoes, socks, and sports gear scattered about, but she often found them on the stairs or on the floor of his bedroom. That home simply felt lived in and cozy.

Maybe that was the problem with Bobby and Judith's house. It was always so tidy and clean, for one thing. They didn't like clutter and never left anything sitting out on the countertops. Everything had its place. They loved a modern style, which further emphasized to Laney that this wasn't her home. She never left her wing of their house without her bedroom and bathroom spotlessly clean. She felt a tiny burn of embarrassment remembering the first evening after she had moved in with them. Judith had knocked on her bedroom door. Laney thought she had come to wish her *sweet dreams*, but she was simply dropping off Laney's purse, which she'd left on the kitchen table. After that, Laney made it a point to never leave her belongings outside of her bedroom.

She and Bobby had been a team. He had only been eight years old when Robert was killed in the collision. Robert had been on his way home from work later than normal that evening. If only he had left work unfinished until the next day. If only he had left work at five o'clock. If only . . . well, she had a long list of *if onlys*.

It had been so many years, but the ache was still there for all the family times he missed, times they didn't share together. She remembered sitting in the emergency room that painful, horrific night, having been summoned by a police officer who, sadly, was a friend of Robert's from childhood. Charlie and Ida had come to the house with Ava, who, as a preteen, had offered to stay with Bobby. Helen, Button, and John had been in the emergency room waiting room when she, Ida, and Charlie had arrived. Her parents and younger brothers were on their way as were Robert's parents and his two brothers, but they all had long drives ahead of them.

From the moment they'd been informed of Robert's passing until well beyond the funeral was time still fuzzy in Laney's memory. Many of her memories were of conversations weeks and months later with Button. She could really lower her guard with Button; talking, crying, planning, and yelling were completely normal and acceptable in Button's company. Laney could tell her anything.

She remembered the day she and Button sat on a park bench at the duck pond near campus. They talked a little as they tossed tiny pieces of bread to the ducks on the shore. "John knows a really nice man; they have business dealings and play golf together," Button had started into a seemingly lighthearted and simple conversation.

"Not interested."

"OK."

Laney turned toward her sister, eyebrows raised.

"Seriously though, let me know if you change your mind."

"It hasn't been that long, Button. Just over a year. I have the house, Bobby, many things to keep me busy. I don't know if I'll ever feel interested. I might. I might not."

"And both of those options are perfectly acceptable," Button insisted.

After sitting quietly for quite some time, Laney broached a subject that had been on her mind. "What do you think heaven is like?"

Button didn't miss a beat. "Joy. Love like we can't understand here."

"But what do you think it's like?"

"Well, despite being thirty-two years old, I honestly have a childlike view of it. I can picture God with little children on His lap, a long line of children waiting their turn for His attention. I picture angels reporting in from their guardian duties and, of course, white-robed cherubs with halos and wings. I see no pain, no illnesses, no concerns or worries. I see dogs. I mean, I think heaven is for animals, too. God certainly seems to love them since He made so many," she said, motioning toward the ducks on the water. "I imagine people of all ages, all nationalities who understand each other, who love each other and watch over us, their families, until it's our turn to join them."

"I can't help but wonder if Robert sees us or knows that we love and miss him."

"I think it's both."

"Do you think he'll be waiting for us?"

"Right at the pearly gate."

"I hope someone was waiting for him. A grandparent, maybe."

"I'm sure there was. I think it's instantaneous. A goodbye here is a hello there."

Laney absorbed those last few words and put her arms around Button. "I could not love you more. I needed to hear that."

Hearing her name, Laney was abruptly pulled out of her thoughts. Lottie was calling to her from the other room.

"Nannie, you have *got* to hear this. Some messed-up lady and her husband on that TV show about finding a house just said she wanted to paint the original wood in this craftsman white. She just said she'd have to paint the fireplace. I say never paint the brick. She is in a gorgeous, historic craftsman and wants an open floorplan and an all-white, modern kitchen. I hope they don't pick this house. It deserves to be admired and kept as it is."

"Charlotte, we have a white, modern kitchen," Judith interrupted. "Don't you think our kitchen is stunning?"

Laney entered the room just in time to see Lottie roll her eyes. "Of course, Mom. Our kitchen is beautiful," she replied with undetected sarcasm. "It's just that our kitchen doesn't really belong in that craftsman house." She motioned toward the television three times as if to underscore each of the words, *that craftsman house.*

Laney loved that girl!

She sat next to Lottie on the sofa, and they jokingly criticized the house buyers on television. "She's never going to find a giant walk-in closet in an older home unless they remodel." Laney judged them without apology.

"Her husband says he wants a turnkey house with no projects. He's lame! The number-one thing on his wish list is a man-cave, but I understand why. His wife is a piece of work," Lottie said as she tossed popcorn in her mouth.

"Charlotte, please attempt to eat something even mildly nutritious for breakfast. It's not even ten o'clock and all you've eaten is popcorn."

"Not true, Mom. I snagged some chocolate Easter eggs from the kitchen island. I promise to eat something in the protein and vegetable category later today."

Changing the topic, Laney said, "I think they'll pick house number three."

"Yep. It's huge, pretentious, and way over their budget," Lottie said as they all laughed, even Judith.

After the show was over, Judith turned off the television and asked what Laney's plans were for the day. "I'd like to take a little Easter basket to Button if you, Bobby, or Lottie have time to join me or give me a ride," she said, feeling quite frustrated and uncomfortable that she had to depend on them for transportation.

"Bobby and I have some errands planned, but we can drop you off and pick you up later," Judith shared, being extra generous today.

"I can take you, Nannie."

"Young lady," Judith started in on Lottie, "you have the 'Learn about Greek Life Day' on campus this afternoon."

"Mom," she said, complaining. "I am going to college in Orlando. I've been accepted. Your sorority is not on campus there. Plus, I know a ton about sororities thanks to you and Nannie. You guys weren't in the same one, but I get the whole sorority thing."

"Well, you might change your mind, and it never hurts to be nice and learn a little about Greek Life. We alumnae have been encouraged to send our legacies to the event," Judith, now standing, said with her hands on her hips. Lottie looked at Laney, who just shrugged. She thought Judith was being way over-the-top *again* when it came to Lottie's college plans.

Fortunately, Bobby entered the living room asking, "What event?"

"Dad, Mom wants me go to a sorority event despite the fact that I'm not going to college here. I am going to Florida College of Theater and Arts in Orlando." Lottie put a major emphasis on the last two words.

Before Judith could start in on one of her tirades, Bobby put his arm around his wife's waist, steering her toward the kitchen and just beyond. "Mom and I are off! I'm taking her for a surprise lunch and some shopping."

Laney and Lottie looked at each other, trying not to smile. Bobby had just saved the day. "Have fun," they called out in unison as Bobby and Judith made their way toward the back door.

"So, Nannie, how about lunch with your favorite girl and then we will drop by to see Aunt Button," Lottie offered.

And again, Laney thought, *I love this kid!* The feeling, she knew, was mutual.

Not long after lunch at their favorite Mexican food restaurant where Lottie insisted fajita chicken and queso were protein and salsa was a vegetable, they arrived at Enduring Grace and walked into Vivian's room to find her sleeping.

"I'm sorry, Nannie. Maybe we should have come here first," Lottie whispered. "Let's stay awhile and see if she wakes up from her nap."

Laney patted Lottie softly on the back, "No, it's fine. Don't worry. Let me walk back down to the nurses' station and ask if they know how long she has been asleep."

After Laney left the room, Lottie sat in the rocking chair and checked her phone. The chair squeaked a little as she rocked.

"Laney?"

Lottie looked up at the quiet inquiry. She smiled at a sleepy Button and leaned toward her. "Hi, Aunt Button. It's me, Lottie. Did you get a good nap? How are you feeling today?"

"My mom was here and the doctors said I'll only have a little scar from the appendectomy. I get to go home in a couple of days and back to school next week," Button shared.

"Oh, um . . ."

"Mom said I will need to rest and take it easy, but I am still planning on going to the sock hop. You always find the cutest dates for yourself! You have to start sharing tips with me. I just feel kind of shy and awkward about it."

Lottie looked over her shoulder toward the door. *Oh no*, she thought. *Where was Nannie?* She decided to try again.

"Hi, Aunt Button. It's me, Charlotte. Laney's granddaughter. Remember?"

Button looked away for a few seconds. She brought her eyes back to Lottie's.

"Do you think I should ask Walter from the Spirit Club? He is a good dancer."

Deciding to just go with it, Lottie answered enthusiastically, "Well, if he is a good dancer, then sure! You can't underestimate the fun and unique opportunity that comes from taking a guy who likes to dance to a dance or, um, a sock hop."

Button smiled momentarily before her attention was pulled away from her sorority sister to rest on the lady entering her room. She looked familiar. "Hi, Lady!"

Laney looked a little confused. Lottie stood up to give her the chair and said with great purpose, "Button and I, Laney," she said, motioning to herself, "were just talking about her mom being here to let her know she won't have a big appendectomy scar. Button will get to go home soon; she may even get to go to the sock hop and, since I, Laney, haven't told her how to pick up guys yet, she is planning on asking Walter, the Spirit Club guy who is a good dancer."

"I see," Laney replied slowly. She was very proud of Lottie for her patience and kindness.

Changing the subject, Laney held up the little Easter basket she'd brought for Button. "Happy Easter. I think the Easter Bunny knows you love chocolate."

Looking at Lottie, Button said, "Do I?"

After attempting to salvage the visit and talking about some random topics as Button barely seemed to be paying attention, Laney stood and said with a forced brightness, "Well, we will see you soon." She leaned over the bedrail and hugged Button.

Lottie leaned in to give Button a hug as well. Button put her arms weakly around Lottie and said, "I love you!" Lottie kissed her cheek while she repeated in her head *do not cry, do not cry*.

They left the Easter basket on Button's bedside table and walked, without words, to Lottie's car. She held her grandmother's hand the entire way. She opened the passenger door, helped Nannie inside, and circled around the car to the driver's seat. She started the car in silence. Then, she turned the car off.

"Dammit, Nannie. This sucks!" Her voice broke slightly.

Laney looked at her granddaughter, failing to keep the pain out of her eyes. "Yes, it does. It completely sucks!"

"You visit her almost every day. Like . . . how?"

"I love her. She would be doing the same for me."

"You know she was hugging *you* in there, saying *I love you* to you, not me."

"I know. I'm sorry, Lottie, so very sorry you had to go through all of this just now. She was much better the other day. Maybe awakening from a nap threw her off. Again, honey, I'm so sorry!"

After a slight pause, Lottie said in a calmer voice, "I'm not. I'm not sorry, not really. I mean, this is so, so sad. It's rough and awful; I don't know how you do it—you, Aunt Ida, and Aunt Helen. I totally admire you. I just learned what love looks like on a really hard, sucky day!"

Before Laney could get a word in, Lottie continued, "Which is just another day in Button's Alzheimer's battle for you."

Looking out the window and shaking her head, she continued with what Laney later called her "true Judith style."

"I'll tell you what. When I meet my Prince Charming someday, he better get the 'for better, for worse, in sickness and in health' part. Like, really get it!" She sat up straighter in her seat and started the car.

"I freaking need ice cream. A giant hot-fudge sundae!" Turning toward Nannie, she asked, "Penny's Ice Cream Parlor?"

Nodding her agreement, Laney finally got to say two words. "I'm buying."

Jennifer

When Mother's Day Is the Greatest Day Ever

"Happy Mother's Day and happy birthday, Mom!" Jen hugged Ava. "Hi, Grandma. Happy Mother's Day and happy early birthday to you too," she said, kissing Ida on the cheek.

May 8 was two celebrations rolled into one for Ava and Ida this year. With birthdays exactly one week apart, they often celebrated together. Jen brought little gifts and cards commemorating both days for them. She also had Mother's Day cards to give her honorary aunts, Laney and Helen, because they were like grandmothers to her. She went back and forth in her decision to buy one for Button. After standing in the store and combing through all the cards, she found one with a cute white puppy wearing a hot pink bow. It wasn't a Mother's Day card, but it felt perfect even if the inside was blank.

Jen had arrived at her parents' house just a few minutes earlier with Jacob Rosales—Jake to everyone except his grandmother. He was the love of Jennifer's life. He fit in with her family, and she with his, so naturally. Right after walking in the door, he'd waved to the ladies and headed straight toward her dad, Joe. They shook hands and patted each other on the back in the weird man-hug that all guys somehow know and perfect by college. As she studied them, she was startled to realize that they looked a little alike. Her dad was mostly gray headed compared with Jake's dark brown. Her dad was a little shorter and had love handles, as he called his wider midsection. They both had brown eyes and tremendous smiles. *Maybe it's the smile*, she thought.

Suddenly, almost as if he could read her thoughts, he looked at her and grinned.

"Jennifer, these are beautiful, sweetie!" Jen swiveled her attention back to her mom, who pulled a silver necklace out of one box and matching earrings out of a second one. They were in the shape of little arrows. She happily showed them to everyone. "I think I'll wear them right now."

Ida opened her gift to discover Jen had bought her the latest romance novel from a favorite author. She couldn't wait to read it. It was the third in series about sisters who grew up in poor circumstances in England in the 1800s and fell in love and married dukes or earls. Helen teased her unmercifully about her love of romance novels, and she had defended herself by replying, "Yes, I love a love story and a happy ending. So, sue me!" Button had loved reading romance novels, too, and they'd shared countless books over the years. Button had come to Ida's defense a couple of years earlier when Helen teased her, and said, "I do believe, Helen, that I saw sappy, romantic Christmas movies on your television recently." Ida hugged Jennifer and thanked her sincerely for the book.

Jake and Joe crossed the room and made their way toward Jen and Ava. Jake stopped to talk to her grandpa, Charlie, laughing at something he said. He came to Jennifer's side and put his arm around her waist.

"Here Mom, happy birthday," Jennifer said, handing the small box to Ava.

"Three gifts? Am I such a wonderful mother that I deserve three gifts?"

Jennifer gave her mom a look. "One is for Mother's Day and one is for your birthday. This is a surprise."

Ava opened the small box, beautifully wrapped in white paper with gold ribbon. It was a ring box, which confused her, and when Ava opened it, she gasped! Inside the box was the most beautiful engagement ring she had ever seen. She looked up sharply at Jen and Jake.

Jen exclaimed, "We're engaged!"

Ava and Ida squealed *yes* at the same time; Ida's arms shot skyward as if she were a football referee signally a touchdown. The entire room erupted in joy!

Jake said, as he reached for the ring box in Ava's hand, "This is how Jen wanted to tell you, but if you have no objections, I'd love to get this ring back on her finger."

Ava cried, which made Ida cry, which made Jen cry. Hugs were shared all around!

Laney and Helen watched from near the fireplace. Laney leaned toward Helen. "This may go down on record as the greatest day in Russell family history!"

"No doubt about it. I am so happy for them. I've been worried since Thanksgiving when Jennifer didn't come home with a ring."

"Or on Christmas, Valentine's Day, or her birthday," Laney added.

"Poor child has been looking for that ring in every present he has given her."

Laney sighed. "She told me she looked at the bottom of her champagne glass on New Year's Eve."

"Well, whatever his reason was for delaying until May, he is utterly forgiven! Jennifer is madly in love."

Jennifer practically skipped up to Laney and Helen. "Do you want to see my ring?"

"Yes!" They all but shouted their responses simultaneously.

Jen shared, "Jake said he wanted to ask me when I wasn't looking for it, wasn't expecting it. Friday night we went to the baseball stadium on campus where we first started dating. He asked me if I wanted to play catch, which is something we've done a few times. You'll be proud to know that I impressed him early on in our relationship by being able to throw and catch. Little did he know then that I had played third base on my high school softball team. Anyway, he pulled out our gloves and bag of baseballs, and we talked a little as we played catch. At one point he said something was wrong with the baseball and asked me to get another one from the bag. When I looked inside, the ring box was on top. I whirled around to find him on bended knee."

"Have you shared all of this with your grandmother yet?" Laney asked with a huge grin on her face. "She may keel over!"

Jen laughed loudly as Ida approached them. "I'll tell her the whole engagement story later. The only comment she has made thus far, beside congratulations, has been to point out my married name will be Jennifer Rose Rosales. I may need to keep my maiden name and go for Jennifer Russell Rosales."

Ida said, "You pick whatever name you like." Looking at Laney and Helen, she asserted, "Isn't this the best day ever? I am over the moon for these two kids."

"Thanks, Grandma!" Jen excused herself as Ava called to her with a wedding question. "Let the planning begin," she said with a wink.

"Congratulations, Ida. You must be so thrilled to welcome Jake into your family," Laney shared, hugging her.

"I was praying he'd be a keeper." Helen leaned in for a quick hug.

"He is. He absolutely is." Ida moved to stand next to Laney, scanning the room. "The only thing that would have made this day better is if Button could have been here. Although I have no idea how she'll react, Jennifer mentioned visiting Button to share the news."

"Just to prepare you, Button thought Lottie was me when we visited last weekend. It wasn't a great day," Laney shared regretfully. "I don't want to bring you down on possibly the greatest day ever, but you should prepare Jennifer just in case."

Ida shook her head sadly. "You know, it was right here in this living room when I first realized Button's short-term memory wasn't good. It was about eight years ago, when Jennifer was seventeen. She and Button talked for several minutes about a little boy for whom she was babysitting that night. He was the grandson of Button's friend from church. They talked about kids, babysitting, and even how much the going rate was for paying a sitter. It was a long chat. Button and I watched Jennifer leave; we waved to her from the front door. Right after dinner with Ava and Joe, we were sitting in here visiting and she said, 'Is Jennifer in her room? I should say hello to her before I go.'"

Laney and Helen didn't reply. Ida offered, "Sorry, now I'm bringing you down on the best day ever."

Charlie asked for everyone's attention. He thoroughly enjoyed making grand announcements. "On behalf of the entire James and Russell family, I'd like to say congratulations to Jen and Jake. It's about darn time, Jacob!" he teased. Everyone laughed, even Jake.

"Happy birthday to my lovely daughter, Ava, and happy Mother's Day to all the mothers, and honorary mothers, here today. And, last but never least, I'd like to wish my beautiful bride an early happy eighty-first birthday with a special little present. Live from New York, it's strawberry cheesecake!"

The following Friday, Ida and Jennifer arrived at Enduring Grace loaded with bridal magazines and wedding-planning material. Ava wasn't free to join them because of a project at work. Jen thought it may have been an overload on Button for all three of them to visit, and besides, a little alone time with her grandmother was long overdue. They made a quick stop at their favorite chicken-finger place for breakfast. Jen was adamant that their chicken biscuit had come into existence thanks to her endless prayers for an egg-free breakfast drive thru option. She could not stand eggs!

Although she was an ever-so-slightly high-maintenance person, Jen was her parents' pride and joy. She was the blessing Joe and Ava had longed for after Ava suffered through a number of miscarriages. This led to Jen being a tiny bit spoiled; she was definitely a kid around which the world revolved.

Thankfully, as Helen said, she "wasn't a brat!" Helen wasn't tremendously fond of children but insisted she adored Ava and Bobby and, therefore, Jen and Lottie. She declared them all major exceptions to the rule.

Button, as another only child, had often jumped to Jennifer's defense. She announced to the group once that she and Jennifer were members of a secret club as Laney, Helen, and Ida had siblings. She had winked at Jennifer, saying, "They don't know the secret handshake and password."

Jen would freely admit to not being the most pleasant when ill, or first thing in the morning. It's not that she wasn't a morning person, she just wasn't a talkative morning person. Her family knew to give her a wide berth until after nine. Her biggest frustration in life was her naturally curly hair, which was unmanageable as a child and worn mostly in ponytails. Luckily, much like the chicken biscuits, she believed hair straighteners were a gift from above. It would have been so much easier if her mother had passed down the blonde hair, minus the curls.

As Jen and Ida made their way through the foyer of Enduring Grace, Jen shared, "Grandma, I am both excited and nervous to see Button!"

"I completely understand." Ida patted Jennifer on the hand as they walked arm in arm. "None of us ever know when we arrive what the day will bring. I did call this morning and Nurse Angela said Button was doing really well. She asked to wear something pink this morning."

"Well, there you go. That's Button personified."

They were directed to find Button in the rec room. When they entered, they found her coloring a picture with her friend, Margaret. Devon was standing nearby as if he'd been circling the room to visit with and assist everyone.

"Hello, Miss Ida," Devon called out as he walked toward them. He looked at Jennifer and asked, "Who do we have here?"

"Devon, this is my granddaughter, Jennifer. Jen, this is Devon, the wonderful nurse I've mentioned. Don't tell anyone, but he is Button's beau."

Reaching out to shake Jennifer's hand, Devon said, "I absolutely adore Miss Vivian; however, I remain single."

"She's engaged!" Ida pointed to the engagement ring on Jen's left hand, visible as she held the bride magazines close to her chest.

"Grandma!" Jennifer looked at her in shock. "I'm sorry, Devon, my grandmother is losing her filter and her manners. It's nice to meet you. I got engaged a week ago, but I do have a wonderful friend you might like to meet. She's pretty awesome."

Devon laughed. "Are you kidding?" He looked at Jennifer's serious face. "Oh, you're not kidding." He paused for a second or two before adding, "OK, I'm in." Devon leaned in slightly toward Jennifer. "Truth is, I don't often meet ladies under seventy-five."

Jennifer laughed. "I'll circle back by when my hands aren't full of magazines and exchange phone numbers with you. I'll call my friend, Payton, and see if she's open to a double date."

"That sounds great." Before Jen could take more than a step or two, Devon asked, "Jennifer, just out of curiosity, did Miss Vivian say something to you about finding me a date?"

"No. I haven't seen her in a while."

"Are you, by chance, in her sorority?"

"Yes. Why do you ask?"

"Just something Miss Vivian said recently. It's nothing. I'll catch you in a few minutes."

Jennifer gave Devon a slight wave as she turned to follow Ida toward Button's table. She caught up just in time to hear Ida say, "We thought this day would never come and just couldn't wait to share the amazing news!"

Jennifer glared at her grandmother for a second or two before moving around her to greet Button. "Hi, Aunt Button. I've missed you!"

Button studied her face and smiled, "Hi, kiddo!"

Jen studied Button in return. She had never called her by that name.

Ida explained, "Button, this is Jennifer, Ava's daughter and my granddaughter. Do you remember Jennifer?"

Button said, "Of course."

Jen wasn't convinced, but she certainly wasn't going to push the issue. "I wanted to give you this card and let you know I got engaged last week. I'm so lucky, Aunt Button. Jake makes me very happy." She held her left hand forward to show Vivian her engagement ring.

Margaret, seated at the table just beyond Button, leaned in toward the ring and said, "Wow, that's beautiful! Congratulations."

Button didn't reply enthusiastically, but she echoed Margaret and murmured, "Congratulations."

Jennifer glanced over her shoulder at her grandmother as if to say *a little help here!*

Ida said, "Thank you, both. Button, Jake is so sweet and handsome. Just like my Charlie. You've met him."

Button said, "Did he come to my house?"

Jen replied, "No, Aunt Button. I don't think he has been to your house. You met him at Mom and Dad's. Oh, and he was at the Fourth of July birthday party for Laney a couple of years ago."

"Is it Laney's birthday?" Button asked, seeming more interested.

"No, but it will be in a couple of months," Jen replied.

"Is Laney getting married?"

"No, Aunt Button. I am," Jen was starting to wilt. "Would you like to see pictures of the wedding dresses I like?"

Button seemed to perk up a little. "I like dresses."

"Yes, you do," Jen and Ida said at the same time. They smiled at each other. Jen pulled out the chair next to Button for her grandmother and circled around to the other side of the table, pulling out a chair opposite the ladies. Margaret leaned in to see the magazines as well.

"I have always wanted to be a June bride because of the song in *Seven Brides for Seven Brothers*," Jen beamed. "The one with Jane Powell. Every time I had a sleepover at Grandma's house, we made popcorn and watched that movie. I wanted to see it over and over. It was my favorite." Jen was surprised to see Button nodding her head.

"A June wedding. Yes," Button murmured.

Jen smiled, feeling like she was breaking through to Button. "So, we'll hopefully get married about this time next summer depending on availability of the church. Jake doesn't want to get married outside in June. I'm just waiting for the lady at the church to get back to me."

She looked at the three ladies whose attention she had amazingly captured. She opened the first magazine to one of many wedding gown photos she had marked with sticky tabs. She glanced up to make sure all eyes were on the magazine. "This one is my favorite. Obviously, I haven't tried it on so I'm not sure how something like this would look on me."

Button studied the picture in the magazine and replied, "Gorgeous!" Jen smiled at Button sweetly.

"You look gorgeous! You do, Button. Simply gorgeous," Laney declared as she walked into the church's dressing room to find Button in her wedding dress. Button was facing the mirror and could see Laney in the reflection.

Button grinned and countered back to Laney, "No, you look gorgeous. I know that bridesmaid dress color wasn't your choice. It was mine. But, Laney, you look stunning in pink. I love your hair pinned up like that."

Making a little twirl, Laney confessed, "I like this soft, pale pink color. It's the bright version I'm not too hip about . . . and thank you. Marie fixed my hair. She, Helen, and Ida are right behind me. The florist just arrived with the bouquets and they are lending a hand. We may be beautiful bridesmaids, but you, sister, are the most stunningly gorgeous bride ever. I mean, I looked pretty exquisite on my walk down the aisle, but gee whiz, look at you."

"Don't make me cry. My mother just left after embarrassing me horribly with a conversation about my wedding night and s-e-x," she cringed, spelling the word. "I wanted to cry it was so uncomfortable. I pledge here and now: I will not wait to have that conversation with my daughter thirty minutes before her wedding ceremony."

"I hope you told her you know more than she does! I shared basically all the details after Robert and I got married last year. That's what sisters are for, you know!"

"Laney! You promised to never talk about that conversation ever again." She swiveled to face Laney with her hands on her hips and asked, "What do you mean 'basically'?"

Laney threw back her head and laughed.

"What's so funny?" Marie asked as she held the door open with her foot for Helen and Ida. They were loaded with beautiful floral bouquets.

Button threw a look at Laney. Interpreting it immediately, Laney answered, "Button thinks I look gorgeous in pink."

"Gorgeous in pink," Button murmured.

"Oh, I don't think it comes in pink, but the traditional white is stunning. Don't you think, Aunt Button?" Jen said, excitedly.

"Stunning . . . yes."

Button's Special Date

When Streamers and Balloons Are Priceless

"Hello?"

"Hi, Miss Laney. It's Mary Carolyn calling from the chapter. I'm so glad I finally caught you."

"Oh, Mary Carolyn, I'm sorry, dear. I'm a horrible cell phone owner."

"No worries, I understand. If you notice a bunch of missed calls from me, just ignore them. Your voicemail box has never been setup so I couldn't leave a message. Anyway, I wanted to let you know that graduation is a week from Saturday. Claire and I are both graduating."

"Congratulations! That's so exciting. Will you be staying in the area?"

"No, we're moving to Orlando. We hope to work at one of the area amusement parks."

"Really? My granddaughter is dreaming of doing that someday. She is a senior in high school now."

"Oh, that's so cool! I grew up there—Orlando, I mean. If you'd like, I'd love to keep in touch. I have your cell phone number and address, and I'll reach out every now and then. My parents are graciously allowing me and Claire to move in with them until we get jobs and find an apartment. I'll keep you posted on everything, and hopefully, we'll see each other in Orlando one day soon."

"I would love that."

"How is Miss Vivian doing?"

"As you know, thanks to all of your really sweet visits, she has good days and bad days."

"Well, don't we all?" Mary Carolyn asked with a little laugh. "Claire and I wondered if we could coordinate a last-minute event with you on Thursday night at seven o'clock. I know this is late notice, but we had a brilliant idea the other day and everyone is on board. The senior class has our final Sorority Send-Off that night before finals start and, if the nursing home will allow, we'd like to do it there in the rec room. We have a little surprise for Miss Vivian. We've been working on a gift for weeks, but thought up this added twist!"

"Oh, sweetheart. You're going to make me cry. I'll call Mrs. Peters at Enduring Grace right away. They don't use the rec room very much after dinner but, if they are that night, we could probably have the dining room. Is it a ritual or anything private?"

"No, ma'am. We will be in dresses and wearing our badges because we also have a national officer coming from Ohio for an operational visit before the semester ends. She said she worked on national committees with Miss Vivian for years and loves her dearly. I'm kind of spoiling part of the surprise."

"Is it Linda Carlisle?"

"Yes! Do you know her, too?"

Laney scanned her mind. "Oh goodness, yes. I've known Linda for about thirty years. She is much younger than me and Vivian, but we worked on national sorority initiatives together. She and Vivian really bonded over committee work and a few trips organized by our foundation. They went to Greece together and Italy, I believe. I truly hope Button remembers Linda when she visits because they were very close at one time."

"They went to Greece and Italy? Wow, that's sick!"

Laney paused for a split second. "Sick meaning cool or uncool?"

"Totally cool!" Mary Carolyn giggled at Laney's question. "Oh, I almost forgot, I want to introduce you to my little sis, Cora, who will be there. She is a junior and will be carrying on with the Adopt-an-Alum program for Miss Vivian."

"Her name is Cora? Do all of you have names starting with a 'C'? I'm never going to be able to keep this straight."

"I know, right? We also have three girls named Caitlin, who spell it three different ways. We have four girls named Maddie and another four named Megan. It's crazy! Have you ever met another Laney?"

"I did once, actually. It was at a restaurant, and they called for Laney's party of four. We all approached the hostess's stand and laughed at the thrill of meeting another Laney."

Laney and Mary Carolyn talked for another ten minutes. They had really bonded over Vivian and over their shared love of sisterhood. She made a mental note to connect Lottie with her. Someday that amusement park networking opportunity could be life-changing.

Jeannie Peters approved the use of the rec room, and Laney pulled Helen and Ida into the loop. Ida was overjoyed and offered to invite Ava and Jennifer. Jen had not done many sorority activities since she lived in the house as an undergraduate, but Ida felt certain she would want to be there for Button.

Thursday finally came. They were all counting the days and holding their collective breath for Button to have a good memory day—as good as was possible for her. Laney checked on Button earlier in the day and stayed for lunch. Judith had dropped her off on her way to work, and Bobby took her home during his late lunch hour.

Laney looked out the window toward the driveway. Helen would be pulling up to Bobby and Judith's any minute to pick her up for the evening. Laney double-checked her appearance and studied her sorority badge in the mirror on the wall. *Always wear it just under your hand as if standing for the Pledge of Allegiance*, she whispered to herself. She had known that since she was eighteen. What she hadn't known or expected at that age was how deeply her badge, its meaning, and everything it represented, would affect her life. She wished sororities were without problems, without a few bad apples that sometimes spoiled and tarnished their worthiness. It seemed more of a struggle for fraternity alumni to keep some college boys from wiping away decades of good; however, girls sometimes made exceedingly bad choices as well. Strict rules were in place and, in this case, rules were not made to be broken. "Bylaws have the word laws in it for a reason," she recalled Button's words with a little smile.

Just then the doorbell rang. Laney grabbed her purse and cane and opened the door to a pleasant surprise.

"Jen!"

"I know. I'm doing an alum thing," she joked with Laney, rolling her eyes. "I told mom that I'd go if I could drive. Sitting in the backseat with Aunt Helen at the wheel freaks me out. Besides, my SUV will easily hold all five of us. Are you ready?"

"I am. And you're right about Helen's driving. Just so you know, she has always been a crazy driver with a lead foot."

A short drive later, Jennifer turned into the entrance at Enduring Grace. "Oh, my goodness, the parking lot is packed! I'll let you out up front and then go find a parking space."

Ava helped her mom, Helen, and Laney out of the car. They walked inside to see Devon and Angela directing the college girls toward the rec room. Laney approached them with a smile. "I know you both had the day shift so I'm surprised to see you this late. It's almost seven o'clock."

"My husband is still doing rounds," Angela sighed. "Besides, I'm a sorority girl at heart. We didn't have a chapter of your sorority on my campus. But I am a sorority alumna, and I totally love this idea. Having Senior Send-Off Night here and including Miss Vivian . . ." She trailed off by simply putting her hand over her heart. "So, I volunteered to work the security system and let everyone inside."

"You're welcome to stay, Angela. It's not ritual," Laney suggested. "We'd love to have you."

"Well, I may stand in the corner. I'm in scrubs and look like I got here at six this morning."

"Please do. And stand by me—scrubs be damned!"

Angela laughed and reached out to squeeze Laney's hand and smile gratefully at all of Vivian's sweet friends.

They proceeded through the living room, down the hallway, and stopped abruptly at the entrance to the rec room, barely recognizing it. The giant room had been cleared of tables and decorated earlier in the afternoon with pink and white balloons and streamers. It reminded all of them of a college sock hop.

"I'm going to cry," Ava said in a choked voice. The others nodded their agreement.

"Too late. Crying!" Jen said, having caught up to them. "Oh scrap," she said for her grandmother's ears. "These college girls are amazing. Now I have to say yes to their request that I serve as finance adviser. Even though no alum in her right mind says yes to being finance adviser!"

"You didn't tell me they'd asked you," Ava chided.

"Well, I was graciously going to decline; I have a job and a wedding to plan." Motioning to the adorably decorated room, she said, "But this has touched my Grinch-like heart."

Ava hugged her daughter. "You have nothing even remotely close to a Grinch-like heart. You should do it, though, if you can find the time. I guarantee you'll be so happy you did."

"Hey, Jennifer," Devon said from behind her.

Jennifer turned around. "Oh, hi, Devon. It's so nice to see you. I understand from Payton that you two have been talking quite a bit. Are you looking forward to dinner and a movie with her, me, and Jake tomorrow night?"

"You know it! Payton seems pretty amazing. She could be way out of my league," he said with a wink.

Jennifer laughed. "You are both awesome. By the way, have you seen the rec room tonight? It's decorated in pink and white and looks like a party."

"I have. I helped a little on my break."

Angela chuckled and spilled the beans. "He more than helped. The sock hop theme was his idea. That sweet red-headed girl over there, Claire is her name I believe, was here one day talking about having a special night for Vivian. Devon gave her the idea."

"Aww, Devon." Jennifer hugged him. "You have my permission to fall in love with Payton and marry my best friend." They both laughed.

Devon seemed a little embarrassed as the ladies gushed over him for a moment. He excused himself by declaring it was time to go pick up Miss Vivian for the dance.

Laney was pulled away from the group by Mary Carolyn. "Miss Laney, Mrs. Carlisle is by the refreshment table, and she is anxious to see you."

"Lead the way. I can't wait to catch up with her!"

The room was a little loud with 1950s music playing and the girls talking; some of them singing to the more famous songs that had stood the test of time. Laney and Linda picked up as if they'd never been apart. The conversation flowed easily and genuinely, and they laughed at many shared memories.

"May I have your attention," Mary Carolyn called from the center of the room. "Miss Vivian is on her way here, so let's keep it to a whisper now." She turned and walked to the entrance doors, peeking down the hallway.

Looking back at her sisters inside the room, she excitedly motioned toward the hall. "She's here!"

Devon, having quickly changed into navy pants, white dress shirt, and a blazer, pushed Vivian into the room. She was dressed in a lovely pink dress, was wearing pearls, and had a corsage on her wrist.

"Ladies, please welcome Miss Vivian, our Rose and White Queen!" Mary Carolyn turned with a huge smile and presented a giant bouquet of pink roses, tied with a giant white bow, to Vivian as the room erupted in applause and cheers.

Vivian looked up at the young girl, taking the flowers into her arms. Her eyes took in Laney, Helen, Ida, Ava, and Jennifer, who had walked up to surround her. She seemed stunned at first.

"Me?"

"Yes, Button, the chapter has named you the Rose and White Queen. Tonight is the Senior Send-Off," Laney shared softly.

"We're having a sock hop, Button. Just for you!" Helen had never smiled so brightly.

The music started playing. Fifties music blared from speakers on the nearby table.

Button gushed, "Oh my goodness! I love a sock hop. I love this song." Devon swirled her wheelchair gently side to side after asking her if she'd like to dance. Everyone joined in.

Linda Carlisle approached Button after her dance with Devon, cautiously optimistic that her sorority sister would remember her.

"Button, I came to see you on your special night. I'm Linda Carlisle."

Button studied her closely. She nodded, smiled, and held out her hand. "My sister from Ohio."

"Yes!" Linda beamed first at Button and then at Laney, standing nearby.

Linda and Button talked for some time. She brought up special times they'd shared over the years and helped guide Button through their conversation. Linda shared with Button, "I flew in to conduct an operational visit, but also to present the chapter with a special award for academic excellence."

"And the award for academic excellence goes to Florida Alpha Chapter," Vivian announced from the podium at their sorority national convention. *She couldn't conceal her extra pride as this was her own collegiate chapter. She hugged the chapter president who had come forward to accept the award on behalf of her sisters. They smiled for a photograph.*

As Button returned to her seat at the banquet table, Linda, who was seated next to her, asked, "How is it possible that they have a chapter grade-point average of three-eight? Are they all straight-A students?"

Button replied with a smile, "Almost all."

She and Linda had become such close friends by working on a variety of national committees. They had been matched as roommates during one volunteer weekend and made that an ongoing tradition. They always tried to schedule their flights with close arrival and departure times so they could share a taxi or rental car and sneak in one last chat at the airport before boarding their flights home.

While at the airport one Sunday following a sorority meeting, several people had called Vivian by name. At first, Button shrugged it off as chance encounters with people she didn't remember from years ago. When the

TSA agent in security said, "Have a nice flight, Vivian," Linda looked at her probingly. Button replied, "He probably just read my boarding pass."

But, as they took a seat in the airport restaurant and the waiter said, "What can I get you, Vivian," Linda looked up in surprise. She suddenly burst into a cackling laugh. "You forgot to take off your nametag after the meeting!"

Vivian looked down to see her name in big block letters on the white paper nametag adhered to her blouse. Ripping it off and wadding it up like trash, Button jokingly said, "And I felt so popular!"

Devon asked, "Miss Vivian, how does it feel to be the most popular girl at the dance?" Button smiled wide at Devon, dimples showing.

The Senior Send-Off was a tremendous success. Linda and Laney made it an extra point to thank Mary Carolyn, Claire, and other collegiate sisters for their tremendous act of kindness in planning such a thoughtful night and naming Vivian the Rose and White Queen.

Claire told Laney privately, "I think she got a little confused because she held her roses in her arms and said, 'I'd like to thank the judges for this honor.'"

Laney smiled and winked at Claire. "Well, she was Miss South Carolina, you know."

They danced, drank punch, ate yummy snacks, and even sang to the oldies. The night was like a dream to Vivian.

It was, indeed, a special night they would all long remember.

All, that is, except Button.

Nick

When a College Boy Likes Pizza Too

Lottie walked into the kitchen mid-morning on Friday in frustration that her growling stomach had not allowed her to sleep later. She looked like she'd just rolled out of bed in hot pink floral pajama shorts and a bright yellow, movie-themed T-shirt. She had thrown her long dark hair into a messy bun on top of her head.

She hit the button on the electric teapot near the stove and spied her favorite blueberry muffins on the counter. She smiled knowing Nannie had made them that morning just for her. She loved that lady! Lottie made a mental note to make Nannie's favorite snickerdoodles soon.

A small sound from the kitchen table alerted her to the fact that she had company. She turned to see her dad sipping coffee, staring into his laptop computer screen. He was dressed in a blue short-sleeve polo shirt and jeans, a little casual for his normal Friday. His once-sandy blond hair was now streaked with silver, but he was still quite handsome. Nannie claimed he looked like his father. He always acted and dressed professionally, proud of his position as a regional manager for a pharmaceutical company.

"Good morning, Dad."

"Good morning, Charlotte," he said, slightly distracted.

"Where is Mom? Where's Nannie?"

"Groceries and Aunt Button." He was succinct with his answers, never looking up.

Lottie put hot water and a tea bag in her favorite red and white polka dot mug. She served herself a muffin, taking a bite as she put her breakfast on the kitchen island. She stood to eat, staring at her father.

"Did you get a muffin?"

"Yes."

"What are you doing today?"

"Work stuff."

"What kind of work stuff?"

"Charlotte, are you not supposed to be in school this morning?"

Had he looked up, he would have seen a half incredulous and half disappointed look on his daughter's face. "No, I finished finals yesterday and graduate tomorrow night. I imagine most fathers know that about their daughters," she offered after swallowing a sip of tea.

He finally looked up, less from the context of her words and more from the tone. He studied her over the top of his glasses. "What are your plans for today then? Shopping with Mom?" He went right back to his work, not waiting for a reply.

Lottie took another bite of her muffin because she didn't really think he was all that interested in her answer. But frustration and resentment had been festering inside her for a while. They were alone together, which was rare, and Lottie made a purposefully snarky reply, "I have a job. Today is my first day. I'm super excited." She paused momentarily. "And again, we're back to the 'most fathers would know that about their daughters' comment."

Bobby jerked his head up from his computer, took off his reading glasses, and glared at his daughter. "You have something on your mind this morning, Charlotte?"

"Ding, ding, ding! Yes, Dad, I do. I really, really do!" She walked over to the table, standing a few feet from him with her hands on her hips. "I have a job this summer. I am working at the community theater as an assistant to the stage manager. I've been talking to them for months after my drama teacher, Mr. Simon, said they were looking for summer help. I was on pins and needles hoping I'd get it since March! I have talked about this repeatedly in that living room," she said pointing. "You were there."

Taking a mere second to breathe, she continued, her voice even louder, "I found out two weeks ago that I got the job, I squealed and danced around the living room. Nannie jumped out of her chair; she and mom hugged me. You hugged me. You even said 'Congratulations, Charlotte'! So Dad, were you not really paying attention that night, just off-handedly patting me on the head so that I'd stop interrupting whatever it was you were more interested in, or do you have Alzheimer's like Aunt Button? From where I'm standing there is no third option, but if you have one, I'd love to hear it!" Lottie crossed her arms and waited.

Bobby's first reaction was to send her to her room and ground her until she was twenty-one. She was way out of line. The tone of her voice was incredibly rude, but her words gave him pause. He closed his laptop. "I do not appreciate being yelled at by you, young lady. You have thrown a spear at me this morning, which I do not deserve. I *do* know and am proud of you about this new job. I recall that evening in the living room with complete clarity, and my congratulations was sincere. I apologize that I did not realize you wrapped up senior year yesterday and your job starts today, but I am slammed to finalize the paperwork on more than twenty performance reviews for staff with an imminent deadline of end-of-business today. I thought I might find peace and quiet and an uninterrupted opportunity in my home to get this done. I see I was mistaken!"

Lottie felt completely deflated. "Dad, of course you can work in peace and quiet in *your* home. I appreciate that your congratulations was sincere but shouldn't you feel concerned that your only child feels a huge disconnect with you? Shouldn't you be freaked out that I assumed you didn't really care?"

"Good Lord, Charlotte! Of course, I love you!"

"I didn't say *love*, Dad. I said care. Deeply involved, fascinated even. When was the last time you and I did anything together, just the two of us? When was the last time you did anything with Nannie?"

Bobby seemed flabbergasted. "Charlotte, I work very hard."

Lottie raised her hand to cut him off. "You do, Dad. You work very hard. You are a great provider, and I appreciate every single thing you've done for me. I'm just asking you to do something *with* me. I'm leaving for college in a couple of months, after all. And, call me Lottie sometimes, like you used to before you changed. It's endearing!" She all but shouted the last two words, made her exit stage left, and never looked back at her dad sitting dumbfounded at the kitchen table.

She showered, dressed, and prepared to leave the house as quickly as possible. Hearing a piece of her mom's advice in her head, she took an extra five minutes to blow dry her hair, leaving it down, and put on a smidge of makeup. Work was casual, but she opted for a cute top, jeans, and sandals. She'd see how casual everyone else was before she dug out her favorite T-shirts and sneakers.

She didn't have work until one o'clock, but hoping to avoid another confrontation with her dad, decided to leave extra early. Upon discovering the kitchen, a dad-free zone, she decided to take a minute to leave the kitchen spotless, thus avoiding a confrontation with her mom. She quickly threw out the cold tea she'd left on the kitchen island. The rest of the muffin she'd left behind was now in a baggie with her name on it for tomorrow. She placed her plate and tea cup in the dishwasher and wiped down the countertop, leaving no evidence of crumbs. The kitchen looked perfect other than some work papers and laptop on the kitchen table. There was still no sign of her dad.

As Lottie got into her car, the hand-me-down Nannie had given her when she quit driving, she realized she'd never yelled at her dad like that. Her mom had, of course, plenty of times. She'd sometimes felt sorry for him, but now wondered if her mom was forced to do so to get his attention. She had so many happy memories with her dad; he was so much fun and the calm after the storm that was often her mother. But, she'd realized something recently about her mom. She was a super-passionate person who really cared about her family and wanted the very best for her daughter. She just came across a little annoying sometimes; her neat freak tendencies were more than infuriating.

Lottie began to notice little things, comments really, that suddenly seemed less pushy and demanding and more like common-sense tidbits. She realized her mom gave great advice—she just gave it as she thought of it, not as Lottie asked for it. Little comments, such as "Don't wash a red shirt in hot water with your white underwear," "Jeans aren't appropriate for a job interview," or even "It's dangerous to mix bleach and ammonia when you're cleaning" were important things to know and not readily picked up in school.

She sighed. It was so weird, but she was seeing her mother in a different light. If only her mom would stop insisting she attend Redding College here in town. She'd even suggested Lottie live at home her freshman year. *Not happening, Mom!*

It was really the addition of Nannie into their home that gave Lottie a fresh set of eyes. She'd always believed her dad and grandmother were very close, but he hadn't slowed down nor taken much time to really spend with his mother. Lottie had not realized how dismissive he was of her until she saw him acting the same way toward Nannie.

A few things had changed for the better. Lottie was spending more time in the living room and kitchen since Nannie had moved in, whether it was to watch television, play games, do puzzles, or bake something.

She wanted all of them to enjoy those things together, and her mom was onboard for the most part. Her dad always passed with a smile saying, "I'll skip this time, but you ladies have fun." How did he not get the fact that she was going to college soon and Nannie . . . well, she was not getting any younger. How many next times did he think he was going to get? Lottie didn't really want to think about that. But, being at Enduring Grace with Button had really opened her eyes. So much could change in one year.

As she pulled her car into the Enduring Grace parking lot, Lottie looked at the front door and wondered if Nannie was inside with Button. She hadn't made a conscious decision to drive here; her car just seemed to make that choice on its own. It made sense, though, to give Nannie fair warning about the argument with her dad.

Thanks to a tip from Jamie, Lottie found Nannie, Button, and Ida in the game room. They were playing the card game Go Fish. Nannie and Button appeared to be a team. Ida had just asked, "Do you have any threes?" Lottie pulled up a chair next to Ida and asked, "Can I be on your team?"

Laney and Ida looked up in surprise. "Lottie, what a nice surprise! Yes, please be on my team," Ida offered.

"Hi, sweet girl. Is something bothering you?" Laney asked the question but she already knew the answer. Lottie wouldn't be here otherwise. This wasn't a social call.

Laney selected a three card from Button's hand. "Give this three to Ida."

Button handed the card to Lottie with a smile.

Lottie handed the card to Ida, leaned over to glance at her hand, and said, "Do you have any queens?"

Laney leaned over to whisper to Button, who leaned forward and said, "Go fish!"

"Do you have any tens? Lottie, what's going on?" Laney figured she could multitask.

"Go fish. I yelled at dad this morning and wanted to give you a heads up. Do you have any aces?"

"Go fish. What did he do to upset you? Do you have any sevens?"

Ida pulled two sevens out of her hand and slid them to Laney. "Shoot!"

Laney helped Button put the cards in her hand. "Any kings?"

Lottie replied, "Go fish. I just got pissed off when he frustratingly asked why I wasn't in school today as I attempted to have a pleasant conversation with him over blueberry muffins and tea. Thanks for the muffins, by the way. Do you have any threes?"

Laney sighed. "Just drew it." She gave the card to Button who happily shared it with Lottie. "Happy to make you muffins. It sounds like your dad deserved it."

Lottie shrugged while Ida inquired with a smile, "Do you have any fours?"

Button sweetly replied, "Go fish" at Laney's prompt.

Ida drew a card and smiled. She had them now.

Laney looked back at Button's hand. "Any sevens?"

"Go fish. How about tens?" Ida was still grinning.

Laney said, "Can you believe that, Button? They get all of our tens!"

Ida put her cards on the table. "That's the game!"

After talking for a minute or two more, Laney suggested, "Ida, why don't you take Button into the dining room, and I'll join you for lunch in just a minute."

"Of course. Are you hungry, Button? I wonder what they are serving today."

Ida thanked Lottie for coming and kissed her on the cheek. As she and Button walked away, Laney asked her granddaughter, "Do you want me to talk to him?"

"No. I just wanted to give you a heads up. I texted Mom before I even left the house, but you aren't great about reading text messages, so I made a quick detour on my way to the theater. I didn't want either of you walking into the mess I started this morning."

Laney nodded. She reached over and squeezed Lottie's hand. "You know, I said he probably deserved your anger, but go a little easy on him. He didn't have his father here to spend time with him, to raise him. It's not an excuse for his behavior but maybe an explanation and a guide going forward. Sometimes pulling gently works better than pushing forcefully."

Lottie nodded slowly. "Thanks, Nannie. I knew you'd have the best advice. My car was so smart to stop here on my way to work." She hugged Nannie. "I'll see you at home tonight. I need to grab a little lunch and be on my way for my first day at the theater. I love you."

"I love you too, sweet pea!"

Lottie blew a kiss to Nannie from the doorway and mouthed *thank you.*

A few minutes later, Lottie pulled through her favorite chicken fingers place. She took her lunch and parked at the community theater about twenty minutes early. She ate her lunch, responded to some friends' texts and social media posts, and was brushing her hair and putting on a little lip gloss when a black SUV pulled into the lot. A really, really cute, dark-haired guy in a pop culture T-shirt, jeans, and black sunglasses got out of the car and walked toward the entrance. Lottie was so glad he never glanced her way because he would have seen her sitting there with her mouth hanging open. She'd never seen a guy like him before.

Lottie entered the building a minute later to find the stage manager, Carson, talking to the cute guy. "Hi, Carson," she said with a friendly, but uncharacteristically shy smile.

"Charlotte. Hello, happy to see you again. Allow me to introduce you to my other assistant, Nicholas. We'll all be working together this summer. He is a theater major in Orlando and is home for the summer."

Nicholas turned toward Charlotte, reaching out to shake her hand and said, "Nice to meet you. Please call me Nick."

"You can call me Lottie." She put her hand in his and thought, *Orlando for the win*!

Work was so much fun it felt unfair to call it work. She and Nick really hit it off, but he'd been assigned to something lighting related, and she didn't see him as she wrapped up her day with Carson. She thanked him for her job for about the tenth time, grabbed her purse, and made her way outside. She was about halfway to her car when she heard her name.

"Hey, Lottie. Wait up!"

She turned to see Nick jogging toward her. "Oh, hi, Nick," she said, trying to be nonchalant.

"Um, listen, I was just thinking, with everyone in the theater being much older than us, maybe you wouldn't mind a new friend or something. Carson told you I'm home for the summer, but truthfully, I'm crashing on my brother's couch to have this opportunity before I go back for sophomore year in Orlando in the fall. My parents live in Atlanta. I don't know anyone here except my brother. Would you be interested in getting some pizza?"

Lottie smiled. Boy, could he talk. Lucky for him, she could not only keep up but she might be able to out-talk him. "Right now?"

Nick nodded.

"OK, sure, I like pizza. Have you ever eaten at Bill's Italian? I know Bill's sounds dreadfully un-Italian, but they make, in my expert opinion, the best pizza in town."

"Sounds perfect! Would you like to leave your car here and ride with me? You can give me directions and then I can bring you back here for your car. I promise I am an upstanding citizen and safe driver," said Nick.

Lottie sort of heard her mom's voice in her head muttering about never getting into a stranger's car, but this was Nick, co-worker, new friend. "OK. I can be co-pilot or maybe it's navigator."

"Navigator," Nick said. "My dad's a former pilot. Much to his dismay, I love stage productions more than airplanes."

They talked all the way to Bill's Italian. She had to laugh when he jokingly accused her of giving *girl* directions. She had told him to turn right just past her favorite clothing store and left at the street before the entrance to the mall.

"Excuse me, pilot's son. Turn east on Floyd Street in two blocks and then turn north again on Mason Street in four blocks. Better?"

Nick laughed. He pulled in front of Bill's Italian and parked the car. "Perfect!"

She opened the car door to let herself out. She didn't want him to think that she thought this was a date. She didn't. It wasn't. They had just met. He was desperate for a friend in an unknown town. She muttered to herself, "Keep telling yourself that, Charlotte."

The pizza was fabulous and the company even better. Nick was so easy to talk to, sharing openly about himself.

"So, that's why I chose Florida College of Theater and Arts," Nick explained. "First, to avoid flunking out as an engineering major at my dad's alma mater and second, to hopefully succeed in stage management, maybe get to New York theater someday. I also think it would be cool to learn projection mapping and other cool technology that amusement parks use in fireworks shows and productions." Nick paused, picked up his soda, and took a sip. "Enough about me. Tell me more about you. Are you an acting major? Vocal music performance? Stage management? How do you like going to Redding College here?"

Lottie's stomach plummeted. She looked away and rubbed her lips together, thinking. Why wouldn't he assume she was in college, his same age? *Scrap!* This was going to be their only date; correction, their only non-date outing for pizza. She had to be honest with him.

"I'm graduating from high school tomorrow night. I plan on being an acting major in Orlando in the fall. I haven't finalized all the paper work, but that's my plan."

Nick simply asked, "How old are you?"

"Seventeen. How old are you?"

"Eighteen. But I'll be nineteen on July 15."

"I'll be eighteen on August 15. Just one month later." Lottie stopped talking, but wondered to herself, *if he is just a year older than me, why is he acting weird all of a sudden?*

It got rather quiet at the table. As they were contemplating their next words, a deep voice interrupted. "Nick?"

Nick looked up to see his big brother standing near their table with a really cute girl with long black hair. He assumed this must be the Payton his brother was looking forward to meeting tonight. "Devon?"

"I didn't realize you had plans tonight." Devon turned toward Payton, explaining, "This is my little brother, Nick." Looking at Nick, he shared, "Let me introduce you to Payton Yun."

"Hi! It's great to meet you." Payton said.

"Nice to meet you. This is my co-worker, Lottie Walsh," he explained.

They were in the middle of greeting each other when another voice, a female one, interrupted and said, "Lottie?"

Turning slightly in her seat, Lottie turned toward the voice she instantly recognized. "Hey, Jen!"

Jen and Jake looked from Lottie to Nick and back again. Lottie took the hint. "This is Nick Nyland from the community theater. We both started working there today. He moved here recently to live with his brother, Devon, who you apparently know, and since he doesn't have a ton of friends yet, I brought him to Bill's for the best pizza in town. Nick, this is Jennifer, my honorary big sister, and her fiancé, Jake."

Jake put his hand on Lottie's shoulder. "Bill's is the best!" He then leaned over and shook Nick's hand. Realizing they were congregating in the aisle, Jake steered Jen toward their booth.

"You kids have fun." Jen looked back over her shoulder at Lottie and grinned as she continued to their table.

Devon said, "Yes, you kids have fun. Nice to meet you, Lottie. Nick, see you later." With a slight wave and a smile from Payton, they joined Jen and Jake to order dinner.

Lottie forced a smile at Nick while her mind grudgingly processed a couple of things. The only thing worse than being called a *kid*, twice, was being on a nondate with a cute guy who introduced you as his *co-worker*.

And then she had a happier thought, remembering Nannie's advice that morning about her dad. She obviously wouldn't *push* the idea on him, but maybe, just maybe, she could *slowly, gently pull* Nick toward the idea of a real date. And that made Lottie grin.

Henry

When a Man Is Dreamy

"What's your problem?" Helen yelled at the driver who honked at her as she pulled into the Enduring Grace parking lot. She'd had her blinker on indicating she was turning right, for heaven's sake!

She was in her car alone. Not that she would have behaved differently if she'd had a car full of friends, but Laney and Ida would have nagged at her about road rage or something ridiculous. Luckily, Laney had chosen, because they were closer to her house, to ride with Ida and Ava. They were meeting for a Monday lunch date with Button.

Helen really loved Monday and cherished these luncheon opportunities. They paid very little for a nice meal and their expenses went straight to an account they'd arranged long ago with Jeannie in the office. Laney managed the account and they each paid their fair share. They wouldn't have set this plan in place otherwise.

Helen found a parking spot right up front and made her way inside where the cool air conditioning greeted her. As she stood in the foyer with her head down to swap her sunglasses for the everyday ones in her glasses case, a deep voice rumbled, "Good afternoon, Helen."

Startled, Helen looked up quickly and felt a little off balance. A warm hand gently touched her elbow to steady her.

"Good afternoon, Henry," she stammered a little. "I didn't see you." Helen always seemed to run into him on Mondays and Wednesdays.

"Easy there," he said kindly. "Are you blind as a bat without your glasses like me?"

"I'm not sure I'd say that. I just had my head down trying to find my glasses case in my purse and was trying to juggle two pairs of glasses without dropping them. I have sunglasses and everyday glasses." Why did she feel like she was rambling? Looking behind her to the clear glass exit doors, she asked, "Are you on your way out?"

"No, I was just stretching my legs a bit. I'm about to make the living room loop. If you're heading to the dining room for lunch, it would be my honor to escort you."

Henry extended his arm to Helen like a gallant, debonair gentleman of yesteryear. She froze.

"I don't bite. I promise."

"Well, of course you don't," Helen said as she took his arm. He started the promenade toward the other side of the living room.

"How is your friend Vivian doing?" He looked down at her face. "Good, I hope."

"She is a conundrum," Helen confessed. "One day she is fairly cognizant of everything and the next she is confused, forgetful."

"That must be very hard. Dementia is challenging. I had a close friend with Alzheimer's and . . . well, again, it's very difficult."

"Thank you. It is. And exceedingly sad. It's painful to lose someone you love slowly."

"And suddenly. Loss is just plain hard. My wife died of a stroke very suddenly several years ago. Are you widowed as well?"

Helen paused.

"Too personal?" Henry asked as they stopped walking.

"No."

"No to *widowed* or no to *too personal*?"

"I was divorced forty-six years ago after being unhappily married for just over ten years. I have no contact with my ex-husband, but last I heard he was still living." Helen looked away from Henry rather baffled that she had just shared that with him. What was the matter with her today? She felt off, but continued her walk with him.

"And you never remarried?

"No."

"My wife and I married very young. We were high school sweethearts, barely eighteen years old. I remember looking at my son when he turned eighteen and couldn't fathom him being a married man at that age. Or my daughter, for that matter. My wife and I had just celebrated our fiftieth anniversary when she died at only sixty-eight years old. That was fourteen years ago. Her name was Virginia." Henry glanced at Helen. *Was he talking too much, sharing too much?*

Helen looked at Henry, studying his face for a moment. "You look very young for eighty-two."

Henry smiled. "And you look very young for . . . ?"

Helen answered, "Eighty-one."

Henry nodded. They continued their slow walk, talking easily, but arrived quickly at the entrance to the dining room. She glanced toward their usual table to find Laney, Ida, and Ava staring at her, or rather her and Henry. She gave them a stern look, thanked Henry for the escort and excused herself to join her friends for lunch.

"I hope to see you again, Helen," Henry said with a little bow. He stood straight and tall, smiled at her friends in the dining room, and walked in the opposite direction toward the residence wings.

Helen watched him walk away for a second and then entered the dining room to join her friends. "Hello," she said, more chipper than usual.

"Who was that?" Of course Laney would jump head first into Helen's business.

"Henry."

"Is Henry a resident here?"

"Yes, Laney."

"Where did you meet him?" Ida chimed in.

"Here. Well, specifically, today I met him by the front door. Previously, I met him very briefly on my birthday and spoke to him again at movie night one evening with Button. We were watching a Cary Grant and Doris Day movie, and Button thought she was Doris Day. Anyway, it made us laugh. I've run into him briefly a few times when I've been here for lunch or to visit Button."

Ava shared her opinion enthusiastically. "That's who he looks like! He looks a little like Cary Grant with gray hair. Maybe he is making an effort to run into you."

"I doubt it. Why would he?"

Ava glared at Helen. "Seriously, Aunt Helen! When you're not being crabby, you're really quite a doll. Have you even looked in a mirror?"

Helen wasn't sure whether to be offended or flattered. "Ava, it's so lovely to have you join us today," she replied sarcastically.

As Helen stood contemplating Ava's comment, Angela entered the dining room with Button, who looked extra summery in green pants, a floral short-sleeved top, and a pale pink lipstick. Angela always went the extra mile to help Button look spiffy on Mondays.

"Here you are. Enjoy your lunch, sweet ladies," Angela said. She passed wheelchair duties to Helen, who took the role gratefully. She pushed Button up to her place at the table. In Helen's opinion, it was time to change the subject. That was more than enough talk about a handsome man she hardly knew. *Did she just think of Henry as handsome?*

Helen wondered if she was coming down with a cold or something. Maybe she should excuse herself and go home, but Button looked so happy to see them and, truthfully, Helen couldn't come up with a single sniffle to support her hypothesis.

Lunch was a delightful chicken salad, pita crackers, and assortment of seasonal fruit. Button looked at her plate, declaring it her favorite lunch. "And we can ask for ice cream or sherbet for dessert."

Laney laughed. "Well, I don't know. Helen might want to watch her figure!"

Ida and Ava joined Laney in a little lighthearted laughter at Helen's expense.

"Button, do you think Cary Grant is a fine-looking gentleman?" Laney smiled as she posed the question.

Button replied, "He's dreamy!"

Ida quipped, "Well, I agree, but I'm not certain about Helen."

"Button, dear, please ignore them," Helen said sweetly. "I know I am!"

Laney leaned back in her chair and all-out grinned. She knew Helen might say she was ignoring them, but she was plotting their demise. Laney did not care one iota; she was going to push hard on this opportunity for Helen to make a nice, new friend. Well, assuming he was nice and Helen-worthy.

Laney made a mental note to learn more about Henry. She couldn't help but wonder if Helen, despite her objections, might actually enjoy a smidge of attention. Lord knew, she really deserved a kind man. Helen's ex-husband, Stanley, had convinced her he was her Mr. Right, but he'd won her heart with lies and deceptions. His professional goals never seemed to materialize. He couldn't hold down a job, blaming a series of lousy bosses or horrible co-workers. He really just wanted to drink beer, play poker, and sleep wherever and with whomever he wanted.

Laney recalled the glorious day Helen finally served him with divorce papers. She was standing on Helen's front porch with Ida and Charlie in case Helen needed them. Stanley was furious; he yelled at her and blamed her for everything. It hadn't taken much time before Charlie intervened with Ida and Laney standing right behind him. Despite knowing that Stanley was wrong and solely responsible for their sham of a marriage, some of his poisonous comments broke through Helen's defenses and she swore off dating. She declared all men not worth the effort, closing herself off from potential happiness.

Of course, Laney had done much the same when Robert died. She understood Helen's sense of loss over the dreams attached to her marriage. Unlike Helen, however, Laney had been open to having someone else in her life. It just never happened. She had Bobby and eventually Judith and Lottie. Helen was alone, and that didn't seem right to her.

Laney's attention was drawn back to her friends at the table as she heard Ida share an unexpected comment, "And then Jen said not only did Devon and Payton seem to have fun on their Friday night date, but so did Lottie." Ida nodded her head at her friends, proud of herself for having gossip to share; not that she'd call it gossip.

Laney leaned forward from her relaxed position in her chair and asked, "My Lottie?"

"Yes, she was at Bill's Italian with a boy. Jen said he was very cute! Did Lottie not tell you she had a date?"

"No, but she wasn't home very much this past weekend. She started her summer job," Laney admitted.

Ida had more information to dish out to her friends. "Jen also said that Devon knew the boy."

Ava stepped in to clarify, "She said he is Devon's little brother."

"Isn't it a small world?" Ida asked. "So many new relationships to explore."

Helen looked up from her plate to see them looking at her with that look on their faces. She knew that look. She rolled her eyes and said, "Button, how about some ice cream?"

After dessert, Helen offered to take Button back to her room for a visit until she fell asleep for a nap. It was a vicious cycle as Button's insomnia led to her need for a nap, which left her less sleepy at night. They tried to keep her nap time to an hour or so. They once made the extreme effort to keep Button from taking a nap, but instead of it leading to a peaceful night's sleep, it led to a complete sundowning meltdown. They vowed to never try that again.

Laney thanked Ava for coming to see Button and sent her and Ida on without her. She asked Helen for a ride home and told her she would meet her shortly in Button's room. She wanted to stay a little longer. She didn't tell Helen, but she was on a mission to investigate a few things, and she hoped Devon was on duty. She found him right away at the nurses' station.

"Hi Devon! How are you today?"

"Miss Laney, I'm doing very well. How are you? Did you have lunch with Miss Vivian?"

"I did. Helen and Ida, too, of course, and Ava joined us. Speaking of Ida and Ava, they had some interesting tidbits to share at lunch today."

"No doubt about my date," Devon said with a chuckle. "Never fear, Miss Laney, it went well. I'm trying to let a couple of days go by to not smother her, but I have high hopes Payton will agree to go out with me again."

"That's lovely, dear."

After a brief pause, she continued, "Ava also mentioned that you all saw my granddaughter, Lottie. She was with a boy they think is your brother."

"Ah, I see. Yes, my brother, Nick, met your granddaughter, Lottie, on Friday at the community theater where they both are working this summer. He is here from Atlanta and staying with me. Apparently, she took pity on the lonely kid and introduced him to our finest pizza establishment in town. Don't worry, Nick is a great guy."

Devon picked up some files, preparing to get back to work.

"Thank you, Devon. If he is anything like his big brother, I'm sure he is an outstanding young man. One last question if you can spare another second?

"Sure."

"Are you familiar with a man who lives here named Henry?"

"There are a couple of men named Henry."

"He is very dapper and looks a bit like Cary Grant, if you are familiar with the actor."

"Perfect description! Yes, he is a resident in the retirement apartment wing. He doesn't live in this wing with skilled nursing. I don't know him well."

"Thank you, Devon. Sorry to delay you from your duties."

"You didn't, Miss Laney. I was taking a brief break. I believe Jamie knows more about Henry if you'd like to be introduced."

"Oh. No, it's not like that. He was talking to Helen earlier, and I was just curious about him."

Devon smiled and nodded. "OK then. I'll see you soon."

Laney turned from the nurses' station in the direction of Button's room only to find Helen leaning against the wall, arms crossed with a furious expression on her face.

A few minutes later, Laney sat in the rocking chair next to Button's bed, crying. She would never forget how Helen looked at her, with both anger and disappointment. Laney had tried to talk to her, to explain, but Helen walked away, slowing only slightly to say, "Button is napping. Find another ride home!" Laney couldn't very well chase after her.

Beside the fact that it was highly inappropriate to make a scene, she couldn't run. Her body wouldn't let her.

"Why are you crying?" Laney looked up at Button, holding a tissue to her nose. She shook her head.

Button repeated her question. "Laney, tell me why you're crying."

The use of her name surprised her. It had been so long since she felt Button was truly talking with her, with *Laney*, her big sister and best friend. It made her cry even harder.

She tried to explain while crying, "Button, I have upset Helen horribly. She is very angry with me."

"What did you do?"

"Earlier today, before lunch, a charming man named Henry who lives here spoke to her. I noticed them walking around the living room together. I thought it looked so right, so wonderful for Helen to have someone be kind to her. He seemed very interested in her. She even admitted that she keeps running into him on Mondays and Wednesdays. That seems like a man who is interested, don't you think?"

Button nodded.

"As much as I want that happiness for Helen, I feel protective of her. I asked Devon at the nurses' station if he knew anything about Henry. Helen overheard me. She stalked off, furious with me for butting into her business. I'm upset that I hurt her just now. I'm upset that she may never forgive me." Laney started crying harder and squeaked out the words, "What if my good intentions to ensure that Henry is worthy of Helen makes her avoid him now?"

"Big sister is protective."

"How do I fix this with Helen?"

"Say you are sorry."

"What if this time I've gone too far? What if I've hurt our friendship? I couldn't bear it if she felt like she couldn't trust me or didn't want to see me much anymore."

"That won't happen. John says we aren't meant to be separated from the people we love. He says our souls are made for eternity and that's why saying goodbye feels so horrible, so wrong."

Laney stopped crying as she stared at Button. "John keeps telling you this?"

"Yes."

Laney leaned in close to Button, studying her. She was completely lucid and in the moment. Laney looked around the room, suddenly wondering if angels were honestly visiting Button. She wasn't sure she believed that; she wasn't sure she didn't.

"Just say you're sorry."

"I will, Button. I will say it, over and over, until she forgives me."

From the doorway, Helen replied, "Good Lord, please don't. I don't want to hear you rambling on forever. You're forgiven. I am going to lay down an unbendable rule, however. Never do it again! I know you have a big sister complex, Laney, but give it a rest. If Henry and I develop a friendship, I will tell you when I want to tell you, but you are not to get involved for even a second. Do you agree to these terms?"

Laney got up from her chair and walked to Helen, who met her in the middle of the room. Laney hugged her and repeated, "Yes, I'm so sorry" several times.

"Button, can you believe how nosy she is?" Helen joked about Laney. They turned to find Button, once again, sound asleep.

Bobby

When Fathers Don't Necessarily Know Best

"Mom, keep an eye on the weather this afternoon," Bobby suggested as he and Laney were seated at the kitchen table together. She couldn't exactly say they were having breakfast *together* as he was sipping his coffee while reading the news from his laptop. He had not even looked at her beyond a glance.

"I'm sorry, dear, did you say something?"

He looked up at her. *Much better*, she thought. "I said we have an almost one hundred percent chance of severe thunderstorms today, and I'd like for you to keep an eye on the weather. It wouldn't be safe to get caught out in a storm. I'm not sure what your plans are later, but I want you to be careful."

"That's very kind of you, son. Why don't you ask me about my plans for today?"

Bobby cocked his head sideways, looking at his mom. "OK. Tell me about your plans."

"It's Button's birthday, and the whole gang is having a little private party in the game room tonight at seven. We've been given permission to bring in a birthday cake from Karen's Cake Company. With the theater closed on Tuesdays, Lottie is off today, and she is going to help me pick up the cake and decorate a little for the party. Jen is bringing a giant birthday balloon, and Helen has some paper plates and napkins. I mentioned it to you and Judith last week. We'd love for you to come."

"Mom."

Laney interrupted. "Bobby. Do not disappoint me and decline. You may be the head of this family, but I proudly and deservedly hold the title of matriarch. As such, I am simply going to say this—I believe tonight will be Button's last birthday with us. When your dad died, she became a second mother to you. She has seen you through good times and bad and loved you with all her heart. She deserves your time and attendance tonight!"

"I know, Mom. I love her too. Very much. I cherish those memories and prefer to think of her as the bubbly, happy, brilliant, and fun second mother she is in my mind."

"Well, that's sweet. But it's also a bunch of crap!"

"Mother!"

"Robert Bradley, life is not always happy and fun; often, it is the complete opposite. You have to accept situations that are in God's hands and honestly deal with all of life's circumstances head on. Button's situation is heartbreaking, son, but you need to be there for her. I'd like to think you will do the same for me, but I'm beginning to wonder."

She put up her hand to stop him from speaking. "Let me finish. Lottie was right to demand your attention the other day. If this family were your company, son, you'd be losing your shirt. No investment, no gain." Laney stood up from the table, tall and proud. "Man up, Bobby! You're blowing it!" She stared at him intently for a second and then departed the kitchen like the queen leaving her throne room.

A few minutes later, Bobby was still contemplating his mother's words when Judith joined him at the kitchen table with a cup of tea. Her light brown hair was pulled back from her face, and she wore glasses this morning instead of her usual contacts. She somehow looked perfectly put together even when casual. She was scrolling through her cell phone and mentioned, "It looks like we can expect severe storms later today."

Bobby looked up in surprise and studied her at length. He suddenly and unexpectedly felt ashamed of himself. "Have we been reduced to talking about the weather?"

Judith looked at him in confusion. "What do you mean?"

"It's something Mom and Lottie said recently. They have both called me out over not being attentive or engaged. Mom just basically said I'm not being the person this family needs."

"I see."

"Do you agree? You haven't said anything."

"Actually, I have. For a couple of years."

"What?"

"I'm sorry, Bobby, but it's true. I have been conducting a science experiment of sorts with you for a long time. I've discovered your tendency to ignore and redirect conversations and situations to fit your narrative. For a time, it worked for me to pick a fight with you. At least I had your attention. But that isn't working so well anymore. I've asked you repeatedly what is bothering you, troubling you; you just push me away."

Bobby stood from the table. Judith thought he was going to stomp off in anger. Instead, he refilled his coffee, brought her a splash of warm water for her tea, and sat back down.

He took a deep breath. "I'm so sorry, Judith. I have tried very hard to be a good provider, a good husband and father. We were older when we married, both career-oriented. We never talked that much about having kids when we were unexpectedly blessed by Charlotte. She is the best thing that ever happened to us. I thank God for her every day."

Judith nodded emphatically.

Bobby continued, "We bought this big house when Mom agreed to move in with us. I still believe it is better for her than living alone and assisted living is beyond both her and our means. When she sold her home, she gave us the money for the down payment on this one."

Judith gasped. "Are you kidding me?"

"No, I'm not. And now I find myself, rather suddenly it seems, at fifty-eight, and things at work are not good. Managers my age are being passed over for promotion. Apparently, I've gone from being a seasoned professional with more than thirty-five years of experience to an old fogey! I think I've reached my earning potential despite giving it everything I've got. We've put money in Charlotte's college fund since she was a baby, but I didn't know then that we'd need about $200,000. We have roughly half that. We have a decent retirement account, but it's not enough should I be pushed out of work before I'm at least seventy. If we take a loan for Charlotte's college education, they'll expect payment until I'm eighty-two unless we can really throw extra money at that debt. And apparently I make too much money for Charlotte to be considered for anything beyond a merit-based scholarship."

Judith took in a huge breath as if she'd forgotten to breathe.

"And, we bought this house when the market was higher than it is now. We can't sell it for what we've put into it."

Bobby paused and stared at his wife.

Judith sat silently with tears rolling down her cheeks. "You've been burdened with financial concerns, worried about your job?"

"Yes. I should have been honest with you, but it all just seemed to come off the rails in the last couple of years."

Judith asked, "But you love me?"

"What? I tell you all that and you ask if I love you?"

"Well, do you?"

"One hundred and ten percent, yes!"

Judith stood up and walked around the table. She sat on Bobby's lap and threw her arms around him. Her soft crying brought tears to his own eyes.

"I love you, Bobby. I thought I loved you way more than you loved me. I thought I was losing you." Bobby shook his head unequivocally no.

Judith smiled at him and continued, "We'll figure out the money. I have a small retirement account that has just been sitting since I left my job, which I guess I was stupid to quit. My ego got in the way of all the young designers with computer skills that I don't have. Home design has completely changed, but I'm only fifty-three. I'd love to work again if someone would give *this* old fogey a chance."

Bobby kissed her. And kissed her again. "I'm sorry. I'm so sorry!"

"Robert Bradley, as long as we love each other, we can figure out the rest."

Bobby grinned, really grinned for the first time in months.

"I don't remember the last time you used my first and middle name. Mom did that earlier, too. Oh, that reminds me," he said. "We have a birthday party to attend tonight."

Judith hugged him. "Indeed we do."

They had no idea Lottie overheard most of their conversation from the living room. She snuck quietly back to her bedroom in tears. She sat on the foot of her bed and tried to process everything she'd just heard.

After a knock on her door and a reminder from Nannie about picking up the cake, Lottie put aside her concerns to focus on Button's birthday party. She drove Nannie across town to their favorite bakery, Karen's Cake Company. They always made the most spectacular creations. Karen, the owner, had started her business in her home, but it had grown into the town's most beloved bakery. They always won the Best of the Best Award, voted on by the community.

Lottie and Laney entered to a little chime at the door. "Be with you in just a second!"

They didn't see anyone, but heard the comment come from the back. They looked around the bakery, simply charmed by the atmosphere. Soon a pretty, young twenty-something entered from the back of the store, wiping a little flour from her hands onto her bright yellow apron with the cute company logo on it. She greeted them with an infectious smile. "Hi, ladies. Are you picking up a yummy cake today?"

Lottie recognized her and said, "Oh, Hi! I'm Lottie Walsh. I met you the other day at Bill's Italian. You were with Jennifer and Jake."

She smiled even brighter. "Yes, you're right. I'm Payton Yun. It's nice to see you again."

"This is my grandmother, Laney Walsh."

"Nice to meet you. You must be here for the chocolate cake with pink icing. I've never had anyone request a cake with mini chocolate pieces on top before, but I loved making it. I hope you're pleased." She circled the display case and picked up a large box from the back counter. "See what you think."

Payton lifted the lid, and Lottie actually squealed and hugged her grandmother. "Nannie, look! Oh my goodness. It's like Button refashioned into a cake!"

Laney clasped her hands at her chest and agreed wholeheartedly. "It's perfect."

"I'm so glad you like it. My mom, Karen, owns this shop, and I had to really convince her that it wasn't crazy to go with a round, tiered cake. First, it feels a little more old-fashioned, and I have a beautiful cake stand you can borrow. Then, I wanted to incorporate a couple of pink icing layers inside the cake instead of a more traditional chocolate sheet cake with pink icing. And finally, piping the top in the swirly motion allowed me to show off the chocolate pieces on the swooping peaks of frosting."

"It is a masterpiece," Laney said. "I must have spoken to you when I called in the order about it being for my best friend's birthday. As I mentioned, she lives at Enduring Grace Assisted Living Center and is suffering from Alzheimer's. I know she will love this cake."

"Yes, I took your call. Actually, a wonderful guy I've been seeing is a nurse there. His name is Devon Nyland. You met him that night at Bill's," she said, addressing Lottie.

"Yes, I sure did. His brother, Nick, is my friend."

"I love Devon," Laney jumped in to share with Payton. "He is a wonderful, wonderful man and an angel to our Vivian."

"I mentioned to Devon that I'd received an order for a chocolate cake with pink icing for someone at Enduring Grace. He said he knew exactly who it was for and that he adored Miss Vivian. I didn't realize it was for her until he said that. I know Miss Vivian. When I was a sophomore in college, I was vice president of programs for our sorority. A national officer recommended Vivian Upton as a speaker. She was so inspiring that I still remember her. Jen, who was president that year, and I took her out to dinner after her presentation and what happened on the way home changed Jen's life forever."

"What happened?" Lottie was completely intrigued.

"Well, it was an uncharacteristically cold night. After we took Miss Vivian home on the outskirts of town, Jen suggested we get hot chocolate from the walk-up bagel place on campus. As we were just about to approach town, her headlights suddenly went out. It was pitch black outside, no streetlights at all, and we couldn't see a foot in front of us. She cautiously moved off the road and put on her hazard lights. Within a couple of minutes, a big pickup truck pulled in behind us and a gorgeous guy came to Jen's window."

Payton continued her story with Lottie and Laney's full attention. "We obviously didn't know him, so Jen lowered the window about an inch. He kindly suggested she might have blown a fuse, told us to sit tight with the doors locked, and he drove to the auto parts store to get a new fuse. He came back, fixed it, and refused to let Jen pay him for the part or his help. They swapped names, so when we got back to the house we did a little private investigative work. We found girls who knew him and reported that he was a really nice guy.

"Jen left a thank you card for him at his fraternity house but didn't see him again, that is, until the first week of graduate school. They were at the baseball stadium for a social event, and they recognized each other. Jen and Jake sat together that night at the game, started dating, and fell in love. And now they are getting married. Oh, and I am the maid of honor!"

Lottie thought that was the most romantic story ever.

Laney said, "I've never heard that story. It's really wonderful! Listen, Payton, I may be overstepping, but Devon will be at the party tonight after his shift. We will start about seven. Why don't you join us?"

"I wouldn't want to impose."

"No imposition at all," Laney insisted.

"Well, Devon did say I should at least peek in the door to see everyone's reaction to the cake. I'm sure I would be a stranger to Miss Vivian, but I definitely remember her."

Lottie suggested, "Yes, Payton, please come. Jen and Jake will be there, too. I even invited Nick. I don't know if he'll come. I just casually mentioned it because he said chocolate cake is his favorite dessert. He also really loves chocolate chip cookies and ice cream."

Laney turned to give her granddaughter an odd look and Lottie responded, "What? Is it weird that I invited him?"

Payton made a little snorting sound and pinched her lips together for a second. "Thanks, I'll be there. Would you rather I bring the cake myself? I can keep it refrigerated, plus I have a delivery van perfect for getting cakes to parties in perfect shape. We can't let the chocolate melt in this June heat. Free delivery for the birthday girl!"

"Thank you, Payton. You are a sweetheart!" Laney made a mental note to tell Devon of her extra kindness. Laney took her credit card bill, added a generous tip, and signed her name with a flourish. They agreed to meet at six thirty that evening.

"Thank you for making this so perfect for Vivian." Laney and Lottie waved to a smiling Payton as they walked out the door.

As they pulled out of the parking lot, Lottie suggested, "Decorations done and cake handled. We have a few extra minutes before we need to get home to change for the party. How about a soda?"

"Sounds great. It's so hot and humid today."

"I know, right? My sunglasses fogged up the minute I put them on as we left Karen's. Payton is so nice, isn't she?"

"She is a delightful young lady. I didn't know we were sorority sisters."

Lottie surprised Laney with her reply. "I've been thinking I might pledge here in the fall. If they were to ask me."

"You mean in Orlando."

Lottie shrugged. "I don't know."

"You are thinking about going to school here? Since when?"

"Since recently. I'm just thinking about it. I mean, Redding is a fabulous university. They have a great theater department. I know I'm kind of late, but maybe I should apply, see if I get accepted and get a scholarship."

Lottie pulled into a drive-in for a drink and parked the car. "Do you want a flavored tea, limeade, or soda?

Laney stared at her, processing the college comments.

"Nannie?"

"Medium peach-flavored tea, please."

Lottie placed the order and dug into her purse for money. "My treat. I'm a working girl now." She looked toward her grandmother, but the smile slowly faded on her face. Nannie looked entirely too serious for someone awaiting a peach tea.

Laney looked worried. "You've been talking about Orlando for a long time. You've been adamant about not going to school here so you can spread your wings. Is this about the boy you met at the theater?"

"No, of course not. I just met him and, besides, he goes to college in Orlando."

"Is it because of me? Because I need a little extra help these days and don't drive anymore?"

"No, ma'am! Although those are good points in favor of me staying here."

"Then why?"

Lottie was saved from answering the question as their drinks were being delivered. She busied herself by setting drinks in the cup holders, offering a straw to Nannie, opening her own straw, and taking a sip.

She changed the subject. "I love that Aunt Ida suggested everyone wear a pop of pink tonight in Button's honor. I mean, I'm not sure that she'll really get the significance of that, but she'll be surrounded by her favorite color. I have that hot pink sleeveless romper and nude flat sandals. What are you going to wear?"

"Lottie, I do not want you to change your college plans for me. I am so excited for you and can't wait to see all you accomplish. I will be just fine. Your mom and dad will take great care of me."

"Nannie, I know they will. I know you will be okay. I'm just having second thoughts. It's not a big deal."

"So, you just want to look at all options?"

"Exactly!" Lottie added as she headed for home, "I think you should wear your floral skirt and pink blouse."

At exactly six o'clock, Laney entered the living room to find Bobby, Judith, and Lottie dressed in splashes of pink, ready for Button's party. She smiled at them with great pride. "Bobby, I didn't know you had a tie with pink stripes. You look so handsome! Judith, you look darling in that sundress, as do you, Lottie, in that romper. Just look at my gorgeous family!"

Judith approached Laney and surprised her by enveloping her in a warm hug. "You are just lovely, and I hope tonight is very special for you, for Button."

"Thank you, Judith," Laney said, a little stunned by her daughter-in-law's compliment.

Bobby offered his mother his arm. "Shall we be off?"

Button's Birthday

When Someone Holds Your Hand

"Sorry we're late!" Jen announced as she and Jake rushed into the game room at Enduring Grace in a flurry of umbrellas and raincoats. Jen was holding a pink ribbon in her hand, while Jake carried the huge, but wet, giant pink birthday balloon that was attached to it.

"I thought this balloon was a goner! The wind is blowing so hard that the rain looks like it is coming down sideways out there," Jake joked as he tied the balloon to the leg of the table near what would be Button's place of honor. "Plus, there was a big traffic jam on Main Street. Right, honey?"

"Oh geez, you guys need to hear this," Jennifer explained, motioning for her parents, grandparents, Laney and her family, and her friend, Payton, to gather around. "So, like Jake just said, we were stuck in a long line of cars. We were going maybe five or ten miles per hour in a forty-five zone. I thought there must be construction or an accident because we could see cars ahead of us passing an obstruction in the road. But, it wasn't an obstruction. It was Aunt Helen!"

They all gasped "no" simultaneously!

"Yes!" Jake insisted. "There she was in her big blue sedan going all of five miles an hour without a care in the world," Jake said with his hands in the air. "Biggest *what-the-hell* moment I've had in a long time! Traffic on Main was backed up far behind us."

Ida tried to come to Helen's defense. "Well, it is raining."

Jennifer shook her head. "Grandma, we hit the edge of the downpour about two miles from here. It was barely sprinkling when we saw Aunt Helen. You need to get her off the road!" Jennifer was adamant.

Ida poked Charlie in the ribs as he laughed, first at Jake and Jen, and then at something Joe had muttered. She and Laney exchanged a concerned look while the rest of the room couldn't prevent their amusement at the hilarious picture Jen and Jake had just painted of Helen.

Laney interrupted, "Someone run out front and make sure she gets safely inside the building. It's raining really hard right now and she might fall."

Just as Joe had raised his hand and offered, "I'll go," Helen entered the room on the arm of her handsome Henry. At least, that's how Laney saw it. Helen was dry as a bone while Henry's gray suit had a few wet spots showing. Unbeknownst to them, Helen and Henry had seen each other a couple of times, and she had invited him to Button's party.

"Good evening, everyone!" Helen looked darling in a new, light gray dress with pink polka dots. They looked like quite the couple with Henry in a complementary gray suit, crisp white shirt, and pink-and-blue-striped tie. "For those of you who haven't met him, this is my friend, Henry."

Henry was an instant hit! He had put a twinkle back in Helen's eyes, and the group instantly adored him. He met everyone, spoke a little with each person, and seemed to feel right at home. He and Charlie appeared to enjoy getting to know each other.

Laney walked up to Helen; they stood side-by-side surveying the room, not even glancing at each other. "You look beautiful. New dress?"

"You know it is."

"It's lovely. Henry looks quite handsome."

"Yes, he does."

"I noticed he looked a little wet from the rain."

"He was at the doors as I pulled under the portico. He insisted on parking my car in the lot for me. He didn't want me to get wet."

"Oh dear."

"What?"

"He might be a keeper."

"Shut up, dear!"

Laney threw her head back and laughed. It felt like the good old days!

Everyone had gathered at the table near Payton and her birthday cake masterpiece. She was blushing at all the compliments and appreciation expressed to her for making something so special for Button. Ida interrupted from the doorway. "Everyone, Nurse Jamie just told me that Devon will be on the way with Button in another minute or two. Let's get ready to light the candles."

Payton helped place two candles, an eight and a one, next to each other in the center of the cake. She pulled out her lighter and was ready to light them when Laney gave her the signal. Jen hugged her friend and gushed over her talent. "You are amazing," she whispered with her head right next to Payton.

Although Ava had been dubbed the night's official photographer, Lottie used her phone to snap a photo of the cake and one of Jen and Payton together. She turned around and scooted closer to them to take a selfie when she spotted Nick walking into the room. She quickly took in how cute he looked in his navy pants and short sleeve blue polo. His shirt had a white collar with a large band of blue and thin line of pink. She'd mentioned the pop of pink plan so casually, and yet, here he was. *He is pretty darn perfect*, she thought as she grabbed Jen's hand and said softly, "He came!"

Lottie stepped forward to greet him with a huge smile. "Hi, I'm glad you could make it."

Nick replied, "Thanks, and sorry I'm late. I hit an unexpected slow down on Main Street. You look really pretty."

"Thank you. I wasn't sure if you'd come. I guess it's a little weird to be invited to a nursing home for someone's eighty-first birthday. I didn't really think of that. But, the cake is amazing," Lottie said, motioning to the table behind her. Jen and Payton waved at Nick, who smiled and nodded at them.

"It might be weird for some people," Nick admitted. "You know Devon is a nurse, of course, but I haven't mentioned that my mom is, too. She is a hospice director in Atlanta. I've volunteered in nursing homes a ton of times."

Lottie smiled at Nick. "Wow, that's amazing. I'm glad you feel comfortable. Button should be here in a minute. Why don't you come see the cake?"

As she and Nick made their way over to the table, a very interested Bobby did as well.

He stepped in between his daughter and her friend as if studying the pink cake. He tried to act cool, but he wasn't really pulling off the vibe. Looking at the cake, he shared, "Aunt Button will love this cake! Don't you agree, Lottie?"

She turned to her dad, her eyes wide. He'd just called her *Lottie*. After a stunned, but brief pause, she agreed, "She will love it, for sure, Dad." Leaning around Bobby to point at Nick, Lottie said, "Daddy, this is my friend, Nick Nyland. We both work at the theater. His brother, Devon, is one of Aunt Button's nurses."

Bobby and Nick faced each other and Nick reached out to shake his hand. "Nice to meet you, sir."

Bobby returned the handshake, a little more firmly than necessary, and said, "My pleasure." He was about to start a conversation that consisted of several interview questions for Nick when his wife interrupted, "Button is here!"

They turned to see the birthday girl enter the room.

Laney, Ida, and Helen were right inside the doorway when Devon wheeled her into the room. She looked stunning! She was wearing a pink lace, floor-length ball gown with a pink and white floral tiara-style wreath in her hair. Her makeup was perfection.

Ida grabbed her friends' hands. "She looks beautiful! Is the wreath in her hair from her wedding veil?"

Laney replied softly, "No, but it looks a little similar. Lottie helped me with an internet search, and it was shipped to the house. The dress was in her closet when we sold her home, and I saved it. We tried it on her a couple of weeks ago and Helen took it in to fit her tiny frame. Ava came earlier this evening and helped Angela get her dressed and do her makeup."

Helen leaned even closer to her friends. "I will never forget how she looks right now. *This* is how she'd want to be remembered."

Devon pushed Button closer to them. He wore a charcoal gray suit with a crisply starched pink button-down shirt and floral tie. He'd had a haircut and looked more handsome than ever.

Behind him was Nurse Angela and her husband, Dr. Marcus Long, as well as Jamie, Jeannie, Button's friend Margaret, and a few other nurses and residents. They all were wearing dress clothes with a pop of pink. They greeted each other in hushed tones.

It was very quiet in the room. They had been coached to not yell *Happy Birthday* as Button entered, choosing instead to greet her a few friends at a time. Laney held her hand as guests greeted her, helping Button by making comments such as "Lottie helped decorate for your party" and "Charlie can't wait for you to cut into your chocolate cake."

They made their way across the room to the table where Devon parked Button's wheelchair in her place of honor. He stared at Payton. "You look stunning tonight, and that cake is spectacular!"

Payton blushed a little. She motioned toward his attire, "Devon, you look . . . just wow." She seemed rather tongue-tied. And, then realizing he'd mentioned the cake, she turned toward it and lit the candles. Laney had never given her the signal, but her timing worked just as well.

"If everyone can gather around," Laney motioned to everyone in the room, "let's sing for our birthday girl, Button!"

They stood in a big horseshoe around the table and sang "Happy birthday, dear Button, happy birthday to you." They all clapped softly.

Laney leaned toward Button and said, "Would you like to blow out your candles?" She waited a few seconds and, getting no response from Button, said, "Shall we blow them out together?" Laney turned toward the cake, looked up, and met Bobby's eyes. He nodded to his mom, and they gently blew out the birthday candles for Button.

Payton and Jen cut and served the cake. They put a small piece with extra chocolate on a pink paper plate for Button and slid it with a fork toward Laney. They continued to serve cake to the guests. Payton cut a piece for Laney and larger pieces for Devon and Nick, who were standing next to Button, talking softly. Lottie served them their plates and then picked up a piece for herself, returning to stand next to Nick. She took the opportunity to introduce Nannie to Nick. Lottie thought, *Wow, she is being way more chill than Dad!*

As they stood talking, Lottie couldn't help but notice that Button seemed so much more interested in Nick than in the cake. She was very focused on him. Lottie whispered something softly to Nick as she knelt down at Button's side. Nick leaned over Lottie's shoulder. "Aunt Button, this is my friend, Nick. He is Devon's brother, and he's here to wish you a happy birthday."

Nick put his hand gently over Button's. "Happy birthday, Miss Vivian. I'm honored to meet you."

Button continued to stare at him. Nick looked at Lottie, Laney, and then Devon with a question in his eyes. Devon shook his head subtly at his brother, who patted Vivian's hand, straightened, and helped Lottie back to her feet.

Laney got Button's attention by asking, "Wouldn't you like to try a bite of your chocolate and pink birthday cake?

As Button remained silent, Laney looked at the group and gave a slight shrug. Devon said, "Let's give her a minute."

Nick couldn't wait any longer. He cut off a bite of cake and popped it in his mouth. He instantly closed his eyes and made an "Mmmm" sound. Button turned her head and looked up at him. She studied him intently and slowly smiled. Lottie put her plate on the table, cut a tiny bite of Button's cake with the side of a fork and offered it to her. When Button did not reach out to take the fork, Devon asked Laney to change places with him, reached over and took the fork from Lottie, giving her a kind smile. He leaned down and fed the bite to Button, who turned back to look at Nick.

Button said, "Mmmm."

"Mmmm."

"Do you always make that sound when you eat?" John was grinning at Button as she thought about his question. They were on their fourth date and sharing dessert at a lovely restaurant in town.

"Only dessert, especially chocolate." Button replied. "How can anyone help themselves from expressing sheer joy in such delights? Don't you like desserts?"

"Sure, I do. I think most people do. But I think you are way beyond like and bordering on love."

Button paused. He was still talking about the cake, right? She decided to test the waters.

"It's hard not to be smitten."

John stopped chewing. He looked at Vivian, recognizing that she knew he wasn't talking about dessert. He swallowed the bite in his mouth, took a sip of water. "It is very hard not to be smitten," he agreed. "I confess that I've never been this crazy about any other dessert. Ever!"

"Me either," Vivian shared, a little shyly.

John glanced outside and realized it was getting late. "Sun is setting. Looks like a gorgeous summer sunset tonight."

Button turned slightly to look out the window. "Oh, it's a Goddess of Love sunset!"

"A what?"

"I call it that. It's really the Belt of Venus, which is a special treat. It turns the sky a pinkish color."

"There is a place up on a high hill, not far from here. You can see the golf course down below, so I call it Golf Ball Hill. Sunsets are beautiful from there if you'd like to go."

"I adore a beautiful sunset. Yes, I'd love to go!"

Just then the waiter approached the table. "Can I get you anything else? Coffee perhaps?"

"Check, please!" John said, his eyes never leaving Vivian's.

"John." Button said his name as clear as a bell. She was looking at Nick.

Laney understood immediately. She could see why Button thought Nick was a young John Upton. They were of a similar size, dark headed, and handsome. She excused herself for a moment.

Devon continued to offer tiny bites of cake to Vivian. It was extremely difficult for her friends to see her have such needs, but at the same time, they felt tremendously grateful for Devon's kindness and care. Lottie saw her dad cringe at one point, but he did not walk away. *This must be so hard for him*, she thought. He had not seen Button in quite some time. Lottie stepped over next to her dad, put her arms around his waist, and hugged him. He put his arm around her shoulders and squeezed.

Laney approached Helen, Henry, Ida, and Charlie, who were talking in the corner. "Gentlemen, if I can borrow these lovely ladies for a moment, please." They didn't even look at the men for comments, but followed Laney to a quiet side of the room.

She blurted out, "Button thinks Nick is John."

Helen said, "Who is Nick?"

"Lottie's boyfriend," Ida shared.

Shooting a stern look at Ida, Laney amended that explanation. "No, Nick is Lottie's friend from the theater. They work together. He is Devon's brother. He is standing next to Button right now, talking to Devon and Lottie."

Helen leaned around Laney to see Nick and really stretched out the words, "Oh, my gosh, I can see why! I mean, he doesn't really look like John, but he is about the same size and coloring."

"And he is about the same age John was when he and Button met at college. What was the story again? They met thanks to a chocolate chip cookie?" Ida inquired.

Laney reminisced. "Well, yes, in a way. I mean, everyone on campus knew John. He was running for student government president; he was quite the politician from the beginning. Button and I were walking to class one day when we saw his picture on a campaign poster. He looked a little too perfect to me, but Button claimed he was the cutest boy she'd ever seen. She volunteered to help his campaign and finally met him at a meeting a week or two later. She told me that she sat in the back and hoped to have an opportunity to meet him. After the room cleared, he approached a tray of cookies at the back corner of the room. Vivian said from the other corner in her charming southern accent, 'Excuse me, but I have had my eyes on those cookies all night. I fear you might break my heart if you eat the last one!'"

Helen commented, "He never knew what hit him!"

Laney chuckled. "To hear John tell it, he turned around, saw Vivian looking at him, and fell in love at first sight."

Helen snickered. "It wasn't love."

Laney shoved Helen slightly with her shoulder before continuing, "Button said he picked up the cookie with a napkin, walked over to her with a smile, and *sealed his fate forever* by breaking the cookie in half and sharing it with her."

Turning their attention back to Button and Nick, Helen said, "Should we go save Lottie's boyfriend?"

Ignoring the boyfriend comment altogether, Laney admitted, "Probably. Let's get the guests to mingle a little. I think if we distract her, she won't stay focused on him all night," Laney suggested.

The party guests mingled and lingered much later than expected. Nobody wanted to leave; they were enjoying each other and the special birthday celebration for Button. Nick and Lottie had wandered away from Button to talk with her parents and other guests. Button did not mention John again. She did not speak at all.

The guests grudgingly acknowledged that Wednesday was a workday and began to depart. As they started to clean up, Payton asked

Devon, "Should I leave the last piece of cake here for Miss Vivian to have tomorrow?"

"I don't think so. Too many sweets are a problem for her. Why don't you give it to Miss Laney? She might want it. I noticed she hardly touched hers." Payton nodded and wrapped the cake in foil.

Jen approached them carrying a large trash bag and called out to Devon, "Excuse me, but I wondered if before you take Button back to her room, we could sing to her." Ida, Helen and Laney were standing behind her. "Payton, can you join us in the Hand-Hold for Button?" Jen looked at Devon, "It's a sorority song, a blessing. We usually sing it at weddings, but I thought we should sing it for Button now."

He smiled. "Of course. Show me where you'd like her to sit."

Jen led Devon and Button to the center of the room. The sisters gathered in a close circle around Vivian and held hands. Jen started the song as the others joined in immediately.

We clasp our hands together as we gather here today.
We ask for special blessings; humbly do we pray.
Grant this precious sister much happiness and love.
Please guard and protect her from so high above.
She is a cherished sister and never will we part.
For we will keep her forever deeply in our heart.

As they sang the song through again, Button's lips began to move, singing along with them. At the end of the song, the only person able to continue singing was Payton. As her solo softly ended and the room was silent, Nick noticed a tear track slowly down Lottie's cheek. Without saying a word, he took her hand in his. She squeezed his hand in return. Nick didn't realize it yet, but he had just sealed his fate forever.

Helen's Comfort Food

When You Would Do Anything to Make a Friend Smile

Laney, Helen, and Ida met for lunch on Monday as usual. They weren't, however, dining at Enduring Grace with Button. They were at Helen's where they'd been, off and on, since Marie had flown in on Saturday morning to see Button for a belated birthday celebration. Unfortunately, there had been no celebration.

Ida was seated on the sofa and Laney on the recliner when Helen called out from the kitchen. "I know it is hot out, but I made a pot of my special potato soup. I think we all need a little comfort food today. Come and get it!"

Laney and Ida made their way toward the kitchen table where Helen set soup bowls, crackers, and iced tea. They had not felt like talking, which was why Ida and Laney decided to stay another night at Helen's. They had no desire to recap the weekend last night with their families; they needed time to decompress.

"Thank you, Helen. I love your potato soup. This is wonderful," Ida shared.

Laney nodded and whispered, "It's delicious."

After they ate in silence for a few minutes, Ida, who had been trying so hard to think of something uplifting and positive to say, shared, "I'm glad Marie got home safely."

Laney was stirring her soup more than eating it. Helen recognized that as a red flag and knew Laney was overwhelmed by emotions that needed to be expressed. She offered, "I'm so sorry Button did not know Marie this weekend."

Laney replied with pain in her voice, "That was actually the least of it."

Helen thought, *Here we go.*

Laney dropped her spoon beside her bowl with a thud. She reached up and rubbed her forehead right in the center like she always did when she was worried or upset. "I just don't understand. She did so well on Tuesday night at her birthday party, but by the weekend, Dr. Long was forced to put her on alternate medications, sedatives even, to battle her delusional state of mind. Did we bring this on with the party?"

Ida countered, "Laney, I think Button loved her party, and it was good for her."

"Good for her or good for us?"

"Laney, don't—"

"Helen, do not tell me not to blame myself!"

"I was going to say, *Don't make assumptions.* Button's battle with Alzheimer's has no rhyme or reason. There isn't a guidebook or rulebook. The last few days may have been bad for Button whether or not we threw her a birthday party!"

Ida reached over to squeeze Laney's hand. "Helen is right. I think it was just a coincidence."

Laney took a deep breath. She looked away from her friends and stared out Helen's kitchen window at the Thanksgiving tree, its leaves now sparse and green. "I hate this damned disease," her voice cracked. "I hate that she never even knew Marie was here. I hate that Marie brought her a cute framed photograph, and Button can't even comprehend it is them in the picture. I hate that Marie's husband, Tim, has developed recent health problems, and Button can't understand that or comfort her. I hate that Marie sobbed on the way to the airport, knowing this was probably her last visit. I hate feeling old, and I hate feeling helpless. And most of all, I hate that God may be taking us home to heaven out of order."

Helen asked softly, "What do you mean 'out of order'?"

Laney cried, "I'm the oldest. I should go first. Why am I still so damned healthy and Button cannot even feed herself or wipe her own butt?"

Ida cringed, but tried to offer her comfort. "You are more than the older sister, Laney. You are the captain. You will go down with the ship only after you have seen Button safely to shore. You can do this because, if you really think about it, you'd have it no other way. God knows you that well."

Laney turned back to look at Ida. She was quiet for another minute. "Thank you! Truly, thank you. I've been so focused on how much this hurts, I never thought of it from another point of view." She cracked a little smile. "Poor God would have a crazed angel on his hands if I were in heaven instead of here to see Button home. You are right, Ida. I can do this."

"*We* can do this," Helen clarified.

Helen patted Laney's hand, got up from the table, and walked to her refrigerator. She came back to the table carrying her famous chocolate silk pie and three forks.

Laney said, "I seriously love you!"

After some much-needed dessert therapy, Ida and Laney declared themselves ready to go home. Helen dropped them off and was driving back toward her house when she had second thoughts. She assumed she'd take an afternoon nap but felt certain she wouldn't be able to rest now. So, she turned away from home and headed to Enduring Grace. She thought it would be a good idea to check on Button and an even better idea to see Henry. When he'd called earlier, he had offered to take her out to dinner. She thought she'd like to take him up on that offer. And in that exact moment, thinking of a date with Henry, Helen realized she'd smiled for the first time in days.

Laney wasn't the only one struggling with Button's depressing, difficult battle. Helen didn't express her feelings as often or as openly as her sisters, but she certainly had them. It had been very difficult to hear Henry share the news, confidentially, that Button was uncharacteristically aggressive at dinner one night. She'd actually pulled a bread knife on sweet little Margaret and yelled wild allegations at her. She hit Jamie for intervening. That behavior wasn't Button and that knowledge distressed her.

Would she follow the same path? Would Laney or Ida? Would Henry? She hated questions without answers. She hated the uncertainty, lack of discernment, and the unease over feelings yet to be acknowledged. She had been trying to put her finger on what frightened her the most so that she could tackle it headfirst. The answer had eluded her until today.

When Laney cried out over the issues haunting her the most, Helen unexpectedly found her answer crystalize into a solved equation. She did not want to be alone!

She knew that she'd have Laney and Ida and their families as long as they all lived but, without Button's care on their calendars, so much would change. She was cognizant of the fact that she shouldn't be driving much longer. Her eyesight was fine when aided by her glasses, but she found her reaction time lagging a little. Giving up Old Blue was going to be so hard, and it would leave her that much more isolated. If she couldn't drive and her friends couldn't drive, when would she see anyone? How would they meet for lunch on Mondays and, without Button, would they even want to do so?

Perhaps Henry was the answer to her prayers. She certainly hadn't prayed for a man in her life, but maybe Henry was a blessing. He certainly *looked* like a gift from God! And that thought made her smile for the second time today.

After parking close to the building, Helen texted Henry and shared her plan to check on Button before stopping by to see him. When Helen entered Button's room a few minutes later, she saw her sweet friend sitting in her rocking chair with a coloring book and pencils on the table in front of her. She was staring out the window.

"Hi Button!" Helen expected no reply.

Surprisingly, Button looked toward her and replied with a tiny smile. "Hi, Lady."

"Can I sit and color with you for a bit?"

Button continued to smile. Helen sat her purse on the foot of Button's bed, pulled up a chair, and selected a deep purple colored pencil. "I love this shade, don't you?"

As they colored, Helen continued to talk about the picture, which resembled a stained-glass window. She talked briefly about the origins of stained glass.

"Did you know during the Renaissance period, stained glass moved from its customary use in many beautiful church windows to also being installed in town halls and homes?"

Helen looked up at Button, who was coloring with a dark red pencil. "That's a lovely color for stained glass."

Button's head was down, and she quietly, slowly, and gently colored the picture. Helen suddenly realized something astounding. Button was coloring within the lines. She wasn't just moving the pencil back-and-forth on the page. She was truly, accurately, and beautifully coloring the picture. *How interesting*, Helen thought.

Helen's attention was suddenly diverted to the television in Button's room, which was on, as always, with the volume very low. She couldn't help but smile as she saw *The Music Man* on the screen. It was a favorite of the four friends, especially Laney who loved Marian the Librarian. Button knew every word of every song of this musical. Or, Helen amended, she once knew every word.

"Button, look at the TV. *The Music Man* is playing right now." Helen turned up the volume, continuing to chat with Button. "Did you know the movie studio didn't really want Robert Preston to play Harold Hill? Can you even imagine? They tried to get Bing Crosby or Frank Sinatra for the movie, both of whom declined. They even attempted to cast Cary Grant; supposedly, however, he not only declined but also said he wouldn't even go see the movie if Robert Preston wasn't in it. I read somewhere Cary Grant saw him in the Broadway production and thought he was brilliant."

Button shifted her eyes toward the television just as the song "Seventy-Six Trombones" began. Helen started singing along, "Seventy-six trombones led the big parade . . ." She saw Button smile and decided to keep singing the song, suddenly remembering a time years ago that they had watched the movie at Laney's, and Button had jokingly marched around the living room, playing an imaginary trombone. *There had been wine involved, obviously!* Helen couldn't help but add that detail in her mind.

Helen stood up from the table where they'd been coloring and, without a drop of hesitancy or wine, she marched to and fro in front of Button, playing her imaginary trombone.

Button laughed out loud! She was grinning widely, dimples show-ing, and clapping her hands. It spurred Helen on, and she sang a little louder and pushed her fist forcefully high into the air as if her trombone skills were the best in the land. She marched toward Button's bed next to the window and turned sharply, only to stop dead in her tracks.

Henry and Dr. Long were standing in the doorway! Helen grabbed the remote and turned down the volume.

Dr. Long's eyes were huge and Henry was leaning against the door in laughter. Dr. Long spoke first. "My goodness, Miss Vivian, you had your own personal performance from *The Music Man* today. Wasn't that spectacular?"

Henry stepped forward with a tremendous smile on his face. He wasn't looking at Button, but at a charmingly embarrassed Helen. "I'm really more of a 'Trouble Right Here in River City' man myself," he declared.

Helen put her hands on her hips and glared at Henry. "With a capital 'T' that rhymes with 'P' . . ."

"And that stands for pool," Henry said as he walked even closer to Helen. "One of my favorite movies," he added with a wink.

Helen suddenly had the insane thought that she wanted to kiss him. *What is the matter with me?*

Dr. Long cleared his throat as if to remind them he was in the room. He stepped closer to Button who returned his regard. He talked to Button, asking her a couple of questions, but he received no replies.

He turned to Helen and Henry. "I'm glad my rounds coincided with your performance, and I got to see Miss Vivian's reaction to your song. So just to update you, we changed her medications recently and, due to weight loss we'd like to avoid, we put her on nutrition shakes. I personally think nutrition and hydration are key components of Miss Vivian's ongoing treatment plan. We'd also love it if she'd rest better at night."

He patted Vivian's hand and smiled at her. As he turned to leave the room, he looked over his shoulder. "Keep it up, Miss Helen! And, if possible, see if you can get her to eat a little better." He didn't wait for a reply, but moved swiftly on to his next patient.

Helen left Henry's side to sit next to Button. She watched in surprise as Henry promptly exited the room.

Making a mental note to buy Button some chocolate morsels, she turned back to the table and selected a colored pencil for Button and one for herself. "Shall we finish our stained-glass window, Button?"

"May I offer my assistance?" Henry stood in the doorway with a chair that he borrowed from the resident across the hall. He carried it into Button's room, placed it at the tiny table, and, upon declaring the hunter green pencil his favorite, began shading in a section of the picture.

Button looked at Henry. Helen watched as she looked from him to the picture on the table. She held her pencil but did not resume coloring. She watched intently as Henry and Helen finished transforming the black-and-white page into a colorful stained-glass picture. When finished, Helen held the picture up for Button's approval. She smiled, but made no comment.

Henry said to Helen, "Excuse me for a moment."

Helen heard Devon's voice from the doorway, "Henry, how are you? Were you just visiting Miss Vivian?" Helen did not hear Henry's reply.

"Good evening, Miss Helen!" Devon strolled into Button's room. "Miss Vivian, do my eyes deceive me or is that a smile I see on your pretty face?" He came closer to the table, viewing the coloring book and pencils.

"She has been smiling off and on all afternoon. We colored this picture, and Henry stopped by to help. His favorite color is green." Helen wrinkled her nose. *Why did I just tell Devon that?*

Devon smiled at Helen. Looking up over Helen's head, he nodded at Henry, who had just returned from the nurses' station with tape. Helen caught onto his plan immediately. She carefully tore the picture out of the book and handed it to Henry. He moved the foot of Button's bed slightly away from the wall in order to tape their special artwork onto the window.

"Miss Vivian, look! You have a stained-glass window." Devon pushed her into a better viewing position.

Henry returned to stand next to Helen, and they took in the sight. It was just a simple page out of a coloring book, but they saw a special work of art.

Helen turned her head and looked up at Henry. "Thank you." She mouthed the words more than actually speaking them. Henry took her hand in his and held it. He didn't let go as Devon turned around. Neither did Helen.

If Devon noticed their clasped hands, he made no mention of it. "It's time for my dinner date with Miss Vivian. Are you planning to join us this evening?"

Henry replied, "Not tonight, Devon."

"Laney will be here tomorrow, and I'll be back on Wednesday," Helen added.

"And I live here, so please let me know if Miss Vivian ever needs a friend or coloring partner if her sisters are not here."

Helen felt her heart melt. Devon turned Button away from the window and pushed her toward Helen and Henry, saying, "Thank you, Henry. That's very kind of you."

Helen leaned down to kiss Button on the cheek.

Looking toward Devon, she shared, "Thank you, Devon. You might interest her in eating more if you could dip her meat or chicken in a sauce such as barbeque or ketchup. She especially likes barbeque."

"I will, Miss Helen. I appreciate that suggestion. Our tiny beauty queen is getting a bit too tiny."

Helen watched them walk out the door. Next to her, Henry asked softly, "Can I take you out tonight for dinner? Do you like steak?"

"I love steak! And, yes, dinner sounds lovely."

Lottie's Big Plan

When Kids Make You Grind Your Teeth

Lottie got out of bed extra early for a Saturday morning. She didn't need to be at work until the afternoon, just before their matinee performance. But she hadn't seen much of her grandmother since Button's birthday party and wanted to spring a great idea on her.

She made her way into the kitchen to the sound of hushed voices. Coming to an abrupt halt, Lottie blinked her eyes. Nannie, her Mom, and her Dad were having breakfast together at the kitchen table.

Noticing her in the doorway, Judith stood. "Charlotte, sweetheart, I thought you were planning to sleep in or we would have waited on you. Can I get you a plate? We have scrambled eggs, ham, and biscuits."

"Yes to everything, but please sit. I can help myself, Mom."

"Orange juice is on the island," Judith added as she returned to her seat.

Lottie asked, "Is grape jelly on the table?"

Nannie replied, "Grape, strawberry, and honey butter. Take your pick."

"What's the occasion?" Lottie couldn't help but wonder.

"No special occasion. I was just hungry for a big breakfast," Bobby shared with his daughter. "We used to eat a big breakfast most Saturdays when you were younger but, with all of our crazy schedules, we were off and running to work appointments or your soccer and softball games."

"Loved softball, but only liked soccer," Lottie clarified as she sat at the table with her breakfast.

"Nannie, you didn't make these biscuits, I can tell, but they look yummy."

"No, your mom made breakfast today. Wasn't that sweet of her?" Nannie replied.

"They are frozen biscuits," Judith offered. "I'm not the baker that Nannie is, you know."

With her mouth full, Lottie quickly assured her mom, "These are so good, Mom!"

"What has you up early this morning?" Bobby asked. "Did you smell breakfast?"

"No, I wanted to catch Nannie and talk about a trip idea for this summer." Looking across the table at Nannie, Lottie shared in her naturally exuberant manner, "Nick and I were talking after work, and we wondered if we can celebrate your birthday with you on the Fourth of July at Big Sky Amusement Park."

"You and Nick?" Bobby was the first to say anything.

"Yes. He has an annual pass because he goes to college there, and the theater is closed for the holiday. I told him that Nannie and I go to Big Sky every year and that we hadn't been yet, so I thought of your birthday. We'll just drive down early in the morning and back after the fireworks. We'll rent a wheelchair, of course. I think it sounds amazing. What do you think, Nannie?"

Bobby repeated, "You and Nick?"

"Why do you keep asking me that, Dad? Yes, Nick! We're friends. Anyway, we live close enough to make it a day trip. Plus, Nannie and I have this shared tradition. What's the big deal?" Suddenly thinking maybe money was an issue, Lottie added, "I have earned enough to pay for my ticket and Nannie's as her birthday gift."

Laney interrupted Bobby by jumping in as he took a deep breath. "Lottie, as lovely as that sounds, a day in the parks is a huge and expensive birthday present."

"Then, how about your ticket is my gift, and you buy your own food?"

"Well, I still think that's overly generous."

"I don't. I mean, I'm going to college in August, and I don't know if we'll get to keep going every year. Let's make this birthday, your eighty-second, a big splash. We could even call it a combo celebration day of my graduation, your birthday, Nick's birthday on July 15, and even my birthday on August 15. I doubt I'll be around on my birthday, anyway, because of recruitment."

Judith's ears perked up! "You've decided to go through sorority recruitment?"

"Sure. You and Nannie have convinced me it will be a great way to make new friends and feel like I have a home away from home. I'll give it a shot!"

Bobby looked toward Judith in frustration. How had this just turned into a sorority conversation? "Lottie, when you and Nannie made your trips over the years, Nannie drove. Even last year, despite you having her car most of the time, she drove. Are you suggesting that you drive this year?"

"I can or Nick can."

"I am unfamiliar with Nick's driving record."

"Fine. I'll drive."

Bobby argued, "Charlotte, the traffic in Orlando can be horrible. You haven't had much highway driving opportunities away from home. Plus, you'd be driving in the dark and coming home late at night!"

Lottie stabbed her scrambled eggs onto her fork a little forcefully. She wondered if he realized he'd just called her Charlotte.

"Dad, how did you think I was going to get to and from college in Orlando?"

Bobby didn't have a response.

Judith intervened, "Charlotte, your dad is just concerned for your and Nannie's safety. And this Nick boy."

"This Nick boy? Good grief, Mom!"

Laney tried to salvage family breakfast. "Lottie, let's talk about it later tonight. I think we need time to think through the plans, but I'd love to go to Big Sky with you if everyone is in agreement. If not for my birthday, then another time this year. When you're in college in Orlando, we will be coming to see you and can go then, too. We will have many more Orlando weekends ahead."

"Will we?" Lottie said sharply to Nannie, reminding her of their recent conversation about Lottie going to Redding College.

Judith pounced on Lottie's comment. "Will we? What does that mean?"

"Nothing, Mom. I've just heard being a college student keeps you pretty busy." Looking at her phone and the time, Lottie hopped up from her seat and took her plate and glass to the sink. "I'm running late. Thank you for family breakfast!"

Bobby, Judith, and Laney looked at each other, but nobody said a word. Judith slowly stood and walked away from the table to start cleaning the kitchen. Laney began to rise from her seat when Judith waved her off. "Nannie, please keep your seat and relax. I'll get everything into the dishwasher in a flash," Judith offered.

Laney studied Judith. She was being kind, gracious, and selfless. Something unusual was going on, and Laney planned to get to the bottom of it. It wasn't that Judith was unkind. She had never been a mean person. She had graciously and selflessly welcomed Laney into her and Bobby's home. But Judith was being down right hospitable!

They suddenly heard music blaring from the bathroom adjacent to Lottie's bedroom. "Uh oh! She's singing Broadway musicals in the shower," Laney shared.

Bobby looked at her questioningly. "So?"

"So, she is upset. She sings at the top of her lungs to over-the-top dramatic music when she's unhappy."

Bobby looked across the kitchen at Judith, who simply raised her eyebrows and shrugged.

"Maybe we can talk about her trip idea for a minute," Laney suggested.

"Mom, she's seventeen. She doesn't need to be driving to and from Orlando in one day, especially exhausted and in the dark. And, how much do we know about that Nick boy?"

"Agreed!" Judith shared her two cents' worth.

"I think you both need to stop saying *that Nick boy*, but other than that, I agree," Laney assured Bobby. "I do, however, feel flattered and honored that she would like to spend my birthday with me at our favorite amusement park. We haven't been this year, and it's a tradition I'd love to keep alive as long as I'm, well, still alive."

"Mother . . ."

Laney interrupted him by patting his hand. "My suggestion is that we all go and, Bobby, you can drive!"

"Wait. What?"

"When was the last time we all shared a fun vacation day together? When was the last time you went to Big Sky and rode roller coasters with Lottie?"

Bobby made a sound of frustration. "Mom, there is no way I can get away from work right now."

"July Fourth is a national holiday, son."

"It will be incredibly hot and crowded."

"So?"

"Well, wouldn't it be more pleasant to go when the weather is cooler?"

"I don't think the weather should dictate spending a joyful, special day with your family."

Judith interrupted, "The tickets are too expensive."

Laney looked at Judith. *Now I'm getting somewhere,* she thought. She was making a mental note to talk to Bobby privately when she had an unexpected thought. *Could this be the reason behind Lottie's sudden, last-minute interest in applying to Redding College? Lottie had mentioned something about seeking a scholarship.*

Mistaking his mother's silence for disappointment, Bobby softened his tone. "Mom, let Judith and me think about it. We'll see."

Laney smiled, thinking back to when Bobby was a little boy. He had whined one day in complaint, "'We'll see' always means no." She had handed him his lunch box, turned him gently toward the door as the school bus was due any minute, and suggested, "OK, then, how about a definite maybe."

Laney stood, pushed in her chair, and thanked Judith for a lovely breakfast. She circled behind Bobby's chair and leaned down to hug him. She kissed him on the cheek and whispered in his ear, "Thank you, son, I'll consider that a definite maybe!"

Bobby couldn't help but smile.

A minute later, with the sound of Laney's bedroom door closing, Judith squared off in front of Bobby. "You aren't seriously considering this idea, are you?"

"I am."

"Bobby, we need to save for Charlotte's future, our future."

"Sweetheart, we can afford to go to Big Sky for one day to celebrate Fourth of July as a family and honor my mom's birthday. We can spend this day with Lottie and get to know Nick. She appears to have a major crush on him."

"Yes, she does," Judith sighed. "Are you sure spending the money is a good idea?"

"It's fine. My concern is not our day-to-day expenses; it's more the shock of discovering myself approaching retirement age without the funds to match the skyrocketing cost of tuition. Let's go ride roller coasters and eat cotton candy, Judith."

"If you're sure. I suppose it could be a special birthday for your mom."

When Lottie barreled into the kitchen a little while later, purse on her shoulder and sunglasses perched on top of her head, Bobby, who was sitting alone in the kitchen, asked her, "Do you have a minute before you need to leave?"

"Yep, like two minutes. What's up?"

"Your mother and I have been talking about Big Sky. If you and Nick would like to go on the Fourth of July for Nannie's birthday, we will all go. I will drive us down early in the morning and back after the fireworks."

"You and Mom want to go?"

"We do. We'd especially like to spend the day with you, Nannie, and, um, Nick."

Lottie was silent.

"I thought you'd be excited."

"Sorry, I'm processing. I think Nick will go for it. I mean, it's a little awkward to be driven like kids on a field trip, but sure, sounds good to me. I'll ask Nick."

"You'll ask Nick?"

"Yes, Dad. It's the polite thing to do. We discussed the idea of going together with Nannie. Adding parental units into the mix is altering the original plan, and I just want to make sure he's cool with it."

Bobby thought, *Why does this conversation make me want to grind my teeth?*

"I've got to get to work. Thanks, Dad. Love you!" Lottie practically bounced out the back door, which led to the garage.

Bobby was still sitting in his breakfast spot, rubbing his forehead, when Laney walked in, dressed for the day.

"Did I miss Lottie? I was going to hitch a ride to check on Button."

Bobby nodded. "She just left."

Laney put her purse on the kitchen table. "That's fine. Helen said she was going to Enduring Grace in a little while. I'll call her back and see if she'll pick me up."

"I can take you to see Button. Ask Aunt Helen if she can drop you back home later. If not, Judith or I will be happy to come and get you."

"Thank you. I will."

"I talked to Judith, and we agreed to take your suggestion and go to Big Sky on the Fourth. I think we're all going. We'll see. Lottie said she needs to *ask* Nick."

"Oh?"

"She said something about all of us riding in one car might feel like we're chaperoning them on a school field trip, and she wants to run it by him."

"I see."

"Really, you see? Because I don't see. She's frustrating the heck out of me!"

Laney sat down at the table next to Bobby. "It's complicated. Lottie sees herself as an adult, but she isn't. You see her as a child, but she isn't."

Bobby nodded.

"Son, just a word of warning. The next few years are new territory. She is weeks, days really, from turning eighteen. She sees that as a rite of passage to adulthood. You see a young daughter, even admittedly a college-age student, who is still your responsibility. Twenty-one is only slightly better. I don't think I thought of you as a grown man until you were almost thirty. You partied a lot in your twenties, missed some bill payments, and wrecked a couple of cars."

"Thanks for reminding me, Mom."

"That's my job!" Laney couldn't help but laugh. "I was hoping you'd agree to go to Orlando, so I checked with Ida and Helen to make sure at least one of us would be here for Button. Ida and Charlie are going to Sarasota to visit his brother and family. Ava and Joe have condo reservations in Destin with Joe's siblings. Won't that be lovely?"

"Yes, Destin is my favorite beach."

"Mine, too. Fortunately, Helen will be here and sounds excited about spending Independence Day at Enduring Grace. They are having a picnic for residents, and they'll be able to see the fireworks that will be shot off downtown from the front patio."

"Sounds like we have a plan. If Nick wishes to accompany us, he is welcome. If he doesn't, we will enjoy your birthday without him."

Bobby finally rose from his seat at the kitchen table. "If you don't mind, Mom, I'm going to grab a quick shower and see if Judith wants to hit happy hour. She gets to be designated driver. I need a beer!"

Jennifer

When Fairy Godmothers Carry Tissues

Lottie looked at Nick and immediately sensed something was wrong. His face looked normal, cute as ever, but his body language seemed weird. They were standing by her car at the end of their long Saturday at work; the last two theater employees left in the parking lot.

"So," Lottie suggested, "we can either pick you up at your brother's apartment or you can leave your car at our house. Either way, we should be on the way by seven or seven thirty that morning to get the most out of our Big Sky day. What do you think?"

Nick shifted his weight, even stepping back a little. He put his hands in his front jean pockets, hunching his shoulders. "Um, right. I haven't had the chance to tell you that I mentioned Fourth of July to Devon. He and Payton thought driving down early and coming back after the fireworks sounded like a blast."

"Pun intended," Lottie quipped.

"What?"

"Nothing."

"So, listen, I'll just ride with them and make it easier on everybody. We can text each other and connect in the park for some rides. You like the Shooting Star Rocket Ride, right?"

"I don't know. I don't normally ride it because it would be too hard on Nannie."

"Well, let's plan to meet sometime that day at the Rocket and ride it together."

"OK. Sure."

"Great."

"Great," Lottie echoed. "So, I'd better get home. See you later." She didn't wait for Nick's reply. She got in her car and was on her way out of the parking lot in record time. With tears welling up in her eyes, she pulled into the lot of a closed auto parts store down the street. She put her car in park and let the tears flow.

She felt like such an idiot. Nick obviously didn't like her and Big Sky was not his idea of a date. Granted, it would have been a really weird date with Nannie going with them, but he'd seemed to understand her reluctance to ditch her grandmother on her birthday. After the way he'd acted at Button's party, he seemed comfortable with elderly people in wheelchairs. She didn't think that was an issue. It must totally be her.

So why did he hold my hand at Button's party? What was up with that? She supposed he was just being a thoughtful friend when he'd seen her in tears. She felt embarrassed for reading too much into it.

Lottie dug to the bottom of her handbag for a tissue, feeling lucky she found one. She blew her nose and dried her eyes. Ugly crying sucked! She couldn't go home looking like this, so she texted Jennifer, who replied that she was home. Lottie typed, "9-1-1, need advice!"

Jen texted back, "Your Fairy Godmother awaits!"

Lottie typed, "Five minutes."

Four minutes later, she pulled into Jen's condo parking lot and saw the young woman she thought of as a big sister sitting on the stairs leading up to her place on the second floor. She didn't see Jake's truck. *That's fortunate*, she thought.

Lottie locked her car and walked toward Jen, who was holding an entire box of tissues.

"I find it's always useful to have snot rags!"

"Thank you," Lottie cried, as she pulled two tissues from the box.

Jen tossed the box on the steps and enveloped Lottie in a huge hug. She pulled back, taking in Lottie's splotchy face. *Poor girl!* Feeling protective, Jen picked up the tissue box and led her up the stairs and into her condo.

Jen motioned for Lottie to have a seat on the sofa. Walking into the kitchen, she said over her shoulder, "Text your folks and let them know I invited you over to watch a movie. Tell them you'll be home by midnight." Lottie pulled out her phone and typed the words Jen had dictated. She received a quick reply from her mom indicating her approval.

Jen sat next to Lottie on the sofa and handed her a glass of lemonade. "When life hands you lemons . . ." Lottie didn't laugh or smile at Jen's feeble little joke, so she offered, "I'm making an educated guess that a boy you thought was a prince regretfully became a frog tonight. Unload, sweetie! Tell me all about it."

Across town, Nick slammed the door on the refrigerator. He'd opened it to look inside after finding nothing appetizing in the pantry. He didn't see anything in the refrigerator either, so he walked moodily into the living room with a soda.

"You want to tell me why you're slamming doors in the kitchen?" Devon turned down the volume on the television. He was sitting on the couch, relaxed in gym shorts and a T-shirt.

"Nope."

"OK." Devon increased the volume thinking perhaps the crime drama wasn't all that boring.

"It's just this thing with Lottie."

Devon hit the off button on the remote. Turning his head toward Nick, he asked, "What thing?"

"She's seventeen."

"Right. And?"

"And we talked about going to Big Sky Park since we're off work on the Fourth of July. We both love it and, I mean, it would be so great to go there with her. But she's seventeen. She doesn't turn eighteen until August 15."

Devon was surprised Nick knew Lottie's birthday.

"When is my birthday?"

"What? I don't know. March something?"

"February something. Anyway, go on."

"At first she was all in. She said she'd love to go with me to ride roller coasters. And then she suggested it would be nice for us to take her grandmother. It will be her birthday on the Fourth, and they have a tradition of going every year. I think she felt guilty about not being with her grandmother on her birthday, so I thought, *sure, why not.* I'm a nice guy. I know how close she is to her grandmother. But tonight, she said her whole family wants to go, and her dad insists on driving. I am not going to sit in the back seat next to his daughter and have him stare at me in the rearview mirror the whole way to Orlando and back!"

Devon opened his mouth, but before he could speak, Nick continued. "So, I told her you and Payton thought the idea was cool and I'd just ride with you. That makes sense, right? I mean, you are my brother, I live here, and it's easier." Nick listed the excuses with his fingers as if numbering them.

Devon didn't say anything for a second, waiting to make sure it was his turn to talk. "What did Lottie say?"

"She said 'sure.'"

"Just that one word?"

Nick nodded. "Then, I suggested we text each other once we get there and meet up for rides. She doesn't usually go on the Shooting Star Rocket Ride, so I suggested that one."

"In my experience, little brother, one-word answers like *fine, sure,* and *great* are dangerous answers from a woman. Even a seventeen-year-old one."

Nick rolled his eyes and took a gulp of his soda.

"My bet is that Lottie got shot down by her parents when she said she wanted to go with you to Orlando—Miss Laney in the plans or not. I lived in Atlanta when I was your age, but I'd never have thought about asking a girl to hop in my car and drive to Nashville for the day. I know you go to college there, and you've driven that stretch of highway several times, but even I see warning flags all over your plan."

Devon walked into the kitchen and put a bag of popcorn in the microwave. He leaned against the counter and offered Nick a little advice.

"Look, I'm sure you and Lottie thought it sounded like a fun way to spend Independence Day, but her parents have only met you once, about three weeks ago, at Miss Vivian's birthday party. I think their offer to go to Big Sky for the day was actually really decent of them. I think they did it to allow you and Lottie this fun time together under the constraint that they not put their precious daughter's safety in your hands."

"Lottie and I have gone out a few times after work or on our days off. It's not like I'm a total stranger. What do I do now? Call her and say I'll ride with them after all?"

"My advice is that you ride with me and Payton and let Lottie ride with her family. But I would let her know you are looking forward to seeing her there. I'd reiterate that if I were you."

"I'll talk to her at work tomorrow. She seemed really tired tonight and was anxious to get home."

Devon walked from the kitchen into the living room carrying two big bowls. He handed one to Nick. "Good plan. Here, have some popcorn!"

Jen said, "Do you want some popcorn?"

"No, I'm not hungry. Thanks though."

"Lottie, like I said, my advice is that you focus on a fun day at Big Sky with your parents and a special birthday for Nannie. I think Nick is sincere and he'll text you, meet up for a few rides. If he doesn't, that's his choice. Don't let that ruin your fun. I think it's sweet that you two have hit it off so well and you want to go to Orlando together. I bet you get to do that several times once you're both at Florida College of Theater and Arts in Orlando."

Lottie's eye suddenly filled with tears again and her voice broke as she said, "If I go to college in Orlando."

"What do you mean? Have you changed your mind?"

"You have to swear not to say anything, Jen. I mean it!"

"I swear."

"I overheard my parents talking a few weeks ago, and college is way more expensive than my dad was expecting, and my parents won't get to retire if I go away to school. If I stay here and live at home, I think they could. I can't go to school in Orlando if it means my dad will have to work until he is eighty just to pay my school loans."

"Oh, Lottie."

"I came to my senses pretty quickly about me and Nick driving to Orlando for the day, which is why I suggested combining it with a trip I've been wanting to take with Nannie. Dad shocked me when he said he and mom want to go, but I think you're right. That's his way of giving me the day I want with Nick and Nannie while staying in his parental comfort zone. It's actually kind of sweet."

"It is. And, just so you know, my dad still grills Jake about driving anywhere with me. He always reminds him, 'That's precious cargo you're carrying, son!' And we're engaged!"

Lottie and Jen shared a little laugh.

Jen squeezed Lottie's hand. "I'm very sorry for the burden you're carrying about possibly living at home and going to Redding instead of your original plan to study in Orlando. I have a couple of friends who might be able to help. Let me connect you with a man I worked for when I was a student here. My job was in the athletic ticket office, and they were fabulous about my class schedule. He is a really nice man. I also have a friend, a sorority sister, who works at the performing arts center on campus in Orlando. I think I've mentioned her to you before."

"You did, but I forgot all about her. Sorry, I'd love to connect with her—with both of them honestly. I've applied and been accepted to Redding , but despite my high GPA, I haven't received any scholarship offers. Maybe I waited too late. I need to figure out what to do, Jen. I'm running out of time and need help."

"That's why I'm here, sweetie. Fairy Godmother to the rescue!"

Lottie threw her arms around Jen, declaring, "I love my Fairy Godmother so much!"

After talking for another few minutes and assuring Lottie she didn't look like a wreck, Jen walked Lottie to her car. "I'll call you tomorrow. Text me when you get home."

Lottie assured her she would check in safely and thanked Jen for everything. She buckled her seatbelt and pulled carefully out of her parking space, waving to Jen as she left. She noticed a white truck pulling in just as she was leaving and slowed down long enough to smile and wave at Jake.

As Jake pulled into the parking lot Lottie had just vacated, Jen was waiting for him on the sidewalk.

"I'd like to think this welcome is for me, but I saw Lottie leaving. I didn't know you two had plans. Hope you had a fun evening." He swooped in for a sweet kiss and Jen put her arms around his waist.

"How was poker night?"

"Well, your dad didn't clean me out for once."

Jen laughed. "Wow, an off night for Dad. He's probably complaining to Mom right now."

"I didn't win much. I think my take was about forty dollars."

"I have an idea where you can spend it."

"Oh yeah? Where's that?

"Big Sky Amusement Park on the Fourth of July. Come inside and I'll talk you into it."

Jake laughed loudly. "I might as well go and gas up the truck!"

Jen hugged him even tighter. *What a keeper!*

Helen's Fourth of July

When You Feel the Fireworks

Helen parked Old Blue in the Enduring Grace parking lot and climbed out of her car looking adorably festive in red, white, and blue. Wearing a lightweight cotton red skirt, navy blue and white striped T-shirt, and a flattering tap of red lipstick, she walked toward the front entrance carrying a dozen chocolate chiffon cupcakes with white buttercream frosting and red and blue sprinkles. She'd picked the chocolate chiffon especially for Button. Henry liked all cakes, claiming his favorite was his famous candy bar cake. *A man who likes to cook!*

Helen entered the lobby, which was much busier than normal. She was charmed by the flags, bunting, streamers, and balloons that turned the space into an Independence Day party. It was lovely to see so many families visiting with each other.

She smiled and couldn't contain her excitement over having plans to celebrate a true Fourth of July. Last year, a ghastly thunderstorm had wreaked such havoc that fireworks had been cancelled. The year before, she'd been sick with a nasty cold, sitting home alone with only cough medicine for company.

Henry had shared similar disappointments with his Independence Day plans in past years, and she gleaned from his comments that he was anticipating this celebratory day as well. Glancing toward the dining room, Helen grinned. *Speak of the handsome devil!*

He looked utterly charming in blue slacks, red short-sleeved polo shirt, and a barbershop quartet-style boater hat with a red, white, and blue ribbon. Helen was smitten with this delightful man, whose charm and thoughtfulness appeared to be genuine.

"Be still my heart," Henry said with an infectious smile. "Don't you look pretty as a picture in your red, white, and blue?"

"Thank you, Henry. You look very dapper yourself today. I love your hat!"

He tipped his hat in appreciation of her compliment. "They have a photographer here today taking pictures in front of an Independence Day banner. Would you do me the honor of having a photo taken with me?"

"Of course!" She motioned to the cupcakes in her hands. "I assume we can find a table to set these down first."

"Yes, there is one in the hallway. I was just over there before you arrived talking with a couple of neighbors. Your cupcakes look delicious. Is that the chocolate chiffon recipe?"

"It is. They are Button's favorite. I brought a couple for you and some for the nurses as well."

"That's very kind. I don't wish to intrude, but I'd be pleased to go with you to see Button if you'd like. I haven't seen her at all lately. I don't eat in the dining room every day, having my own kitchen in my apartment, but I haven't seen her nor have any of my friends. Perhaps we could color another picture with her."

Helen accepted his offer as they walked toward the photographer. She set her purse and cupcakes on the small table nearby and slowly walked toward Henry, who was already standing in front of the sign. She slowed her steps as she suddenly questioned how to navigate this photo opportunity. Should she stand next to him, arms at her side? Should she put her arm around his waist? *Heaven help me! Why am I always so socially awkward?*

Henry reached out his arm and gently pulled her into his side. She slowly wrapped her arm around his waist, looked up toward the photographer, and gave him her best smile.

"Now let's add in a fun shot," the photographer suggested. "Why don't you take off your hat? You two face each other and, sir, hold up your hat as if you're cloaking a private kiss from the world."

Helen pulled slightly away from Henry and turned to look up at him. He'd already removed his hat and stood there with a question in his eyes. He positioned his hat for the photo, put his other hand on Helen's shoulder, leaning in for a kiss. Helen met him halfway.

"Great, thanks. That's going to be really cute. I think you might frame that one," the photographer said. After a brief pause, he repeated, "OK, thank you again!"

Helen pulled back from Henry. He whispered, "Heck of a first kiss!"

It was! But Helen certainly wasn't going to talk about it as if such things were casual conversation. She retrieved her purse and cupcakes and turned toward Henry. "Are you amenable to having a cupcake and a visit with Button now?"

"I am amenable, yes."

They stopped at the nurses' station to offer cupcakes to Angela and Jamie and a few other nurses Helen did not know well. Angela told her Devon was off today, but they would put one in plastic wrap and save it for him.

When she and Henry walked in to see Button, they found her sitting in bed in her nightgown, staring out the window.

"Happy Fourth of July, Button!" Helen shared, trying to catch Button's attention. With no response, she offered, "I made you a choco-late cupcake. It's your favorite, the chocolate chiffon." She walked closer to her friend, peering around the foot of the bed in hope of making eye contact. Button just stared out the window with no emotion reflected on her face.

Henry offered to take the cupcake tray from Helen, and he sat it down on the table near Button's bed.

"Hello, Vivian," Henry said softly. "Happy Independence Day. Do you like fireworks? We'll be able to see them tonight. The sky is clear with no rain in the forecast. That's very lucky, indeed. It rains almost every afternoon in Florida during the summer."

He looked at Helen, who sadly shook her head. She walked back to Henry's side, whispering to him, "God bless her, she looks so thin, so gaunt. Devon has had some success in getting her to eat, but it's not much. I thought she might perk up at the mention of chocolate cupcakes."

"She still may. Let's see what the day brings."

"You don't have to stay, Henry. I can meet you at your apartment in a bit."

"I'll stay." He offered Helen the rocking chair and pulled up a desk chair to sit near her. He noticed the television was on and increased the volume just enough to hear it. He pushed the channel button to surf the lineup and found an action movie just starting. "My son and daughter love these hero movies. They suggested I'd like them, but I was skeptical at first. Now I've seen all of them. Have you seen any of these movies?"

"I have. I love the new one with the female agent the most. She is my favorite. Do you get to see your children very often?"

"Not as often as I'd like. Visits have mostly been when I have flown to the west coast to see them. I think at first it was hard to come home with their mother gone and then I moved in here and there is no room for guests. I've offered to pay for them to stay nearby in a hotel, but it's not the same. Plus, it's just one airline ticket for me to purchase. It's much more of an expense on them if they come with their spouses. My four grandkids are grown and married now. I wouldn't be surprised to find myself a great-grandfather in the near future."

"That's wonderful."

"It is. Although I don't see them often, we talk and I know they love their old Pop."

Helen gave Henry a weak smile and nodded. "I never had that."

"With your ex-husband?"

"With him or my family," she clarified. "We became quite estranged, my parents, siblings, and me over the years. It started when I came to Florida for college. Well, honestly, it started before that. It ate at me to have my life separated from them, especially my mother, but the situation was so toxic, so unhealthy for me."

Helen told him everything. She talked about growing up in Macon, working at the drug store, and boarding the bus for Redding College. She shared with him how Button and her sorority sisters had brought stability and happiness into her life and how her work at the museum had challenged her, empowered her, providing such a tremendous feeling of achievement and accomplishment. She spoke briefly about Stanley. He wasn't worthy of more than a few sentences after all.

After she shared her thoughts, they remained silent for a moment. Henry leaned toward her and took her hand. "I like you very much."

"I like you very much, too."

"I'm sorry life has been so hard on you. You're a very strong woman, Helen. I really respect that. You're extremely intelligent, keeping me on my toes. I would like to keep getting to know you and spend more and more time with you, if you're open to that development. And, just so you know—I hate ketchup!"

Helen scooted forward in the rocking chair, leaned forward, and kissed Henry, toppling his hat off his head. She laughed, "I am amenable to that. I would say, *Let's take it slowly*, but we're no spring chickens."

Henry smiled, kissed her hand, and then kissed her on the lips one more time.

"You kissed." Button shocked Helen and Henry with those two little words!

"Button! Hello, dear. I've missed you. Henry and I came to have a chocolate cupcake with you. Would you like a treat?" Helen didn't wait for a reply, but opened the top drawer of Button's nightstand for one of the napkins she knew was stashed there after her birthday party. Helen put three napkins on the rolling table near Button's bed. She set out three cupcakes, one for each of them. Button watched as Helen handed one to Henry. He took a bite and declared them delicious. Helen did the same.

When Button did not accept the cupcake on a napkin, Helen returned it to the table, reached into the drawer and pulled out a fork wrapped in plastic. She shed the wrapper, put a tiny bite of chocolate cake on the fork, and lifted it to Button's mouth. She waited there patiently until Button slowly opened her mouth, trying a bite. She didn't make her usual yummy sound of delight but opened her mouth for more.

Henry suggested he get Button some water and excused himself to fill a plastic pitcher in her room. When he returned, he poured Button a tiny sip, held the cup to her lips and watched carefully for her to swallow.

Despite only eating about a third of the cupcake, Helen and Henry felt such elation at Button's willingness to eat even a little bit. Helen talked to Button as she busied herself with cleaning up. "So, Ida and Charlie are in Sarasota, Ava and Joe are in Destin. Laney, Lottie, Bobby, and Judith are at Big Sky Amusement Park. Can you believe that, Button? Bobby and Judith are riding roller coasters today. I hope they're having a fun birthday celebration with Laney. When she comes to see you tomorrow, can you wish her a happy birthday?"

Suddenly having an idea, Helen went to Button's wardrobe and searched for her small, silk red scarf. Finding it, she returned to Button and said, "How about we fix your hair and take a picture for Laney?" She found Button's hairbrush near the sink and brushed her hair back from her face. She rolled the scarf into a thin strip, tucked it behind the hair on her neck, and tied the ends on top of her head. She returned to the sink, found a pink-tinted lip balm, and added a little color to Vivian's pale lips. "You look lovely, Button. Let's take a red, white, and blue birthday picture for Laney. I can text it to her."

Helen asked Henry to take a picture of her and Button with her cell phone camera. He was happy to help and more than a little surprised that when he said, "Smile," Button actually joined Helen in doing so. He took several photos from which Helen could select her favorite.

Looking through the pictures, Helen said, "These are darling! Button, look at how cute we are!" Although she didn't speak, her eyes moved as if taking in the pictures. Helen selected her two favorites with their heads touching and smiles on their faces. In those two pictures, Button's eyes were even on the camera. They were adorable shots, far better than she thought they'd get. She texted them to Laney, wishing her a happy birthday and fun Independence Day with love from Button and her.

"There is a picnic in a couple of hours, Button. They are serving hamburgers and hotdogs. I heard they'll have watermelon, too. Why don't Henry and I let you rest for a little while? I imagine when you awaken, Angela or Jamie will help you dress in something red, white, and blue . . . or pink." She kissed Button on the cheek.

Henry patted Button on the hand, leaned toward her, and whispered, "I'm hoping to get more kisses from Helen, Button. What do you think?" She didn't reply, but looked at him and her lips seemed to soften as if she thought momentarily about smiling.

He joined Helen at the door, taking the cupcake platter from her. He carried them in one hand as he offered her his arm.

Helen tucked her arm in his and said again, "I like you very much."

Later that night, just after dark, Henry and Helen pushed Button in her wheelchair into position on the front patio to watch the fireworks.

She had eaten a little at the picnic with Angela's kind assistance. Angela had also been so sweet to help Button dress in a red top and white pants. She still had the silk scarf in her hair.

Helen knew this day was going to long be remembered as a special day and a pivotal one in her friendship with Henry. "I'm so excited to see the fireworks," Helen said just as the first one soared into the sky. The colors burst forth with sounds of excitement in the crowd. The fireworks were just far enough away to be lovely without craning one's neck to look skyward. The booming sounds were more muffled, allowing for people to talk.

Helen checked Button's face for a reaction. She appeared to be looking in the direction of the fireworks, but Helen couldn't ascertain if she was absorbing the beauty and excitement.

When the firework show came to an end, the residents, guests, and staff on the patio clapped and cheered. "That was spectacular!" Henry said to Helen. "A great way to top off the best Independence Day in years!"

Angela offered to take Button inside, and Helen and Henry said goodnight to her. Helen had intentionally left the remaining few cupcakes in Henry's apartment. She knew she could pick up the platter in a day or two. Despite the glorious day, Helen felt a little tired and was trying to ignore a headache. She and Henry snuck into a private alcove to say their goodnights.

Henry accompanied Helen to her car and waved as she pulled away. He was walking into the building when he stopped to talk to a friend. If not for that brief delay, he would have missed the horrible, sickening sound of tires screeching, truck horn blaring, and the heart-stopping sight of his Helen's blue sedan demolished and smoking in the intersection.

Henry took off running as fast as he could, shouting at his friend to get help! *Please, God,* he prayed.

Henry

When You Didn't See That Coming

Lottie and Nick were holding hands as they walked behind all seven of the family and friends who had chaperoned their day at Big Sky. Bobby, pushing Nannie in a wheelchair, was surrounded by Judith, Devon, Payton, Jennifer, and Jake. The group strolled just ahead of them along the themed Rainbow Road toward the exit following the Starry Sky Fireworks Show.

"Today was so awesome!" Nick said, his head close to Lottie in order to be heard.

"It was. Nannie told me she felt positively spoiled for her birthday. I'm glad it worked out for us to hang out together."

"Sort of together," he corrected with a chuckle. "I've never been here as a party of nine."

Lottie laughed. "I still don't know how our original plan to come here by ourselves turned into a family reunion."

"Me either, but I had fun. Your dad still kind of freaks me out, but his obsession over beating me at the Celestial carnival game made my day. I gave him some tips, and his score doubled from his first try; it was still below mine, but he said he could live with it."

"And check out my mom! I'm in shock. She rode Ghostly Orbit three times, and now she looks like a kid in her Spooky Sky shirt and ball cap. It's so out of character for her!"

"I love that she's holding that giant churro like a weapon to ward off ghosts. I think that's her second one."

"It is. She said that one is her to-go churro. I can't believe she and Dad haven't been here a dozen times. They had so much fun today."

"Devon had a great day hanging out with Payton. He isn't much of a roller coaster fan."

"No kidding! They cracked me up on the Shooting Star Skydiver coaster. Devon was screaming like a girl, way louder than me, and Payton was laughing hysterically. I love the picture you took of them with Jen and Jake in front of the sign after we all got off. Payton said she needed a commemorative photo of the experience."

"What was your favorite ride?"

Blushing a little, Lottie said, "The Skyway Gondola."

"Same." Nick had kissed her on that ride, in the dark, when they were finally alone. She was a little embarrassed when Jen had grinned and given her a knowing look as soon as they got off the ride. It was like she could read Lottie's mind.

"Our first kiss has to be my moment of the day."

Before Nick could respond, Devon motioned for their group to step off the main thoroughfare and over to a corner where they sold balloons and popcorn. He gestured for them to wait, took Payton by the hand and stepped with her a few steps away. He was talking on the phone. He said something to Payton, who ran to Jen, and then she ran and whispered something to Bobby.

"What's going on?" Lottie watched in confusion.

Nick shook his head. "I don't know."

"Something is wrong." Lottie walked to where her dad was kneeling in front of Nannie's wheelchair with Judith's hand on her shoulder. When Lottie stepped closer, she could see her grandmother crying.

"Dad?"

"Honey, Aunt Helen has been in a horrible car accident tonight. We need to head home right away."

Devon approached the group, motioning with his arms for them to huddle in closer. "Jamie just called from Enduring Grace. The accident happened right out front in the intersection. They assume she didn't see the truck coming."

Laney said in tears, "There isn't anyone in town to be with her."

Jen said, "I'm calling Mom as soon as we get to the car. Do you want her to call my grandma or do you want to call Ida yourself, Aunt Laney?

"Have her call your grandma for me, Sweetie."

Devon moved closer to Laney. "Before you leave, Miss Laney, I want you know that she isn't alone. Henry is with her. Jamie said he rode in the ambulance."

Henry sat alone in the corner of the emergency room. His thoughts looped continuously from the accident scene to ambulance ride. He'd last seen her, on a stretcher, as emergency room staff had taken her from the EMTs and pushed her frantically behind the huge door that said, *No Admittance.*

She was unconscious when he'd run up to her car door. Her head was slumped over to the side away from him. He kept calling her name as he pulled on the door, but it was so crumpled and misshaped that it would not open. Her driver's side window was shattered, the windshield cracked into thousands of tiny pieces, but still in place.

A frantic voice caught Henry's attention. "Oh God, sir, she rolled out of the parking lot right in front of me and just didn't move. I couldn't stop. Is she alright?"

Henry looked up at the truck driver, a younger man who appeared to be in one piece. Henry couldn't believe he'd never given the other driver a moment's thought. "She is breathing, but I can't get to her. The door is jammed. Are you injured?"

"Nah, I'm OK. Just freaked out!"

Others from the nursing home ran to the car. They informed Henry that emergency vehicles were on their way. They kept talking as Henry continued to search for a way into the car. Finally, the back passenger's door creaked open enough for Henry to squeeze inside.

"Henry, let me!" Jamie said from behind him. "I'm a nurse."

Henry barely replied to her. "I've got it." Henry scooted carefully toward Helen while Jamie rested her knee on the backseat and leaned in to see.

Henry quickly assessed that the blood on Helen's face appeared to be from a bloody nose. He didn't see major head injuries. Most likely the deployed airbag had been too strong with her small frame close to the wheel. He could hear and see her breathing, but he reached to check her pulse, satisfied for the moment. The sound of sirens was getting closer, thank God.

He turned back to Jamie. "She's unconscious, but it appears the blood is from her nose, not from a head injury. Hopefully fire trucks get here with equipment to pry her door open." They both looked up as flashing red lights swirled in front of them.

Jamie patted Henry on the shoulder. "Let's climb out so first responders can do their job."

The scene went from chaotic to an utter frenzy as police, firetrucks, and an ambulance arrived on the scene. Henry remained nearby, but respectfully out of the way. He overheard the truck driver give his account of the accident to police officers. He repeated the same story. "She pulled slowly out of the parking lot right in front of me and just stopped. I don't know if she had car trouble or what, but the car was rolling forward as if in slow motion. I tried to avoid her but I couldn't stop in time."

Henry moved into a better view of the car and watched intently as they got the door open and EMT professionals moved forward to assess Helen's injuries. They appeared to be stabilizing her left arm as they moved her onto a stretcher and into the ambulance.

He turned his head toward Jamie. "I'm going with her in the ambulance. Can you try to notify her friends?"

"I will, Henry, but I don't think they'll let you ride in the ambulance."

"They'll let me." He walked toward the ambulance, said something to the police officer and EMTs, and climbed in, sitting near the door and out of the way.

Henry was drawn out of his thoughts as he heard voices near the front desk in the emergency room. They'd said Helen's name. He stood and walked closer to them and realized it was Laney. She was standing on the far side of a younger man in shorts and a T-shirt.

"Laney?"

"Henry. Oh, Henry, bless you for coming to the hospital with Helen. How is she?"

"She is stable and in surgery for a compound fracture of her left arm. She regained consciousness in the ambulance. She showed signs of having a possible TIA, a mini-stroke. They are treating her as such, pending further tests, but they had to address that arm immediately. An orthopedic surgeon was called in and they said to anticipate a two- to three-hour surgery. We should get an update about three or four in the morning."

Bobby respectfully interrupted, "Henry, thank you for the update. I'm Laney's son, Bobby. We met at Button's birthday party very briefly. Forgive our appearance. We've been at Big Sky Amusement Park all day."

Henry shook his hand. "Yes, Helen mentioned that your whole family was there. How did you get word of the accident?"

Laney replied, "Nurse Jamie called Devon. He was with us."

"That was so kind of her. She said she would get in touch with one of you."

Bobby shared, "My wife and daughter are waiting in the car for a text from me to either wait or go home. Mom, I think since Henry is here, and it will be a couple of hours before she is out of surgery, I will take Judith and Lottie home, grab a shower, and come back in just a few minutes. Do you have your phone? Can you text me if you get any updates before I get back?"

Laney dug around in her purse, finding her cell phone on the bottom. She looked at it and her face registered surprise. "I have a text from Helen."

Henry recalled the afternoon mini photo session with Button. "She sent you pictures."

Laney's eye filled with tears as she saw the Fourth of July photos and happy birthday message. She shared her phone with Bobby, who put his arm around his mom.

"Button ate a little today," Henry shared. "She seemed aware of activities. I'm sure this is a horrible moment to say it, but I hope your birthday was a special one."

"It was, Henry. Thank you. I'm just distraught over Helen's accident."

"Trust me. I understand. Can I get you a cup of coffee?"

Bobby left Laney with Henry and jogged back to his car in the parking lot. He shared what he'd learned from Henry with Judith and Lottie and headed toward home.

Henry led Laney to a seat in a quiet corner. "I'll be right back with your coffee."

Laney looked at her cell phone again at the precious pictures of Helen and Button. It was uncanny how those two little pictures had boosted her strength and fortified her. She called Ida with an update. She and Charlie were driving home and would be at the hospital about the time Helen got out of surgery. Laney was still processing the possible stroke. That word was horribly scary. One thing was for sure, Helen was going to need extra help and support.

Henry returned with coffee in two small cups, little packets of sugar, and creamer. He pulled a plastic-wrapped spoon from his pocket. "I wasn't sure how you took your coffee."

"This will be perfect. I don't see a coffee station. Did you have to walk far?"

"No, not too far."

Henry and Laney talked comfortably and passed the excruciatingly long wait the best they could. Bobby returned just before Devon came to the emergency room to check on Helen's status. Ida and Charlie entered just after Devon arrived, and they all hugged and went over the accident and Helen's injuries again.

Just before four in the morning, a nurse asked the family of Helen Chastain to follow her to a private waiting room. She indicated the surgeon would be right in with an update, but Helen was in recovery, in stable, good condition.

A few tense moments later, a middle-aged women entered the room in scrubs. "Good morning, for those of you that don't know me, I'm Dr. Melinda Murphy. Your sister is in recovery, and surgery went well. She has been admitted, obviously, and in addition to her arm, Dr. Ryan Barrett, our lead neurologist, will be following up on some TIA (Transient Ischemic Attack) systems reported by the EMTs who transported her to the hospital. Can I answer any questions?"

Nobody said anything, shaking their heads. "OK, then, if you need anything, let the nursing team know once Ms. Chastain is moved to her floor. She'll be in recovery for a little while." She motioned respectfully toward Henry. "And I'm sure Dr. DeCamp can answer questions as well." She smiled at Henry and departed the room as swiftly as she'd entered.

All eyes turned to Henry as Laney asked in a shocked voice, "Doctor? You are Dr. Henry DeCamp?"

Henry nodded. "Retired."

Devon

When Heroes Show Their True Strength

"And that's when we discovered Helen's Henry was a doctor, a retired neurologist of all things!" Laney looked at Button for a reaction even though she knew there wouldn't be one. She was awake, sitting up in bed, but her head was turned toward the window.

"Test results proved she'd had a mini-stroke that night, which we assume led to the car accident. Speaking of the car, Old Blue was totaled. The insurance adjuster told Helen on the phone that damages exceeded the value of her car. Although she can no longer drive, it sure felt like the end of an era to say goodbye to her special sedan. Henry is still driving, but I don't know how much longer he intends to do so. He told me he can take Helen home when she is released from the hospital."

Laney continued, "So, Lottie brought me by on her way to work at the theater. She loves her job and guess what, Button? She has a boyfriend! He is Devon's brother, Nick, who you met at your birthday party. He goes to school in Orlando, and I think it's lovely that she'll have him to help her acclimate to college."

She paused momentarily before saying, "When she goes away to school, I will probably have to request a taxi more often. It's so hard, Button, to be what others consider old. It's been hard for me to give up driving when I still have the desire and ability to get out of the house. I don't want to be a burden to Bobby or Judith, but I just cannot sit in their house staring at the walls. Ida is in the same boat and now Helen will be, too. None of us are driving any longer. What do you think we should do, Button?"

Laney couldn't help but sigh as her beloved little sister simply stared out the window.

Devon announced from the doorway. "I'd hire a limousine so you sweet ladies can go wherever you want, whenever you want. Or, I'd move here. One of the retirement apartments would be wonderful for you, Miss Laney. You already have friends here, and there are lots of activities."

"Devon, how good to see you. I know it's only been a few days, but it feels much longer."

"It certainly does. How is Miss Helen today?" He walked into the room with Button's medicine on a tray.

"A little irritable, but otherwise, she was much improved when I saw her yesterday afternoon. Jennifer checked on her as she went to work this morning and reported that she is still grumpy, but doing better. She rested well in the night thanks to a different pain medication. Henry has been an absolute angel, and she is much more agreeable to his suggestions."

"Does she know he's a doctor?"

"I don't know and it's driving me crazy! I mean, I can't just come out and ask her if he hasn't told her. I wanted to ask him if he's had a conversation with her, but I haven't seen him in a couple of days. He usually takes a break to eat, shower, and the like while I'm there."

Devon nodded. "As I told you that night, you could have knocked me over with a feather! I had no idea he was a doctor. Obviously, I don't know him that well since he has a retirement apartment and doesn't live in the assisted-living wings, but it's rare to meet a doctor who introduces himself as just Henry."

"I like him," Laney insisted.

"Me, too."

"Speaking of men I like, can I rave about Nick for a minute? I enjoyed our day at Big Sky, of course, and yesterday evening he came over for dinner and game night. He and Bobby were ridiculously competitive over a board game. Lottie beat them both in the end!"

Devon laughed.

"Nick is very sweet to Lottie. That earns him many points in my book."

"I'm glad to hear it! He is a good kid, although he hates it when I call him that." Devon moved closer to the bed and set his medicine tray on Button's table.

Laney stood. "Let me move this chair so you can help Button with her medicine."

"Here, please, allow me." Devon moved the rocking chair to a convenient spot and assisted Laney comfortably back into her seat.

Turning back toward the bed, Devon inquired in a cheery voice, "Miss Vivian, how's my favorite girl this afternoon?"

Button did not respond.

"Vivian, I brought you some applesauce." Devon stroked the side of Button's face softly. His touch seemed to get her attention. She turned toward him, and he tapped her lips with a tiny bite of applesauce on a plastic spoon.

"Did she refuse to eat today?"

Devon answered Laney, but his focus was solely on Button. "She ate a little for breakfast and drank some of the nutrition shake. She didn't eat her lunch. We've tried taking her to the dining room and bringing trays here, but so far we've seen no pattern of her preferring one over the other."

Button opened her mouth and Devon began to slowly feed her tiny bites of applesauce. He cooed encouraging words to Vivian as she ate.

"The applesauce helps us get meds into her system. She can't swallow pills anymore. She's lost understanding of that request, although she will still swallow food and drink. Some of her meds are available in a liquid form and the others get chopped up into tiny bites. They are small enough to go down with applesauce, gelatin, and ice cream."

"She adores ice cream!"

"Not really anymore."

It saddened Laney to hear that. After a minute, she asked in a hushed, depressed tone, "Devon, how much longer?"

He turned to look kindly at Laney with sympathy in his eyes. "I don't know. A few months, maybe. I know it's agonizing to see how much this talkative, vibrant, loving lady has declined, but she still has a few decent days mixed in with these bad ones. I've seen patients like Vivian linger, but I think this precious soul has other plans. She said a few months ago that a goodbye here is a hello there. She talked a little about heaven."

"Button told me the same thing, years ago, after my husband passed away."

"She also explained to me, not all that long ago, that it feels unnatural to our souls, which are programmed for eternity, to be separated from those we love."

Laney arose from the rocking chair and came to stand next to Devon at Button's bedside. "We discussed that as well. I don't know if she'd been hallucinating or actually in the presence of an angel, but she said that John . . ."

Devon said John's name at the same time and finished her sentence, "John told her."

"Yes!"

"She has so much faith, Miss Laney. I admire her."

"Me, too. She always has had a love of God, church, bible study. The only thing she didn't do was sing in the church choir. She can't carry a tune!"

"Our Miss South Carolina can't sing?"

"No, she played the piano for her talent. At church, she also taught Sunday school for many little children and enjoyed our Ladies' Circle. I think her comments on how our eternal souls feel pained by separation is something we heard in a bible study once. I had forgotten, but Ida remembered. I honestly hope it is a visiting angel coming to comfort her. That comforts me as well."

As Button finished her applesauce and Devon gently gave her a sip of water, Laney shared more with him.

"My favorite poem is 'The Road Not Taken' by Robert Frost. Are you familiar with it?"

"I am."

"When we were all eighteen years old, Button, Helen, Ida, and I came, in our own ways, to a fork in the road. We were blessed to have taken the path less traveled. Many, many girls did not get the opportunity to go to college back then. Fortunately, our paths converged and that has made all the difference in the world for each of us. We needed each other and found the love, support, acceptance, and happiness we all craved. To us, Button wasn't only a beauty queen or Ida just Charlie's girl. I was no longer weird, and Helen was no longer alone. We became sisters, and we haven't let go of each other since. Knowing I have to let Button go is ever so slightly less painful to face if she is right about heaven. And, based on my experience, Devon, Button is always right."

Across town at the hospital, Helen grudgingly admitted, "You're right, Henry. The pain meds are helping. I just hate how they make me so groggy and stoned."

"I'm glad they are giving you relief, Helen. That's what they're intended to do. I'm so glad I was right." Henry squeezed her good hand as he, again, adjusted her light blanket.

He really must stop smiling and winking at me, she thought. "You aren't always right."

Henry studied her face. "Are we circling back to this morning's disagreement? You know I'm correct in this too, Helen. There are only two paths forward: I stay with you at your house, or you stay with me in my apartment at Enduring Grace. You must see reason. I am not trying to dishonor you by living with you out of wedlock. At our age, does that really even matter?"

"I know Ida and Laney will come by my house to help me."

"They don't drive any longer. How are they going to get groceries, do laundry, prepare meals, or clean the kitchen? You shouldn't be doing much of anything. Your wrist fracture involves a long rehabilitation. Currently, you need immobilization, but after you heal, physical therapy will most likely be prescribed. You also had a TIA and need to be monitored closely to decrease the likelihood of a stroke. I can manage your recovery better than anyone."

"Because you're a doctor?"

"No, because I like you very much!"

That took the wind out of Helen's argument. "It's asking too much of one person, Henry. Are you safe to drive? You're a year older than me.

Maybe I could hire a home health nurse to stop by a few days a week. How can I allow you to help me in and out of the shower, to dress? I'll die of embarrassment!"

"OK, *now* my answer is because I'm a doctor! I'll close my eyes if you insist. And, as for my driving, I'm still confident in my abilities."

"What will people think? What will your family think?

"I'm sure I don't care what people think. My family would be surprised if I didn't suggest we live together."

"What? Why? They don't even know me."

"They know of you and they trust my judgment."

"Henry, I don't want to be a burden."

"It's my idea, Helen."

"I'm afraid you'll discover that you don't like me within a week. I'm very picky!"

"Your house or mine?"

After a few seconds of silence, Henry repeated sweetly, "Your house or mine?"

Helen muttered, "Mine."

"Am I interrupting?" Henry turned and Helen peeked around him to see Ida walking into the room as if entering the field of battle.

"Come in, Ida. Is Charlie with you?" Helen reached out her good hand to her friend as Henry moved toward the foot of her bed.

"He stayed home this afternoon, but told me to give you his love. Ava is multitasking in her car and on a conference call in the parking lot. I'm just here for a quick visit. Your color looks much improved. How are you feeling?"

"Well, my bossy personal physician here assures me that I am on the mend."

Henry lifted his eyebrows at Helen. *Is she still trying to pick a fight?* In answer to Ida's question, he shared, "She is doing exceedingly well.

Consensus is that she will most likely go home day after tomorrow. We were just discussing arrangements."

Helen's eyes narrowed on Henry. *He's going to get it!*

Ida shared, "Well, that's one of the reasons I stopped by. Helen dear, as you know, Button isn't doing well at all. Laney and I are concerned for her and believe it's imperative that someone check on her every day. Ava, Jennifer, and even Bobby and Judith have offered to help. We have figured out, we think, how to alternate our days between you and Button. Don't you worry for a second that you're a burden in the least."

Helen frowned. "No, Ida. If you and Laney can be with Button, that would make me happy. I don't want you exhausted from adding in my needs; nor do I want everyone jumping through hoops to help me."

Ida offered a counter argument. "But, Helen, we love you, dear, and want to assist you in your recovery."

"Thank you for your sweet offer, Ida. I love you for it, but Henry's medical background makes him tremendously capable and qualified to help me during my recovery."

"But what about your meals?"

"Henry is an excellent crook, um, cook!" Helen looked baffled as her medicine was really taking over.

"Are you, Henry? That's wonderful!" Ida beamed. "And I suppose you can handle a little laundry. Groceries can be delivered so you don't have to leave her alone."

Henry suppressed a smile. He saw right through Ida's little game. Helen probably would have noticed Ida's ploy if not for the pain medication she took a little earlier. Henry could see she was relaxed and more than a little loopy.

"Well, it's settled then. I will leave you to finalize your plans. Helen, I think it's wise to have Henry move in with you." She nodded her approval at Henry.

Helen murmured, "I like him very much." She finally gave into the pain meds and closed her eyes for much-needed sleep.

Henry motioned that he would follow Ida into the hallway. He pulled Helen's door closed. He turned toward Ida. "You little schemer!"

"Why, Dr. DeCamp, whatever do you mean?"

"I sense your friends have greatly underestimated you."

"No, they know me quite well. Helen is far too sharp when not under the influence of drugs. So, Henry, you are clear to move, at least temporarily, into Helen's house. Take care of yourself; this is a big step for Helen. Meds or no meds, she wouldn't allow this if she didn't want to be with you. She was making up excuses for propriety's sake."

"I know."

Ida handed Henry a slip of paper. "This is contact information for me and Laney. Try me first. Laney often forgets to have the volume up on her cell. My daughter, Ava, has already created a plan for meals. She, Judith, and Jennifer will be dropping things off after you get settled. I understand you are more than capable in the kitchen, but we want to do this for you and Helen."

"Thank you. You are a wonderful . . . sister."

"I love being called that. Good luck, Henry." Ida smiled and turned toward the elevator.

"Ida, thank you again. I care about Helen very much."

She turned after entering the elevator and smiled knowingly at Henry. "I know you do."

Lottie, Laney, and Change

When You Overthink Everything

Lottie was singing and dancing to songs from a favorite musical as she dried her hair and selected a cute outfit for Nick's birthday dinner date. She'd invited him to pick dinner plus a movie, miniature golf, or bowling. He selected Bill's Italian for pizza and miniature golf. *Fun choice,* she thought. She had offered bowling, but truthfully, she was horrible at it, always throwing a series of gutter balls or occasionally knocking down a single pin. Miniature golf seemed to require more luck than skill, and it wasn't something they'd ever done together.

She changed clothes a few times, ultimately deciding that she was trying too hard. Ultimately, she chose denim shorts, a blue and yellow floral tank top and comfortable sandals. She pulled her long hair into a high ponytail, which she thought looked cute and was cooler for the warm July night. With frustration, she tapped concealer lightly on a couple of blemishes and added mascara and a berry-colored lip gloss.

As Lottie was putting her wallet and other things in a small cross-body bag, she heard a knock on her bedroom door. "Come in," she offered.

She looked up to see Nannie enter her room, carrying an envelope.

"Hi Nannie. How was your day? Jen called earlier and mentioned she'd stopped by to see Helen and Henry. She said they seem to be getting along well."

"Yes, they are. It's been a week since she went home and Henry is still there."

Lottie chuckled. "That's great and kind of amazing!" Looking at her watch, she sat down on the corner of her bed. "I'm leaving in about ten minutes to pick up Nick. I'm treating him to birthday pizza and miniature golf." Pointing to the gift-wrapped box sitting next to her bag, she added, "I got him a Big Sky T-shirt. The design is super cute."

Laney nodded, "I'm sure he'll like that. I thought I saw a small box in the kitchen too."

"Yes, you did. I bought a couple of Payton's cutest cupcakes this afternoon. His cupcake even has an edible chocolate candle he can eat instead of lighting it and blowing it out. Payton is so creative!"

"She sure is, and it sounds like you've thought of everything. Lucky guy!"

"Thanks, Nannie. Is that envelope for me?"

"Yes, it is." She handed Lottie the envelope from the Redding College Office of Financial Aid. Watching Lottie closely, she shared, "I couldn't help but see the return address."

Lottie tossed the envelope, unopened, on her dresser. "I told you that I needed to look at all options."

"You did. My question is why?"

"What do you mean?"

"Sweetie, you've been talking about going to Florida College of Theater and Arts for more than two years. Why the sudden change of heart?"

Lottie shook her head. She didn't want to answer. She didn't want to lie.

Laney didn't want to push, so she softly offered, "You know you can talk to me about anything that's bothering you."

Relenting a bit, Lottie shared, "I know, Nannie. Thank you. It's just that there is a tremendously high price tag attached to my plans for college in Orlando. I thought it might be smarter to stay here. It's probably the right decision."

Laney took a deep breath. "Why don't you keep thinking about it? We can talk another time. But, sweetheart, saying, 'It's probably the right decision,' with tears in your eyes and despair in your voice means it probably is not the right decision at all. Go enjoy your date with Nick. Please tell him I wish him a happy birthday. Things have a way of working themselves out."

Lottie grabbed her purse and Nick's gift and hugged Nannie. "I'll see you later tonight or in the morning."

Laney followed Lottie out of her bedroom, turned out the light, and closed the door. She made her way to her bedroom and sat quietly for a few minutes. She could almost hear Helen's voice scolding her for intruding into business that wasn't hers. Laney could argue that Lottie was her business, but she respected that Bobby and Judith's finances were not. She didn't have much, but she would gladly offer funds toward Lottie's education. Would it be welcome or rejected, she wondered?

She debated the questions in her mind. In the end, Helen won. Laney knew she shouldn't get involved in this unless she was specifically asked for help or advice. She just needed her brain to communicate with her mouth!

Laney made her way through the quiet house to the kitchen. With Bobby and Judith also out with friends for the evening, she made herself a plate of cheese, crackers, and fruit. She took her plate to the living room, sat in her favorite chair, and turned on the television. Clicking through numerous channels, she found nothing very interesting. The contestant on a game show somehow guessed the correct answer, *jar of peanut butter*, winning lots of cash and a shiny red sports car. Laney switched the channel to find lottery winners trying to decide which mansion they'd like to buy and then decided everyone else's money was annoying her! She turned off the television.

She'd never tied success, joy, or contentment to money and the things it could buy. She couldn't care less about designer-label clothes, jewelry, or fancy new cars. She'd just wanted a home, health, and a simple, happy life. Without a doubt, God had answered her prayers.

She'd been terrified when her husband, Robert, had died, leaving her to raise Bobby alone. But, their needs had been met and, thanks to some budgeting and frugality, she had managed just fine. She had an unexpected thought, a memory actually, recalling an opportunity Robert had to transfer to Denver for a promotion just after Laney discovered she was pregnant. Despite loving the beauty of the mountains, Laney felt and Robert agreed that *who* they lived near was more important than *what*. It punched her in the gut to think what might have been had they moved. What if they had moved to Colorado? Would Robert have lived? Would he still be with them? Should they have chosen that path?

Realizing that her mind was drifting into dangerous territory, Laney looked around the living room. Nothing in this room belonged to her, and yet she'd been happy with her family. Should she remain here? The house felt so quiet and empty tonight. It hurt to know she would soon be feeling Lottie's absence on a daily basis. Button's, too.

Would living elsewhere alter her feelings of loneliness? Despite Devon's suggestion that she live at Enduring Grace, she couldn't afford it. And even that thought, as depressing as it could have been, was not her main concern. She wanted to help Lottie get her college education without the crushing debt Bobby and Judith, and Lottie herself, were surely facing. She didn't have much money in savings, living mostly on social security, but she'd give it to them in a heartbeat.

Thoughts continued to swirl through Laney's mind. She looked around, sitting in the dark except for a little light streaming in from the kitchen. *Good Lord*, she thought, *I'm staring at the walls!*

Laney took her cheese plate and glass back to the kitchen, loading them into the dishwasher. *When stressed, bake*, she thought. *I'll make snickerdoodles for Helen and Henry.* She gratefully pulled ingredients out of the cabinets and refrigerator and pushed play on her CD player. "Sugar, butter, flour."

A short time later, a delightful cinnamon aroma filled the kitchen as Laney put the cookies on a rack to cool. She heard her cell phone's ring tone over the music playing in the kitchen, turned down the volume, and answered the phone.

"Miss Laney, how are you? This is Mary Carolyn."

"Mary Carolyn, what a lovely surprise! I'm doing well. How are things in Orlando?"

"Out of this world!"

Laney laughed. "You got a job at Big Sky!"

"I did! I start training in a few days. I'm going to be working in guest relations. I'm so excited; it's my favorite park."

"I'm thrilled for you, Mary Carolyn! Has Claire found a job there as well?"

"Not yet, but she will. She has her heart set on being a performer. If she could dance or even be a character who waved to kids from a parade float, she'd be in heaven. She's been to some auditions, so she's hopeful."

"I'll keep my fingers crossed for her."

"Fingers and toes," she laughed. "There's another reason I wanted to get in touch with you. Our chapter is in need of a ritual adviser. As you know, it's not a tremendous time commitment and much of it can be handled over the phone, answering questions and the like. You don't have to go to the house on a weekly or even regular basis. I know you aren't driving, but if you are needed at the house, one of the sisters would pick you up and take you back home. And, even that would be limited, for example, to Initiation or Founders' Day. You would be amazing at teaching new initiates about the history, meaning, and tradition behind our ritual. Everything is scheduled well in advance for you to put on your calendar. And, most important, Claire's mom, Gina, is chapter adviser, and she and other advisers would cover for you anytime you aren't available. Would you be interested in sharing a little wisdom and sorority love with the chapter?"

"Mary Carolyn, I'm eighty-two years old."

"Yes, I know. So what? My grandmother is eighty-five, and she and my grandfather are on a cruise right now. I think you'd love it, Miss Laney, but it's up to you. If it feels like too much for you to take on, that's fine."

Laney started to thank Mary Carolyn for thinking of her. As she opened her mouth to kindly decline, her eyes turned to the darkened living room and her unwelcome feelings of loneliness and isolation.

"Please ask Gina to call me. I think I might be interested."

"Oh, Miss Laney, I'm so excited for the chapter! They will adore you and they really, really need you!"

And I need them, she thought.

Laney cleaned up the kitchen, leaving it sparkling clean. She put the snickerdoodles in a plastic container for Helen and Henry after stealing just one. She put a piece of masking tape on top and wrote Helen's name in permanent ink. She would ask Bobby if he could drop her by Helen's house tomorrow, just long enough to drop off cookies.

She bypassed the living room, not wishing to dwell there, and went to her room. It wasn't very late, but she felt more tired than usual. She prepared for bed and, upon climbing under the sheets, she opened a book she'd pulled off her shelves. She'd had it for years and remembered it fondly for the words of encouragement it contained. As she thumbed through the pages, a piece of paper, now yellowed with age, fell into her lap.

It was the poem "The Road Not Taken" by Robert Frost. Her Robert had cut the clipping with the poem on it out of their local newspaper. They had debated in college, working in the school library, about the true meaning of the poem. Laney believed it was about choices in life, uncertainty when making a decision on which way to go. Robert had argued it was about being a nonconformist and choosing to go in a unique direction despite societal pressures. Laney could almost hear his voice. *That's it*, she thought.

Laney climbed back out of bed, dug through her side table for a piece of paper, pen, and tape. She adhered the poem to the paper and wrote a note, which she then placed on Lottie's pillow.

Lottie,

Life often leaves us standing at a fork in the road to choose the path that's best for us. Most likely either direction you pick will work out fabulously in the end, but I think choosing the road less traveled, unique, and perfect for you will be the path you someday realize made all the difference in your life.
Have faith!

Love,
Nannie

Lottie's Decision

When You Face a Fork in the Road

Lottie sat down on her bed and read the note and poem Nannie left for her a second time. She'd looked down the hall toward Nannie's room to see if her lights were on. Her room was dark and it was past midnight. Lottie knew she was most likely sleeping.

With one month to her eighteenth birthday and the start of her freshman year in college, it was time, past time, for Lottie to make a decision. She was officially enrolled in college in Orlando; she had her class schedule and dorm assignment with a potluck roommate. She had registered for recruitment, knowing she could cancel at the last minute. None of these checklist items were done if she changed course and stayed in town to attend classes. If she needed to cancel her plans and rearrange everything to go here, it was time to make a decision.

Nick's birthday night had been so much fun! Everything had gone as she'd imagined it would, except that he easily beat her at miniature golf. Apparently, a little skill was involved after all. She'd like to see Nick and her Dad have a putt-putt battle sometime.

He loved the Big Sky T-shirt and promised he'd wear it next time they went to the park. The birthday cupcakes were delicious, and they both made Button's famous yummy sound when biting into them. He talked all night about things he wanted to show her on campus or in Orlando. She hadn't realized that he noticed her dampened enthusiasm and was surprised when he'd called her on it.

"What's going on, Lottie? Something is bothering you about college."

She had attempted a bright smile. "I'm very excited about college."

"Try again!"

"I am. I love everything about it."

Nick cocked his head and stared at her. They were sitting on a park bench overlooking the lake as the sun went down. He turned his body further toward her and raised his eyebrows as if waiting for an answer.

Lottie blew out a breath. "I don't know if I'm going to Florida College for Theater and Arts after all."

"Why? What happened?" Nick ran his hand through her ponytail.

"I heard my parents talking, weeks ago, and college is twice as expensive as my dad thought it would be. They will have to take out loans and take on major debt for me to go there. If I stay here and live at home, they can probably cover it. If I go to Orlando, I will be forcing my dad to work until long after he wants to retire, and I can't be that selfish."

"I'm sorry. I understand. My parents have taken out loans for both me and Devon to pursue our dreams. Our deal with them is that we will help pay back half once we have jobs and sufficient income after college. I haven't asked, but I assume Devon is already paying some toward those loans. I don't make a lot, but I work on campus in the fitness center at the front desk."

Lottie nodded. "Jen has a sorority sister who is a manager at the performing arts center on campus, but she sent a nice reply to my email explaining that there aren't any openings. She said if she heard of something, she'd let me know. She suggested I go to the job fair when school starts. She was confident I'd find something."

"I'm sure you would."

"I just feel stuck, frozen. My mind is caught in this loop of constant *what-if* scenarios. What if I go to Orlando? What if I stay here? I wish I had a magic crystal ball."

"Or a fairy godmother."

"Oh, I have one of those. Jen has been my confidant and adviser for years. We joke that she is my fairy godmother. Nick, what do you think I should do?"

"I think I'm the last person who should chime in on this decision."

"But do you want me to go to Orlando?"

"Yes, of course. But, whether you are here or there isn't going to change how I feel about you. It will complicate things, but we'll figure it out. This decision has to be between you and your parents."

Lottie leaned in and kissed him. "It's wonderful to hear that your feelings about me won't change. Mine won't change either, but I've read articles about long-distance romance tragedies. It's high on my *what-if* list of worries!"

He kissed her back. "No worries."

With her mind back on the poem in her hand and a decision to be made, Lottie left her room and tiptoed to her parents' bedroom, where she could see a soft light glowing under the door. She knocked softly.

"Come in."

Lottie opened the door to find her parents sitting in bed reading. Her dad had papers surrounding him, and her mother was looking at her cell phone.

"Charlotte, sweetheart, is everything okay? Are you feeling sick?" Her mother was concerned.

"I'm fine. I wondered if we could talk."

"Of course." Her mom motioned for Lottie to take a seat at the foot of the bed.

She climbed up on the bed, but positioned herself, just like when she was little, between them. Her parents pushed their pillows together behind her.

Looking at her in concern, Bobby, only slightly joking, but hoping to lighten her mood, asked, "Do I get to punch Nick now?"

"No, Dad. He's perfect."

Bobby rolled his eyes. "How nice. Then, what's bothering you?"

Lottie took a deep breath. "The cost of college. Listen, I apologize, but several weeks ago I was walking toward the kitchen and accidentally heard you guys talking about college expenses, finances, and retirement. I should have walked away from a private conversation, but it kind of involves me, so I stayed. I heard everything."

"Charlotte Leigh Walsh, you know better!" Her mother was shocked.

"I do. I'm sorry, Mom. But, now that I am aware that college expenses are higher than you expected, and you're facing such a huge financial burden to send me to Florida College for Theater and Arts, I can't go. I will change plans, live at home, and go to Redding College. They have a fairly decent drama department, so it'll be fine. I was offered a scholarship and can get $5,000 a semester in financial aid, which I will pay back when I graduate and have a job."

Lottie expected to see her mom leap with joy, but neither parent said a word. She looked left and right at her parents' faces. There was no joy.

Bobby put his arm around Lottie and hugged her. "I'm sorry you overheard all of that, sweetheart. Truthfully, it was about me and some concerns I'd been keeping that were weighing me down. Part of it was just frustration with work and some displaced jealousy over younger co-workers succeeding at such a high level without putting in the time and paying the dues I had to pay. Getting older isn't easy sometimes, Lottie. But, you heard one conversation on one bad day. We can afford to send you to Orlando for college, sweetheart."

"Charlotte, read this." Judith handed her cell phone to Lottie.

She read the first sentence: *Judith, we are pleased to offer you the position of designer.*

"Mom! Oh, my gosh, congratulations!" Lottie turned and hugged her. Staying snuggled next to her mother, Lottie added, "You'll love doing this, and they are so lucky to have you, but I know you are going back to work to pay for my education."

"Charlotte, I'm thrilled to be given this opportunity. I love decorating! And, if some of my earnings help you, then I'm thrilled even more. I don't know how long you were in the living room eavesdropping on your dad and me, but I hope you heard the most important part of that conversation. We love each other, and we're a team. Your dad needed a little sense knocked into his head, and I mean that lovingly, but this family is not solely his responsibility to support. I am strong, smart, talented, and capable, and we are partners, equally, in the care and keeping of this family. And we love you very much, Lottie!"

Tears sprang to Lottie's eyes when her mom used her nickname. She hugged her even harder.

Her Dad leaned in for a group hug and asked, "What's that paper in your hand?"

"Nannie left this on my pillow tonight. She doesn't know anything about the conversation I overheard, but she has noticed that something has been on my mind. I applied to Redding, just to see if I'd get accepted and receive a huge scholarship offer. I did get accepted, but the scholarship was less than the one I'd get in Orlando. The major savings comes from me living at home."

She handed the note and poem to Bobby. Judith leaned over to read it.

Bobby shared, "'The Road Not Taken' is my mom's favorite poem."

Judith added, "I see what she is saying, and I have to agree. You should take the path that's calling you, even if, or maybe because, it is the road less traveled. Go to Orlando, Lottie, and go after your dreams. I don't think you will ever look back and wonder *what if* you had chosen the other path. You may, just out of curiosity, but never with regret. I know I suggested you stay here, time and time again, but every time I did so, I saw your resolve and desire to go elsewhere grow stronger. You made the right decision long ago, sweetheart!"

Bobby said, "I completely agree. Don't worry about the money, Lottie. We're fine in that regard, I promise. And besides, things have a way of working themselves out."

Lottie's tears turned into an all-out ugly cry. She saw tears in their eyes, too. "Thank you so much. I love you!"

They talked a little longer before she hugged them both one last time and scooted off the bed. She leaned back and picked up the poem and note Nannie had left for her.

"Mom, after I thank Nannie for this in the morning, could you help me get it framed?" Judith nodded. "I know the perfect place."

Lottie smiled and left her parents' room, closing the door behind her. She went to the kitchen to get water and pain reliever. She'd cried herself into a headache. It was well after one o'clock, but she texted Nick, "I talked to my parents. Happy tears. Next stop, Orlando."

She pulled out paper and a pen and wrote Nannie a note, which she slipped under her door. As she finally climbed into bed, her phone chimed with a text reply from Nick. "Best birthday present ever!"

Button's Influence

When a Little Visit Is a Big Deal

"I can't stop eating these snickerdoodles," Henry complained.

"How many have you had?" Helen asked.

"Today? Two. And two yesterday."

"That's nothing. I once ate four in one day. I told Laney to stop delivering cookies. This is the third batch since I was released from the hospital. Of course, she knows I don't mean it. Wait until you try her Thanksgiving mashed potatoes!" Helen cringed at what an awkward and presumptuous thing that was to say.

She offered, "I'm not implying you should spend Thanksgiving with me or assuming that you'll still be living here. Laney just makes the most amazing mashed potatoes, which is all I meant by that statement."

Henry looked up from his book. "Thanks for the clarification." He lifted his book as if reading something very interesting simply to hide his smile. "I make an amazing honey-glazed ham."

"Do you? We don't usually have ham, but it would be a lovely complement to my roasted turkey."

"I am also the king of cornbread stuffing!"

"Then, perhaps you should be here for Thanksgiving to share your culinary talents."

"OK."

Helen looked at Henry in surprise. She couldn't help but smile. "OK," she agreed.

The doorbell rang and Henry stood to answer the door. "Are we expecting company?"

"Not that I recall."

Henry opened the door to find Lottie on the porch, holding a small, purple box.

"Hi, Henry. Sorry to drop by unannounced, but I brought something for you and Aunt Helen. Is she awake?"

"She is! Please come in. It's so hot out today. How are you not melting?"

"Seriously! August is brutal. It's so humid today." Lottie spotted Helen in her living room recliner and showed her the box she was carrying. "I am making my rounds to say goodbye before I leave for college on Saturday. I stopped by to hug Payton at work and, voilà, cupcakes!"

Helen looked over Lottie's head to smile at Henry. They certainly didn't need more dessert in the house. "You are such a dear, Lottie. Thank you. Can we offer you a drink? I believe we have tea, lemonade, ice water."

"No thanks, I have a soda in the car that I've been sipping as I run errands."

Henry offered to take the cupcakes, excusing himself with a slight bow. "I will leave you ladies to your visit. Call me if you need anything."

Lottie pulled the footstool from a nearby chair closer to Helen. "So, you seem to be feeling well. And you look so happy! Henry is such a nice man. It's awesome that you two have fallen in love with each other."

Helen's eye widened. *In love?*

Lottie continued to tell Helen about her day in her charming, enthusiastic way. "I've been on a tour around town the last couple of days. Nick and I said goodbye to Carson at the theater last week, but I stopped back by earlier to thank him again for the opportunity. He said to let him know by March if I plan to be in town next summer and want to work there again. He is such a nice guy.

"I saw some high school friends yesterday. We are scattering all over the country for college, but promised to stay in touch. Last night, Jen asked me to meet her at Aunt Ava and Uncle Joe's house. Aunt Ida and Uncle Charlie were there. Jen surprised me by asking if I'll be a bridesmaid in her wedding in June. I've never been a bridesmaid before and I'm so excited. You were a bridesmaid for Nannie, weren't you?"

"I sure was! For Ida and Button as well. I have a large scope of experience as a bridesmaid if you need any guidance."

Lottie smiled and nodded. "Payton is maid of honor. I am so glad I've gotten to know her. I love her already. I gave her a big hug when I got the cupcakes. And now I'm here to see you."

"Well, I'm delighted you stopped by. Are you packed and ready to go?"

Lottie nodded. "Everything is lined up around the edges of my room with my bedspread, sheets, and towels washed and ready in the laundry room. Mom and I have had so much fun the last few weeks getting me set for college. My roommate and I connected and she seems to be super nice. She loves amusement parks, so we have that in common. She said she signed up for sorority recruitment, too, which makes me happy that I'll know at least one person. It's going to be so hot next week. At least we get to wear a simple recruitment T-shirt they'll give us with whatever shorts we want and sandals or sneakers the first day. Nannie said my dressiest day, Preference Day, is equivalent to her most casual day. I still can't believe you all wore hose and high heels with fancy dresses."

"And gloves. You know the story about Button and the black gloves?"

Lottie giggled. "I do. Poor Aunt Button. I would have been mortified to realize I had given myself a mustache."

"Oh, she was definitely mortified. I thought she was going to faint!"

She and Helen laughed. After talking for a few more minutes, Lottie looked at her watch.

"So, I think I'm all set. Mom and Nannie have given me a little recruitment advice such as be myself, enjoy making new friends, wear comfortable shoes. Do you have any tips I should know?"

"Just one. Smile, dear. All day long." *God bless sweet Button*, Helen thought.

"I will. I'll keep you posted and text pictures of my dorm room and everything. I'll be home by Thanksgiving at the latest and I'll see you then."

Lottie carefully hugged Helen to avoid bumping her arm. "No, please don't get up. I can see myself out. Please tell Henry to take great care of you. He's a keeper!"

Helen smiled at Lottie, but suddenly felt a huge wave of sadness. Despite the excitement Helen had for her college adventures ahead, she would miss this precious child. *No, not child*, she thought, correcting herself. *This young woman*. She couldn't imagine how Laney was feeling and made a mental note to call her much more often.

She shook off her morose thoughts and purposefully brightened her tone. "I love you, sweet Lottie. I can't wait to hear all about your college experience. It seems as though you've matured into a young woman, but I'm having a hard time believing you are now the age I was when I came to Florida for college and met my sisters. I will pray you find the same special people in your young adult life. I do believe you've already met one very special boy."

"Yes, I have."

"Good. Go take the world by storm, Lottie. Our world needs more young women like you."

"I will do my best! I love you, Aunt Helen. Thank you."

Lottie waved to her as she left. As the door closed, Henry came back into the living room to sit on the footstool, pulling it even closer to Helen. He took her hand and kissed it. "Did I happen to hear the word *love* attached to my name a few minutes ago?" He chuckled at the look on Helen's face. This was going to be fun!

Lottie took a sip of the drink in her car. She had one more stop to make, but she wasn't looking forward to it. When standing at the cash register to buy cupcakes for Payton, Lottie noticed petits fours in the cabinet. At the last minute, she added one for Button.

She hadn't visited Button much since she moved to Enduring Grace. It was so hard to see her losing this battle with Alzheimer's, but she didn't want to move to Orlando without seeing Button; she worried she'd regret that decision.

She pulled into the parking lot just as it started sprinkling and jogged inside with her purse, tiny cake box, and umbrella. She skirted around the edges of the living room, which was mostly empty. Someone was playing the piano at the other side of the room. Lottie knew, if not for Alzheimer's, Button would have enjoyed playing that piano very much.

Lottie pushed the giant button on the wall that led to the residence wings and slowly entered, feeling horribly uncomfortable.

"Lottie?"

She turned at the sound of her name and saw Devon standing near the nurses' station. Walking up to him, she got right to the point. "I came to see Button."

"I'll walk with you." He motioned toward the hallway where they moved slowly toward Button's room. "She was awake a few minutes ago. She ate a little today and even replied, 'No,' when I asked if she liked her lunch. She still has a bit of impishness inside her. I think all four of those eighty-year-old sorority girls, as they call themselves, are the definition of feisty."

"They have been as long as I can remember. I think it was because of them, and women like them, that so many things have changed. My generation owes them our thanks."

"Agreed."

Devon stopped at Button's door. "I'll leave you for your visit. If you need anything, just push the call button on the control pad attached to her bed."

"Thanks, Devon. I brought her a petit fours, but I don't really feel comfortable feeding her."

"I understand. One tip I'll suggest is to put a tiny bit on a plastic spoon—there is one in her drawer—and see if she'll lick the spoon. I can come back in a few minutes to help you."

Lottie nodded and turned to walk into Button's room. She was sitting up in bed, dressed in a pink T-shirt, looking out the window at the falling rain.

"Hi, Aunt Button. It's me, Lottie. I brought you a pretty petit fours. It's white with a beautiful pink flower on top. I also wanted to say good-bye before I leave for college on Saturday."

She was shocked to see Button turn and look at her. She didn't say anything, but seemed to be studying her very closely. Lottie wondered if Button thought she was a young version of Laney. It was fine if she did.

Lottie approached Button's bedside, put her purse and umbrella on the nightstand, and opened the box to reveal Payton's delightful tiny cake. Button's eyes moved from Lottie to the cake, so she set it down on the table stretching across the bed and reached into the drawer for a plastic spoon. She unwrapped and dipped the spoon into the edge of the cake, offering it to Button for a taste. At first she didn't move, but slowly Button's tongue reached out ever so slightly to lick the spoon. As she gave Button tiny tastes of the petit fours, she talked to her about her plans for college, starting with her dorm room color choice in their shared favorite color, pink.

"My bedspread is white, which my mom didn't think was a great idea, but it looks super cute with the pink and white polka dot sheets. I have one polka dot pillow case and then an all-white pillow sham, so I think it won't be too over the top. I like it. It's bright and cheery. My roommate, who I haven't met in person yet, is from Houston, Texas. She said her bedding is a bright floral, so we'll have a pretty colorful room."

Lottie put the spoon down on a paper towel, deciding a few bites was probably plenty for now. She put the lid back on the box and pulled the rocking chair close to the bed where she sat for a chat.

"Aunt Button, I'm going through recruitment at the end of next week. I have no idea what I'll decide or who will offer me a bid. My mom, whose sorority isn't on campus in Orlando, never stayed tremendously close to her sorority sisters, but Nannie obviously did. I don't want my expectations to be too high; like what you four have had all these years. That might not be realistic. But, I'm an only child, like you, and I love the idea of having sisters to share some of the special moments coming in my life." She told Button about Jen's wedding plans and her excitement about being a bridesmaid.

Lottie saw Button nod slightly. *Oh my gosh, is she listening to me?*

"Has Nannie told you about my boyfriend, Nick? We met at the community theater at the beginning of the summer. He is so sweet and super cute. He makes me laugh. He says the same about me, which is crazy. I never thought I'd have a boyfriend because I'm such a nerd! But, he is too. I guess that's why we click. Dad was acting weird about Nick at first, but they've bonded over these silly competitions they've been having. Last week, Dad blew the dust off our old video game player and challenged Nick to a few rounds of a racing game. It's a video game that Dad and I used to play. Anyway, Dad beat Nick, and Mom and I were in hysterics at his goofy victory dance. They're already talking about a rematch sometime when we're home."

Button's attention drifted back to the window as Lottie chatted about Nick. She guessed she had carried on about him a little too long. Lottie noticed the rain had stopped and thought she should probably head home during a break in the weather.

"Aunt Button," Lottie couldn't talk beyond a lump in her throat. She folded her hands together and leaned her hands and elbows on Button's bed. She cleared her throat, but couldn't battle the tears in her eyes.

"I love you, Aunt Button. I have nothing but fabulous, amazing memories of fun times with you and Nannie. You've always been an extra grandmother in my life, and I just wanted to thank you for everything. Thank you for being there on big days like birthdays and Christmases and for cheering for me in school plays and at soccer and softball games. I wish I had been talented enough to learn piano from you, but there is no denying I was your worst student ever."

Lottie's head fell to her folded hands on Button's bed, and she wept. She suddenly felt a hand on her head, gently stroking her hair. "Don't cry," Button whispered.

"Oh, Button!" Lottie looked at her with tears streaming down her face.

Button put her hand on Lottie's hands and said softly, "Love."

"I love you too, Aunt Button." Lottie believed with all her heart that Button would be the most fiercely loving and protective guardian angel heaven will have ever seen! And Lottie felt blessed to know Button would be watching out for her when that time came.

As Button's attention was pulled back to the window, Lottie saw Devon in her periphery. She turned toward him and saw tears in his eyes.

"I heard her speaking to you when I walked in just now. I hope you know how special and incredible that was, Lottie."

"I do, Devon. It's so weird. I was at Payton's to buy cupcakes when I suddenly spotted the petits fours and knew I had to buy one and come see Button today. I wanted to tell her I loved her and say goodbye. It's amazing how all of our lives have become so linked together."

Lottie stood and hugged Devon. "Thank you for taking such good care of her."

"You are a loving, generous, and strong young lady, Lottie."

"Thank you. I've had the most amazing role models!" She gathered her belongings and looked lovingly at Button one last time.

Henry and His Lunch Dates

When Your Telephone Finally Rings

"Thank you, Henry." Helen reached over and squeezed his hand as he sat in the driver's seat, buckling his seatbelt. He had carefully and sweetly assisted her into his car, preparing to take her, Laney, and Ida to have Monday lunch with Button. They had not been consistent in having Monday lunch since Marie's disappointing weekend visit and Helen's accident. Helen had mentioned how much she missed these lunch dates, and Henry offered to play chauffeur and see them to Enduring Grace and home.

"It's my pleasure to drive three beautiful women around town. Besides, it will give me an opportunity to check on my apartment while you're having lunch."

"Would you like to join us?"

"Yes, but no. I think you four need to have this day together. I will make a plate to go and see to a little cleaning. Just text me or walk to my place when you've concluded your lunch. There is no rush, so enjoy yourself."

"You are so thoughtful. I can't wait to see Laney, especially. Lottie has Bid Day today at one o'clock, and we'll finally find out what sorority she pledged. She hasn't shared much information, but that's normal. It's such a busy, crazy week."

They stopped at Ida's house first. Henry went to the door, visiting briefly with Charlie, and then escorted Ida to his car. She looked so stylish in a vintage southwest-style skirt in bright colors of red, yellow, and turquoise. She matched it with a yellow T-shirt and sandals. Helen felt a little frumpy in her short-sleeved, button-up blue blouse and denim wraparound skirt. They were simpler to put on with her arm in a cast.

"Ida, you look so pretty!" Helen exclaimed. "I love that skirt!"

"Thank you. Ava found it at a little shop downtown." She started to suggest she and Helen visit the store soon, but Helen had never cared that much about fashion.

"Let's go together and check it out as soon as my arm is out of this stupidly frustrating cast!"

"I'd love to do that," Ida replied, more than a little surprised.

Henry backed out of the driveway and turned toward Laney's, which wasn't far. He never said a word, simply enjoying Ida and Helen's conversation. He wondered if they realized how often they finished each other's sentences and answered questions with just a look.

"So, we know nothing on Lottie's decision, right?" Ida asked from the backseat.

"Not to my knowledge."

"Is Laney on pins and needles?"

Helen turned and made a face at Ida that answered those questions.

Ida shifted and leaned slightly forward. "Jen has talked to her a couple of times. I understand her roommate is darling, and they are getting along very well."

"Yes, Lottie texted me a picture of her room and shared a little. I've been texting her encouraging messages this week."

"You have? That's really sweet of you, Helen."

"Well, she's such a sweet girl." Scrolling through her texts, she found the one from Lottie. "Here is the picture. Her bed is the white bedspread with pink polka dot pillow, and that's her and her roommate sitting on the bed. She wrote, 'My roommate's name is Mayson Winslow and I've already started just calling her May. She has a thick Texas accent, loves movies, horses, and dogs. She can't believe I've never ridden a horse. The first day of recruitment was exhausting but fun. Yes, I loved your sorority a ton! Others too. More soon.'"

"I'd say you know more than me. Oh look, there is Laney waiting on the porch. She always loves sitting in the sunshine no matter the heat."

Henry parked the car and met Laney on the walkway.

"You are such a sweetheart of a man," Laney said, accepting his arm to walk the remaining steps toward his car. "Do you happen to have a brother for me, Henry?"

"He remains happily married and lives in Florence, Oregon."

"Well, isn't that the way it always goes?" Laney smiled after her comment and climbed into the car. Looking at Ida and Helen, she quipped, "Before you ask, I know absolutely nothing!"

They arrived at Enduring Grace in no time. Henry pulled under the portico and helped the ladies out of the car. One of the residents asked him why he had three dates. He replied with a cheeky grin, "Because my fourth date is already inside." He smiled when he heard Helen laugh out loud.

Upon entering Enduring Grace, they were pleased to see Jeannie Peters talking with Nurse Angela, who was out of scrubs and looking very professional.

"It's lovely to see you two. You both look very classy today," Laney shared sincerely.

Jeannie looked at Angela, who gave her a nod. "Ladies, please meet Enduring Grace's new director, Angela Long. I couldn't be more thrilled for her to take over here as I move into a regional director role."

Everyone hugged and shared congratulations with both ladies.

Angela explained, "Jamie has been promoted to director of nursing, so congratulate her when you see her. I'm transitioning this week and will start fully next Monday. I'm excited for this opportunity to move into a new role, which will include working with nursing staff to continue providing the best care for our residents."

They shared the news with Henry as he joined them after parking his car. He stayed to congratulate them as the three sisters excused themselves to meet Button in the dining room. They could see her and Devon already at their table by the window.

Sharing their hellos and hugs with Button, the ladies talked briefly to Devon about Angela and Jamie's job promotions. He shared that he had also received a promotion with more responsibility in the resident wings. They asked him to stay and have a celebration lunch, but he kindly declined. "You four deserve your special Sisterhood Monday Lunch. Isn't that what you call it?"

"It is," Laney confirmed. "Thank you, Devon, we will help Button with lunch and see her back to her room. Perhaps she will eat lunch today."

Devon helped Button take a sip of water before going back to work. Helen noticed that he stopped to talk to Henry in the living room, laughed at something he said, and patted him on the back. She wondered what was so funny.

They enjoyed their lunch together immensely! Helen thought it was just what the doctor ordered, her doctor. He'd suggested it would do her a world of good to get out of the house. She looked around the table and smiled at her sisters. Did they all suddenly look younger and healthier from their shared laughter, or did she simply see them as young in her mind? Even Button was looking at those who were speaking and eating little bites of food.

After finishing her meal, Helen texted Henry. Looking up at her sisters, Helen shared his idea. "Henry is suggesting we bring Button and walk over to his apartment. We can walk the corridors inside or take Button out for some sun and fresh air and enter through another door."

"What a fabulous idea! I know Button would love to be outside," Laney replied.

"I'd love to do that," Ida said. "I saw one apartment here in the past, but I've never seen Henry's."

They thanked the dining room staff for a lovely lunch and helped clear away their dishes. Ida volunteered to push Button. They walked outside in an area with a gazebo, sitting areas, gardens, and even lawn games such as cornhole and croquet. They walked slowly and enjoyed the sunshine.

Upon entering the corridor of apartments, Helen led the way. She knocked lightly on the door with her good hand and Henry answered immediately, welcoming them into his humble abode.

Ida gasped. "Henry, this is darling! Your floorplan is larger than the one I visited when we were looking at options for Button."

Laney agreed, "Your kitchen is very large with full-size appliances. Do you have one bedroom?"

"I have two bedrooms, but the second is quite small. I use it for a study. My children and grandchildren would never fit in this apartment, so I didn't worry about extra beds. Some residents have a double bed in their second bedroom. And, I have one bath."

They were suddenly interrupted by Laney's cell phone. "Sorry, I turned the volume up so I wouldn't miss Lottie's call." She answered with all eyes on her.

As they watched closely, Laney's face bloomed into a huge smile. She kept saying over and over how happy she was for Lottie and ended the call by saying that she couldn't wait to see pictures.

"We have a new Sister!" The squeals of delight could be heard, as Henry teased, all the way to Orlando. He would never have believed it if he hadn't seen it with his own eyes, but three of the four eighty-plus-year-old women were hugging each other and jumping up and down.

Tears were flowing freely with smiles all around. Button was right in the middle in her wheelchair, and she seemed to love all the squeals, hugs, smiles, and tears.

Laney's phone chimed with an incoming text. She took her arms from around her sisters and opened the message. She turned her phone around. "Look!"

The photo was of Lottie in their sorority's Bid Day T-shirt with a tremendous smile on her face. She was holding gifts her new sisters had given her.

The next photo was of Lottie with her roommate, Mayson, wearing the same shirt along with two sisters they knew must be their Bid Day buddies, most likely sophomores who would be potential big sisters.

Helen and Ida leaned forward and, at the same moment, said, "Love it!" Laney leaned down to show Button the photos of Lottie, and her eyes looked from one picture to the other. After another minute or two of sharing their joy and elation, Laney's phone chimed again. She read the text out loud. "Let me read Lottie's message to you. She says, 'I pledged here for so many reasons. I love it so much. The girls are super friendly, but also funny and genuine. Most of all, they called me Lottie instead of Charlotte like a real sister would!'"

"I love that girl!" Helen said emphatically. "I can't wait to buy her a cute sorority gift."

"Yes! Won't that be fun? I say we go shopping soon," Ida offered cheerfully.

Laney joked, "Ida, something tells me you know the best store on campus for gifts."

"Of course I do, dear!"

They all laughed out loud and suddenly heard Button giggle. They looked at her in shock.

"Button, your laugh is the best. It just makes my day all that more fabulous!" Laney squeezed her hand.

Laney's phone chimed once again. "My goodness, I've never received so many texts." She looked down at her phone, suddenly covering her mouth in surprise.

"Laney, what does it say?"

"It's two more photos. The first one is of Lottie and Nick. He looks so happy for her. But, the second one is of Mary Carolyn and Claire. They volunteered to help the house with recruitment." She turned her phone to show everyone the cute pictures.

One more message from Lottie appeared. "It says, 'I just met these two alums that know you and said to say hello. They want you to know they both work at Big Sky now, Claire just started, and they have offered to help me find a part-time job. They said seasonal hiring is coming soon. We just exchanged cell phone numbers, and I cannot stop smiling!'"

Little did Lottie know, her eighty-year-old sorority sisters could not stop smiling either!

Button and Her Family

When You Love Someone More Than Anything

Football season kicked off at Ida and Charlie's with a lively brunch on the first Saturday in September. The entire "fam-damily," as Joe described them, arrived dressed in a variety of team spirit gear. The kitchen counters were filled with an assortment of muffins, bagels, fruits, and juices. Ida put scrambled eggs, hash browns, bacon, and ham in large warming trays, along with flour tortillas wrapped in foil. Jen and Jake brought a large tray of chicken nuggets, but the most popular item, by far, was Joe's annual batch of monkey bread. It was simply biscuit dough, cut and made into balls, rolled through a mixture of cinnamon sugar, and layered in a fluted tube pan. The result was scrumptious! He made four pans of monkey bread this year to meet the high demand. Jake had insisted he could eat half a pan of monkey bread by himself.

The kitchen and living room were filled with extra seating and a few old-fashioned beanbags. It was crowded with their growing family. In addition to Ida and Charlie's crew of Ava, Joe, Jen, and Jake, Helen and Henry had come with Laney, Bobby, and Judith. Lottie and Nick, who were visiting for Labor Day weekend, were there as well. Football watching wasn't Lottie's favorite pastime, but family brunch was high on her list of fun. Devon and Payton would be staying for only the first half and then they both had to head to work. The family was ready for the noon kickoff!

As they all gathered in front of the television, eating from the football-shaped paper plates on their laps, Charlie turned down the volume and asked if he could say a few words. "First, welcome to football season!" The room erupted in cheers. "Second, Henry and Nick, we are happy you joined us this year. We will allow you to root for the other team, but you may wish to leave early if it appears they will win. At the very least, don't sit next to my wife." Charlie winked at Ida as everyone laughed.

"Any conversation not related to the game in current time is a personal foul. You will be flagged and penalized fifteen yards to other rooms in which to chat. Please put your phones on vibrate. Do not walk in front of the television to refresh drinks, retrieve snacks, or visit the restroom. Your exit is along this path around the back of the recliner and circling the sofa. Any questions?" Scanning the room, Charlie smiled. "Seeing none, I declare it game time!"

Ida could not love him more. She kissed him as he joined her on the sofa. They had been forced to make the difficult decision to release their season tickets, and this was the first home game they'd missed in decades. With Button's decline and Helen's accident, Ida did not share much about this decision, which they'd solidified during baseball season.

They'd begun to have a series of challenges when climbing stairs and sitting in the bleachers. Charlie's hearing had been helped with hearing aids, but he'd had a series of back spasms that coincided with either climbing stairs or standing for long periods. His back did not bother him nearly as much at home, but after baseball games, he'd found himself in quite a bit of discomfort. Ida also struggled with random bouts of dizziness, which is why she had stopped driving. It appeared as though stairs were going to be an ongoing challenge for her as well after misjudging steps and falling twice over the summer. She and Charlie had ventured into conversations recently about their two-story home. With their bedroom on the first floor, they managed, but Charlie had asked her why they needed such a large home now, especially when the upstairs was all but forgotten. She hated the thought of giving up their happy, sunny home.

"Block in the back," Ida shouted at the television, just before the ref tossed his yellow flag on the field. Nick sat up from lounging on the beanbag next to Lottie to turn and look at Ida.

"You know your football, Miss Ida." Nick had just paid her the highest compliment.

"Son, you have no idea," Charlie replied.

Throughout the game, Nick heard Ida's comments, looking at her with astonishment. Just before halftime, he squeezed in next to her on the sofa, going over the first two quarters as if they were coaches studying film after the game.

During halftime, everyone surprised Lottie with a birthday cake and a few gifts. Her birthday, August 15, was the day after Bid Day, and Nick had taken her out to dinner and a little shopping. Her parents and Nannie had come down the following afternoon for a quick celebration, returning home that night. Eighteen was a milestone birthday, and Lottie was thrilled to stretch out the celebration over several days. She was especially happy that Nick could stop saying, "but you're only seventeen."

For her halftime party, Payton had made her a special red velvet cake with cream cheese frosting. It was her favorite. Her mom brought paper plates and napkins with the number eighteen on them. They all jokingly agreed that, between brunch and birthday cake, they wouldn't be able to eat again for a week.

In the third quarter, Lottie fell asleep on the beanbag and Nick moved to stand behind the sofa, near Ida, to watch the game. He couldn't stop laughing at Ida's funky cuss words, and he didn't want to wake Lottie from her much-needed nap.

"Tartar sauce! That was pass interference," Ida yelled from the sofa, pointing at the television.

"Nope. Good no-call decision by the referee," Nick argued.

"Defensive back had his hands all over our receiver," Ida countered.

"He can put his hands on the guy as long as it doesn't restrict him from making a play on the ball."

Ida turned to hand Nick her cup. "Nicholas, dear boy, would you mind bringing me a lemonade. You may need to check our second refrigerator out in the garage where we store extra drinks."

"Yes ma'am." Nick took her cup and went on a lengthy search for lemonade.

"You know we don't have any lemonade," Charlie said quietly to Ida.

Ida just smiled. "Don't we? How disappointing. I may need to send him to the store."

And thus began the years' long, *mostly* friendly football clashes between Ida and Nick.

Midway into the fourth quarter, the game was tied. The living room was a hotbed of pacing, jumping, cheering, and groaning. All eyes were glued to the television. Even Lottie couldn't sleep through this level of fandom. Henry moved to stand next to Nick, physically showing camaraderie, as they were rooting, silently, for the visiting team.

Feeling his phone vibrate in his pocket, Nick grabbed it and glanced briefly to see a text from Devon. Nick frowned. Devon never texted during a work shift. He read the words and handed Henry his cell phone, whispering, "Read this." Henry read the message, nodded, and returned the phone to Nick. He leaned over and said something to Charlie, who had dubbed himself king of the remote control, and the volume on the television was muted.

Henry said, "Everyone, Devon just texted Nick from Enduring Grace. It's Button." Turning toward Helen, he said, "Sweetheart, you, Laney, and Ida need to come with me."

They were out the door in less than a minute.

Devon led Laney, Bobby, Helen, Henry, Ida, and Charlie into a private waiting room. Dr. Marcus Long and his wife Angela, in her new role as director, came in a few minutes later. Angela sat next to Laney and took her hand. Dr. Long pulled a chair around to sit in front of the group.

"I'm sorry, but we have regretfully reached a difficult decision point with Miss Vivian," Dr. Long shared softly. "We have been incredibly concerned the past several days as she has become dehydrated. Her swallowing issues, known as dysphagia, have been problematic for several weeks. She is not swallowing because, as this disease progresses, memory to perform what should be a somewhat-automatic action is forgotten. When we reach this point, we have two options. A feeding tube could be inserted, which is not my recommendation, or we can call in hospice."

It was completely silent in the room. Dr. Long suggested, "Angela and I are happy to give you time to talk about this and discuss it with other family members."

Helen, holding tightly to Henry's hand, spoke first. "Thank you, Dr. Long. We don't need to confer with others. Button's wishes were expressed clearly to us a long time ago."

Laney was holding both Bobby's and Angela's hands as they sat on each side of her. "Helen is right. We would appreciate your help in contacting hospice. Thank you for everything you have done for Button, for our family."

Dr. Long nodded. "We will take care of it right away."

Angela added, "You are welcome to stay with Miss Vivian. I will be in and out to check on her as well. That little lady holds a special place in my heart." She hugged Laney, expressed her sympathy to everyone, and followed her husband out the door, closing it softly.

After a quiet moment, Henry kissed Helen's cheek and said, "Excuse me for a few minutes. I'll be right back."

As they watched him close the door, Devon sat in the now-open seat next to Laney. "I'm so sorry. I've tried, we've all tried so hard, to help her fight this damned disease. I hate that she is losing this battle, but she has been such a warrior."

Laney looked kindly at Devon. She adored him; they all did. He was the best, most compassionate person in the world for Button to have caring for her. She said gently, "Devon, remember, a goodbye here is a hello there. She is going to win in the end. God is about to slay this beast of Alzheimer's for Button. I'm so grateful for that."

Devon nodded and simply patted Laney's hand.

Ida cried, "I had not thought of it like that."

Devon took Ida a tissue box. "She has taught me so much. You all have. Is there anything I can get for you?" As they each shook their head, Devon offered, "I'm going to head back to the floor. I will check on you throughout the day."

As Devon turned to leave the room, Henry opened the door. He said, "The apartment next to mine is currently vacant, and Angela has kindly agreed to make it available to you. If bedding can be brought here for two full-size beds, we can set up a place for you to rest. This could take several days; we will know more after the hospice evaluation. I am happy, of course, to drive you to your homes at any time."

Bobby agreed. "Henry, this is incredibly thoughtful of you. Let me call Judith. She will set up this apartment for you all in a heartbeat."

Charlie offered to Ida, Laney and Helen, "You three go ahead and sit with Button. We will make some phone calls and see to everything."

And they did. Henry, Charlie, and Bobby coordinated with the rest of the family to set up the apartment for Ida and Charlie in one bedroom and Laney in the other. Ava and Judith brought nightgowns, changes of clothes, and toiletry items for Ida and Laney. They also delivered a few groceries. Henry collected similar things from Helen's house and moved her in with him.

The next day, Marie arrived and she and Laney took turns standing vigil at Button's bedside, circulating the use of the apartment's second bedroom. Marie had insisted, "One of us will be holding her hand, Laney. If either of us is not there when she passes, we were not meant to be there. Button would want us to take care of ourselves as well." It bolstered Laney tremendously to have Marie's strength and bright spirit, and she was so thankful she had dropped everything to fly to Florida.

Button had been in an unconscious state when they'd arrived on Saturday. She never opened her eyes, but they continued to talk to her. As she appeared to sleep peacefully, covered in the T-shirt blanket Mary Carolyn and Claire had given her, they shared special memories, told funny stories, read scripture verses, and prayed. They sang their favorite sorority songs softly for Button. Family came in and out to share their love. Jamie pushed sweet Margaret from down the hall into Button's room after Margaret heard that Vivian was under hospice care. Laney smiled at Marie when she quipped, "You know Button would be loving all this attention under different circumstances."

The hospice nurses were tremendous, and their care was felt and appreciated by everyone. One of them commented that Vivian was moving through the dying process so much more quickly than many patients.

Laney shared, "That's our girl. She is sprinting for home."

In the end, on a beautiful September evening, two days later, Button took her final breath. Her sisters were at her side along with Henry, Charlie, Bobby, and Devon. When the hospice nurse confirmed her passing, Devon walked to the other side of her bed, to the window she had so often looked out longingly, and he opened it wide.

"I believe it is a Danish tradition, but many people believe in opening a window for their loved one's soul to pass through, and I think Miss Vivian would appreciate my doing this."

In tears, through their shared and overwhelming grief, they looked toward the window at the beautiful sunset as the sky was turning stunning colors of purple and pink.

Laney cried, "It's a pink sunset. Look at those pink puffy clouds." She glanced at Helen, fully expecting, despite her tears, a scientific explanation, but Helen simply nodded.

"It's Button's sky, for sure," Helen murmured.

They wrapped their arms around each other and stood in silence, simply looking out the window.

The room was peaceful, and Button was finally at rest.

Sisters Minus One

When a Little Wine Never Hurt Anyone

Laney packed her small suitcase to go home to Bobby and Judith's house. She wasn't folding anything, and it would all be horribly wrinkled, but she couldn't have cared less. Her mind kept playing a loop of the last few days, especially Button's funeral. The service was just what Button wanted—a celebration of her life and tribute to her charming personality. It was a beautiful service for the most beautiful person Laney had ever known.

Laney was interrupted by a brief knock at the apartment door as Helen entered asking, "Have you found one of my shoes by chance? It's a black sandal. Henry swears he walked me next door last night hobbling in only one shoe."

Laney looked at Helen sympathetically. "I think you and Ida were discussing shoes, so check the other bedroom. The whole night is fuzzy!"

A couple of minutes later, Helen returned with her sandal and a pink scarf. "Found it! Thank you for loaning me your pink scarf, Laney, which I apparently left here as well. It was a perfect smidge of pink for Button's memorial service. I love that we all wore a bit of pink yesterday."

"Me, too," Laney agreed. "Helen, did Henry buy you the pink necklace you wore to the service? I've never seen it before."

"He did. He went on a run to buy wine and came home with wine and jewelry. I started crying all over again. God bless that man. He has held me together the past several days, weeks . . . months."

"I've been meaning to ask if Henry paid for this apartment for us to all stay here with Button. Do you know?"

"He did. He negotiated a fair daily rate with Angela and then she added in a huge discount. It was sitting empty until the furniture could be moved. They are doing a refresh of carpet, paint, and the like."

"We all like him very much, Helen. I'd say we love him, but I know how squirmy you get around that word. We should do something grand to thank him. You'll have to give us some suggestions."

"Let me think on it. Perhaps a restaurant gift card."

"Grander than that."

Hearing a noise at the door, they looked up to see Ida and Marie enter the apartment carrying large vases of pink roses and white carnations.

"After sending flowers home with the whole fam-damily, the remaining flowers from the church have been donated or distributed as a thank you to several people who cared for Button here. We saw Angela, Jeannie, Jamie, and sweet little Margaret. The nurses' station looks like a Valentine's Day delivery. I think Button's memorial service was perfect, but I've never seen so many flowers in my life," Marie shared as she set the vases on the coffee table and took a seat in a living room chair.

Helen suggested, "I suppose we should have said 'no flowers allowed' instead of in lieu of flowers, please make a donation to the foundation."

Ida shrugged. "I think some people do both. Plus, Button would have adored these pink roses."

Pointing to the flowers she and Ida had placed on the table, Marie offered, "These four vases are for us. Please take one home. I'm going to try to board my flight with flowers or press them into a book to save as, well, pressed flowers. Wow, I'm tired, and we old girls drank way too much wine last night."

"We needed it," Helen stated emphatically.

"We did," Laney agreed. "It was wonderful of Henry and Charlie to watch a couple of movies next door and leave us this apartment for a much-needed sisterhood night. We simply lifted our glasses and said a toast to our precious Button one time too many."

"Many times too many!" Marie corrected.

"Other than the headache and brain fog, I feel so much better after spending a little time talking with you three last night," Laney offered.

"Agreed," Helen nodded. "I released so much emotion last night."

"And you lost a shoe," Ida said, making them all laugh.

After a minute, Helen posed the question. "What do we do now? As much as I feel like I could curl up in bed and sob forever, Button would not want us to conduct ourselves in such a manner."

"No, she wouldn't. Being Jewish, the sentiment I most often hear is 'May her memory be a blessing.' It's hard to embrace that right now, but it's the best path for us to take. So, I am flying home tomorrow afternoon, but never fear, my loves, I will be back soon."

Laney reached over to squeeze Marie's hand. "We'll miss you so much! I have no energy and zero enthusiasm for anything right now, but I have an initiation workshop at the sorority house next Saturday. I know Button is smiling from heaven that I will be serving as ritual adviser."

"Yes, she is," Marie agreed.

Helen shared, "Henry and I are going back to my house, and I have doctors' appointments early next week. I think the cast is coming off, and I can't wait. What about you, Ida?"

Looking around the apartment, she replied, "I'm going to move in here—with Charlie, of course."

"Are you serious?" Helen was incredulous.

"Yes, very serious! Staying here the past few days has showed Charlie and me that we need less space than we thought. We need to simplify, downsize, and minimize our responsibilities. I love it here. They have football watch parties, holiday events, and excursions. We can always go to Ava and Joe's for family times. The lobby is a sunny yellow with light blues and corals, which are my favorite colors. Angela even said we could paint this apartment if we want."

"You've already talked to Angela?" Laney was as surprised as Helen.

"We have. We've also talked to Jen and Jake, who have said many times to let them know if we ever decide to sell our house. They are so excited, and Jen is talking about redecorating to create more of an open concept and remodel the master bath. They will want to change many things, I'm sure, to make it feel more modern and their style. We'll probably make it part sale and a tiny part wedding present. It's a fabulous family neighborhood with great schools. It will be perfect for them."

"My head is spinning again!" Marie made them all laugh.

Ida suggested eagerly, "Helen, sell your house and move in with Henry next door. And, when an apartment opens up next to one of us we'll snatch it up for Laney."

"Hold on a minute," Laney interjected before Helen could respond. "I enjoy living at Bobby and Judith's house and, besides, I can't afford to live here. I will visit often though. Lunch every Monday?"

Ida nodded enthusiastically. Helen didn't reply, but Ida knew she was thinking and processing. Change was hard for Helen, but Ida had planted the seed, and she'd wait to see whether it grew into anything. Ida glanced around the room at her sisters and thought again. Change was at the heart of *all* of their concerns.

Laney shared a sudden idea. "Oh, Lottie's initiation is in mid-October. I am going to be there even if I have to take a bus. Would any of you want to attend?"

They all raised their hands. Marie laughed. "See, I told you I'd be back soon."

"Wouldn't it be easier if you and Tim finally moved back to Florida?"

"It might," she said with a smile.

"It would," Ida insisted. "Laney, I'm sure Ava or Jennifer would want to go and would drive. I will ask them. We'll just sit in the back of the room and try not to embarrass Lottie that her whole fam-damily is there." They all laughed, feeling a teeny bit sorry for Lottie.

Laney said, "There is one more thing I've been putting off that I need to share with you. I was going to do it last night, but it didn't feel like the right time."

Helen asked, "What is it?"

"Button left a small fire safe with me and the key. She gave it to me even before her health declined and she moved here to Enduring Grace. We had quite the argument when she said that I should share it with you three after her death. I told her I would surely go well before she did, but she insisted I keep it. Bobby delivered it here yesterday. We need to open it."

"I do believe this would have been better with wine," Helen debated.

Laney offered, "Do you want to wait for tonight?"

"No, please, let's do this now. I don't want to board my flight tomor-row feeling like I do right now," Marie insisted.

After receiving reluctant agreement from Helen and Ida, Laney asked Marie if she could help her move the box onto the coffee table. Laney put the key in the lock and opened the lid. The box was filled with papers and envelopes. She pulled out the first small envelope and opened it. "It's a variety of pink buttons!" Laney laughed. "Her note says, 'I hope you don't mind the play on words, but I wanted you to have a little pink button to make you smile. Don't cry for very long, dears. I love you!'

"Then she wrote a post script. 'P.S. I know which button each of you will pick.'" Laney put the buttons on the table, and the sisters leaned forward to look.

"Well, of course she knows I want the fancy, ornate one," Ida said.

Laney mentioned, "It looks like it's been dipped in pink glitter."

Ida, Marie, and Helen insisted vehemently and simultaneously, "Never speak of glitter!"

Laney chuckled to herself that the dreaded golden glitter storm from hell was still a touchy subject more than sixty years later.

"I love the one that looks like a small, shiny stone if nobody else wants it," Helen said.

Marie picked up the button that caught her eye. It was predominantly pink, but swirled with a little rainbow of blue and purple. "This one is mine."

The final button was the largest, most sturdy, durable, and brightest of the bunch. Laney held it tightly in her hand. "This one is perfect for me. Button was always right."

They made their way through the box, finding photos and memories for each of them. At the back of the box was a tiny box wrapped in pink paper and a thick, white legal-size envelope. Marie, Ida, and Helen insisted Laney open the box first.

She tore off the wrapping paper and lifted the lid to find a tiny piece of pink paper folded on top of her sorority badge. Laney opened the paper and burst into tears. Helen quickly leaned forward to take the piece of paper from Laney and cried, "It says, 'For Lottie.'"

Marie gasped. "Button must have put her badge aside for Lottie two or three years ago. Oh, Laney!" They were all moved to tears.

Ida took the tissue box off the side table and handed a handful of it to Laney before passing the box all around.

"I can't even open that large envelope," Laney said, wiping her tears.

Marie offered, "I'll do it."

She opened the envelope, pulled out the thick papers, and scanned them. With an expression of shock on her face, Marie said in a soft voice, "I can't believe what I'm reading. It appears she left her estate to the four of us and named us the beneficiaries of a whole-life insurance policy."

They sat in stunned silence.

Finally, Laney said, "I knew nothing of this. She gave me power of attorney to assist with the sale of her home, bill payments, and medical records."

Helen was in tears, and Ida kept repeating, "You're kidding me."

"I'm in shock," Marie stated softly, still looking through the papers. "It appears, in addition to leaving a substantial amount to our sorority foundation, our Button is doing her best to take care of us. We're going to need legal advice and probably a financial adviser, but at first glance, Laney, I'd say Button wants you to live wherever you want."

Laney the Adviser

When It Feels Like Home

Laney climbed the two steps leading up to the sorority house's beautiful double front doors and turned to wave at Bobby. He would be back to get her when the ritual workshop was over. She rang the doorbell and was greeted by a young lady dressed with charming bohemian flair. Her red-framed glasses highlighted her lovely brown eyes. Her dark hair was worn in one long braid, which curved and rested on the front of her colorful blouse. Her smile was immediately endearing. She welcomed Laney inside where the foyer and grand staircase, updated over the years, instantly brought back many special memories. Laney could practically see herself, Button, Helen, Ida, and Marie running up and down those steps in their poodle skirts, rolled-up jeans, bobby socks, and saddle oxfords.

"You must be Mrs. Walsh. I'm Maya Cardenas, ritual chair, who you spoke with on the phone. It's really nice to meet you. Thank you for agreeing to serve as my adviser."

"It's lovely to meet you as well, Maya. Please call me Laney."

"I will, thanks. I am anxious to introduce you to my committee. We're set up in the small meeting room. We're supposed to call it that now, but truthfully, we still all call it the TV room. We will start in there, but between our committee meeting and the afternoon workshop, we're hosting a Snack Attack."

"Snack Attack? You need to fill me in on that one."

"It's just a dessert function, kind of a reception. We're having it to honor our senior class. It helps to get them to come to activities they've already done several times if there is food involved, especially dessert. Who doesn't love dessert?"

Laney couldn't help but smile. "Nobody I know."

They walked through the main living room, decorated to be both lovely and functional. Several seating areas of sofas and chairs were complemented by tables large enough for study groups or committee meetings. It looked so familiar to Laney despite the new furnishings. As she scanned the room, her mind replaced the current décor with that from her Redding College days. She had been here many times since college, but not in recent years.

They walked beyond the living room, down the corridor, and into a room that was part of an addition and a remodel that had been completed since Laney was a student. It was beautiful, and she was happy this much larger group of young ladies had the extra space. As they entered the small meeting room with the giant flat-screen TV, Maya shared, "Hey, everybody, this is Laney Walsh, our ritual adviser."

When the six girls in the room all smiled at her, Laney felt hopeful she'd made the right decision to accept the role as an adviser. As they introduced themselves and she shared a little about herself and her time in the house years before, she felt welcome and inspired by her ongoing sisterhood. When she walked them through the steps of initiation, she had the sense of being home.

As the committee meeting concluded, and they walked to the dining room for Snack Attack, Maya shared, "I need to run upstairs to my room. I need a few things for our workshop, but I left them on my bed. Our chapter president, Ari, is looking forward to meeting you." Maya waved to a girl across the room, who smiled and indicated she'd be there momentarily.

Laney offered, "Maya, please go ahead and get what you need. I'll wait right here for Ari."

"Thanks. I'll be right back."

Laney looked around the gorgeous dining room with large round tables and chairs. It was funny how much this room reminded her of the dining room at Enduring Grace. It was charming and bright with sunshine pouring in from the windows. The tables were covered with white tablecloths and the chairs were a combination of wood and white paint. The walls were covered with an exquisite floral wallpaper. Laney nodded to herself. She now knew with certainty that Button had been here in her mind numerous times during her stay at Enduring Grace. When Button had revealed what she was thinking with word clues, she'd given Helen, Ida, and herself a glimpse into her flashbacks to this sweet, special place and time.

As she looked around the room, the photos and plaques on the wall caught her attention. She stepped closer to see a plaque listing the names of the chapter's recipients of the Vivian Kinkaid Upton Scholarship. Laney felt the harsh loss of Button, but also tremendous pride. She wished Button could know that soon a second scholarship also would be made in her name. She, Marie, Helen, and Ida were already working with their sorority foundation to endow a scholarship with some of the money Button had left them. The Vivian Kinkaid Upton Memorial Scholarship would be open to sisters nationally, both collegiate and alumnae, to be awarded in the area of art, performance, and entrepreneurship. Laney could not wait for everything to be finalized. *Look at what you did, Button*, she thought.

Laney was pulled from her thoughts by a kind voice. "Hello, I'm sorry to keep you waiting." Laney turned to smile at a beautiful young woman, who was slightly taller than she was. She wore a red tunic over black leggings with such a cute necklace and earrings, Ida definitely would have quizzed her on where they were purchased. Her light touch of red lipstick made her sweet smile that much brighter.

"I'm Arionna Brooks, but everyone calls me Ari. I'm so happy to meet you. Thank you for coming today and for helping us out as ritual adviser."

"It's so good to meet you. I'm Delaney Walsh, but everyone calls me Laney. You can call me that as well, if you'd like."

"OK, thank you." Looking up at the plaque on the wall that Laney had been studying, Ari motioned toward it. "Our chapter adviser told me you were super close to Vivian Upton. I am one of the recipients of her scholarship," she shared. She motioned to a dining room table nearby. "The two sisters seated at that table were awarded scholarships, too, and we'd love to hear about Mrs. Upton, if you'd like to join us. We're saving a chair for Maya as well."

Laney nodded in agreement and, as they made their way toward the table, Ari leaned in toward Laney and shared, "I got here early and snagged some mini cakes and punch for our table so we wouldn't miss out. Dessert goes fast around here. That's how Snack Attack got its name."

Laney replied, motioning toward the cakes sitting beautifully on a plate in the center of the table, "They're petits fours."

"Yes, you're right. We get them from a bakery, Karen's Cake Company, and I love that you can eat two of them without blowing your diet!"

Ari introduced Laney to the sisters at the table after they took a seat. She shared with Laney, "I talked to Mary Carolyn, who was president before me, and she said she knew you."

"Yes, I love Mary Carolyn."

"She said the same thing about you. I understand you are Mrs. Upton's big sister."

As the girls at the table listened, Laney replied, "I am her big sister, and the first thing you need to know is that everyone called her Button and her favorite color was pink."

Maya had just returned, taking the seat on the other side of Laney. "You called her Button? How did she get that nickname?"

"We didn't give her the name, her family did because she was a cute as a button. But we kept it going for more than sixty years. Have you heard that expression?" They all nodded.

"That's adorable," Maya answered. "Now I want a nickname. I'm just Maya."

One of the other girls at the table promised they would come up with something perfect for her.

Ari passed the plate of petits fours, and Laney served herself one. After everyone had been served, she and Ari picked up their cakes and smiled at each other in anticipation. They took a bite of their petit fours at the same time, briefly closing their eyes and making a similar sound.

"Mmmm," said Laney.

"Mmmm," echoed Ari.

Their eyes popped open, and they laughed at each other.

Laney leaned slightly closer to Ari to ask, "What are you studying? What do you want to do after college, Ari?"

"I want to go to medical school to be a pediatrician," she answered.

Laney went around the table to learn about her young sisters and their interests. She was more than a little impressed. Their goals and aspirations were well beyond anything her generation of girls had considered possible. In addition to Ari's plans to be a pediatrician, Laney was sitting with a future aerospace engineer, architect, and college professor. Maya shared that she worked at the university library and loved everything about books and learning. "I'll probably pursue teaching humanities, but I love history as well." Laney loved that they had that in common.

Ari suggested, "Laney, please tell us more about you and Mrs.," she stopped herself and instead said, "Button."

Laney took a sip of punch, sat the cup down, and turned toward her. "If you've ever seen a picture of Adolph Hitler, then I trust you're familiar with his little mustache?"

They all nodded, their curiosity piqued, and leaned forward to hear her story. They laughed out loud as they heard several stories about the one and only Button Upton. Button stories became Laney's favorite thing to share with the chapter during her years as ritual adviser. And those stories were passed down for years to come and even embellished a little. Button's legacy not only lived on, it flourished!

As they started the initiation workshop after dessert, Laney looked around the room at all the young girls and thought again of her sisters. They say that the more things change, the more they stay the same. And she saw her now-eighty-year-old sisters in these girls. *I am going to call Mary Carolyn tonight and thank her for talking me into this!* Laney knew that every minute she gave to this chapter, they would be giving back more to her in return.

A month later, their initiation ceremony was tremendously well done and truly lovely. Laney was so proud of them. She made it through the ceremony without internalizing her feelings of loss over Button and didn't shed a single tear. The same could not be said of Lottie's initiation a few days later.

Marie flew to Orlando the Friday before Lottie's initiation on an early morning flight and she, Helen, Ida, Ava, Jen, and Payton drove over to pick her up at the airport. Ava borrowed Joe's giant SUV that seated seven comfortably. It may have seated seven, but the luggage compartment barely held overnight bags for seven women. Ida offered to put her bag at her feet, claiming it made a nice footstool for her legs.

They reserved a few hotel rooms near campus for the weekend and felt as if they were on a special girls' trip. They saw Lottie's dorm room, met Mayson for the first time, and considered themselves brilliant for asking for the small, private room at the local seafood restaurant for dinner. They were way too loud to be anything less than annoying if they'd been seated with other customers.

As Laney simply said, "Close families are loud families. I wouldn't have it any other way!"

After dinner, Lottie and Mayson came to their hotel and they shared much about their great experience as pledges. They loved their big sisters and were excited to be initiated. Laney pulled Lottie aside into the adjoining bedroom to give her the box from Button, which Laney had wrapped again in pink paper with a pink and white striped ribbon.

"Dearest, this is from Button. She left it for you."

Lottie looked surprised and confused. She unwrapped the little box, opened the lid, and saw the badge. "Is this Button's sorority badge?"

"It is."

Lottie opened the little slip of paper, which had been on top. *For Lottie*, she read. She choked out the question, "Button's handwriting?"

At Nannie's nod, Lottie burst into tears.

Hearing the crying from the adjacent room, Marie said, "Like grandmother, like granddaughter," and she passed a box of tissues around the room as everyone else shared in the tearful moment.

Lottie's family of sisters did indeed sit in the back of the room during her initiation the next day, but their presence was strongly felt and never forgotten by Lottie. As Button's pin was secured in place, she silently thanked Button, her sister now, for her precious gift.

Very early the next morning, Laney sipped her coffee in the hotel dining area while waiting on the others to join her for breakfast. She'd risen before the sun to see Marie off for her early flight home. Insisting the others not awaken at three thirty in the morning, Marie hugged everyone goodbye the night before. She wasn't surprised, however, when Laney got up to go downstairs with her to meet the taxi driver.

After the car pulled in front of the hotel and the driver greeted Marie, Laney hugged her warmly. "Thank you so much, Marie, for coming to Lottie's initiation. It truly means the world to me."

"I wouldn't have missed it. And never fear, I'll be back again soon. I love you more than my luggage," she jested, borrowing the line from *Steel Magnolias*.

Missing Marie already, Laney distracted herself with a second cup of coffee. Helen and Ida joined her as she made her way back to the table.

"The others will be down in a few minutes," Ida shared. "If you ask me, we are better travelers than the girls in our family. My bag is half the size of Jen's! Listen, I've been giving it some thought, and I think we should start planning a trip to celebrate our birthday season."

Laney offered her opinion after another sip of coffee. "I may pack light, but I'm no spring chicken."

Ida countered, "We will build our itinerary with age-appropriate parameters. Not too much walking, with plenty of downtime."

Helen agreed with Ida on taking a birthday-season trip. "Let's come up with a top three list of destinations we never thought in a million years we could visit. We'll call it the Button birthday-season expedition. She has given us the world, and we should go see a little of it while we still can."

"I love that idea, Helen! I am at my happiest when I have something exciting to plan and anticipate." Ida pulled paper and pen from her handbag. She pulled the cap off the pen and sat poised to write down a list of suggestions. "Do either of you have somewhere on your bucket list you never thought you'd have the opportunity to go?" It was quiet for a moment while Helen and Laney gave it some thought.

"France," Helen shared, sitting up straighter. "The wine would be magnificent, plus I have all my French ancestors to thank for my existence."

"Yes, indeed!" Ida enthusiastically wrote it down on her list. She looked at Laney inquisitively.

Laney considered Helen's suggestion with a great deal of unexpected interest. She suddenly imagined visiting a patisserie, a French bakery, and said almost reverently, "Croissants, eclairs, petits fours."

Helen and Ida looked at Laney in wonder and revelation. Helen whispered, "Petits fours."

Ida nodded slowly as the connection to Button inspired her, too. "And I'll buy a pink beret."

Laney grinned first and then Helen. Ida smiled, giving them a firm nod. She put her pen and paper back into her purse.

Just then, Ava, Jen, and Payton joined them for breakfast. "Good morning, all my grandmothers," Jen enthused. "You three look pretty deep in thought. What's up?"

"We're going to France," Ida announced. Helen and Laney smiled and nodded.

Jen looked at her mother, Ava, in confusion. Ava simply shook her head and stated, "I need coffee, lots of coffee, before I can dive into this conversation."

They served themselves a light breakfast and revisited their favorite moments from the weekend. Jen shared, "Obviously, initiation was spectacular, but I really loved meeting Mayson and seeing their dorm room. Lottie seems so happy here."

"She is very happy," Laney agreed.

"Speaking of Lottie," Payton interrupted, "She just walked into the lobby," Payton gestured toward the front door.

They all turned to see an exuberant Lottie, wearing a Go Skydiving at Big Sky T-shirt, leggings, and sneakers, and jogging right toward them. Her smile was contagious. She held up her phone for everyone to see an email message she'd received and practically shouted, "I just got a part-time, seasonal job at Big Sky!"

Ida, Charlie, and Moving Day

When Everything You Own Brings You Joy

"I'm sorry," Ida apologized again. "I thought we had downsized enough to fit into this two-bedroom apartment." She and Charlie's November 1 moving day had not gone quite as well as planned. The movers had shoved the last of their belongings into the kitchen and entryway of their Enduring Grace retirement apartment and walked off the job, claiming there was nothing else they could do.

Although she couldn't see Charlie through the mound of boxes piled well over her head, she heard his reprimand.

"I told you we needed to lay out the room dimensions on paper with everything measured and our furniture placed in advance. Who was it that mentioned we should rent a storage shed for the Christmas decorations alone?"

"You. But, we did leave the bedroom furniture from Ava's old bedroom behind. Jen said she wanted to refinish it and use it. It will look precious in a nursery someday. We left the lawnmower and yard care equipment as well as the washer and dryer for her and Jake. We sold the patio furniture. I thought the rest would fit."

Charlie didn't respond. Ida assumed he was praying for patience. As she started to apologize for the third time, she heard a voice from the hallway calling, "Hello in there! Anybody home?"

Charlie answered, "In here, Henry. Enter at your own risk!"

"Helen and I have lunch and water bottles for you, but I think you'd better come next door to eat, if you can find the exit."

Charlie started laughing and couldn't seem to stop. He tried to talk to Henry, but his words were barely discernable through his hysterics. Ida heard Henry from the hallway, trying to reply, but he was apparently overcome as well.

"Well, really!" Ida stomped her foot and then recalled neither of them could see her for all the tall boxes in the way.

Henry finally caught his breath. "See if you can pull Ida out and come over for a lunch break."

Getting out of the apartment was not as difficult as Charlie had made it out to be. Ida said those exact words to him as they walked the few steps next door. While they snacked on sandwiches and fruit, Henry made a suggestion. "When I first moved here, I rented a storage shed about a mile away to store things my children didn't want, but that I couldn't give away. Over time, my grandchildren chose some items, and I finally released the rest. I imagine they have units available."

Charlie agreed. "I knew I should have rented space. I'll call them right away. That will give Ida a little extra time to decide what to do with some of the belongings that we simply cannot hold on to any longer. We already know we can't put up our big Christmas tree. The apartment doesn't have room for something that size."

"I don't put up my tree anymore, Ida. You know that. And I don't feel a lack of Christmas spirit from having made that choice," Helen said to her sister. "I know you can find something smaller and make your apartment just as charming and festive as ever."

Henry shared, "I started with photographs. My wife had a million picture frames, which I had nowhere to display. I kept my favorites and my daughter helped me by putting the pictures in a photo album and giving away the frames."

Helen tried to offer advice. "I read something about de-cluttering. It was recommended that we should look at an item in our house and ask, 'Does this bring me joy?' and, if it doesn't, then out it goes."

"But everything I've brought here brings me joy," Ida cried.

"Honey, surely an entire box of plastic ware doesn't bring you joy!" Charlie insisted.

Helen asked Ida gently, "Would it still bring you joy if some possessions were at Ava and Joe's and you could still see them put to good use?"

"I've already offered so much to Ava, and she says she has taken everything of mine that she wants. I've apparently put her and Joe in a position of now having to de-clutter their own home. How did I collect so much?"

Charlie tried his very best to sympathize with his wife. "Sweetheart, you have many things that belonged to your mother and grandmother. Those are not items that can be thrown out easily. I really do understand, but if you want us to live here, we have to somehow fit within a thousand square feet."

Helen shared, "And you took many things, as did Laney and I, when Button's home was sold. Items that brought joy to loved ones bring joy to us. You can tell by looking at my house that I really understand and sympathize with you. The idea of moving and trying to downsize terrifies me. My books would take up more space than Henry has here."

Charlie noticed Henry flinch slightly. He seemed deep in thought after Helen's comment.

"Maybe this was a bad idea," Ida lamented.

"No, it's not a bad idea, love," Charlie insisted. "We're going to be very happy here. As a matter of fact, I don't know how it happened, but you're already down on the list to call bingo numbers at game night tomorrow evening."

"I simply volunteered," Ida shared with a shrug.

"Of course, you did," Charlie and Helen said together.

"I'll make some calls and see if we can get a storage shed and if Joe and Jake can bring their SUV and truck and lend a hand. I know Joe has a moving dolly. Helen, maybe you could help Ida decide what furniture and things we should keep here."

Henry suggested to Helen, "Your cast is off your arm, but please don't use it. Don't lift or move anything."

"Yes, Doctor DeCamp," she replied with a grin.

About three hours later, after securing the lock on his new storage shed, Charlie looked at Joe, Jake, and Henry. "I can't thank you enough for all your help. I don't know what Ida and I would have done without you. I am never moving again!"

Joe patted Charlie on the back and laughed. "I've heard that from your own daughter, and we're in our fourth house now. Ava says moving is like childbirth. Everyone always says they'll never do it again, but then a house with a pool comes on the market, and suddenly they forget all about the pain."

Henry snickered, nodding in agreement.

Jake threw his arms in the air. "I'm doomed. Jen would move in a heartbeat for a house with a pool."

Charlie suggested, "Put in your own pool, son. Save yourself the misery. Start saving now. Listen, I'd love to buy everyone pizza and beer for dinner if we can just postpone it for a couple of nights. I'm exhausted, and I'm sure Ida still needs help at the apartment."

Joe suggested, "Let's all head back to Enduring Grace and make sure you can at least sleep in your bed tonight. You know you can stay with me and Ava if we still can't find floor space for your bedframe and mattress. How about pizza and beer at next Saturday night's poker game? Henry, would you be interested in joining us?"

"Thank you for the invitation. I accept. I should warn you, however, that I'm not a very good poker player."

Charlie snorted as he patted Henry on the back. "Oldest trick in the book, my friend!" Henry simply grinned.

After returning to Enduring Grace, the four men opened the door to Ida and Charlie's apartment and double-checked the number on the door. It didn't look like the place they'd left a few hours prior. Everything was cleared away from the kitchen and living room, and the boxes were gone.

Charlie took in the pale yellow walls and oatmeal colored sofa, which was draped with a yellow and blue throw blanket. Their two blue chairs and coffee table looked elegant in the space. The small end table next to the sofa looked freshly polished. A favorite lamp was sitting atop the table with light glowing beneath a new, soft yellow lampshade. Their television was resting on a small entertainment table; it was already plugged in and connected to cable with oldies playing from the speakers. Glancing to his left, he saw their small kitchen table against the wall with two chairs and their mixer and coffee maker sitting on the otherwise-clear countertops.

"Are you sure this is your place?" Henry couldn't believe his eyes.

As they walked further inside, they heard singing and looked toward the larger bedroom. Judith was standing on a step stool hanging a picture over their bed, which had been freshly made with a gray, white, and yellow comforter and pillows. Laney was hanging clothes in the closet as Helen handed them to her with her good arm. Ida was dusting and arranging a few items on their dresser.

Charlie was stunned, but with all the boxes gone and the furniture rearranged, everything fit. It was snug, but he'd describe it as cozy more than crowded. The women were singing along to the tunes coming from the television as they worked.

"How did you manage this?" Charlie's voice broke through the sound of their singing.

Ida turned in surprise toward Henry. "Welcome home, honey! I called for reinforcements," she said in explanation, motioning toward her friends. "Judith is an absolute wizard! Thanks to her, Laney, and Helen, we can call our apartment home tonight. Just please, whatever you do, don't open the door to our second bedroom. We'll get to that over the next several days."

Henry asked, "But how did you move all the furniture and boxes?" Looking directly at Helen, he said, "Please tell me you didn't pick up anything heavy." Helen vehemently shook her head and smiled at his concern.

Judith shared, "We used sliding disks. If you can get a disk under the legs of, say a sofa for example, it takes hardly any effort at all to push it. As for the television, I saw Devon on one of my runs to and from my car and, on his break, he offered to lift it and put it in place. He plugged it in and even got it running. Your remote is on the coffee table. I know our football team had a bye week, but you should be able to watch a different game tonight if you want, Aunt Ida."

Ida grinned and nodded appreciatively, as Judith continued, "Devon also helped take our empty boxes. We broke them down and he dropped them in recycling on his way back to the nurses' station. The rest is piled in the second bedroom. Like Ida said, don't open that door. We aren't quite finished."

Looking around in satisfaction at the charming, little apartment, Judith added, "You're all set for a few days." She turned to Ida. "I'll call you and run by a sample of the hanging shelves I suggested. If you decide you like that idea, I can order them at wholesale for you."

Ida hugged Judith. "Like I said, you're a wizard. I'll add creative genius to my accolades for you. Can you make suggestions for curtains as well?"

"I'd be happy to help." Judith beamed as Laney put her arm around her daughter-in-law's waist to hug her.

Charlie looked around in total surprise. "Thank you, Judith, Laney, Helen. I'm completely flabbergasted! It looks beautiful."

Ida nodded, standing next to Charlie and taking his hand. "It looks like home to me."

Charlie smiled and looked around the apartment. "Then I guess the only thing left to say is call all the fam-damily. I'm not too tired for Bill's Italian pizza tonight after all—and it's on me!"

Thanksgiving Reimagined

When Change Is Actually Good

"Helen, which of these two bowls would you prefer I use to serve my cornbread stuffing? The glass one works, but this fine china would look beautiful on the table."

Henry was in Helen's dining room the day before Thanksgiving, where they'd already started preparing for the arrival of what Helen described as a record number of guests. He had helped her dust and vacuum and cleaned all the china and crystal. He'd even buffed the silver until it gleamed.

Helen called out to him from the living room. "Which one do you mean? I don't think I have more than one serving dish large enough for stuffing."

He held up the large red and green oriental bowl with the matching lid and leaned into the living room. "This one!"

Henry waited for a response, but Helen didn't immediately look up from a project in front of her. She'd been so quiet since Henry's family had come to town the previous weekend for an early Thanksgiving visit. Helen had gone from new acquaintance to part of the family in a matter of days.

Henry studied her from across the room. She was seated at a long, white folding table Ava had loaned them with six matching folding chairs, which were padded and quite comfortable. With a guest list of fifteen people, she'd taken his advice and set up card tables in the living room. She owned one small square table that would seat four guests, and Ava and Joe had a six-foot table that would seat Lottie, Nick, Devon, Payton, Jen, and Jake. Lottie had not been sure of her work schedule until a few days ago, but she was surprisingly off on Thanksgiving Day, which meant that now Nick, Devon, and Payton were coming as well.

Devon and Nick's parents would be driving in from Atlanta and arriving after dark. They had graciously offered to stop by for pie and were planning to celebrate Thanksgiving with their sons over the weekend. Because Payton had to run the bakery all weekend, she had been excused from traveling to see her great aunt. Next to the long kids' table, as Helen called it in jest, she planned to have Ava, Joe, Bobby, and Judith at her card table and to have Laney, Ida, and Charlie seated with her and Henry at the dining room table.

"Helen?"

Finally looking in his direction to see the dish he was holding, Helen rested her hand over her heart and shared, "That special serving piece was Button's. She and John got it on a trip to China many, many years ago. I'd love for you to use it."

"Would you like me to take the Thanksgiving tree photograph off the mantle from last year and put it on the counter where we're setting up the buffet?"

"That's a wonderful idea!" Helen said in a teary voice.

He put Button's serving dish on the dining table, walked into the living room, and took a seat near Helen at the long table. "And wonderful ideas make you cry? How can I help, sweetheart?"

"I'm just making those name cards, which look like colorful turkeys. I'm almost finished with all the names, but you can help me set them at each place setting in a minute."

"Happy to do that, but I wasn't referring to the name cards. Do you want to talk about what's troubling you?"

"Oh, I'm just tired, I think. Maybe we took on too much by offering to host Thanksgiving for everybody. I have always loved doing it and can't wait to see everyone tomorrow. The event just feels a bit daunting this year, and it never has before. I guess I just don't have the energy I used to have."

"Maybe it's too much after hosting my family here last weekend."

"No, that was my favorite weekend in a long time. They are just delightful! I think it comes down to the fact that I'm not as young as I used to be."

"Helen, you have been through so much in the last few months. You've been good about setting boundaries and not overdoing it, but, if you feel this way, you should listen to your body. I think it's telling you to slow down."

"I can't get any slower than sitting in a chair, Henry! Life is just so puzzling. I think I'm ready for a few changes one day and, by the next, I feel like I'm not ready at all. On one hand, I don't want to give up hosting Thanksgiving, but on the other hand, I think it would be fine to hand over my recipes to Jen and nominate her as Thanksgiving committee chair."

"Then talk to her about it. She and Jake may be wishing to host family holidays in their new home, but they might not feel comfortable taking away something that is so special to you."

Helen shrugged. "Change is hard sometimes."

He leaned forward to kiss her. "I know. Sometimes change is good." Taking a deep breath, Henry said, "I love you, Helen." He couldn't help but chuckle at the shocked expression on her face. "Surely you've known that I love you for some time. I've been certain since the day you played your imaginary trombone and sang to *Music Man* in Button's room."

"Really? I was horribly embarrassed!"

"I know. I think that's what sealed the deal for me. You loved your sister so much you did whatever you could to bring a smile to her face."

"I love you too, Henry," Helen replied shyly. "I've known since we colored the stained-glass window picture with Button. I've just been scared to say it, but I do. 'I like you very much' has meant I love you very much for a long time!"

"Yes, it has."

"You make me smile, laugh, and feel special. I'm not sure what I did to deserve you, but I'd very much like to keep you."

"Good, because I'm all yours!"

The next morning, Thanksgiving dawned brightly with a chill in the air. As Helen sipped a cup of hot tea, she looked out her kitchen window at her Thanksgiving tree. "Is it my imagination or did that tree turn a more vivid color overnight?"

"It appears with the colder weather, chlorophyll production has begun to wane." Helen smiled at him. She'd found a man who loved science and was a wiz in the kitchen! His culinary skills impressed her greatly. Together they managed to prepare two large turkeys, a beautiful honey-glazed ham, and stuffing for the Thanksgiving feast.

Helen decided to wear a new, cute outfit instead of her Thanksgiving pants. She chose a brown floral skirt and teal blue sweater, matching them with a cute pair of brown boots. The skirt was stretchy like her pants, but gave her the fashion flare she felt she'd often lacked. Henry wore khaki pants and a plaid shirt just like every other man at Thanksgiving that day.

The extended family poured into Helen and Henry's, as she thought of their home now, carrying platters of food. It was as if a storm—a very loud storm of smiles, hugs, and laughter—had suddenly blown through the front door, and Helen felt a sense of joy and lightness come over her.

"You look gorgeous, Helen," Ida exclaimed as she strolled into the kitchen with her amazing pumpkin pie, starting a dessert overflow section on the kitchen table.

"Thank you. It's a new skirt and sweater," Helen shared. "And I bought boots, which I love. They are so comfortable and they keep my feet warm."

"Very stylish and cute on you, but I think it's something else."

"Oh, I bought a new lipstick. The color is new for me. It's called nutmeg frost and has a bronze, autumn tint to it."

"Also lovely, but no, it's not that either. Let me see . . ." She tapped her chin and paused as if to study Helen, but she already knew where she was going with this conversation. "I know, it's your smile, dear, because you are madly in love."

Helen smiled tremendously and hugged Ida. "I am. I'm happier than I've ever been."

"I couldn't be more thrilled for you and Henry. Ever since he came into your life, you've brightened from the inside out. You have a down-right sunny disposition, which is taking some getting used to, I might add," Ida teased.

As Helen giggled, Laney entered the kitchen, agreeing with Ida's statement. "You are entirely darling and enchanting. I could just kiss Henry!"

"Do so at your own peril," Helen jested, and they all chuckled.

Laney's attention was drawn to the kitchen window and the colorful tree in the backyard. "I see your Thanksgiving tree is picture perfect today." As soon as she said it, she felt Button's absence more intensely.

Helen and Ida came to stand next to her, looking out the window. "I miss our beautiful Thanksgiving Queen," Laney shared.

"We all do," Helen said softly. "As much as I miss Button, I don't miss watching Alzheimer's steal her away day by day. It's much easier for me to picture her celebrating Thanksgiving with John in heaven today. You both know, from the day she met that chocolate-chip-cookie-sharing boy, there was no one Button adored more."

Ida nodded. "My instincts tell me that Button is at peace."

"Your extra-sensory perception, you mean," Helen said.

Ida giggled. "Joe calls it that too. He says I freak him out sometimes."

"We're used to it," Laney said as Helen chuckled. Changing the subject, she complimented Helen, "I love your new skirt, by the way."

Helen replied, "Thank you. It's soft, stretchy, and has pockets." She demonstrated by pulling something from her pocket, showing it to her sisters by opening her hand. It was her special pink button.

Laney and Ida pulled their buttons from their own pockets.

"Our lucky charms," Laney offered as her sisters nodded in agreement. "Here's to our sweet angel. Happy Thanksgiving, Button. Please give Robert a kiss for me."

"Aunt Helen?" Lottie, who was calling Helen's name, grabbed their attention as she swept into the kitchen. "Hey, Aunt Helen, Payton made a totally sick pumpkin spice cake, and we can't find room for it in the dining room."

"Sick?" Helen questioned in confusion.

Laney exclaimed, "Oh, I know, I know! Sick can mean awesome."

Helen said, "Well, that's new to me. Here, dear, put it on the kitchen table."

It took some maneuvering, but they found room for the delicious items everyone made. As they enjoyed their Thanksgiving feast, they declared which recipes were their favorites. Helen smiled when Henry voted for Laney's famous Thanksgiving mashed potatoes. He had asked Laney twice, "What on earth did you put in these potatoes?"

After the lovely meal was enjoyed by all, Ava positioned herself at the kitchen sink. "I am chief dishwasher today." As she picked up the first plate to give it a good scrub, she added, "It never fails to astonish me how much less time it takes to eat the Thanksgiving feast than it does to prepare it."

Charlie took a towel and started to dry dishes as she handed them his way. "I'll never forget, Ava, when you were about five or six, you didn't particularly like Thanksgiving and declared it your least favorite holiday. I remember it clearly, you put your hands on your hips and griped, 'So that's it? Thanksgiving is just food and there aren't cards, presents, or chocolates?'"

"Funny, Dad. I seem to remember Jen saying much the same thing when she was little," Ava replied, poking fun at Jen, who was next to her at the sink. "She just wanted chicken nuggets."

"I still love chicken nuggets, just not on Thanksgiving. I have, thankfully, matured."

"And next Thanksgiving you and Jake will be married and living in your new home," Ava offered.

Helen, who was putting leftovers in the refrigerator, glanced at Henry. He shrugged and nodded at Helen's unspoken question. She turned toward Jen and offered, "Jennifer, I've been thinking about it, and if you'd be willing, I would love to pass the role of Thanksgiving coordinator to you, that is, if you and Jake wish to host the holiday at your house."

Jen splattered a little soap and water on Ava as she turned quickly to speak to Helen. "Sorry, Mom. Aunt Helen, you're feeling okay and doing well, right?"

Following her train of thought, Helen assured her, "I'm doing very well. It has nothing to do with my health. I simply see our family growing and I'm not sure how much longer I'll live here," she glanced at Henry. "Henry and I may move into his apartment at Enduring Grace and be next-door neighbors with your mom and dad. I'd love to see our family Thanksgiving tradition continue, and I think you're just the person to manage that. You don't need to decide today, obviously. You and Jake can think about it."

Jen walked over and hugged Helen. "I doubt I'll ever be as lovely a Thanksgiving hostess as you, but I'm honored you think I can do it. When you are ready to pass the baton to me, Aunt Helen, I'm your girl. I've got this."

Helen teared up. "Ignore the tears. I seem to cry all the time these days. Thank you, Jen."

"There is just one giant problem," Jen added, putting her arm around Helen and gently turning her toward the window.

Helen asked, "What's that?"

"How are we going to transport and replant your Thanksgiving tree in our backyard? Before you sell this house, that tree is moving to the Rosales house. I can't very well host Thanksgiving without it!"

The tree was shining brightly in all its autumn regalia as Ava took numerous photographs to commemorate the day. She took pictures of cute couples, which everyone agreed was a category won by Helen and Henry, as well as families and friends. The photo of all the men in their inadvertently matching plaid and khaki attire proved to be Ava's favorite of the day.

As Laney looked over Ava's shoulder to see the photos on her computer, she asked, "Ava, can I have copies of all of these? I'm afraid I can't pick just one."

"Of course, Aunt Laney. Obviously, you must have the big group shot, and this adorable one of you, my mom, and Aunt Helen. This picture is super cute of you with Devon. And, this one—this one takes the cake! I still can't believe Bobby pulled Nick into your Walsh family photograph. Look at the shocked expression on Nick's face."

Laney giggled. "Lottie's face is priceless. Bobby surprised all of us. He seems to be doing that quite a lot lately, in a good way."

Ava nodded. "I don't know how you, my mom, Aunt Helen, and Aunt Button ended up on a path that led to this amazing group we've dubbed our fam-damily, but thank God you did. It's made a tremendous difference in all of our lives."

Laney smiled and winked at her. "Keep it going, Ava. I believe you know the way."

Cocoa and Christmas Carols

When Great Things
Come in Small Packages

As Lottie walked into the kitchen, humming a Christmas carol, she smiled when she saw her mom and Nannie baking together. It was great to be home!

Although she loved school, sharing a room with Mayson, and seeing Nick as often as class and work would allow, she was happy to be home to celebrate an early family Christmas. Scheduled for a late shift on Christmas Day, she'd be driving back to Orlando in the morning, giving them just this one day together.

"Good morning, fam," she said, peeking over her mom's shoulder to see what she and Nannie were baking.

"There she is," Judith said. "We were just wondering if we should check on you."

Laney couldn't help tease her. "Hey, sleepy head. I'd barely consider it morning; I've been up for hours."

Lottie replied with a sigh, "Oh, the pleasure of sleeping in one's own bed!" As she turned on the electric teapot and pulled her favorite polka dot mug from the cabinet, she said, "It smells amazing in here, kind of like snickerdoodles."

"We're making pecan sticky buns," Judith offered. "They'll be out of the oven in a few minutes."

Lottie peeked in the oven. "These look amazing. Where did you get the recipe?"

"Henry. He's trying to convince me to reveal the secret ingredient in my Thanksgiving mashed potatoes. I'm not sure how much longer I'll be able to hold out. His recipes are stupendous," Laney shared with a chuckle.

"You've got everyone thinking it's just one thing, Nannie. That's pretty sneaky! Never fear, your secret is safe with me." Lottie pledged. "Speaking of Henry, how awesome is it that he has coordinated family caroling tonight? I cracked up when I got an email with music and lyrics. As if I need music and lyrics! So, what is the plan for later?"

Judith shared, "We're supposed to be there at seven o'clock. We've decided that we'll have brunch, decorate Christmas cookies, and open our gifts to each other here and then head over to Helen and Henry's for cocoa, caroling, and secret Santa gift exchange. Whose name did you get this year, sweetie?"

Lottie answered enthusiastically, "I got Jen, and I'm so excited, Mom! I've never drawn her name before. I found her a shirt that says 'Yes, I'm a Fairy Godmother.' It's perfect. Who did you two get?"

Judith replied, "I have Helen, so that was an easy stop for wine."

Laney shared, "I have Jake, which was simple as well. He's getting a Bill's Italian gift card."

Lottie was curious. "Who did Dad get?"

"He didn't say," Judith shared. "He says it is called secret Santa for a reason. He never tells me."

"Where is Dad?" Lottie asked, looking toward the living room.

Judith replied, "He is finishing his Christmas shopping. He should be home any minute since the stores all opened so early today. I have no idea why he puts it off until the last minute, but he always does."

"Like father, like son. Robert did the exact same thing," Laney explained.

"After Dad gets home and we eat brunch, can we bake and decorate Christmas cookies? Nannie, I know you said you already made two dozen."

Laney explained, "Oh, that batch is gone. I sent a dozen to Marie and your dad polished off the rest." As Judith raised her eyebrows at Laney's comment, she admitted, "And I ate a few of them."

"We can make cookies today, if you'd like. Did you say Nick was stopping by? I love that boy," Judith said with a decisive nod.

Lottie shared a look with Nannie, trying not to laugh. It hadn't been all that long ago she'd referred to Nick as *that boy* in a less than friendly way.

"He'll be here later. He and Devon are driving to their parents' house really early in the morning. His mom has to work today, so they'll celebrate on Christmas night."

The timer started beeping on the oven. Judith turned off the annoying sound, checked the buns, and declared them perfect. Mere seconds later and with impeccable timing, Bobby shouted, "Ho, ho, ho," as he entered the back door from the garage. He had a couple of gift bags in one hand and coffee in the other. "Santa is starving," he said. "And ready for sticky buns!"

A few hours later, Henry was setting up a cocoa bar on the kitchen counter with foam cups, stirring sticks, marshmallows, and candy canes. He sang along with Helen's Christmas CD as he worked. "Have yourself a merry little Christmas, let your heart be light."

"From now on your troubles will be out of sight," Helen sang as she joined him in the kitchen. "Everything looks ready? Can I do anything?"

Henry took one last look to see that everything was ready for their guests. "Yes, you certainly can. Please come with me." Henry took Helen by the hand and escorted her to the living room sofa where he invited her to take a seat. "You can open this Christmas present," he said, offering her a gift, which was wrapped in red paper with little snowmen. "But first, I would like to know what manner of gift opener you profess to be. Are you slow and careful, trying to save the paper, or are you a ripper?"

"One hundred percent, I'm a ripper! What about you?

"I'm king of the rippers!"

Helen chuckled. "Well, as I am the queen, it appears we are compatible."

"Yes, I would certainly say so," he said with a huge smile. "Please, open your present."

Helen tore the paper quickly off the box and opened it to discover a series of computer lessons guaranteed to have her speaking French in no time. "Magnifique! Merci, Henry. This is perfect for me to learn a few more words and phrases before Laney, Ida, Marie, and I go to France this summer." She gave him a quick kiss on the cheek. "This for you."

Henry took the package from Helen and shredded the festive green wrapping paper in record time to discover wireless earbuds, perfect for his favorite music and podcasts. "I've really been wanting a pair of these." He thanked Helen with a return kiss. "One more gift," he offered. "I hope you like it."

Helen went a little slower in unwrapping her second gift, trying not to let the special time pass too quickly. She opened the box to discover an e-reader inside.

Henry explained, "I took the liberty of downloading many of your favorite books and a few you haven't had the opportunity to read yet. I thought you might enjoy having all of your books at your fingertips since you mentioned they won't fit into my apartment."

"Henry, this is so thoughtful and generous of you. I mentioned that once in passing. When was that?"

"It was the day Charlie and Ida moved in next door to me. I did not realize until that moment that you were concerned about the space needed for your belongings. The e-reader holds all the books you want in something barely larger than a piece of paper. Additionally, you'll have a tremendous number of books to read on your flight to Paris and back."

"It's brilliant! You are the most thoughtful man. Thank you. I fear you'll find my head in a book, so to speak, constantly."

"I will endeavor to earn your attention."

Helen smiled sweetly at him. "Here, I have a second one for you too. I'm afraid it's not as fantastic as an e-reader."

Henry pulled the paper off a box. Inside, he found a picture frame containing pictures of Helen and him. The largest photo in the frame, which held three pictures, was from the Independence Day party at Enduring Grace. It was the picture of their first kiss behind Henry's hat. He didn't know she'd ordered it. The second photo, taken at the park, was with his children and grandchildren, who had come to visit before Thanksgiving. The last one in the bottom right corner was their picture together in front of Helen's Thanksgiving tree.

Helen said softly, "I know you don't have room for many frames, but I thought this one would look pretty on the table next to *our* couch in *our* apartment." She smiled at his surprise of her carefully chosen wording. "Yes, Henry, I will be ready to move in soon and enjoy a different lifestyle."

Before Henry could say anything, the doorbell rang and he heard singing from the front porch. "That must be Charlie. He's horribly off-key," Henry chuckled. He opened the door to find his new friend belting out "We Wish You a Merry Christmas."

After everyone arrived, Henry held a brief rehearsal before they went caroling in the neighborhood. He put Devon and Payton in the middle, declaring their voices beautiful. He put Charlie next to Joe on the back row, with Ida and Ava in front of them and Lottie and Nick on the front row. He had everyone else fill in the available space.

Although the sidewalk was well-lit, the older members of the family were carefully matched with someone to carry a flashlight and keep a safe hand on them. Bobby walked at Laney's right side with Devon on her left. Laney squeezed Devon's hand as he offered to assist her. "I've missed you very much, Devon; I used to see you almost every day. I'm thrilled you have allowed us to pull you into our crazy family."

"I've missed you too, Miss Laney. I'm so happy to be here. I told Nick not too long ago that if he and Lottie ever break up, heaven forbid, I'm keeping her and this family anyway."

Bobby said, "I've warned him not to break my baby's heart. But, all joking aside, I'm embarrassed to admit, I think it would break my heart to see them split up."

Laney said, "We are all in agreement. I must say, Devon, we think Payton is just darling and are rather hoping you two will stay together as well."

"Mother," Bobby said, cautioning her.

"Not that I'm meddling or it's any of my business!"

Devon chuckled. "Right! You wouldn't want to meddle. No worries, Miss Laney, I'm crazy about Payton. Between her and her thoughtful mom, Karen, I've gained about ten pounds. It's just the two of them, you know. Payton's Dad passed away from a sudden heart attack when she was in high school. She is really close to her mom. When I'm around her, I just feel insanely lucky," Devon shared, looking at Payton as she laughed at something Jen said.

Bobby looked toward Judith, strolling with Lottie and Nick. "When you find the right woman, that lucky feeling never goes away." Bobby gave Devon a knowing look.

As they walked up to the first neighbor's home and rang the doorbell, Henry led them through their songs like a choir director. Laney couldn't believe how good they sounded for such an unrehearsed, amateur group of singers. They sang four songs, rotating two at each house, returning to Helen's with loads of thanks, smiles, and Christmas spirit.

With cocoa shared all around, they kicked off secret Santa according to age, youngest first. Lottie gave Jen her gift and, at the moment Jen squealed in delight, she signaled a touchdown with her arms high in the air. Lottie was certain it was the gift of the year until a few minutes later when Bobby announced in a serious tone, "My gift is for Nick." Lottie snickered under her breath as Nick took the brightly wrapped package as if it might bite him. When he tore off the wrapping paper, Nick discovered old-fashioned board games. Bobby stated emphatically, "These are my generation's games, and I challenge you to beat me."

Nick threw back his head and roared with laughter, "You're on!"

When it was finally Henry's turn as the oldest in the room, he offered his secret Santa gift to Laney. She thanked him for both the gift and for being older than her by a few months. She liked not being last. As she slowly unwrapped her package, Henry leaned toward Helen and smirked, "She's definitely not a ripper."

Laney opened the box to find a blue shirt, her favorite color, with blue, yellow, purple, and pink buttons. When Laney pulled the shirt out of the box and turned it for everyone to see, Henry explained, "I hope you like it. It reminded me of you, Helen, Ida, and Vivian. You often wore those colors when I saw you having lunch together on Mondays at Enduring Grace,"

Ida offered, "Those are our favorite colors."

Henry nodded, suddenly feeling bashful with all eyes on him.

"Thank you, Henry. I love it so much," Laney said, touched by his thoughtfulness.

"I hope you all won't mind tolerating me for a moment more," Henry entreated. "This is my first Christmas with you, and I would like to ask your indulgence as I have one additional gift to share." Henry opened a drawer in the living room side table and presented Helen with a beautifully wrapped gift.

"Why Henry, we've already exchanged our gifts. We said two gifts, and you are breaking the rules we established," Helen scolded.

"Just open it, please," he replied.

Helen pulled off the paper and opened the box. Inside was another smaller box, a ring box. She froze.

"Allow me," Henry offered as Helen said nothing, staring at the box.

Slowly bending down on one knee, Henry opened the ring box, held it toward Helen and asked, "Helen Renee Chastain, will you share the rest of your life with me and allow me to share mine with you? Will you marry me?"

With everyone on the edge of their seats, ready to jump for joy, the family held their collective breath and awaited Helen's answer.

"Yes!" she replied with a tremendous smile. As she launched herself into Henry's arms, Helen cried, "I love you, Henry. You just made me the star of my own sappy Christmas movie!"

Les Sœurs

When Someone Gives You the World

Just over five months later, Marie stood, waving gleefully, as she watched Laney, Helen, and Ida clear customs at the Paris Charles de Gaulle Airport. "Bonjour, mes belles sœurs!" She'd arrived two hours earlier from Washington Dulles and had been anxiously waiting for their flight to arrive.

Helen leaned closer to Laney and Ida in order to be heard, "She said, 'Hello, my beautiful sisters.'"

Ida looked at Laney with a slight eye roll. They already knew Helen was planning to be the official translator for their birthday-season trip in France. They would be here for ten days; ten days of Helen telling them what's what despite the fact that many Europeans spoke English.

"Marie!" They called her name in chorus, hugging her while unintentionally blocking the walkway for fellow travelers, oblivious to dirty looks.

"I've already figured out where we meet our driver, so follow me," Marie suggested. A few minutes later, they were in a car speeding toward their hotel and the much-anticipated sights of Paris.

"As the travel guide suggests," Helen instructed, "despite only having a couple of short naps on the plane, we should do our best not to think about our loved ones who are fast asleep in the middle of the night at home. It's ten o'clock in the morning here, so that's our reality. No sleeping, if we can manage it, until an early bedtime in Paris. It will help us adjust to current time and ease jet lag."

As all three of them nodded, Ida admitted from the front seat next to their driver, "I'm so excited. I couldn't sleep right now if I tried."

"I can't believe I'm in France," Laney murmured in wonder as she looked out the window. "I've never been out of the United States before. I always loved Button's stories of her and John's travels and lived vicariously through her, through her pictures."

Marie squeezed Laney's hand. "And now you are here, living a dream *because* of her."

Laney glanced at Marie in awe. She was such an amazing, strong woman. She had somehow weathered the gut-wrenching months that her husband, Tim, had battled pancreatic cancer, calling Laney to come on the first day of February. Tim passed away the next night. At one time, Marie had enjoyed a tremendous circle of friends and family in Bethesda, but found herself much more alone as those closest to her moved or passed away. Her circle had become quite small there, and Laney suggested her support system would grow tremendously with a move back to Florida. "Come home, Marie," she'd insisted. "The whole fam-damily would love to have you, and I think it would make a tremendous difference—for both of us."

Laney's eyes refocused on the majestic sights of Paris as Helen cheered, "The Arc de Triomphe!" In true Helen style, she shared, "This was a project started by Napoleon I in 1806 to salute French army victories at the Battle of Austerlitz. He didn't live to see it completed. It wasn't actually opened officially until 1836 by King Louis-Philippe."

Marie quipped, "I'm so glad we brought her."

"No need for sarcasm, Marie dear," Helen replied.

"I'm not being sarcastic; you are in the company of three history nerds."

Helen sat up straighter and grinned widely. "That's right, I am. You will appreciate everything I've learned."

Ida clarified, "Although I may slug you if you keep translating every single word. I know *bonjour* is hello and *au revoir* means goodbye."

Laney and Marie burst out laughing at the driver's hilarious expression in the rearview mirror.

Helen gasped, "The Eiffel Tower! See it there on the right? I never thought I'd live to see the day."

After pointing out a few places they wouldn't want to miss, their driver turned down the street leading to their hotel. Ida thanked him again for going a little out of the way to show them famous sights of Paris. What a great introduction to the City of Light! They pulled into their hotel, which Ida had suggested after much research. It was an eighteenth-century, beautiful boutique-style hotel with balconies offering stunning views of the city. It had its own private garden-like outdoor café.

They were greeted warmly by the staff at the front desk, who began the conversation in French, but quickly switched to English despite Helen's best efforts. A charming young woman checked them in promptly and asked for only a moment to retrieve their keys. Ida had splurged and booked them a suite with a living room, balcony, and two bedrooms with double beds in each. There were also two bathrooms. It wasn't that much more expensive with them splitting it four ways, and the view from the balcony was swoon-worthy.

The employee distributed their key cards, and as they turned toward the elevator, she called out softly, "Madame DeCamp?" With no reply, she repeated, "Madame Helen DeCamp?"

Laney tapped Helen on the shoulder. "Madame DeCamp. That's you, Helen."

"Oh my goodness, c'est moi!"

Laney, Ida, and Marie could not prevent their merriment as Helen practically skipped to the desk to retrieve her credit card she'd accidentally left behind. She'd been a married woman for more than three months now, but seemed to be struggling with her new last name. Helen and Henry were married on Valentine's Day in the small chapel at their church, which they both admitted was tremendously cliché, but perfect for their romantic natures. Helen wore a beautiful white suit and carried a small purple calla lily bouquet. Henry donned a sharp gray suit, white starched shirt, and purple bow tie. His children and grandchildren all came for the ceremony, welcoming Helen into their family. She was now a mother, grandmother, and soon-to-be great grandmother. Henry's son and daughter were honored to serve as their attendants.

As Helen returned to the desk, she introduced herself to the employee who had her credit card. "*Je m'appelle* Helen DeCamp." She put her credit card safely in her purse, replied, "*Merci beaucoup*," and turned to look at her sisters with a proud, somewhat smug look on her face.

With keys in hand, they took their luggage to their rooms and freshened up quickly. They agreed to not linger for long; they would get a snack nearby before starting their afternoon tour of Paris. Based on her internet research, Ida had a plan. She knew there was a highly rated bakery just down the street.

As they strolled in that direction a few minutes later, enchanted by Paris' unique charm, Laney said, "I suppose it's outlandish to be so excited about food, but I want nothing more right now than a giant, flaky croissant from a beautiful Parisian bakery."

"It's not crazy to have food on your Paris list. It's on mine, too. My entire suitcase is full of stretchy pants, and I can't wait to try . . ." Marie suddenly stopped mid-sentence. "Oh, look," she sighed as they took in the precious, charming little bakeshop. The shop window was clear glass with the words *Boulangerie* and *Viennoiserie* etched across the middle in gold script. From the window, the sisters drooled over the rows and rows of French breads, including a variety of croissants. Laney bought two. As far as she was concerned, their birthday-season trip was off to a perfect start.

That afternoon they cruised down the Seine River in an open-air boat, Bateau-Mouche, truly enchanted with the sites of Paris. Unapologetically tourists, they captured photograph after photograph, saw the Eiffel Tower again as well as the Musée d'Orsay, and the Louvre Museum. After an early evening meal of wine, baguettes, and cheeses at a charming sidewalk café, they declared themselves exhausted. They didn't even take a moment to linger in the living room or admire the view from the balcony. They simply brushed their teeth, donned pajamas, and were fast asleep within minutes.

The next few days were like a dream! They visited all the sites of Paris—the museums, art galleries, shops, bookstores, and restaurants. They collected a variety of gifts to take home to their family, but not many things for themselves. Marie had purchased an inexpensive print of her favorite Paris street by a local artist. Helen selected wine glasses she hoped would make it home safely in her suitcase. Laney selected an elegant French cookbook full of pastries. She knew she couldn't understand it, but she wanted it for her collection. She also bought a CD of music she'd heard playing most evenings in the hotel garden bistro, which would always remind her of her trip to Paris. Ida found a darling, bright pink beret.

On their tenth and final full day in France, they hired a driver and scheduled a special trip to a large winery out of town where the view from the vineyards was famously shared on many postcards. Marie climbed into the car carrying a box from a nearby patisserie, but nobody seemed to notice.

The views on their drive in the country were incredible, and Helen declared from the front seat, "J'adore France. I wish I could come back with Henry and stay a month. I'd love to see Burgundy, Champagne, Normandy, and the French Alps."

"Why can't you?" Ida insisted. "You sold your house and moved into Henry's apartment, where there is no upkeep or maintenance. You have no obligations other than to be happy. We have all managed the physical demands of this trip quite impressively. Don't convince yourself, Helen, or allow anyone to suggest that you are too old. That's poppycock! Viva la France!" She raised her right arm high in the air as did the driver, following her lead. The backseat erupted in hoots of laughter.

A little while later, they pulled into the winery. Their typically loud manner of talking was replaced with hushed, almost reverent voices. "Wow, I just got goosebumps," Marie said.

"I think I'm in heaven," Helen agreed.

As they took in the stunning view of the vineyards, they stood almost frozen by the car. An employee walked out to meet them and directed them to the starting location of their tour. The facilities were top-notch, and their visit was tremendously well organized. They sampled many different wines, trying to identify the specific characteristics. Laney admitted, "I never taste the different aspects, I just know what tastes the best to me."

Ida made arrangements well in advance for them to have dinner on the lovely back deck of the winery, where they often hosted private parties. It was set up to offer a spectacular view of the vineyard.

As Helen started her second glass of wine, she announced, "I'm not saying I'm an expert, but this wine is phenomenal. Actually, an expert in the scientific aspects of wine making is an oenologist."

"I thought that was a sommelier," Marie said, as she pulled off a piece of a baguette and took a bite.

"A sommelier is the professional in a restaurant who advises customers on pairing wine and food," Helen clarified. "An experienced wine maker is sometimes referred to as the master vintner, but the official term is oenologist.

"Cheers to all of them!" Laney lifted her glass for a toast.

"Here, here!" They all joined in their salute.

"Cheers to Paris," Helen offered.

"Cheers to Button," Laney said, perhaps a bit too loudly. Marie stood up so that she could reach Laney and they could clink their glasses together. She turned, a little wobbly, to share clink glasses with Ida and Helen.

After dinner and a little more wine, Marie turned to where her purse and the patisserie box were sitting on the empty chair to her left. She put the box on the table and opened the lid, gently removing four pink petits fours with tiny, intricate white flowers on top. She sat them on a small plate in the center of the table.

"Happy birthday to Button," Marie said softly. "I know we already spoiled ourselves with petits fours soon after we arrived, but I thought we should have one this evening. Besides, these are chocolate cake under pink icing."

"As they should be," Ida insisted, slurring her words just a teensy bit.

They each took a petit fours and, after taking a bite, purposefully and all together made an "Mmmm" sound. With tears in their eyes, but sweet smiles on their faces, they ate, drank, and toasted their darling Button, who had given them the world.

As they paid their tab, gathered their belongings, and were preparing to meet their driver to return to their hotel, Laney glanced behind her toward the vineyard one last time. "Oh Button," she cried.

Her sisters turned quickly toward the vineyard to see the most beautiful pink sunset. It looked like a huge strip of pink in the sky with purple clouds above. They walked to stand closely together, putting their arms around each other's waists, to face the sunset.

"That's the most beautiful sight I've ever seen," Helen sobbed.

Ida and Marie wept and wiped tears from their cheeks.

"She knows," was all Laney could say.

Marie jested, "Seriously, Button? Next time, catch us before we polish off a couple of bottles of wine! You know I'm an emotional drunk. This could be considered well over the top, dear!"

The manager of the winery took a photo of the four ladies leaning on each other as they faced the setting sun. It was the most beautiful sky he'd seen in some time, and he found their camaraderie endearing. Laney, Helen, Marie, and Ida never saw the photograph, but it hung near the front entrance of the winery for decades to come.

The next afternoon, they were at the airport, checked in and awaiting their flights. Marie was flying home to Washington Dulles Airport. After much thought and discussion over the past ten days, she told Laney she would start cleaning out her home and preparing to sell it. She would be coming to Florida soon to find a new home near her sisters. It made it so much easier to hug her and send her on her way.

Being Marie, she departed in style, "Au revoir and never fear, mes amours. I'll be home with you soon!"

While Ida and Helen looked through the duty-free shops for last-minute gifts, Laney bought Paris T-shirts for both Lottie and Nick and hoped they'd have the opportunity to come here someday themselves. Ida and Helen were waiting for her as she exited the store.

"Are you ready to go? We'll be boarding soon," Ida shared.

"I'm ready," Laney replied.

"Henry and Charlie will be meeting us at the airport. They asked if we'd need two cars for all our souvenirs." Helen chuckled as they walked toward their gate.

"We need to get home and get some rest. Jen and Jake's wedding is in two weeks," Ida said.

"Our great-grandbaby will be here in a couple of months," Helen mentioned.

"And the second annual Fourth of July Big Sky Amusement Park trip for my birthday is coming soon," Laney shared. "I'm glad you all are coming this year. "

When the airline representative called their boarding group, Ida turned to them and asked, "Are you ready for everything that's coming next, sisters?"

Helen replied, "Absolutely!"

Laney smiled and nodded. "Lead the way home."

Epilogue

Teh Years Later . . .

Lottie walked into the storage facility where Aunt Ida and Uncle Charlie had warehoused their apartment overflow items after moving to Enduring Grace many years ago. Lottie smiled a little as she remembered how Ida always insisted it was her *off-site, giant walk-in closet of joy*. Lottie rubbed her chest for a second, just over her heart. The anguish of losing Ida, less than a year after Charlie, was still a recent and fresh grief for all of them.

"Jen, where are you?" she called.

"End of the hall on the right," Jen shouted in reply.

The entire family had teamed up to move Ida and Charlie's belongings out of Enduring Grace, donating much of it to local charities. Recognizing her mom Ava's sorrow and exhaustion, Jen had offered to tackle her grandparents' storage shed and volunteered Lottie to help her.

As Lottie reached the end of the long hall and peered into Ida and Charlie's unit, she leaned left and then right in an attempt to find Jen in the sea of boxes. Spying her in the back left corner, Lottie gingerly made her way through the maze and asked, "What's up? I got your text, Jen. I'm normally the one sending out '9-1-1 urgent' messages to you. Thanks for clarifying that no bodily injury was involved."

"You won't believe what I've found," Jen eagerly shared as she tugged Lottie gently by the arm to a stack of boxes she'd separated from the others. "Look!"

Lottie peered into the boxes Jen was pointing toward in confusion. "Books?"

"Not books. Diaries," Jen replied with an almost whispered emphasis.

"Ida's diaries?" Lottie sank to her knees to lift one out of the box. A little puff of dust flew up as she opened it.

"No! They are Button's diaries. It appears that pink one was the beginning of college. She talks about meeting her new sisters."

Lottie glanced at the pink diary in the pile, but her attention was pulled back to the rosy floral one in her hand. She shared with Jen, "Button wrote in this one, 'Laney and Helen might be in trouble for their shenanigans the other night. They kept my name and Ida's out of their confessions, but the whole thing was my idea.'"

Jen threw her arms wide. "Why are we just now finding out about these diaries?"

Lottie pondered, "Why did Button entrust these to Ida, and why are they here in storage?"

Jen answered, "Button knew my grandmother, Ida, would never throw away a single thing." She added with a laugh, "It's not surprising in the least that Button was right."

Jen knelt and began to pack the diaries she'd set aside back into an almost empty box. "Lottie, help me load these boxes in the back of my car. I'll call my mom and tell her to meet us at Enduring Grace."

Lottie enthusiastically agreed. "You've read my mind."

As Jen closed the back of her SUV with the boxes of diaries inside, she wiped her dusty hands on the legs of her jeans. She turned to Lottie. "I wonder if Laney, Helen, and Marie know about Button's diaries. Button used the word 'shenanigans.' I think they have some stories to share and a lot of explaining to do."

"They sure do. I'm taking notes!" Lottie walked toward her car, talking to Jen over her shoulder. "I'll meet you at Enduring Grace. I'm going to dash home quickly and pick up my laptop."

Jen smiled at her. "I can't wait to read every word Button left behind to share with us. She would not have given these diaries to my grandmother if she didn't want us to find them one day. It may sound crazy, but it's like Button knew this sisterhood story needed to be told. I think, Lottie, you are the perfect person to do it."

Lottie shrugged. "I'm absolutely taking notes, but I wouldn't have even an inkling of how to write this story."

"Well, what's the first thing you'd say if you tried to describe Button?" Jen asked.

After a brief pause, Lottie grinned widely and said, "Her favorite color was pink."

About the Author

Yes, Robin is a sorority alumna, and she would love for you to guess to which sisterhood she belongs after reading this book. There are a few clues, but also loving references to many National Panhellenic Conference sororities. She did not name her sorority, nor create an imaginary one, so that every sorority woman would feel it was written especially for her. No matter the letters, colors, emblems, or creeds, this book is for all the sorority "girls" out there.

Robin has served in officer positions for her sorority and Alumnae Panhellenic. She has said for many years that Thanksgiving at her home could be considered a Panhellenic meeting with the different sororities represented in her family.

She graduated from college in 1985 with a degree in journalism/public relations. She believes it was her sorority experience which led her to a career in public relations/community relations with non-profit agencies and corporations. She wanted her work to be meaningful and helpful to others. That desire to make a difference led her to become a writer.

Robin is now a three-time author with two previous books under her belt. She wrote her first book in 2010 following the amazing success of her daughter Jillian's vision therapy treatment. *Jillian's Story: How Vision Therapy Changed My Daughter's Life*, and her second book co-written with her daughter in 2014, *Dear Jillian: Vision Therapy Changed My Life Too*, are found in many optometry offices around the world.

The Eighty-Year-Old Sorority Girls is her foray into fiction writing, but it, too, grew from a desire to share her personal perspective of loving someone with Alzheimer's. Her mother, June, passed away in 2017 after struggling with the disease for several years. This story also blossomed into one about sorority sisterhood, thanks to the examples of many special sisters in Robin's life. One constant thread these sisters shared was their belief that they were sorority girls at heart no matter their age, thus the title of this book.

Robin lives in the Midwest with her husband Brian, and they have two adult daughters, Annelise and Jillian. She loves to travel and credits her 1984 experience on Semester at Sea for creating the adventurer in her. She is a tremendous Disney fan, and it will become obvious to the reader that Big Sky Amusement Park was inspired by that love. She also enjoys her Bible study circle and can be found several days a week in her local YMCA's water aerobics class.